I0735241

RECOMMENDED

74 Bible Mysteries Solved

"ALIENS FACT OR FICTION?"

The word of the LORD came expressly unto Ezekiel the priest, the son of Buzi, in the land of the Chaldeans by the river Chebar; and the hand of the LORD was there upon him.

And I looked, and, behold, a whirlwind came out of the north, a great cloud, and a fire infolding itself, and a brightness was about it, and out of the midst thereof as the colour of amber, out of the midst of the fire.

Also out of the midst thereof came the likeness of four living creatures. And this was their appearance; they had the likeness of a man.

And every one had four faces, and every one had four wings.

And their feet were straight feet; and the sole of their feet was like the sole of a calf's foot: and they sparkled like the colour of burnished brass.

And they had the hands of a man under their wings on their four sides; and they four had their faces and their wings.

Their wings were joined one to another; they turned not when they went; they went every one straight forward.

As for the likeness of their faces, they four had the face of a man, and the face of a lion, on the right side: and they four had the face of an ox on the left side; they four also had the face of an eagle.

Thus were their faces: and their wings were stretched upward; two wings of every one were joined one to another, and two covered their bodies.

Tommy Bruce Jones

WORKBOOK PRESS LLC
187 E Warm Springs Rd,
Suite B285, Las Vegas, NV 89119, USA

Website: https://workbookpress.com/
Hotline: 1-888-818-4856
Email: admin@workbookpress.com

Ordering Information:
Quantity sales. Special discounts are available on quantity purchases by corporations, associations, and others.
For details, contact the publisher at the address above.

Library of Congress Control Number:
ISBN-13:   978-1-954753-79-2 (Paperback Version)
                978-1-954753-80-8 (Digital Version)

REV. DATE: 23/03/2021

All quoted scriptures are from the Holy Bible, King James Version Cambridge Addition: 1769; King James Bible Online www. kingjamesbibleonline.org.

Commentaries used are "from HOLY BIBLE, INTERNATIONAL VERSION Copyright 1973, 1978, 1984 International Bible Society and used by permission by Zondervan Bible Publishers

INTRODUCTION

In the King James Bible, the word Mystery is used 71 times, and it has created a curiosity in me to seek out some of these mysteries and try to find a possible answer to them. Here in this book, I have included some I have found for your evaluation. One, in particular, is the possibility that alien cultures are mentioned in scriptures. People have performed many deceptions, and well-meaning people have misunderstood many natural sightings. Still, there is a great deal of sightings by very trustworthy professional individuals. Many professional pilots have experienced sighting UFO and some flying in close proximity to their aircraft, confirmed by ground radar tracking of the same UFO contact. Many military pilots and NASA astronauts have experienced UFOs and are not permitted to speak of their experience. But a few have come forward with their death bed confessions of alien events, and they were told to keep silent under penalty of law.

There is a lot of earth history that confirms exceptional events by old drawings and sculptures depicting unusual individuals; and space vehicles. Many scholars have investigated these phenomenal events and have concluded that aliens have and are visiting earth. Many people have seen and testified seeing UFOs worldwide: are we to disbelieve all of these people?

In the Dark Age of history here on earth, we know anyone who disagreed with the Pope edicts was executed for heresies. So much knowledge was denied at that time; the earth was slow in coming to some truths. These same traditional influences are still present today.

We have been told by religious leaders and some scientist that "all this UFO information is a Hokes," but if true, would change our religious concepts; *which it will not*. This is more fear tactics. However, they cannot explain with a more convincing explanation of these events. But, I have found information for your appraisal in the Bible on aliens, and it will not change but explain some Biblical concepts. The Gospel of Jesus and salvation by faith will not change. Lastly, I would ask you to test my Spirit as commanded in scriptures in **1st John**.

1 John 4:1 *"Beloved, believe not every spirit, but try the spirits whether they are of God: because many false prophets are gone out into the world." (KJV)*

DEDICATION

This book is dedicated to my loving wife, who demonstrated great patience with the time it has taken out of our lives for me to write this book. And the encouragement she has provided during the process.

I also want to dedicate this book to my son Kerry and daughter Jill, whom I hope will benefit from these words and doctrine. May God bless them and keep them in his Love and protection.

To the men in my prison ministry, I hope and pray that the time we have spent together studying God's Word has made a positive impact on your lives to accept Jesus as your Lord and Savior

Consider all dates approximate in this book. There are no date calculations that can give accurate times to these dates used here in this book. However, history dates are workable because the older the dates, the less precise the dates will be.

My Prayer for You

Lord, for these correct and true things, I pray that you place them in our minds and hearts. Help us to apply them correctly in our everyday life for the benefit of your Kingdom. For those things that are not correct or not true, I pray that you reveal those erroneous things and replace them with the correct ones. Remove that which is incorrect and not true from our minds and hearts.

Amen

This book can have a depressing effect on the sensitive, week, or lost, but those who know Jesus as our Lord and Savior can joyously be reassured in our future with Jesus. God's plan for you is so fantastic, and the depth that God has gone to reveal his love for you, so take courage! Take comfort in your soul, assurance of protection, and peace in your heart. Jesus said, *"For my yoke is easy, and my burden is light."*

MY DICTIONARY

Over time words tend to take on a different meaning. So here at this juncture, I would like to give you words to consider in this book. Many words used in scriptures are not capitalized and lose the power and focus of a noun. If I said the words Paris, London, or Chicago, you would focus on those cities. But if I said rapture, what power or focus would a non-believer have. Therefore, I have capitalized on certain christian words. Notice, I spell *christian* with the small letter c because our dictionaries do not specifically *address this word's spiritual depth and many more Christian words.* I see two types of Christians revealed in the Bible. Here are some simple definitions for the words and the meanings I used in my books.

> **1. church** = is not a building but *a group of individuals* who believe (faith) in God, but may not believe in Jesus, or they have performed no works (*deeds*) for Jesus. (*See Pew-Sitters*)
>
> **2. Church** = is not a denomination or a building, but *is a group of Christians* that have <u>*faith in Jesus*</u> and <u>perform works (*deeds*) for Jesus.</u>
>
> **3. ½ christians** = is *a group of individuals* who are saved by faith in Jesus but are *disobedient to works* (deeds) and the Great Commission. (They are *half righteous?*) They are righteous in Faith but not in Deeds.
>
> **4. Christians** = *are a group of saved persons* who are saved by *faith in Jesus* and *do the works* (*deeds*) for the Great Commission. (*Righteous*)

5. Pew-Sitters = *is a group of individuals* who have claimed Jesus and are saved by faith. However, they do not perform works (*deeds*) for the Church or the Great Commission. *(Half Righteous, disobedient)*

6. The Great Tribulation = *is a name* for the time of the seven years of God's greatest wrath against *non-believer* in Jesus.

7. The Great White Throne Judgment = *is the name* for the final day of judgment for all *non-believers*. They are from all the earth's humans past to present. This event occurs before the New Earth and New Universe are created, and eternity begins. And they are cast into the Lake of Fire.

8. Hell = is a *generic name* for a place of punishment or grave. It is a location for *non-believers and evil entities,* who are held awaiting the Great White Throne Judgment and finally the *Lake of Fire.*

9. Lake of Fire = *is the name* of the final location for eternal punishment for those *non-believers* in Jesus and blasphemed the Holy Spirit. (*Unrighteous*)

10. Torment = *is the name* of a place where *non-believers* are held awaiting the Great White Throne Judgment. (Hell)

11. Paradise = is the name of 2 locations. One is in the bowls of the earth, and the other is with Jesus in Heaven.

12. heaven = *is the name* of 3 sites: sky, space, and God's abode.

13. Heaven = *is the place* of God's residence.

14, Saints = *is a name* for all saved individuals. (*Righteous*)

15. Old Testament Saints = *is the name* of all individuals saved by God's Grace in Old Testament times. From Adam to Jesus (*Righteous*)

16. Church Saints = *is a name* for all believers in Jesus and who do the Works of Jesus. (*Righteous*)

17. Tribulation Saints = *is the name* of the converted individuals who have converted to Jesus during the Great Tribulation and/or *who have faith in Jesus* and have not received the Mark of the Beast (a mighty deed for the Pew Sitters). During those seven years of the Great Tribulation.

18. Saved = *is a word* for individuals *saved by faith* from the Lake of Fire. (*Righteous*)

19. Non-believers = *is the name* for those who have rejected Jesus as their Lord and Savior. And for those who have blasphemed the Holy Spirit. (*Unrighteous*)

20. Rapture = Christians who will be taken to Heaven to avoid the Great Tribulation; but, ½ christians (deedless) will miss this treasure.

21. Our Soul = is our eternal spiritual body that houses our Spirit.

22. Our Spirit = is who we are. Our character, our unseen abilities to understand spiritual concepts, such as Love, beauty, ideas, likes, dislikes, reasoning, forgiveness, and more. This characteristic is especially true in reflecting the light of Jesus.

23 Our Bodies = houses our soul, which houses our spirit while present in this carnal state on earth.

24. god = is any false god of a pagan religion.

25. God, GOD = is our supreme creator, covenant-keeping, and final Judge. The same applies to the Lord and LORD.

26. Living Creatures = Aliens. This word alien was not used the same way in the time scriptures were written. It surfaced during the time of Jules Vern's SFI books.

27. Sons of God = is all entities that are obedient to God and Jesus.

28. Half Righteous = are those who believe in Jesus (saved) but are disobedient and perform no deeds for Jesus' Kingdom. They have no treasures.

I am sure some of you may take exception to the word *Half Righteous.* This word you have never heard in Church doctrine. I use this word to hopefully explain the cause of those left behind at the Rapture. You will read more on the word in the chapter on Deeds versus Faith.

I must add some more information here to help with understanding these different mysteries. Hopefully, they will give you focus and directional power in interpreting the scriptures when you read these words. Dictionaries are man's interpretation of words and are not adequate to reveal spiritual meanings. You will also notice I have underlined some scriptures which are not underlined in the Bible. I have done this to bring your attention to these verse's words. You will also see reference scriptures in bold to help find that verse or verses when looking back.

Note

Keep in mind the English language does not have specific words to explain the Bible's translation adequately. For example, the Greek and Hebrew language have several words for God, Love, and Hell. Traditions by teachers have used the word Hell for all the lost souls' final destination. *But the Bible is clear; the final destination is the Lake of Fire* **(Rev.20:14–15).** Several books of translation (Concordance) have every word mentioned in the Bible and its meanings. And I suggest you have one if you are a serious student of the Bible.

In the *Old Testament* (KJV), God has ten (10) different names. The one most used is:

"**Elohim;** plur. 433; *gods* in the ordinary sense, but epec. used (in the plur. esp. with this art.) of the supreme *God*; occasionally applied by way of deference to *magistrates*; and sometimes as a superlative: - angels, X exceeding, God (gods) (-dess, ly), X (very) great, judges X mighty[2]."

Notice this word is plural (*gods*) but also in connection with a **single** *supreme God*. Therefore, this supreme God is three Gods in one: the Father, the Son, and the Holy Ghost. Also, we read that Elohim is the magistrate of his creation. He is an official empowered to enforce the law, both physical and spiritual.

In the New Testament, we see twelve (12) different names for God. This word is used often, the word is:

> "**Theh-os**; of uncert. affin.; a *deity*, espec. (with *3588*) the supreme
> *Divinity*; fig. a *magistrate*; by Heb. *very*: - X exceeding, God, god
> [-ly.-ward][2]."

The three keywords here are God, Divinity, and Magistrate. Therefore, Thehos refers to the divine power of the magistrate we have seen above. It also applies to the total (X exceeding) absolute supreme power of Divinity (GOD). We know this word Thehos first used in Genesis 1:1 through Genesis 6:4, revealing the unlimited power God used in Creating. And God is the ultimate magistrate for the complete duration of his creation.

In Genesis 6:5, we see the name of God as:

> "**Loo'-o;** a prim. verb; to *bathe* (the whole *person*; whereas *3538*
> means to wet a *part* only, and *4150* to wash, cleanse *garments*
> exclusively):- wash[2]."

Notice the two meaning "*bath the whole body*" (Protestant) and "*wet a part only* "(Catholic). It seems both are acceptable. But baptism must be that individual's choice, not the parent.

God used this name to reveal God's Divinity as the ultimate magistrate to destroy humanity with the flood's bathing. And God did execute this punishment on humanity, but God has created a home for his righteous Old Testament children. Also, notice a possible reference to baptism in the words *"cleanse garments."* It is a baptism that visually reveals our filthy garments' cleansing to white as snow as all sins are forgiven.

You will also see god, God, and GOD, along with lord, Lord, and LORD. The *god* is pagan, where the others are basic and increase in impact.

I hope you can see the different characteristics of God used to give meaning to scriptures. A Concordance Book information is essential to understand better God's foundation in that particular verse or verses of scriptures.

For example: in **Genesis 2:1**, God uses the word HOST, which we usually think of as a person who provides for a group of guests. But, let us look into the meaning of that word in a Concordance for the Hebrew language.

> **Host** = *tsed-aw-aw:* from 6633; a mass of persons (or fig. things), espec. Reg. organized for war (*an army*); by impl. a campaign, lit. or fig. (spec. hardship, worship);-appointed time, (+) army, (+) battle, company, host, service, soldiers, waiting upon war (-fare)[2]."

As you can see, God created us (in the beginning) as an army waiting for spiritual warfare. Somewhat different from the previous words I mentioned. As you, no doubt, have surmised, this meaning can affect many understandings of future scriptures.

It appears God has a plan for the destruction of all evils. It also appears God is telling us that the only way to remove corruption from the earth is to kill it by mortal death and Spiritual Death.

You will notice, chapters of Major Mysteries which are supported by Minor Mysteries to help solve the Major Mysteries. All total is 74 Mysteries.

CONTENTS

MYSTERY ONE --- *ALIENS FACT OR FICTION*

1. MY DICTIONARY TRADITIONS ----------------------------------- 16
2. SAINTS -- 22
3. #1 ALIENS --- 25
4. #2 ALIENS --- 38
5. #3 ALIENS – Ezekiel's Wheels ------------------------------- 41
6. THE CREATURE --- 57
7. SHEEP FOLD --- 66
8. INHERITANCE -- 77
9. ADAM and EVE FALL -- 83
10. MAN'S CREATION --- 95
11. AGE of ACCOUNTABILITY -------------------------------------- 97
12. PARADISE, TORMENT, and ABYSS ------------------------------ 101
13. SPEAKING IN TONGUES --------------------------------------- 108
14. PREDESTINED --- 111
15. THOSE OUTSIDE THE CITY ------------------------------------ 115
16. UNIFORMITARISM -- 119
17. TIME OF FORGIVENESS --------------------------------------- 121
18. BLASPHEME THE HOLY GHOST ---------------------------------- 126

B. MYSTERY TWO --- 135
C. MYSTERY THREE – *THE MYSTERY OF THE SAINTS* ---------- 222
D. MYSTERY FOUR – *OF THREE CLOCKS.* -------------------- 240

E. ATTACHMENTS
    REFERENCES CHARTS

A Third Heaven -- 439
B Places in the Earth --------------------------------------- 440
C Completion Chart -- 441

PREFACE

This book is an attempt on my part to explain a concept that occurred to me hopefully from the Holy Spirit. I will use scripture to support my conclusions, and I will share those scriptures with you as the concept develops. I pray that I do not take those scriptures out of context and make every effort to prevent that from occurring. I will be asking questions for your consideration to provoke you into considering some ideas of your own before I address my answers. I have found that a thought-provoking question can be an excellent tool in getting our minds into gear, and it can sometimes readily reveal the answer in itself.

You will find diagrams that will have visual information relating to the previously written information. Many people can visualize written concepts and need not any visual aids. However, others benefit from such charts or graphs. The diagrams will build in their complexity, and a complete compilation diagram D1 is in the book near the end.

You will notice specific passages of quoted scripture are <u>underlined to center your attention on that word or words,</u> but the actual scriptures are not underlined. Also, keep in mind that the original scriptures were without chapter and verse numbers. These were added later to facilitate the ease in locating a particular verse. The best example is in chapters **Mat. 24** and **25,** as **chapter 25** is a continuation of the concepts written in **Mat. 24.** Also, you will see a word or words in parenthesis to help clarify the sentence.

One last thing I would like you to be aware of is my use of the words: Israel or Israelites, Jews, and Hebrews. Today we have been bombarded with Israel as that is the name of their country. But in the past, when scriptures were written, there was; first, the Hebrew Nation made up of God's elect, the Hebrews. Later the Hebrew Nation split into two nations. The one to the north was named Juda, from which came the Jews, and the south was named Israel, called Israelites.

So when you read Israelites or Jews, it is synonymous with the Hebrew people, both Jews, and Israelites. However, there are some caveats (exceptions) to this statement; But not entertained here.

When you see "the elect," it refers to those individuals God predestined for his service in both the Old Testament and New Testament times. The first elect was the Hebrew nation. The second elect is the saved Gentiles.

Note

Keep in mind the English language does not have specific words to explain the Bible's translation adequately. For example, the Greek and Hebrew language have several names for God, Love, and Hell. Traditions by teachers have used the word Hell (traditionally) for all the lost souls' final destination. *But the Bible is clear; the final destination is the Lake of Fire* **(Rev.20:15).** Several books of translation (Concordance) have every word mentioned in the Bible and its meanings. And I suggest you have one if you are a serious student of the Bible.

In the *Old Testament* (KJV), God has ten (10) different names. The one most used is:

> "Elohim; plur. 433; *gods* in the ordinary sense, but epec. used (in the plur. esp. with this art.) of the supreme *God*; occasionally applied by way of deference to *magistrates*; and sometimes as a superlative: - angels, X exceeding, God (gods) (-dess, ly), X (very) great, judges X mighty.[2]"

Notice this word is plural (*gods*) but also in connection with a **single** *supreme God*. Therefore, this supreme God is three Gods in one: the Father, the Son, and the Holy Ghost. Also, we read that Elohim is the magistrate of his creation. He is an official empowered to enforce the law, both physical and spiritual.

In the New Testament, we see twelve (12) different names for God. This word used most often is:

> **"Theh-os;** of uncert. affin.; a *deity*, espec. (with *3588*) the supreme *Divinity*; fig. a *magistrate*; by Heb. *very:* - X exceeding, God, god [-ly.-ward]²."

The three keywords here are God, Divinity, and Magistrate. Therefore, Thehos refers to the divine power of the magistrate we have seen above. It also applies to the total (X exceeding) absolute supreme power of Divinity (GOD). We know this word Thehos first used in Genesis 1:1 through Genesis 6:4, revealing the unlimited power God used in Creating. And God is the ultimate magistrate for the complete duration of his creation.

In Genesis 6:5, we see the name of God as:

> **"Loo'-o;** a prim. verb; to *bathe* (the whole *person*; whereas *3538* means to wet a *part* only, and *4150* to wash, cleanse *garments* exclusively):- wash²."

God used this name to reveal God's Divinity as the ultimate magistrate to destroy humanity with the bathing of the Flood. And God did execute this punishment on humanity, but God has created a home for his righteous Old Testament children. Also, notice a possible reference to baptism in the words *"cleanse garments."* It is a baptism that visually reveals our filthy garment's cleansing to white as snow as all sins are forgiven.

You will also see "god, God, and GOD, along with lord, Lord, and LORD. The *god* is pagan, where the others are basic and increase in impact.

I hope you can see the different characteristics of God used to give meaning to scriptures. A Concordance Book's information is essential to understand better God's foundation in that particular verse or scriptures.

NAMES OF THE PLACES OF THE DEAD

These names of the places of the dead have been a throne in the side of interpreters for years. There is also a distinction between death and Death. In this book, I use death as the *death* we are most familiar with; the death of our mortal body. Here we are separated from our body into our spiritual soul. And our Spirit is in the spiritual resting place in peace or a place of punishment.

Death is the destruction of all souls from a place of lesser punishment (a holding area) awaiting the final Day of Judgment; it is similar to our prisons, awaiting their death sentence. However, God holds prisoners in a location where they can see and experience the heat from the Lake of Fire. For far too long, we have been bombarded with Hell as the final place of eternal punishment. But, **Rev. 20:14** reveals, *"Death and Hell are cast into the Lake of Fire."*

Revelation 20:14–15 "(14) And <u>death and hell</u> were <u>cast into the lake of fire.</u> This is the second death. (15) And whosoever was not found written in the book of life was cast into the lake of fire."

If this is a true statement, **and it is**, then there have to be different locations for Heaven and Hell. This condition should not surprise us, as God's law did the same for a prisoner before the crucifixion. Jesus was held in a cell until he met with Pilate in the morning. We do the same today with our death row prisoners.

Here are some names of locations of the dead.

1. **Gehenna** = a permanent place where body, soul, and Spirit are placed in the unquenchable fire. **(Mar.9:43)** [Lake of Fire]
2. **Hades** = the temporary abode of the dead. [Paradise and/or Torment.]
3. **Sheol** = the place of the abode of the lost souls waiting for the final Day of Judgment. (O.T.) **(Luk.16:23)** [Torment / Hell]
4. **Tartarus** = temporary holding place for fallen angels [Abyss].

5. **Lake of Fire** = the permanent place where Hell (Torment) and all lost souls are thrown into the Lake of Fire. **(Rev.20:14)** Satan, fallen angels, demons, Antichrist #1/#2, and the False Prophet are also there and captured for eternity.

JESUS' RETURNS

For clarity, I must place here the returns of Jesus to affect the earth.

1. The **first time** is Jesus visited the earth was to die for our sins and become our savior.
2. The **second time** he comes, He does not touch the earth but collects all His believers and workers. It is called the Rapture.
3. The **third time** Jesus comes to earth as our Lord and King for 1,000 years. It is called Jesus' 1,000-year Kingdom.

TRADITIONS

I am sharing this chapter first with you to challenge you because of old hidden traditions or misunderstood Biblical understandings. Hopefully, we together can find the truth from the scriptures.

Traditions have been passed down from before Jesus to today. And they are still used in our teaching and preaching. Many of our decisions we use in our everyday life are based on traditions, be they in spiritual or common usage. For example: in our celebration of Christmas, we decorate a tree, put lights on our outdoor roof, and send Christmas Cards. This celebration is acceptable as there is no scripture against celebrating Jesus' birthday. But, Santa Clause could be a different matter. If you look closely at Christmas cards, you will see camels and Wise men also at the birth scene. The Wise Men came later to Joseph's home, about one year after Jesus' birth. So we innocently pass on this tradition to our children. But for righteous traditions, must be supported by scripture.

First, let us look at the definition of tradition in Concordance[2] and Funk and Wagnall Dictionary[3].

Concordance "3862 = par-ad"-os-is; from 3860: transmission, i.e. (concr.) a precept; spec. the Jewish traditionary law: ordinance, tradition[2]."

F & W = tradition 1) The knowledge, doctrines, customs, practices, etc., transmitted from generation to generation; also, the transmission of such knowledge, doctrines, etc. 2) The body of unwritten Christian doctrine handed down through successive generations. 3) Among the Jews, an unwritten code said to be handed down orally from Moses. 4) The historic conceptions and usages of a school of art, literature, etc. 5) *A custom so long continued that it has almost the force of law*[3]."

This last definition is the worst as we take them for granted and do not challenge them. So many traditions are based on false assumptions and are passed down initially by word of mouth. Many are old wives' tales created to protect their families. One is *"cleanliness is next to Godliness."* This quote is a good tradition, but it is not true, except cleanliness through the blood of Jesus. Many half-truths have become traditions.

The concordance definition speaks to the time of Jesus when the religious leaders considered him to be a fake and a hieratic, as Jesus did not follow the incorrect traditions these men espoused. In **Mat.15,** we read of a Jewish traditional law of washing hands.

Matthew 15: 1–3 "(1) Then came to Jesus scribes and Pharisees, which were of Jerusalem, saying, (2) Why do thy disciples transgress the tradition of the elders? For they wash not their hands when they eat bread. (3) But he answered and said unto them, Why do ye also transgress the commandment of God by your tradition?" (KJV)

As you can see, there is a non-scriptural tradition for cleanness for washing hands before eating. Not a bad practice, but it is not Biblical written law. It is called the Tradition of the Elders. Jesus uses this example to teach these

Pharisees a lesson about these non-Biblical traditions. The lesson is found in **Mat.15.**

Matthew 15:11 "Not that which goeth into the mouth defileth a man; but that which cometh out of the mouth, this defileth a man." *(KJV)*

To get a full understanding of this encounter, please read the complete **chapter 15**. Here Jesus reveals that it is not that which goes in the mouth that defiles a person, but the evil words that come out of the mouth that defiles that person. Because it reveals that person's condition of their heart, be it good or evil. And evil words will defile. Jesus continued by telling these Pharisees they are transgressing God's law by performing some traditions against God's Law. Jesus was referring to **Mark7:7–9** and **Mat.15:1–4.**

Mark 7:7–9 *"(7) Howbeit in vain do they worship me, <u>teaching</u> for <u>doctrines the commandments of men. (8) For laying aside the commandment of God, ye hold the tradition of men,</u> as the washing of pots and cups: and many other such like things ye do. (9) And he said unto them, <u>Full well ye reject the commandment of God, that ye may keep your own tradition."</u>* *(KJV)*

Jesus here is referring to the tradition of not teaching children to respect their parents. And some of these Traditions of the Elders directly contradict God's command of **Deu.5.** We see this failure in our society today. There are too many fatherless families—teenagers who totally disrespect seniors and including their parents. Once disrespect finds its home, then it spreads to systems of non-authority (anarchy).

Deuteronomy 5:16 *"<u>Honour thy father and thy mother,</u> as the LORD thy <u>God hath commanded thee;</u> that thy days may be prolonged, and that it may go well with thee, in the land which the LORD thy God giveth thee. " (KJV)*

There was a tradition that said a person could give to God's (Priest) service instead of supporting that person's parents. **(Exo.20:12)**

Many traditions have continued down through history have been founded on the original Roman Catholic Church doctrine. However, so does other denominations. I was raised in a Southern Baptist Church, and we had traditions that said: we cannot drink alcohol. There is no such law or scripture against liquor, except for drunkenness, but also gluttony **(Deu.21:20–21).** We could not get drunk, but we could get fat. "MMMMMMM?" Jesus himself turned water into the best wine for his first miracle. These drinkers knew good wine at the wedding and called it the best wine and not grape juice.

Also, we were not allowed to dance with a girl or woman. But no scripture says this. So these are church-directed (elder's) traditions. The most significant number of traditions came down through the original Roman Catholic Church ("Sacred Traditions"), and many have no or very little foundation in scripture. Here are some for your preview. But remember, those that contradict the Bible must be considered invalid.

1. The Pope is infallible. Only the triune God is infallible.
2. Purgatory, a place to pay for sins.
3. Penance, deeds to pay for sins. What is sin, and how many and how much?
4. Indulgences; pay the Priest or Pope enough Money, and he will pray you into heaven. Not possible.
5. Praying the Rosary, standard repetitive prayers.
6. Praying to Saints and Mary instead of to Jesus or God.
7. The wearing of the scapulars.
8. Mary is also a savior equal to Jesus.
9. Mass was initially in Latin; it was babble to most uneducated people, and in scripture is not permitted unless there was an interpreter present to reveal what is being said.
10. Only the Priest and Jesuits could own or read a Bible.

These traditions and many others are not found in the Bible. Many oral traditions started in the time of the Apostles as they moved around the land.

But, the correct ones were eventually written down in the scriptures. Those traditions that contradict with scriptures must be considered invalid. The ones that do not contradict are OK, such as washing your hands before eating. *Jesus, at no time, spoke well of the traditions*. Jesus' Gospel contradicted the traditions of the Elders and Priest, which eventually caused his death. In **Col. 2,** we can read what Peter had to say about Traditions.

> **Colossians 2:8** *"Beware lest any man spoil you through <u>philosophy and vain deceit, </u><u>after the tradition of men,</u> after the rudiments of the world, and <u>not after Christ."</u> (KJV)*

So we see that we are to remain strong in scripture and not in the traditions of men. This concept requires the study of the Bible. But what types of traditions are there? There are oral, written, and doctrinal. The most misunderstood is doctrinal.

The doctrinal traditions come from well-meaning teachers, scholars, and priests; trying to prevent people from sinning. *However, God gives individuals their exclusive right to exercise their own self-will, be it for good or evil.* Also, there are hidden scriptures in the Bible that will not be properly interpreted until God releases them to man. This causes teachers and Priests to establish questionable traditions that temporarily answer a question. Remember, the Popes had to remain infallible to retain power. He could not say, "I don't know! So here comes a new tradition. One such restricted scripture is found in **Dan.12.**

> **Daniel 12:4** *"But thou, O Daniel, shut up the words, and seal the book,* even *to the time of the end: many shall run to and fro, and knowledge shall be increased." (KJV)*

This verse has caused many old scholars problems as God has kept it secret until now. Some of the ancient interpretations were incorrect, and the incorrect became traditions for teachers. This concept is nothing new as Jesus had to break through old traditions being taught to people; to bring in the truth. We have experienced these ancient traditions ourselves. We were told by the Pope the world was flat, and if you sail far enough, they would fall off the earth into oblivion (infallible?). Isaiah even knew the earth was round (see **Isaiah 40:22**). But the infallible Pope's tradition said it was flat. Many of the Pope's rules continue to follow us today. *Ezekiel's wheels corrected the Pope's traditional doctrine* (**Eze.1** and **10**) *that we are not the only people in the Universe.* Many Jewish traditions were formed by the elders that had no basis in the Scriptures. Some of the Jewish traditional celebrations are not in the scriptures. They are OK because they do not contend with scriptures and can be historical celebrations, like our 4th of July.

Interpretation of scriptures is very difficult to perform as it must come from the Holy Spirit. We humans can be affected by many outside influences and our pre-disposition. It can affect our knowledge, such as: are you conservative or liberal, are you motivated by logic or artistry, are you loyal to your denomination or the Bible, are you open-minded or closed-minded, and are you motivated by learning or not? Interpretations must be supported by scripture, and the more scripture, the better. But, some scriptures can stand by themselves. **(John 3:16)** The deeper the traditions have been entrenched in us, the more difficult it will be to accept new knowledge. One of the Pope's oldest traditions is *"we are the only living creatures in the universe."* Nowhere is this located in the Bible, but the Bible eludes to alien's presents.
Most traditions will disappear or be revealed by an earnest study of the Bible. God tells us this in **2 Tim 2.**

> **2 Timothy 2:15–16 *"(15) Study to shew thyself approved unto God, a workman that needeth not to be ashamed, rightly dividing the word of truth. (16) But shun profane* and *vain babblings: for they will increase unto more ungodliness." (KJV)***

Notice *"shun profane and vain babbling,"* which can refer to vain traditions created for selfish desires like religious power, especially during the Great Tribulation. This vanity will rear its ugly head during the false religious times spoken in Revelation. The False Prophet will use erroneous doctrine and using traditions to control the masses. When receiving information, remember what James said in **Jam.1.**

James 1:19–20 *"(19) Wherefore, my beloved brethren, let every man be swift to hear, slow to speak, slow to wrath: (20) For <u>the wrath of man worketh not the righteousness</u> of God.*

Some people take offense very quickly when their beliefs or knowledge are perceived as being challenged. And that is why we have *a tradition of not discussing religion or politics in public.* Here is another utterly wrong tradition. These two are the most important subjects for our knowledge and understanding. But it angers some people quickly. We see this all the time on our TV news media; people screaming at each other, interrupting each other, and even calling the other names. This is not the attitude of a Christian. **(Jam.1:19)**

I have placed this chapter first to prepare you for challenges you might encounter in my book. But, I desire you to understand that I am trying to give knowledge truthfully as it has been given to me. I want you to challenge my concepts, and you are told to do so in **1 John 4.** <u>That way, two heads can be better than one.</u> "MMMM." Is that a tradition?

1 John 4:1 *"Beloved, believe not every spirit, but try the spirits whether they are of God: because many <u>false</u> prophets are gone out into the world." (KJV)*

SAINTS MYSTERIES

First, I would challenge your understanding of Saints. A Saint is a righteous individual **saved by God's GRACE** and not selected through a committee. God's grace is given to his children that attempt to please God in their daily walk. The proof is found in **1 Cor. 6:2.**

1 Corinthians 6:2–3 *"(2) <u>Do ye not know that the saints shall judge the world? And if the world shall be judged by you, are ye</u> unworthy to judge the smallest matters? (3) <u>Know ye not that we shall judge angels?</u> How much more the things that pertain to this life?"(KJV)*

Notice that *"ye"* (you), we, <u>all those in Jesus (Saints)</u>, shall judge the world and angels. *Paul is writing to all the Corinthians believers* in Jesus. Therefore, who are these different classifications of Saints? These are *my classifications*, which help me to understand scripture.

Old Testament

1.   **Pre-law Saints** – These are the individuals that found **Grace** in God's eyes for trying to do good **deeds** rather than evil deeds, and their heart's worshiped God. They are from Adam to Moses and the Law.

2.   **Law Saint** – These are the individuals who also found God's **Grace** by trying to follow the **deeds and theirs's hearts love** of God's. They followed God's Laws as best they could. The Pre-law Saints and Law Saints are both saved by deeds and their heart's attitudes.

3.   **Church Saints** – These are the Saints who have professed *faith in Jesus* for their salvation and have *performed the deeds* of spreading the Gospel. These individuals are also called the Bride of Christ and the Queen of the Universe.

4.   **Tribulation Saints** -- These are the left behind Church Pew Setters that <u>performed no deeds but are saved by faith but have no treasures (no deeds)</u>. And the Hebrew and Gentile converts by the 144,000 Jewish missionaries; that proclaim faith in Jesus as their savior. They now see the proof of the *<u>necessity to perform deeds</u>*. They are found under the Temple Altar beheaded for not accepting (deed) the Mark of the Beast or worshipping Satan.

I have given you a brief look at Saints to help you understand some Biblical concepts. You will be given more information on Saints later. If you would like, you can go to The Saints Mystery for that information now.

ALIENS

FACT

OR

FICTION

ALIEN MYSTERY #1

Based on Mat.18:11–14

I approach a very controversial subject. Many people do not believe in aliens but believe in angels. To those that do not believe in aliens, please bear with me. Here I am presenting verses of scripture that can or does reveal an alien's presents. Please hear me out. Also, keep in mind that there was no word for *aliens* when the scriptures were written. It appears that the scribes used Living Creatures to represent living aliens.

We have been taught this _tradition_ for eons from religious leaders and nonreligious leaders; we are the only planet in this entire universe with life. To disagree with the Pope was a death sentence for heresy. A powerful motivation not to disagree with religious leaders. This religious attitude caused the Dark Ages, where millions were murder under the guise of heresy.

A universe having extreme distances measured in light-years, with uncountable galaxies, with even more Stars and planets within those galaxies. With more habitable capable planets to those suns (stars) similar to our solar system; and we think we are alone in this unmeasurable Universe. There is overwhelming historical and present time evidence on earth that points to a different possible conclusion. The possibility is there are other life forms in the universe — Aliens. One consideration is the possibility concept of probabilities or the odds.

Computing odds has been a well-established scientific math procedure of computing the possibility of something happening. And if one calculated the odds of the earth being the only inhabited planet in our galaxy alone, the odds would be phenomenal. Just in <u>our galaxy</u>, if one star out of a million stars had one habitable type planet comparable to earth, and if one of those habitable planets, only one had life. We would have over one million ± habitable planets capable of life just in our galaxy alone. But there are over an estimated 2 trillion galaxies in the universe, and each contains billions of solar systems.

Science tells us (2018) that the seeable Universe is 46.6 billion light-years in-depth (radius from the earth). That is a diameter of 93.2 billion light-years with 2 trillion galaxies. Our galaxy alone is estimated to have 300 billion Stars (suns) with planets. And we are the only star (sun) with an inhabited planet? Ancient traditions from the Pope say we are alone. If anyone disagreed, they were a heretic and burned at the stake. And many were burned for their conflict with the Pope's words. Death was a powerful motivation to keep silent.

Keep in mind that the speed of light is: 186,000 miles per second; 11,160,000 miles per minute; 669,600,000 miles per hour; 16,070,400,000 miles in a day; 5,849,625,600,000 miles per year and 157,939,891,200,000,000,000,000,000 miles in 27,000 light-years to the center of just our galaxy. We cannot fully grasp the magnitude of this diameter distance in the universe. *And we are the only occupants within this Universe?* How think ye? Is our government keeping truths from us?

It seems our government is concerned about how our population would react, knowing there are superior knowledgeable aliens in our atmosphere. It is right to consider the ramification of possible aliens, be they hostile or friendly. Since we have survived for millenniums without any known massive unified aggressive action from aliens, why would they do any now? Since we have developed the atom bomb, we now have a power source that they may be concerned with our application.

The governments on earth appear to be concerned with their population's potential panic if they knew aliens exist. Aliens have not invaded our planet since 1938 in Orson Welles's fictional radio program "War of the Worlds." His radio program was so believable many people believed America was under attack by aliens. Many people were frightened, and very few did panic to some degree, but there was no national panic by people: running amiss down city streets; destroying property; running over people, stealing food, or trying to escape. There were mostly people who did not panic, and some disbelieved. In 1938 mainly were agricultural families and not all that familiar with aliens (except Jules Verne's writings), and people only had a radio for their electronic entertainment. Many people in Sardis, Tennessee (my grandparent's home) had minimal electricity; Grandfather had three overhead single swinging light bulbs for light; a hand crank (party line) telephone. And these lights were located: one in the parlor, one in the dining room, and one in the kitchen. Kerosene lamps provided other Lights. Grandfather had to tie in to the one light in the parlor to serve his radio.

We are told that the occupants of this earth could not handle knowing aliens are present. But America did not panic in WWI, WWII, or at 911 attacks. On the contrary, we came together as one people to fight. Also, we are told this knowledge of the presence of aliens would change all religious concepts.

And the Gospel of Jesus would change. *However, nothing could be farther from the truth.*

Aliens are already present in the form of angels, and additional aliens will not change the Gospel but possibly clarify some of the mysteries of the Gospel of Jesus. Our primary belief that our faith in Jesus is our way to eternal life is permanent, unchangeable, that goodwill eventually conquer evil, and Jesus' 1,000-year earthly Kingdom will exist. We, who accept Jesus, will rule with Jesus, and we will become kings or lords and priests. We will be heirs with Jesus of *all God owns, which is everything in the Universe!*

These entities in the universe are waiting for our brothers and sisters to accept Jesus and become the Sons of God **(Rom.8:19–23).** God's plan for the universe will come to an end. But God will again create an entirely New Universe and a New Earth. All souls will have a new home, be it Heaven or the Lake of Fire. However, many Bible scriptures would become clear with the presents of aliens.

Note

From this point forward, it will be difficult to distinguish between children of men and children of God's sons (aliens). Both children are carnal and will experience mortal death. This mortal death is because the women born to the sons of Man are mortal, too. After all, Adams's curse (death) is in the children of the earth.

Here we see verses that alien presence would clarify.

Genesis 6:1–4 *"(1) And it came to pass, when <u>men began to multiply</u> on the face of the earth, <u>and daughters were born unto them,</u> (2) That <u>the sons of God</u> saw the <u>daughters of men</u> that they were fair; and they took them wives of all which they chose. (3) And the LORD said, My Spirit shall not always strive <u>with man, for that he also is flesh:</u> yet his days shall be an hundred and twenty years. (4) There were giants in the earth in those days; and <u>also after that,</u> <u>when the sons of God</u>* (aliens) *came in unto the <u>daughters of men,</u> and they bare* children *to them, the same became mighty men which* were *of old, men of renown."(KJV)*

Note

In **Rom. 8:14,** *"For as many as are <u>led by the spirit</u> of God, they are the sons of God." (KJV)*

This verse clarifies that those led by God's Spirit (obedient) are the sons of God. There are five names for God's Spirit: 1) Spirit of God; 2) the Holy Spirit; 3) the Holy Ghost; 4) the Spirit of the Lord; and 5) the Spirit of the Lord God **(Isa.11:2)**. Spirit is used many times in the Bible. In **Rom. 8:14,** the word used here is *<u>"pnyoo'-mah,"</u> which <u>means a blast of breath from a rational soul about a vital principle from God or Christ Spirit.</u>[2]* But, remember the Holy Spirit (God's Spirit) came to earth, for the Church at Pentecost, which was many years later after creation. Therefore, in **Gen. 1:2,** *"sons of God"* could be righteous angels or aliens *who are obedient to God's will.*

Please notice the verbal distinction of the *daughters of men;* and *sons of God* (aliens) in **verses 2** and **4.** This is a curious statement by God. First, who are *"the sons of God?"* In **Rom. 8:14,** we just read they are led by God's Spirit. It is my understanding that all individuals created by God are his children (sons and daughters). But also notice that initially, the daughters were born to **men** (not lead by the Spirit of God); and not to the *Sons of God* (aliens); until after the *sons of God* (aliens) saw the *daughters of men* and took them as wives. Here again, there seems to be a separation of the classification between *daughters of men* and *Sons of God.* These *Sons of God* (aliens) took all the wives they desired. Today, we call this a Harem, which is not permitted by some religions in the world and those countries' laws. [More on this subject later.]

And so, being that God created all things, *would not obedient aliens be sons of God* created in his image? We know angels have appeared to us in the human form **(Heb.13:2)** that we are familiar with. But angels are known to fight **(Dan. 10:12–13** and **20)** Satan in the spiritual world, which indicates a universe of at least two dimensions, mortal and spiritual. Angels are spiritual, but sons of God are mortals. When you are reading Genesis, remember, Jesus was with God before God started his creative efforts. I know of no mention of the creation of angels except in the possibility of a verse of **Genesis 2:1,** " *the host.* "

If angels are not created like us, then they must have the ability to assume our appearance. In SIFY terms, they would be called Shape Shifters. This Shape-Shifting appears to be an unnecessary condition. Angels are separated into two groups. One group is righteous, and one is unrighteous. The righteous have been obedient to Jesus and God and, therefore, are sons of God; the unrighteous angles are disobedient to Jesus and God. If righteous angels can appear to us, can also unrighteous angels appear to us (poltergeist)? Here is another reason for **1 John 4:1** tells us to test the Spirit. So is it possible both groups of angels can appear like God's form [head, torso, arms, hands, legs, and feet]?

We can read in **Exo. 33:18–23** God placed Moses in the cleft of a rock, and God put his hand over Moses' face so Moses cannot see God's face and die. In these words of scriptures, we read of God's physical backside appearance. God has 1) a face, 2) a hand, 3) an arm (assumed), locomotion (legs/feet?), and 4) back parts. Back parts indicate recognizable body parts to Moses, or he would have been surprised and would have mentioned it. Therefore, if we are made in God's image, then God must appear somewhat like us, and we appear like God.

Notice also, these children of the sons of God (aliens) are also flesh due to both aliens and mothers (women) being flesh, and now their children have become human. Otherwise, we would have had more than one virgin birth! And being flesh, they have a limited life span to carnal death, and they too will become corrupt. We see Jesus' birth made Jesus mortal also.

Jesus referred to himself many times in the Bible as *"the Son of Man."* From his statement, it appears he is defining his *distinction between God's sons* (aliens) *and man's sons (earthlings).* This statement is in agreement with Genesis' different classification between *"sons of God"* (aliens) and *"daughters of men."* **(Gen. 6)**

> **Genesis 6:1–4** "(1) *And it came to pass, when men began to multiply on the face of the earth, and daughters were born unto them, (2) That the sons of God saw the daughters of men that they were fair; and they took them wives of all which they chose. (3) And the LORD said, My Spirit shall not always strive with man, for that he also is flesh: yet his days shall be an hundred and twenty years. (4) There were giants in the earth in those days; and also after that, when the sons of God came in unto the daughters of men, and they bare children to them, the same became mighty men which were of old, men of renown." (KJV)*

Verse 2 is a _clue_ as to the daughters of man. Scientists, through the theory of Darwinism, tell us; we evolved from apes. But notice that "*the sons of God saw the daughters of men that they were fair*." Beautiful is another word for fair. If we were made in God's image and so are all beings (aliens), how could they think an ape was beautiful and want to procreate with them. This idea is against one of God's later laws, where a harem is not. And what is the possibility of the offspring of an ape and an alien? Today we know that this is not possible as apes and humans are not in the same species and unable to interbreed.

Now we read of the offspring of the sons of God (aliens). Notice they produced _children of flesh_ because the daughters of men were flesh, and the children would have the DNA of both the sons of God (aliens) and daughters of men. Now the statement "*with man, for that he also is flesh.*" This appears to inform us that these Sons of God (aliens) are flesh. Their children became flesh, just as Jesus became flesh. Therefore, these sons of God (aliens) must be flesh, or their son's birth would be from a virgin birth, which I doubt very much; as Jesus was the only virgin birth and Jesus too was a carnal man. Their children would be of flesh, and apparently, they were as they died in the Flood. However, nowhere does it say that these sons of God (alien fathers) died in the Flood, just their children. But, notice that these sons of God (aliens) reappear after *that*, which refers to the Flood. But notice verse 2 and verse 4 reveal two different times that the Sons of God took daughters of the sons of man for wives.

Note

One other consideration is, where did all the different colored races on earth come from? Science tells us that food and other atmospheric conditions cause these different colored races. However, we have evidence today that mixed marriages cause a change in the baby's color. Over time we have seen white and black have produced lighter and lighter shades to a golden brown. Some blacks are not black externally at all. Could the different colored aliens cause these different colored races? This color change is proven, where food and the atmospheric conditions are only a week theory.

In **Gen.6:3 / 7 / 13,** man had only 120 years to live until the Great Flood. Also, **verse 4** says, *"and also after that,"* where *"that"* refers to the Great Flood. Where did these sons of God (aliens) go to avoid the Flood? In **verse 4,** we read the sons of God (aliens) returned to daughters of men, and they bear children who became *"giants"* and *"became mighty men of renown."* This event must have occurred after the sons of God (aliens) return to earth and after man's daughters produced more sons of Man. Here too, this statement proves they were mighty men of flesh. Their children would have a higher level of knowledge taught them from their alien fathers, making them appear superior to ordinary people, making them mighty men. Some were giants, which would infer some of God's sons (aliens) were giants too.

Notice also these sons of God (aliens) took as many wives as they desired. There is no mention of one husband and one wife, but apparently, they had harems of wives just like before the Flood. Is it possible these sons of God (aliens) taught man the concept of harems, which we see occurring in our history, and even today.

Remember at this time there is no law from God with the exception of the laws of *1) "to not eat from the Tree of Knowledge of Good and Evil"* (but now it is gone); 2) make lots of babies (replenish); 3) subdue and 4) to rule. These laws were given to Adam and not the Sons of God (aliens). However, these laws were passed down to Adams's offspring, the sons of Man.

The statement in **Gen.6:3,** *"for that he is also flesh,"* also creates the concept that the offspring of these sons of God (aliens) *are also made of flesh and blood, just as we are carnal flesh and blood.* Therefore, it would appear these mighty sons, of the sons of GOD, were also of flesh, and they became corrupt just as earthly humans. Now we know that angels do not die. Therefore, angels are not flesh, as Satan is a fallen angel and has been with man since creation. One-third of all angels **(Rev.12:4)** have also become corrupted and have joined Satan in his attempt to become like God. But the righteous angels have been obedient servants of God for good and have brought us messages from God. They, too, appear to us as humans, as they are in God's image. In **Col.1,** we read that every creature is made in the image of God.

> **Colossians 1:14-15** *"(14) In whom* (Jesus) *we have redemption through his blood,* even *the forgiveness of sins: (15) Who is the* <u>*image of the invisilbe God, the firstborn of every creature:"*</u> *(KJV)*

Pay attention to these words, especially *"every creature,"* as we have redemption through Jesus' blood. And Jesus is the image of God; Jesus is the firstborn of <u>every creature</u>. [This is not referring to animals.] *Therefore, all created living creatures are made in the image of God.* But it appears that the sons of the sons of God (aliens) on earth are now carnal; to be able to have children.

In **Job 1:6** and **2:1,** we read of a meeting with God, *sons of God (aliens),* and Satan. How is this possible if the Sons of God are humans? It appears this is a repeating event, and those present are spiritual. Remember in **Rev.2:4;** John was in the Spirit to go to Heaven. This being in the Spirit was a one-time event as John returned to Patmos to live out his incarceration.

> **Job 1:6–7** *"(6) Now there was a day when the* <u>*sons of God*</u> *came to present themselves before the LORD, and Satan came also among them. (7) And the LORD said unto Satan, Whence comest thou? Then Satan answered the LORD, and said, From going to and fro in the earth, and from walking up and down in it.*

In **Job 1:7,** Satan has been walking up and down the earth (legs and feet?). But, *what of the sons of God (aliens);* where did they come from? And can the carnal (woman) individual procreate with the spiritual (angel) creature? I think not, only God! What is the Spirit?

John went to Heaven in Spirit, in **Rev.4.** Here is a very subtle statement from God and easy to be overlooked. How can a mortal body be converted to a spiritual body and instantly transported across the universe to the 3rd Heaven? Today we know of no material way this can happen. But nothing is impossible to God. It appears the spiritual soul of man will have no boundaries or limitations.

Notice later in this chapter the elders, which are the Church's leaders (now spirits), and the seven spirits of God. This scene is spiritual; therefore, the Sons of God must be spiritual or converted, as is John. How is it angels can have solid bodies and spiritual bodies? Can they procreate with solid bodies? Questions, questions, and questions!

But also, angels can appear as human beings. **Heb.13**.

> **Hebrews 13:2** *"Be not forgetful to entertain strangers: for thereby some have entertained angels <u>unawares.</u>" (KJV)*

This verse clarifies that we are being visited by angels unaware because they have the shape and form of us and not little gray men. These angel visitors speak the language of the people they are visiting; know the customs, courtesies; traditions; history; government, and all necessary information to fit perfectly into that society. If we are created in God's image, then the angels are made in the image of God. In **Rev.22,** we read of a fellow servant and <u>brethren</u> that appeared to John.

> **Revelation 22:8–9** *"(8) And I John saw these things, and heard (them). And when I had heard and seen, <u>I fell down to worship before the feet of the angel</u> which shewed me these things. (9) Then saith he* [angel] *unto me, See* thou do it *not: for I am <u>thy fellowservant, and of thy brethren the prophets, and of them which keep the sayings of this book:</u> worship God." (KJV)*

This individual is so remarkable in appearance John falls to his knees, before his feet, to worship him. But please grasp the reply of this supposed angel. *"I am thy fellowservant and <u>of thy brethren the prophets.</u>"* Angels are indeed God's servants, but the following description leaves no doubt; he was human at one time by his statement about being a *"prophet";* as only prophets are from man, humans. It appears that there are tasks for those who have died and are in Paradise. This statement is supported by the parable of the rich man and Lazarus **(Luk. 16:19–31).** There you will find Lazarus in the bosom of Abraham being comforted, which reveals Abraham and Lazarus are in

Paradise, and the rich man is in Torment. Notice Abraham is tasked by Jesus to bring comfort to the son of man, Lazarus.

Also, notice that these sons of the sons of God (aliens) bear children. Are these sons of God, angels? We know that our created forefathers bear children, but can angels bear children? In Greek and Hebrew language, words have a masculine or feminine inference to the word. I understand the word "angel" has a masculine inference and nowhere is it used in a feminine context. *(Here is an example of traditional input, as we see female angels everywhere)* But, can angels procreate with women of the earth to produce children? I know of no evidence of this in the Bible that answers this question. But it would be possible if the other entities (aliens) were created, like us, to procreate with earthly women and produce children. We humans here on earth have had our string of knowledge interrupted due to the curse of language confusion at the Tower of Babel. **(Gen. 11:7–8)**

These aliens' accomplishments would be staggering as they would have: one language, long life, and there would be nothing they could not accomplish. They also would, most likely, live long lives, as did Adam and Eve. We see this revealed in our planet earth at the Tower of Babel; they all spoke the same language **Gen.11**.

> **Genesis 11:5–6 *"(5) And the LORD came down to see the city and the tower, which the <u>children of men</u> builded. (6) And the LORD said, Behold, the people is one, and <u>they have all one language;</u> and this they begin to do: and <u>now nothing will be restrained from them, which they have imagined to do."</u> (KJV)***

Here again, we see the inference of *"the children of men"* (verses the *sons of the sons of God)* who were building a tower to heaven. But, who are the architects with the knowledge of the construction of large structures, understanding how to move extremely heavy stones for long distances? Where did they get the knowledge to create bricks?

This knowledge is a very revealing clue for us to consider, the movement of heavy objects. Scientists today cannot agree on how the sons of man could accomplish this task. Why would man forget such a valuable tool? We have not forgotten the use of the wheel, which proved to be a valuable tool for ordinary people. The wheel is simple to understand for man. The movement of very heavy objects must have taken complicated and massive tools made from unknown metals or some form of levitation, too complex for man to retain in his memory. But the sons of the sons of God (aliens) would keep this knowledge taught to them by their fathers (alien). The children of the sons of God (aliens) were destroyed during the Flood, and their knowledge died with them. However, when the sons of God (aliens) returned after the Flood, they would train their new children in construction techniques.

Now Noah and his sons had to move and manipulate some hefty logs during the Ark's construction. The Ark was: 45 feet high, 75 feet wide, and 450 feet long. Scaffolding had to be used to work the sides, and some form of crane would be needed to hoist timbers up to a 45 feet high deck. The logs to do this would have to be longer than 45 feet and very thick. Which also would be required to be mobile to move forward or aft of the 450 feet long ark. And the cross timbers (one top side across to the other top side) had to be 75 feet long or spliced together. What a job for three men, and one was old.

But what of the architects building the Pyramids? They had to move extremely heavy stone many miles, across the Nile River and up hundreds of feet. This knowledge of moving and building survived many years, for we see this in the stepped Pyramids around the earth. Are these architects the sons of God (aliens) or their children? All through history, we see the claim of men to be gods. And the lower status of the sons of man performed the labor for these supposed gods. From where did this knowledge of government structure come? Who informed man that there is a God or gods? When was God not present and visible to the sons of Adam? Apparently not for most, but they were taught of God by Noah's forefathers, Noah, and his sons-in-law.

Apparently, God wants us to know that our planet earth *("the sons of man")* has been denied this increase in knowledge for some reason, but not the *"sons of the sons of God."* God may have planned it this way. Another mystery to be solved by someone. We see that the Flood destroyed all individuals on earth, and if the aliens were here, they too would die if they did not have a way to escape. But the knowledge of building large structures and moving heavy objects survived the Flood. So there must be some way that this knowledge survived the Flood. It is possible Noah and his Sons-in-Law, but more likely by the returning sons of God (aliens).

Now it appears our earth fell into mortal death by the temptation of the fallen angel Satan. In this fall, inherited sin and a short life span entered into the world for all of Adams's offspring. See **Rom.5 and 1st Cor.15.**

> **Romans 5:12** *"Wherefore, as by <u>one man</u> sin entered into the world, and death by sin; and so death passed upon all men, for that all have sinned." (KJV)*

> **1 Corinthians 15:21–22** *"(21) For since by man came death, <u>by man</u>* [came] *also the resurrection of the dead. (22) For as in Adam all die, even so in Christ shall all be made alive." (KJV)*

We know this loss to sin has happened here on earth. Death proves we are the Lost Sheep, both Jews, and Gentiles. Death has been with us as we read in Genesis the life spans and the deaths of our forefathers[1] from Adam to the present time. Man has been given a natural life of 70 to 80 years on this earth at the current time. Here is another *clue* as in Adams day, man lived hundreds of years. Another *clue* about time movement is; over the year's man's life span decreased from 100's of years to 50 years, and today we are in the prophet period of 70 to 80 years of life expectant period. **(Psalms 90:7–10)** God has given us: Jesus, the Holy Spirit, teacher, pastors, prophet, and his Love Letter, the Bible, to help us on our journey through this life. God wants you and all individuals with him in Heaven for eternity. But, who are these sons of God (aliens) and their children?

To summarize: the Sons of Man became unrighteous earthlings, and the Sons of Gods are righteous earthlings and aliens. Both Sons of Man and the children of the Sons of God are human carnal. *The children of the Sons of God may live very long lives, as did the early children of man.*

ALIEN MYSTERY #2

Test, to understand this mystery, we must look at the players in this mystery. We will find them in The New Testament, **Rom. 8.**

> **Romans 8:14–18** "*(14) For as many as are <u>led by the Spirit of God, they are the sons of God.</u> (15) For ye have not received the Spirit of bondage again to fear; but ye have received the <u>Spirit of adoption,</u> whereby we cry, Abba, Father. (16) The Spirit itself beareth witness with our spirit, <u>that we are the children of God:</u> (17) And if children, then heirs; <u>heirs of God, and joint-heirs with Christ;</u> if so be that we suffer with him, that we may be also glorified together. (18) <u>For I reckon that the sufferings of this present time</u> are <u>not worthy</u> to be compared with the glory which shall be revealed in us*" *(KJV).*

One thing to consider is, to whom is this passage of scripture written? It is written to the Living Creatures, the Old Testament Saints, Church Saints, and Tribulation Saints. To any creature that is obedient to God. I'm sure the Holy Spirit worked from time to time with different individuals during the time before Pentecost. But after Pentecost, the Holy Spirit comes to earth and is present to every soul, especially for those who have faith in Jesus. So those who are led by the Spirit of God are now called the sons of God. To be led assumes obedience to God, Jesus, and the Holy Spirit. The *"children of Man"* are disobedient, but *"Sons of God"* are obedient.

Here we see the two players again named: *"sons of God"* and *"children of man"* **(Gen.6)**. *The sons of God* are those led by God's Spirit **(Rom. 8:14)**. But those _not_ led by God's Spirit *(children of man)* are carnally minded and will die both mortally and spiritually **(Rom. 8:13)**. Now notice the combining of *sons of God and the Children of God* in **Rom. 8:16–17**. The _clue_ here is: *"heirs of God."* Christians are in Jesus and will inherit with Jesus all God possesses. This unique *being in Jesus* is only for the sheep and goats of earth, and Jesus came to save all souls on earth.

Now keep in mind the statement *"they are led by the Spirit of God."* This statement identifies who is led by the Holy Spirit, which came to the Christian Apostles at the time of Pentecost **(Acts 2:1–21)**. And the Holy Spirit leads all Christians until the Holy Spirit is removed just at or before the Rapture **(2 Thes.2:6–8)**. Therefore, those after Pentecost are to be led by the Holy Spirit, but what of those righteous individuals before Pentecost? It appears that Noah, Elijah, and Enoch found grace in God's eyes to save them and Noah's family from eternal death. Was Noah lead by the Spirit of God? It would appear so, as God told Noah to build an ark. And God's Holy Spirit would have given Noah the necessary building instructions.

We tend to forget that Adam's lineage[E] found in **Genesis 5,** is of righteous men. One, in particular, is Enoch **(Gen. 5:21–24)**. Enoch walked and talked with God and did not die, for God took him to Heaven. So Enoch was led by God. Therefore, Enoch could be considered a son of God. Could *all the righteous people* who lived during that time before Moses' law be regarded as sons of God? ---- Yes! God's grace has spared many of them from the Lake of Fire, and they are in a place in the center of the earth, called *Paradise*. This Paradise is the location Jesus went to preach to those souls after his Crucifixion **(Luk. 24:23 / 39–43)** and **(1 Pet. 3:19)**. The prison mentioned in **1 Pet. 3:19–20** is called *Torment*. See the Parable of Lazarus and the rich man. **(Luk. 16:19–31)**

One other point to consider in this mystery is the statement of God in **Gen. 6**.

> **Genesis 6:1--3. *"(1) And it came to pass, when <u>men began to multiply</u> on the face of the earth, and <u>daughters were born</u> unto them, (2) That the <u>sons of God saw the daughters</u> of men that they*** were ***fair; and they <u>took them wives of all which they chose</u>. (3) And the LORD said, My <u>Spirit shall not always strive with man</u>, for that <u>he also</u> is flesh: shall yet his days be an hundred and twenty years"</u> (KJV).***

Did you catch the words *"he also is flesh"?* Here God is comparing both the sons of God to man, *as both are flesh.* And it is **the flesh** that has 120 years to live before the Flood. Therefore, the sons of the Son of God will die in the Flood.

Here we see again the distinction between Man and sons of God. If the sons of God are led by God's Spirit, then there seems to be a problem with the one husband and one wife concept. Remember, there is no <u>Law of Moses</u> given to man initially on earth. Notice that God is not pleased with man, but he is OK with the sons of God. Apparently, the Sons of God harems did not displease God, with the concept of one husband and one wife. As it is not a central theme at this point in history. Could this be like when God limited what foods the Hebrew people could eat and later removed that limitation? This is another mystery in itself.

Now, God shows his displeasure with the sons of Man as *their thoughts are continuously evil* **(Gen.6:5),** but not the sons of God who committed polygamy. Does this not appear to be Lust of the Flesh and Lust of the Eyes? It seems more than one wife for one husband was permitted by God. Possibly this was to aid the *"replenish the earth"* command. And God limited man's life to 120 years. This 120 years is the time it took Noah to build and provision the Ark. But polygamy continued for over 1,650 years until the Flood. And it continued again after the Flood and even today. So the sons of God (aliens) continued by their surviving the Flood. **(Gen.6:4)** If aliens, where did they go and when? Therefore, *Noah was a son of God* as he was led by God to build the Ark, and he was obedient. But, is Noah, an heir to God? ---Yes!

The Gospel declares we are heirs with Jesus (**Rom.8:16–17)**, as *we are now these children of God.* The foundation of the children is based on Jesus. It is in the faith of Jesus salvation through his death on the Cross. These children make up the true Church of God (all believers in Jesus) who are inheritors The main strength I see in the Sons of God is they are *righteous and obedient* creatures to God. They did not have the failure of being disobedient, as did Adam's offspring. But now enters another obedient player in this mystery— Ezekiel.   In Ezekiel, we find a fascinating subject, *Alien Wheels, in Chapters 1 &10.*

ALIEN MYSTERY #3 (EZEKIEL WHEELS)

This mystery starts in the Book of Ezekiel **Chapters 1 and 10.** Keep in mind that Ezekiel is trying to explain what he is experiencing in words of his day. There were no words for helicopters, rocket, space ship, airplane, spacesuit, or any modern device we have today. So the best we can do to understand is to surmise just what Ezekiel is trying to reveal in his comparative words of his day. Remember that these creatures, if aliens are far superior to our technical knowledge of today, most likely due to their single language and long life on their planet. However, we can see more possibilities today than Ezekiel could in his day. So there most likely will be things Ezekiel saw that we, even today, cannot understand or explain. But we have experienced many similar events. One is the whirlwind effect.

> **Ezekiel 1:4** *"And I looked, and, behold, a <u>whirlwind</u> came out of the north, a great cloud, and a <u>fire infolding itself,</u> and a <u>brightness</u>* was *<u>about it, and out of the midst thereof as the colour of amber,</u> out of the midst of the fire." (KJV)*

First, we read of a whirlwind that reveals some exhaust or forceful wind; but this wind appears to be in a cylindrical shape motion. We might say this is caused by a helicopter, as that is one of our experiences of today. Or from a craft using its engine thrust to move over the terrain stirring up a cloud of dust or sand. Ezekiel could be seeing wing-tip or propeller tip vortices that are circular in motion. And this fire infolding could be the engine exhaust hitting the ground and bouncing back onto the ship as the craft descends to land. Of course, any fire of this magnitude would also create an incredible light even in the daylight.

Next, Ezekiel describes the color of the ship within the exhaust as being amber. There are two colors of amber. One is Honey's color, and another is the color of yellow, such as the traffic light color of warning of a signal changing to red. We use yellow as a foundation color of warning signs in many applications. Is it possible Ezekiel sees yellow lights to warn ground personnel of dangerous exhaust temperatures as the ships land? Next, we read of the creatures that exit the single craft (or possibly four craft joined into one) after the landing.

> **Ezekiel 1:5** "*Also out of the midst thereof* came *the likeness of four living creatures. And this* was *their appearance; they had the likeness of a man*". (KJV)

Ezekiel sees *Four Living Creatures* that appear like men. They are also created in the image of God; at least they have a head, shoulders, torso, arms, hands, legs, and feet. But clothed in what? That is not mentioned here, but later we will read about their clothing. They are Living Creatures meaning they have the breath of life **(Gen.2:7 / 6:17 / 7:15, and 7:22).** Next, Ezekiel explains (in limited description) of their faces and wings.

> **Ezekiel 1:6** "*And every one had four faces, and every one had four wings.*" (KJV)

Today, it is common practice to paint organizational icons on flight helmets, but Ezekiel would not know this practice. Many ancient drawings and sculptures show a single-headed man in a space helmet with clear glass in the front for him to see through and for us to see his face. Now Ezekiel knows what a face looks like, with facial features we are familiar with. So it appears the Living Creatures have a face like ours; if not, I'm sure he would have mentioned the difference. It is possible Ezekiel sees the face of the living creatures through this transparent helmet material. As for these four faces, that will come later.

As for the four wings, Ezekiel's experience with flight was with birds and flying insects that use wings to fly. So this would be his way to explain these creatures' ability to fly and not design their flight mechanism. And for us today, we may not know what devise the creatures were using, possibly some personal powered flight devices. These devices have been created even today but are not cost-effective to mass-produce at this time. It also is possible that these wings are part of a suit that we have today where individuals can glide down from mountains tops. These wings mentioned here appear to be used in powered flight but not flapping their wings like a bird in flight. Ezekiel next describes their feet.

> **Ezekiel 1:7 "*And their feet* were <u>*straight feet*</u>*; and the sole of their feet* was *like the <u>sole of a calf's foot</u>: and they sparkled like the colour of <u>burnished brass</u>." (KJV)*

Straight feet reveal these creatures' feet are just like ours and God's feet. But Ezekiel was used to seeing people wearing sandals and not boots. He sees their soles of their boots as calf's feet with stiff soles (hoofs). And the color of these soles is burnished brass. This material may be made of a metallic woven material of brass as it is an excellent corrosion-resistant metal. It is also an excellent germicidal and antimicrobial agent. Researches are being performed today for the use of brass for these two qualities of brass. Many times in ancient documents, Brass and Bronze are used as one.

> **Ezekiel 1:8 "*And* they had *the <u>hands of a man</u> under their wings on <u>their four sides; and they four</u> had their faces and their wings." (KJV*

Ezekiel continues to reveal the hands of these Living Creatures are like our hands. Also, keep in mind that this description could be of a flight suit and not of the creature's body. He knows what hands look like, and they have the hands of a man. These hands are under the wings at the regular spot. But notice these four wings are on four sides. These four sides include the four Living Creature's sides, *"and they four had their faces."* So this description is of all four, and their personal flight devices. God created man in his image, and we only have two arms with hands. It appears from scriptures that God created these living creatures in God's image also. Remember, the wings are representative of some device for locomotion, possibly like the wings of a Dragon Fly separated but together at their base. They could also be like those flight suits of today that permit gliding but with a power source to allow continuous flight. But you must notice there is no mention of the wings flapping like a bird's wings.

Ezekiel 1:9 *"Their wings* were *joined one to another; they turned not when they went; they went every one straight forward." (KJV)*

Here we read of an event that these Living Creatures have joined their wings together and travel. When they travel, the creatures remain in formation, facing forward. They also do not turn individually; as they move, they remain all facing forward. It appears these vehicles can move in any direction without turning to face the new direction of flight. From military videos and individuals' observations, these UFOs have demonstrated this ability to go in any direction without facing the new direction. And they can do this change in the blink of an eye.

The wings joined together is a fascinating concept. The only time we can to be touching another aircraft is in mid-air refueling. However, in the USAF, we called this Close Formation. To one not familiar with this formation, it would appear that wings were touching, much like the U.S.A.F. and Navy Flight Demonstration Teams fly. But, the following verse reveals their faces, which is a piece of in-depth hidden information.

Ezekiel 1:10 *"As for the likeness of their faces, they four had the face of a man, and the face of a lion, on the right side: and they*

four had the <u>face of an ox</u> on the left side; they four also had <u>the</u> <u>face of an eagle.</u>" (KJV)

I covered a Man's face (in front) previously as the actual face Ezekiel saw through the helmet or faceplate. You will find these Living Creatures have a completely clear ball-shaped helmet in **verse 22.** The <u>face</u> of this living creature is like our faces. All these icons' faces on the sidc and back represent the *four Gospel of Jesus.*

This face of man **<u>represents</u>** the humanity of Jesus. Jesus referred to himself many times as the "Son of Man." Jesus was both the son of God and the son of Mary (Man). Jesus chose to reveal himself as the Son of Man**,** proving that he was God and man. There are so many examples of Jesus humanity that it will be difficult to include them all, but here are some examples from the *Book of John: the waters of life* **chapter 4:14***; our intercessor* **17:1–26***; defender of the weak* **3:15***; model sufferer* **18:11***; great physician* **5:1–9***; the light of the world* **19:1–39***; our comforter* **14:1–3***; divine teacher* **3:2–21***; the good shepherd* **10:1–16***; the true vine* **15:1–16***; the conqueror of death;* **20:1–31***; the bread of life* **6:32–58***; the prince of life* **11:1–44***; the giver of the Holy Spirit* **16:1–15***; the restorer of the penitent* **21:1–17.** Here is the characteristic or picture of the **<u>Gospel of John,</u>** Jesus' humanity.

<u>The face of the Lion</u> (right side) represents the King of Beasts, and Jesus is in the Kingly line of Joseph and will be our King eternally. This is reflected in the *<u>Book of Matthew.</u>* Initially, in Matthew, is the revealing of the lineage of Kings. Of which Joseph and David are named in this lineage of Kings. Therefore, this is showing us Jesus would have been king and the heritor of the kingship of the Hebrew people. Matthew's writing reflects the character of the perfect King in Jesus. In **Mat. 2:2,** Jesus is born king; **21:5** says *"behold thy king cometh";* **25:34** *"Then shall the king say":* Jesus is called the king eight times and *"the son of David"* (a king) nine times. This lion represents the **<u>*Gospel of Matthew*</u>**

<u>The face of an Ox</u> (left side) represents a beast of burden or *servant to man.* This characteristic of Jesus is defined in the *<u>Book of Mark</u>***.** In **Mark 6:2,** Jesus demonstrates his mighty works, helps, and mercy. *"Straightway"* is used many times, indicating Jesus did not lauder but accomplish the task quickly. Most of all, Jesus carried our sins into his death in order to conquer spiritual death. *Jesus performed many tasks to help people. He healed the sick, gave life back to individuals, and taught the people, including his disciples,* just to name a few. This Ox is the ***Gospel of Mark.***

The Eagle (backside) represents in the *Book of Luke* the reflection of the characteristic of *Jesus as Savior.* Jesus is both a friend to sinners and outcasts. *In Luke, we read Jesus came to seek; and save sinners* **Luke 19:10;** *he is the good Samaritan* **10:30–37;** *seeks the lost sheep* **15:4–7;** *a story of prodigal son* **15:11–32;** *the Pharisee and Publican* **18:10–14;** *seek the lost Zacchaeus* **19:2–10** *and the penitent thief* **23:39–43**. This Eagle is **the *Gospel of Luke.*** The Eagle is a mighty bird of prey seeking food for its self and its young. A pair of eagles will help protect each other and their young. They are also capable of carrying heavy loads in flight. They can soar very high and, with keen eyesight, spot any birds or animals threatening their nest and their babies. It is an awesome site to see two eagles working in concert attacking a threat. It is as if they can communicate with each other. They are savior for their children just as God and Jesus are hovering over waters in **Gen.1:2,** and God is creating a nest for his children and saving us from Satan and his demons. We see the Eagle as a rescuer of the Hebrew people in **Rev. 12:13-–14**.

> **Revelation 12:13–14 *"(13) And when the <u>dragon</u>** (Satan) ***<u>saw that he was cast unto the earth, he persecuted the woman</u>*** (Israel) ***which brought forth the man child.*** [Jesus] ***(14) And to the <u>woman were given two wings of a great eagle,</u> that she might fly into the wilderness, into her place, where she is nourished for a <u>time, and times, and half a time,</u>*** [3½years] ***from the face of the serpent."* (KJV)**

The Dragon (Serpent) is Satan, and he is permanently cast out of heaven onto the earth **(Rev.12:9).** *This casting out will occur just before the Rapture of the*

Bride of Christ, as Satan cannot be in Heaven together with the bride. And Satan will not be a guest at the wedding of Jesus to his bride.

Satan will try to destroy the Hebrew people (The woman). But *she is given the wings of an eagle to fly to safety* to a place prepared for her **(Rev. 12:13–17).** I hope this eagle is America. Also, notice that this eagle is on the back of the helmet. What an appropriate location, backside, for this icon! Satan would see the eagle as the Hebrew people escape from Antichrist #2 (Satan's) grasp. One other exciting fact; is the proof that in **verse 14,** the *"time and times, times, and a half time" is 3½ years,* which is synonymous with **verse 6,** where she fled into the wilderness for *1,260 days.* In the Jewish lunar calendar, *1260 days is equal to 3½ lunar years.* This time mentioned here is the last half of the seven years of the Great Tribulation of the Book of Revelation. So these four faces are the portraits or characteristics of *Jesus' 4 Gospel missions on the earth.*

You will see these same four faces in other verses in the Bible. When you see these creatures' faces, remember they are living examples of the four Gospels of Jesus. But you will notice in **Eze.10:14** the same four faces, but a Cherub replaces the ox. A Cherub is a class of angels and appears to be warriors or guards. In **Gen. 3:23--24,** God ejected Adam and Eve from the Garden of Eden and placed Cherubims and a flaming Sword to isolate the Tree of Life from Adam and Eve. Also, in Solomon's Temple, Cherubims were carved into wood and stone throughout the Temple. The Ark of the Covenant had two Cherubims, one each on the top end of the Ark's lid.

You might ask why is there a change from the ox to Cherubim? To answer this, remember what the ox represents, the Servant Gospel of Mark. The Cherubim is also a servant of God, as are all righteous angels. But, at this point in earth's time, Jesus has not been on the world; and the Cherubim Face is pointing to the time of Jesus who will be the servant and warrior for man on earth. These Living Creatures do not turn as they change direction but face forward.

Ezekiel 1:12 *"And they went every one straight forward: whither the spirit was to go, they went; and they turned not when they went." (KJV)*

These Living Creatures face in one direction (forward) when they move. Now helicopters can do this maneuver by sliding left or right, and apparently, so can the Creatures. Also, by facing forward, they keep their vision on a point of interest just in front of them. These creatures are showing Christians not to be distracted from our focal point of the Holy Spirit. Do not let these world temptations or Satan's attempt to take our eyes off Jesus for a moment of pleasure or prosperity. We are to be the light (lamp) to the lost in this world. **(Mat.5:16)**

Ezekiel 1:13 *"As for the likeness of the living creatures, their appearance* was *like burning coals of fire,* [and] *like the appearance of lamps: it went up and down among the living creatures, and the fire was bright, and out of the fire went forth lightning." (KJV)*

What can we compare this vision today? Is this a vision of their spacesuits or a uniform? Is it the appearance of reflective material like polished aluminum reflecting sunlight? As they moved, the sunlight would appear as flicking flames of fire with their movements. The shiny metal attachments (burning coals) on the suites; maybe devises to attach something to; or to keep something secure, and would appear, in sunlight, as burning coals. Polished aluminum will reflect light just like a mirror, and as they moved, the suit material will fold and wrinkle, reflecting sunlight, which appears as lightning flashes. But their wheels are the most difficult to describe.

These wheels (revealed later) are going up and down, but it does not allude to their movement's magnitude. Ezekiel may be seeing the hover movements where these wheels are moving slightly up and down as a helicopter moves in a hover.

But what makes the lighting come forth? Today's flying machines are required to have Pulse Lights on their wings, tips, and tail. These Pulse Lights put out intermittent and very bright flashes of light to be seen at long distances. These lights could appear to Ezekiel as flashes of lightning, especially if reflected in the dust created by the engines. As you can see, he has no common knowledge of anything earthly he can identify, just as with Ezekiel. It could be a spiritual vision. But remember, these are Living Creatures and are carnal also. Next, we read of their quickness in their movements.

This lighting could be the static electricity created between the vehicle and the ground. If you remember the German's Hindenburg Airship, it was destroyed by static electricity when trying to land. This static phenomenon was taught to us in Viet Nam about rescue recovery using a Jungle Penetrator Seat from a helicopter. The helicopter built up static while flying through the atmosphere.

Ezekiel 1:14 *"And the living creatures ran and returned as the appearance of a flash of lightning." (KJV)*

These Living Creatures' movements appear to be extremely fast. This fast movement has been reported by respectable persons that a UFO changed direction very quickly and accelerated out of sight extremely fast. Military pilot flying Mach 2 (1500 mph) aircraft have reported not keeping up with UFOs. We had never experienced anyone or thing moving like lightning and not turning when they moved. Just the accelerations alone would be deadly to humans. Somehow, they are not affected by our gravitation pull of the earth or the pressures of acceleration. With this information, we would think these living creatures are spiritual rather than carnal. But remember, they are Living Creatures. Next, we read about their vehicles.

Ezekiel 1:15--17 *"(15) Now as I beheld the living creatures, behold <u>one wheel upon the earth</u> by the living creatures, with his four faces. (16) <u>The appearance of the wheels</u> and their work* was *like unto the colour of a beryl: and <u>they four had one likeness:</u> and their appearance and their work* was *as it were <u>a wheel in the middle of a wheel.</u> (17) When they went, they went upon their four sides:* and *they turned not when they went". (KJV)*

This is a curious statement as it appears that these wheels came from the mother ship of **Eze.1:9** (wings joined) and **10:1** (sapphire stone). But, there is no mention of them coming out of the mother ship. However, in **Eze.1:5,** the 4 Living Creatures came out of the midst of the whirlwind. It may be possible that these wheels are an integral part of the mother ship or can attach and detach from each other. It is possible; they are capable of interstellar flight individually or coupled together.

Interestingly, only one of the four wheels is on the ground. This can be a little confusing as there are four complete units of two wheels in each of the four units. Also, we see one Living Creature comes out of each of these four units. Each of these living creatures has a personal vehicle (assumed) with them; however, one wheel is on the ground, and not all wheels and the wheels remained by each creature. There is no mention of feet or landing gear for this wheel on the ground.

And these vehicles appear as wheels the color of beryl. Beryl is the colors of green, light blue, yellow, pink, or white, and some are used as gems. I'm glad Ezekiel cleared that up! But he does say that all wheels appear the same. These four-wheel units work as a wheel within a wheel. Some take this to mean the two wheels have a larger one on the outside and a smaller one on the inside perpendicular to each other. One is horizontal, and one is vertical. However, they both could be vertical or horizontal. Now, these wheels could be solid interior or with spokes. Most common wheels in Ezekiel's day were solid but expensive wheels had spokes. Both solid horizontal wheels would appear as a saucer. **Verse 17** explains that these wheels can go in four directions, and they seem not to turn in the direction they are going, just as the Living Creatures did not turn in **verse 12. Verse 18** adds information about the rings of these wheels. A round object in flight generally does not appear to rotate. A baseball is rotating in flight, but most people do not perceive its rotation. Also, a Frisbee spins for flights, but we normally can't perceive its rotation, and yet, we know it spins. But, there is no mention of these wheels rotating.

Ezekiel 1:18 *"As for their rings, they were so high that they were dreadful; and their rings* were *full of eyes round about them four." (KJV)*

Here Ezekiel explains the size of these wheels as being dreadfully high. He may be referring to the actual size of the vehicle. It is not clear if Ezekiel is speaking of the width of the horizontal band of the wheels. Or the diameter above the ground the wheels are in at a normal wheel position vertically. Or the height or thickness of the complete horizontal wheel. Also, these rings are full of eyes on all four vehicles. Now, this can mean the eyes are all in a row around the wheels or scattered around at different locations on these wheel's perimeters. It would appear these wheels are horizontal rather than vertical as the eyes would be on the ground if wheels are vertical; unless they can hover. If the wheels were spinning, these eyes would be a blur and not recognized as eyes.

If the wheels are both horizontal, then the center wheel diameter must be a little smaller in diameter than the outer wheel. This could be that the horizontal wheels' inner wheel could be above and/or below the outer wheel. Like two two-layer wedding cakes joined together with the base layers, and one is turned upside down. But if the wheels are rotating very quickly, Ezekiel would not have seen their eyes. They would have been a blur.

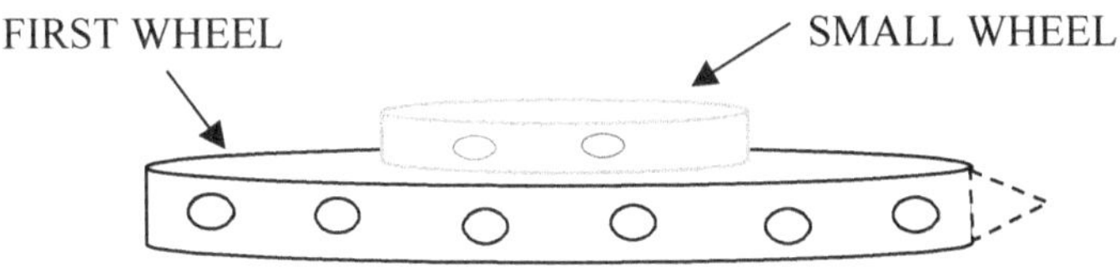

These eyes could appear circular (eyes) and maybe windows or lights. It would appear that if these are windows, then they would be only visible with very slow turning or stopped wheels. It also could be that Ezekiel saw the eyes of the crew or passengers looking outboard. Lights (lamps) would seem most appropriate due to **verse 13.**

Now keep in mind that we think of moving wheels because Ezekiel says they appear as wheels. Normally think these wheels are rotating as wheels, and forget wheels can be stationary too. Remember, these wheels are humongous in size. And the overall movements of these wheels are tied to the Living Creatures movements.

Ezekiel 1:19 *"And when the <u>living creatures</u> went, the wheels went by them: and when the <u>living creatures</u> were lifted up from the earth, the wheels were lifted up." (KJV)*

When the Living Creatures moved, the wheels moved with them, and if you remember in **verse 12,** these living creatures did not turn as they went. They either slid sideways or turned in unison rather than individually, for all to face forward continually. Now, these wheels move in concert with the Living Creatures. If the creatures are lifted up, so are their wheels. If the Living Creatures are slightly lifted up for their turn, so would the wheels. We see this in **verses 20** and **21**.

Ezekiel 1:20–21 *"And when the living creatures went, the wheels went by them: and when the living creatures were lifted up from the earth, the wheels were lifted up. (21) When those went, these went; and when those stood, these stood; and when those were lifted up from the earth, the <u>wheels were lifted up over against them</u>: for the spirit of the living creature was in the wheels." (KJV)*

Notice when the Living Creatures are lifted above the earth; these wheels are moved against (touching) the living creatures. Could this be a tractor beam securing the creatures to the wheels? Now above the earth indicates seeable height, and not in outer space. It appears these wheels are for the living creature's transportation. And that the Living Creature's spirit is in the wheels directing its movements. This statement may indicate other living creatures are inside these wheels controlling the wheel's movements through commands through an intercom system within their helmets. Ezekiel would not have heard any words spoken between the two. Interestingly, there is no mention here of the use of the living creatures' wings.

This is a curious statement; *"spirit of the living creature* was *in the wheels,"* which appears that the wheels within a wheel may have a fuselage for the spirit of the Living Creature to reside and to control the wheels. Ezekiel may not have sight of the operator and assume the living creature's spirit controls the wheels or vessel. If this is true, then the vessel center inside wheels would be the best place for a cockpit or flight control station. Control of this vessel could be by the Living Creatures' thoughts or by a personal electronic control panel. It could be located on the wheel's surface or, more likely, by a detached hand control, like our Ipad or IPods. That way, the wheel would need to move close or against the Living Creature for the creature to reach the control panel or secure them safely to the vehicle. However, this hand control unit would most likely be remote like our cell phones or computer game controllers.

Now Ezekiel continues the description of the Living Creatures.

Ezekiel 1:22 *"And the likeness of the firmament upon the heads of the living creature* was *as the colour of the <u>terrible crystal, stretched forth over their heads above."</u> (KJV)*

Here Ezekiel tells us about the Living Creature's helmet. The firmament is the sky shining through the crystal helmet. Terrible would indicate a film or built-in shade protection from the sun, making it look unclear on top. This helmet is transparent all around and over, which is somewhat different than our space helmet of today. However, ancient carvings show a man in a round helmet, much like a commercial underwater divers helmet, with a clear faceplate.
I have a question that might create some discussions. *Who built Ezekiel's wheels and devices?* I know God could do it in the twinkling of his eye but would he? God has given man knowledge and has given us specifics in designs. God gave Noah the Ark's plan, but Noah and his stepsons had to build the ark. Nehemiah was to make the wall around Jerusalem with God's specifications, but men had to build it. God gave information on building the first temple, but

men had to do the work to make it. So it would appear that God would provide these Living Creatures the information needed to build these wheels, but it had to be the Living Creatures to do the work. <u>And *where would this construction take place?*</u> Not on earth? I think not.

There is more in Ezekiel about these Living Creatures; I would recommend more study into the book of Ezekiel.

Note

You will find a similar event with the whirlwind in **2 Kings 2:11–12.** There Elijah (who walked with God) was taken to Heaven in a chariot of fire. Elijah did not die but will return to earth with Enoch, who also did not die. These two events happened many years ago. Enoch and Elijah's return is revealed in **Rev. 11:3–12,** *the two witnesses during the 1st half (3½ year) of God's Great Tribulation.* Here they are killed after witnessing against the Antichrist #1, but after three days, they will come back to life and be taken into Heaven. Remember **Heb.9:27,** for all men are appointed once to die; then their judgment.

Another verse in **2 Kings 6:17** tells about numerous chariots of fire that appear to be cloaked until Elisha prayed to God to uncloak the chariots of fire for his servant to see. Also, chariots of fire are mentions in **Psalms. 68:17** and **Isa. 66:15.** The same questions apply to these chariots as with Ezekiel's chariots. There are many other writings and pictures around the world revealing flying objects, and in India, there are many drawings of war or fighting in the sky. Many oil paintings from the middle ages (thousands of years ago) show UFOs in paintings. Also, many large structures appear around the earth.

Building, structures with huge and heavy stones fitted together so precisely that science today cannot explain how they were cut, moved, and fitted. Normally you would think that while cutting out the stone, the mason would not pay particular attention to the smoothness of the rock from which the cut-out stone will come. But, in many places where these stones are cut-out, the remaining cut corners reveal perfectly clean square pointed corners where the stone was removed. Not only are the remaining corners square, but *all sides* of the waste cut-out stone are smooth and square. Why would the remaining waste stone cut-outs be so perfectly smooth and geometric? The tools of that day would require a great many wasteful working hours of labor to accomplish this task. And what would be the purpose of performing this to the waste stone? But there is so much more information that points to a very knowledgeable group of Living Creatures.

Many items are found in Mexico, and one which is very old is a perfect replica of an aircraft, made of gold. It has a Jet aircraft fuselage, a bubble canopy, delta shape wings, a vertical rudder, and a horizontal elevator. It is very accurate and is an uncanny representation of a fighter jet aircraft of today. There are thousands of artifacts and documents from history revealing individuals visiting earth.

So who are these creatures flying in these machines and building these massive structures? Where did they come from? And why is it so hard for earthlings to understand; we are not alone in this incredibly vast Universe? What are we Christians afraid of, or is it vanity?

Note

At no time is the skin color of these Living Creatures mentioned or their sizes, except some, are giants. Possibly, the suits and gloves they wear cover their skin, but the helmet appears clear except the top, and there is no mention of the little grey creature. But this omission does not deny the possibility of different colors of skin. Where did our skin color: white, black, red, yellow, and brown come from?

Romans 8:38--39 *"(38) For I am persuaded, that neither death, nor life, nor angels, nor principalities, nor powers, nor things present, nor things to come, (39) Nor height, nor depth, nor any other creature, shall be able to separate us from the love of God, which is in Christ Jesus our Lord." (KJV)*

Isaiah 60:8 "Who are these that *fly as a cloud, and as the doves to their windows?* "*(KJV)*

Isaiah 66:1 *"For, behold, the LORD will come with fire, and with his chariots like a whirlwind, to render his anger with fury, and his rebuke with flames of fire." (KJV)*

In **Eze. 10:20,** there is a caveat I must include, which appears opposed to the concept of the Living Creatures being aliens. There you will read that Ezekiel knows they are the Cherubims (angels). Cherubims are warriors of God, and God is present.

THE CREATURE MYSTERY

First, I want you to know there are 18 scriptures speaking about creatures. And four specifically speak of Living Creatures. One, in particular, is in **2 Cor. 5:17.**

2 Corinthians 5: *17 "Therefore if any <u>man be in Christ, he is a new creature:</u> old things are passed away; behold, all things are become new." (KJV)*

This scripture tells us that every human being that has Repented and been Baptized in Jesus is a new creature (born again). And those still alive are Living Creatures. Even those individuals who have gone to Jesus in mortal death are still Living Creatures as they have escaped the Second Death

It appears that all Living Creature have God's breath of life given to them. If the Bible calls them Living Creatures, then they have life. If Adam transmitted Satan's sinful nature, would he not have conveyed the Breath of Life from God? **(Gen.2:7)**

Now, let us look at the Hebrew word for "Creature" definition3.

Creature = "5215 ***neh' fesh;*** from 5314; prop. <u>A *breathing* creature</u>, i.e. *animal or (abstr.) vitality;* used very widely in a lit., a commondated or fig. sense (bodily or mental):- any, appetite, <u>beast,</u> body, breath, <u>creature,</u> X dead (ly), desire, X <u>[dis-] contented,</u> X fish, <u>ghost,</u> + greedy, <u>he, heart (-.y), (hath, X jeopardy of)</u> life (X in jeopardy), lust, <u>man, me, mind, mortally,</u> one, own, <u>person,</u> pleasure, <u>(her-, him,</u> my-, thy-), <u>self, them,</u> (your) –selves, + slay, <u>soul,</u> + tablet, <u>they,</u> thing, (X she) will, X would have it[2]."

5214 = "***naw-fash;***'a prim. Root; <u>to *breathe*;</u> pass., *to be breathed* upon, i.e., (fig.) *refreshed* (as if by current of air):- (be) refresh selves (ed)[2]."

Here again, God has a sense of humor. I have underlined some points for your consideration. Notice this definition ends referring to *"beast, creature, he,*

man, *persons, him, her, self, them, your, selves and they."* But initially, it speaks of a breathing discontented creature, in jeopardy of life. And we know from **Gen. 2:7** that God breathed the breath of life into Adam, and he became a living soul. Notice the first meaning is *a breathing creature.* So it would appear that these Living Creatures (not animals) are also living souls in a convoluted way. If so, then this mystery has been hidden from Biblical searchers for years. But this next mystery is found in **Rom.8.**

> **Romans 8:19–23** *"(19) For the earnest <u>expectation of the creature waiteth for the manifestation of the sons of God.</u> (20) For <u>the creature</u> was <u>made subject to vanity,</u> not willingly, but by reason of him who hath subjected the same in hope, (21) Because the creature itself also shall be delivered from the bondage of corruption into the glorious liberty of the children of God. (22) For we know that the <u>whole creation groaneth</u> and travaileth <u>in pain together</u> until now. (23) <u>And not only they, but ourselves</u> also, which have the <u>firstfruits of the Spirit,</u> even <u>we ourselves groan within ourselves, waiting for the adoption,</u> to wit, the redemption of our body."* **(KJV)**

WOW! The magnitude of these verses of scripture should blow your mind! We read of this creature waiting in <u>earnest expectation</u> for the Children of God (Christians = *"the first fruit of the spirit"*) to be liberated from bondage. Apparently, these creatures think and feel. The creatures are placed into vanity unwillingly. Notice the creatures know that they will be released from bondage (death) with the children of God. How do they know this? Who told them? Notice they all know this by the pain for the whole creation (every living creature). Next, we are given *a clue* as to their physical condition as compared to earthlings. They all groan and feel pain like humans (ourselves). But, a *clue* is in **verse 23,** in which we both groan inward ourselves, waiting for our adoption into God's family, which is the result in the redemption of our bodies, and we will receive an inheritance. It appears the creatures will also have redemption of their bodies too. Is this the time of our fellowship mentioned in **Eph.3**? More on this later).

In **Genesis 1:24,** we read God created these Living Creatures. Most of these creatures to be primarily land animals. And that is partly true as there are also sea and foul creatures. Notice, however, that the earth is to bring forth all creatures after its kind. There is no mention of God creating any aliens, just animals. However, remember this information in Genesis is primarily for earth's creations, except possible for Day 4. Next, in **Gen. 2:7,** God breathed the breath of life into Adam, and he became a living soul. So as of today, there is no specific statement of aliens being created in the universe as there was no such word (alien) in Hebrew. However, in **Gen. 2:1,** God reveals his work includes the *entire host in heaven and earth*, all living creatures.

> **Genesis 2:1** *"Thus the <u>heavens and the earth</u> were finished, and all the <u>host of them</u>." (KJV)*

Host in Hebrew "6635 means: *tseb-aw-aw;* from 6633 <u>a mass of</u> <u>persons</u> (or fig. things) espec. Reg. <u>organized for war</u> (an *army*): by impl. *a campaign,* lit. or fig. (spec. *hardship, worship*):--<u>appointed</u> <u>time,</u> (+) army, (+) battle, company, host, service, solder, <u>waiting</u> <u>upon, war</u> (-fare)[2]."

6633 *"tsaw-baw'*; a prim. Root; <u>to mass (an army</u> or <u>servants):</u>-assemble, fight, perform, muster, <u>wait upon, war</u>[2]."

These definitions are clear this host is an army of all living entities *("Mass of persons")* waiting upon *warfare,* and <u>they are *from the Heavens and Earth.*</u> They are living persons and not solid objects like stars or planets, but life. We are told in many places in the Bible of this war, Armageddon, which will occur near the end of time. **Rev. 19** is the final words on Armageddon. In **Eze.39:11–15,** he tells us that it will take seven months to bury the dead. This time is where the Host is prepared for battle and destroys all evil. So who is this Host? And when will this battle occur? The Host is all the righteous Souls in Paradise (be it heaven or center of the earth), under the Alter and the universe's (Heavens) obedient alien (Living Creatures). The 1st Harvest **(Rev. 14)** will be the Old Testament Saints and Tribulation Saints, which will be Harvested (resurrected) to meet Church Saints, angels, (creatures?) and Jesus; to fight Satan and his army of unrighteous souls and unrighteous angels **(Rev.19:14–21)**. And Satan's army will be destroyed! Satan will be locked in the abyss for 1,000 years.

After 1,000 years **(Rev.20:7–10)**, Satan and his army will be destroyed by God with fire. Satan, fallen angels, and all lost soul since the beginning will go to the Great White Throne Judgment and then to the Lake of Fire

But in **Rom.8,** there appears to be a contradiction that reveals this creature. Notice in **verse 19,** *this creature is waiting for the revealing (manifestation) of the children of God.* This means the complete revealing *of all the children of God.* Also, this creature desires liberty, as do we, the children of God. And this liberty of the children will be shared with these creatures. Therefore, this creature must have life. This creature is waiting for you and me to be revealed (born again into Jesus); we call the Church. *Why? So the creature, too,* will *be rescued from corruption* (death)—[More on corruption later]. But, let us look at the mystery within a mystery.

The words in **Eph. 3:9–10** allude to those individuals (principalities and powers) in Heaven (Space – the 2nd Heaven) who need to be *taught by the Church.*

Note

<u>1st heaven</u> is our sky, our atmosphere where birds fly (**Gen. 1:20**).They need oxygen to survive.

<u>2nd heaven</u> is space, Lights (stars) in the firmament (**Gen. 1:14–15**).

<u>3rd Heaven</u> is God's abode (**2 Cor. 12:12** and **Rev. 4:1**). [See attachment A]

Ephesians 3:9–10 "*(9) And to make <u>all</u>* men *see what* is *the <u>fellowship of the mystery,</u> which from the beginning of the world <u>hath been hid in God,</u> who <u>created all things by Jesus Christ;</u> (10)*

To the intent <u>that now</u> unto the <u>principalities and powers in</u> <u>heavenly</u> places might be <u>known by the church</u> the <u>manifold</u> <u>wisdom of God</u>," (KJV)

WOW again!

Verse 9 makes a very provocative statement, *"the fellowship of the mystery"*-- *"which hath been hid by God."* And God chose to hide this from us until now. This letter was written to the Saints of the Ephesians' Church. This fellowship is between the Church and the Living Creatures, *"in the principalities and powers in heavenly places."* Now a fellowship is usually considered between two or more people (living entities). And typically, it includes conversations and participations of sorts. But where are our fellowship partners? There are three heavenly places in the Bible. Since we see at present no principalities or powers in our sky, it must be in space. It would appear there would be no need for the Church to bring knowledge of God or Jesus to God's abode, so these references must be referring to space or the universe. And this event is in the fellowship of Living Creatures, angels, Church Saints, Old Testament Saints, New Testaments Saints, aliens (?), the Holy Spirit, Jesus Christ, and God.

But why would God hide this fellowship from earthlings until the Church is created? This fellowship may be one of the rewards set aside for the Church. In any case, it is in God's perfect timing as now appears the plan of man's salvation is to be revealed. And God's future Kings, Lords, and Priest (Church) are to be announced; then sent to the principalities and power in heavenly places (space).

There are apparent organizational structures in the universe (2nd Heaven) of positions of power, but with a lack of information about Jesus and or God's plan! Not God's and Jesus' existence and authority, but why God is doing this for all entities in the universe. How is this possible? If it is angels, then the Church (in the fullness of time) will reveal God's plan through each individual's life (light) of those chosen by God for his *Bride*. But angels are messengers of God, and it would appear that these angels would remember the messages God has sent by them to earthlings and would, in that sense, receive some knowledge from God. In Revelation, we read that angels are prepared to perform deeds God has prepared for them to perform well into the future. Now back to **Romans 8.** Most important, angels do not die (corruption).

The verse in **Rom.8:20** is another mystery in itself, so let us look at the Greek definition[3] of the word *"vanity."*

> "1. **Vanity** = 3153 μαραιότης mataʊtēs, *mat-ah-yot-ace*; from *3152*; *inutility*; fig. *transientness*; mor. *Depravity*, vanity[2]."
> 2. **3152** μάραιότης matalʊs, *mal-ah-yos;* from the base of *3155:* empty, i.e. (lit) *profitless,* or (spec.) an *idol:*--vain, vanity[2]."

Vanity mention in these definitions is a human or a living creature's emotional trait of moral depravity. If this is the case, then this creature is a living entity. And apparently, *this entity was not willingly subjected to this vanity or moral depravity.* But, notice the hope of these Living Creatures is to be liberated *(delivered) from this depravity or corruption when the children of God are finally and completely liberated.* This statement implies some relationship between children of God and the Living Creatures. This liberty of the children will apply to the creatures, as well as God's children. This liberation will occur after the 1,000-year Kingdom of Jesus. This time is when God will destroy Satan, evil angels and his evil human army, death (corruption), the Great White Throne Judgment, and creates a New Earth and New Universe **(Rev. 21).**

Is this Living Creature mentioned here, all of the natural elements of creation? In Strong's Concordance, we read the Greek word used here for the creature.

Creature = *"2932 **Ktisis,** ktis-is; from 2936; original formation (prop. The act; by impl .the thing, lit. or fig.):- building, creation, creature, ordinance[2]."*

This formation implies original creation; and that both "creation and creature" are to be considered. In **Rom. 8:19–23,** those verses of scripture are very enlightening. First, notice this creature is of the original creation, just like us (the Host). What is this creature, and why is it waiting for the Sons of God to be revealed *(manifestation)*? In the Bible, we read that the creature is mentioned as *"the living creature."* Therefore, this creature pertains to the body, soul, and spirit of all living entities in the universe. **Col.1:15–20** covers all creatures, but particular governments, but **Rev.5:13** goes so far as to include ever-mortal creatures living and dead. Notice all these creatures are spoken of here in these two scriptures.

> **Colossians 1:16** *"For by him were <u>all things created,</u> that are <u>in heaven,</u> and that are <u>in earth</u>, visible and invisible, whether* they be *<u>thrones, or dominions, or principalities, or powers</u>: all things were created by him, and for him" (KJV)*

> **Revelation 5:13** *"And <u>every creature which is in heaven,</u> and <u>on the earth, and under the earth,</u> and such as are <u>in the sea</u>, and all that are in them, <u>heard I saying</u>, Blessing, and honour, and glory, and power, be unto him that sitteth upon the throne, and unto the Lamb for ever and ever." (KJV)*

First, let us look at the definition of heaven used here. This word is defined as the Sky, space, or the Place of God's abode. This word's main thrust appears to be all three locations due to the different locations mentioned in these scriptures. However, the statement *"under the earth and in the sea "* appears to reference the righteous dead on earth; because of the words " *heard I saying, Blessing, and honour, and glory, and power, "* which are voices of all humans or all Living Creatures. So this word heaven could be a reference to all three: sky, space, and God's abode; due to the statements: *birds fly in our sky (our atmosphere); Sun and Moon are in space, and God's abode is in Heaven.* A copy of **Rom.8:19–23** is repeated here for your convenience.

> **Romans 8:19–23** *"(19) For the earnest <u>expectation of the creature waiteth for the manifestation of the sons of God.</u> (20)*

> *For <u>the creature</u> was <u>made subject to vanity,</u> not willingly, but by reason of him who hath <u>subjected</u> the same <u>in hope,</u> (21) <u>Because the creature itself also shall be delivered from the bondage of corruption into the glorious liberty of the children of God.</u> (22) For we know that the <u>whole creation groaneth</u> and travaileth <u>in pain together</u> until now. (23) <u>And not only</u> they, <u>but ourselves also, which have the <u>firstfruits of the Spirit,</u> even <u>we ourselves groan within ourselves, waiting for the adoption,</u> to wit, the redemption of our body." (KJV)*

Are these verses in **Rom. 8:19–23** referring to God's created items, including inanimate objects? Notice these creatures are in hope and vanity **(verse 20).** Do animals have hopes? All things in the universe are indeed in bondage to decay, as this is revealed in the 3rd Law of Thermal Dynamics. But does an inanimate object have feelings of pain, groaning, travailing, *vanity, moral depravity,* bondage, waiting, and expectations of liberty when the Sons of God are revealed? It appears all lost souls are not concerned with this knowledge. Where did these creatures get this knowledge of being delivered from bondage with the children of God? Also, these living creatures are mortal and in the bondage of decay and experience death. However, if they were created like Man was originally, they could have very long life spans, as did Noah's forefathers. But, what of the inanimate objects such as rocks?

A rock has none of these feelings (vanity, moral depravity), as it is not a living creature. But Genesis only speaks of eternal (mortal/spiritual) Living Creatures (humanoids) being created on earth on Day 6 (**Gen. 1:24).** Please notice that **Rom. 8:23** refers to living beings by comparing ourselves to these creatures *("not only they but ourselves").* These verses here are referring to other creatures (Host of **Gen.2:1)** like ourselves with the same corruption (death) occurring. These words reveal the living creatures of God are like us, and fellowship begins in **Revelation 21.** This fellowship beginning will happen after the *1ˢᵗ Harvest.* It is in Jesus' 1,000-year Kingdom that is when we will fellowship with the Principalities and Powers in the heavenly places (universe). This time is when Christians and Living Creatures will go from corruption to incorruption *(No decay but liberty)*. All dead righteous individuals and Living Creatures are changed from corruptible to incorruptible **1 Cor. 15.**

> **1 Corinthians 15:52–54** *"(52) In a moment, in the twinkling of an eye, at the last trump: for the trumpet shall sound, and the dead shall be raised incorruptible, and we shall be changed. (53) For this corruptible must put on incorruption, and this mortal must put on immortality. (54) So when this corruptible shall have put on incorruption, and this mortal shall have put on immortality, then shall be brought to pass the saying that is written, Death is swallowed up in victory." (KJV)*

It is clear that these verses are talking about earthlings and other living created humanoids; and not inanimate objects which cannot die. If this is also to aliens in heavenly places, then we have a dilemma in our Christian doctrine. But keep in mind that angels are alien to earth. But angels do not die. Corrupted by Satan, yes, but physical death, no, as they are spiritual.

For centuries we have accepted *traditions* from well-intentioned Christian leaders that the earth was flat (wrong), and if you sail far enough, you will fall off the earth's edge (false). Then the earth was round but in the center of the universe (wrong). (Appears the Pope's *traditions* were fallible.) Are we the only planet God infested with people? Today we know the earth is not flat or in the center of the universe; we are not even in the center of our galaxy but 27,000 light-years from the center of our galaxy. *These traditions were created by religious leaders of the past and are still present on earth today.* These mistaken leaders were overtaken by *VANITY.* This vanity is revealed in their need to be the religious leaders of all creation. They had power over the earth but not over space. Therefore, they had to believe aliens do not exist. But, what of the evidence that points to the fact; they do exist?

There is so much evidence present today of visitors to earth with extreme knowledge and special tools or abilities. To ignore this possibility of other created entities like us seems erroneous and verges on vanity. If we have angels (aliens) visiting earth as strangers who appear as we do, could we also have other aliens visiting us that appear like us? So is it <u>possible </u>we are not the only species created in God's image? One last thought is: from where did all the different races on earth come?

Science has tried to clear this subject up for years. Is it possible that these races came from the Sons of God (creatures from other 99 planets) when they intermarried, spoken of in Genesis? Interestingly, our different races have no barrier to child reproduction, as do the different animal species. Such as primate species appear not to be able to procreate with other primates. Man is a primate (named by scientists) and apes, and there is a barrier between these two. Could this be because they are different species? But Man and the Living Creatures (sons of God) must be of the same species to procreate the children. Living Creatures are Aliens and of the other 99 folds.

THE SHEEP FOLD MYSTERY

Please be patient with me as I may be repeating some previous information. As you read this chapter, I want to prove to you that sheep refers to all who believe in and follow Jesus.

The 1st scripture we need to keep in mind is **John 12:47** during this section, as it reveals a central point in God's plan.

> **John 12:47** *"And if any man <u>hear</u> my words, and believe not, I judge him not: for <u>I came not to judge</u> the world, <u>but to save the world."</u> (KJV)*

God is clearly revealing, and Jesus is telling us of God's plan **to save the world**, which pertains to all humans on the earth for all times.

In **Eze.34**, we read the desires of God and his plan to accomplish his wishes.

> **Ezekiel 34:16** *"I will seek <u>that </u>which was lost, and <u>bring again that which was driven away,</u> and will bind up* that which was **broken, and will <u>strengthen that which was sick</u>: but I will**

destroy the fat and the strong; I will feed them with judgment."
(KJV)

This verse speaks of two groups: Hebrews and Gentiles. *"That"* refers to today. And the *"bringing again"* was in 1948 when Israel won back the location of their homeland. But *"bring again"* spiritually is more correct when the 144,000 Jewish missionaries convert all Israel to Jesus. Remember, this was in God's plan for man. **(1 Tim.2)**

1 Timothy 2:3–4 *"(3) For this is good and expectable in the sight of God our savior; (4) <u>Who will have all men to be saved, and to come unto the knowledge of the truth."</u>* *(KJV)*

These verses are unmistakably clear; God wants *<u>"all men"</u>* (<u>Jew and Gentile</u>) to be saved and not one over the other. Jesus is bringing a new and better covenant to earth. Man was unable to live by the Laws of God, but Jesus could. For all men to be saved, salvation must be simplified, and the debts of sin paid for by the perfect, sinless man. In **John 10,** Jesus gives us a peek at his care and leadership.

John 10:11--16 "(11) *<u>"I am the good shepherd: the good shepherd giveth his life for the sheep.</u> (12) But he that is an hireling,* (paid false leader) ***and not the shepherd, whose own the sheep are not, seeth the wolf coming, and leaveth the sheep, and fleeth: and the wolf*** (Satan) ***catcheth them, and scattereth the sheep. (13) The hireling fleeth, because he is an hireling, and careth not for the sheep. (14) <u>I am the good shepherd, and know my sheep, and am known of mine.</u> (15) As the Father knoweth me, even so know I the Father: <u>and I lay down my life for the sheep.</u> (16) <u>And other sheep I have, which are not of this fold: them also I must bring, and they shall hear my voice; and there shall be one fold,</u>*** and ***<u>one shepherd.</u>***

In **verse 15**, Jesus clearly tells us," *<u>I lay down my life for the sheep,</u>* " and Jesus did perform this sacrifice *<u>on earth</u>* (the world) *<u>for both Jews and Gentiles.</u>* We have been taught that **verse 16** (*"other sheep I have"*) pertains to the sheepfold of the Gentiles, for this is the tradition we have been taught. But, keep in mind **1 Pet. 2:9–12 & 25,** which specifically identifies Israel **(verse 12)** as the lost sheep. But in **1 Pet.2:1–3,** God speaks of the Gentiles *(newborn babes)* now borne again into Christ Jesus *("desire the sincere milk of the Word")*. Also, most Israelites turned their backs on Jesus *(the stumbling stone)* from the beginning of Jesus' mission and even up until today. So they are the sheep that left the fold. So the Jews are one half the lost sheep on earth to be considered in **Mat.18:11–14,** and the Gentiles are the other half that got lost too.

Notice the scripture its-self speaks that the fold of Jew and gentiles (earth) are a fold, but Jesus has other folds apart from this world that *"are not of this fold."* Therefore, who are these different folds? Also notices the plural word *"them also I must bring."* So how many folds are *"them"*? 99? Does this oppose the *traditions* we have been taught?

We read in **Mat.10:5,** Jesus tells the apostles to go to the Jews and not the Gentiles.

> **Matthew 10:5–6 *"(5) These twelve Jesus sent forth, and commanded them, saying, Go not into the way of the Gentiles, and into** any **city of the Samaritans enter ye not: (6) But go rather to the lost sheep of the house of Israel." (KJV)***

Notice the apostles were to go only to the *"lost sheep of Israel."* This proves that one-half of the lost is Israel. But in **Mat.28:18–20** (*"teach all nations"*), Jesus includes both Gentiles and Jews that are lost sheep because of the sin entered into all of earth's humanity by Adam's sin. Keep in mind these words of Jesus were at a specific juncture in Jesus' mission before the Church was established (*Jesus' resurrection*). So it would appear Jesus came to the Jewish sheep first (family) and secondly to Gentile sheep by Paul **(Acts 9:15)**. It seems Jesus knew that the most challenging individuals to convert to Jesus are those who worship a similar but different religion (Pharisees). By going to the difficult 1st, the other Gentiles would hear and be more receptive to the new information. But the Apostles were more open-minded and converted to Jesus, so these groups of converted souls by the Apostles were Jews and Gentiles. This then *makes up the total lost sheep of the earth (one fold)*. Did Jesus not die for the sins of both the Jew and the Gentile? Since there are no other sheepfolds on this earth, we now have a complete fold of sheep. With this being said, does it not appear that Jesus' words are for the planet earth (that which is lost)? ----Yes! Now let us look into these words with a new perspective. It is unquestionably clear Jesus came to save all the lost souls of the earth **(John12:47).** We see Timothy understood this in **1Tim.2.**

> **1 Timothy 2:3–4 *"(3) For this* is *good and acceptable in the sight of God our Saviour; (4) Who will have <u>all men</u> to be saved,* (Jews and Gentiles) *and to come unto the knowledge of the truth". (KJV)***

Interestingly, this verse says, *"all men,"* which includes both Hebrews and Gentiles. Is it possible God does not include animals? I hope he does! I love my pets.

All these words are talking about the people of the earth, and if so, would it mean that the individuals on the other 99 planets have maintained their righteousness by obedience? ---Yes. But I must allow a Cavite for Satan and his demons.
Satan (the red dragon) has received a third of all the Angels created by God. And these falling angels do not follow God, Jesus, or the Holy Spirit, but only Satan. And all these fallen angels will eventually be cast to earth and be conquered there. **(Isa.14:12–16** and **Rev.12:3–4)**. Up until **Rev.12**, Satan has had the freedom to the universe. And his followers *are not righteous* in Jesus and *will not* be included in the 100 sheepfold fellowship.

Who is Jesus talking to here? He is talking to his apostles, you and me. Here are the New Testament writings revealing salvation: through *faith in Jesus,* brought through the *Holy Spirit's power,* and through the *deeds (gospel) of the Church* (true believers). The apostles were Jews, but they are the beginning of the Bride of Christ, the Church. The Church is made up of some Jews but mostly Gentiles at this present time. Jesus came to save <u>the Jews initially</u>, but the Jews are blinded by God **(Joh.12:40)**. **1 Pet.2:25** identifies the Gentiles also.

> **1 Peter 2:25** *"For ye <u>were</u> as sheep going astray; but are now returned unto the Shepherd and Bishop of your souls." (KJV)*

Keep in mind that this verse includes <u>all the lost individuals (sheep and goats)</u> who are to be saved. Be they past, present, or future. This mass of saved souls will not be fulfilled *until just before* **Rev.20:7–9** and will be in the *1st Harvest* **(Rev.14:13–16)**. Other verses in the Bible speak of these lost sheep, and one is in **Luk.15:7–9** but especially in **verse 7**.

> **Luke 15:7** *"I say unto you, that likewise joy shall be in heaven over one sinner that repent, <u>more than over ninety and nine just persons, which need no repentance"</u> (KJV)*

These verses in **Luk. 15:3–7** are the same as in **Mat. 18:1–18,** but **Luk.15:7** is different than **Mat.18:14**. Luke adds or clarifies **Mat.18:14** by revealing *<u>the 99 sheep are just</u>* **persons** *<u>that need no repentance.</u>* Interestingly, Luke uses <u>99 just persons</u> in almost the same reference as in **Mat.18:13** for the <u>99 *that went not astray.*</u> There Mathew speaks of *"these little ones should not perish."* **Sheep are not the object spoken of here**. Persons have souls *(man and living creatures)*. Does this mean these creatures are *righteous persons?* ---Yes! As they may not have had the Tree of Knowledge of Good and Evil; and are obedient to God's will. The 99 *righteous persons* will be with Jesus and need no salvation, as they are not lost. Earth can be seen as a metaphor for the prodigal son of **Luk.15:11–32,** which is a continuation of **Luk. 15:3–7**. Jesus' parable in **Mat.18;** has been miss-read for many years. *Therefore, we must recognize **Mat.18** as the anchoring scripture to reveal these 99 other planets.*

In **Mat.18**, Jesus makes a curious statement through a parable that has created some interest but can be easily overlooked.

> **Matthew 18:11–14** *"(11) For the Son of man is come <u>to save that which was lost.</u> (12) <u>How think ye?</u> if a man have an hundred*

sheep, and one of them be gone astray, doth he not leave the ninety and nine, and goeth into the mountains, and seeketh that which is gone astray? (13) And if so be that he find it, verily I say unto you, he rejoiceth more of that sheep, than of <u>the ninety and nine which went not astray. (14) Even so it is not the will of your Father which is in heaven, that one of these little ones should perish.</u>" (KJV)

Interestingly, Jesus uses this parable to explain a truth. A parable must be truth to explain a parallel spiritual truth. If the parable is not true, then it is a fabrication or fiction. Fiction is not truth but fantasy or an untruth. Why would Jesus or God need to fabricate when he insists on the truth? Plus, God and Jesus know every human's life story that has ever existed (trillions and trillions). *Jesus can call upon these true human stories that actually happened.* So Jesus asks us, **"How think ye?"** It appears Jesus wants you to know if you are aware the Holy Spirit has been revealing these mysteries to you, and why do you not know this? Is it a lack of study? God has blinded the Hebrews, so it seems these words are pointing to Gentiles. These words appear to be an intellectual <u>challenge by Jesus of *our old traditions,* too. This tradition of no aliens, go way back in history to the early days of the Catholic Pope's decrees; that we are the only planet with human life and we are the center of the universe.</u> And anyone who disagreed with the Pope was a heretic and was burned at the stake. Pretty strong motivation to believe there are no aliens. But the Bible does create an intellectual mystery here. So *"<u>how think ye?</u>"*

In the Dark Ages, many scientists knew the world was round. The bible also confirmed this in **Isa.40:22** to the Pope. But he ignored this to maintain his infallible power (vanity). So he remained silent. In the Pope's silence, some scientists were burned at the stake by Priests for heresy. And this was murder! And what does **1 John 3:15** and **Mat.18:12** say? *So how think ye? Are you still stuck in traditions?* Now back to the 99 sheep.

Please notice that this Shepherd departed from the 99 other sheep. A Shepherd's primary job is to protect his flock and lead them to food and water.

This flock he left behind must have had protection from rustlers, wolves, and lions; because that Shepherd would lose more than one sheep to those rustlers, attacking wolves or lions. So this Shepherd had to be assured of their protection. Also, the 99 sheep could wander off just like the lost sheep. What protected them and kept them together? Could this be God's protecting and guiding? Or is it *these sheep (aliens) are obedient* and retain their *righteous position?---Yes!* Angels have provided this protection and guidance for earthlings from God, so why not the other 99 planets?

Now let us look again into these words with a new perspective. It is unquestionably clear Jesus came to save all the lost souls of earth. Who are these other sheep not of this fold of the earth?

Is Jesus telling us that he created 100 planets in total during his creative efforts, and we are the only planet that ate from *"The Tree of Knowledge of Good and Evil"* immediately? Or is our planet the only planet to be given The Tree of Knowledge of Good and Evil**?** This concept runs in the face of the traditions we have been taught by well-meaning Christian Leaders over the ages. But this tradition is nothing new as Jesus himself ran into these same problems when he tried to introduce new knowledge of salvation. *Jesus' teachings appeared to be diametrically opposed to the Torah* (first five books of the Bible) *teachings and especially traditions of the elders, Hebrew Rabbis, and Priests.* Could these scriptures refer to the living creatures on other plants who are waiting for the revealing of the *"sons of God?"*
So how think ye?

The scriptures in **Rom.8:19–23 / Eph.3:9–10 /** John **10:14–16, and Mat.18:11–14;** I repeated for your convenience as it should be more revealing to you now.

> **Romans 8:1–23** *"(19) for the earnest <u>expectation of the creature</u> <u>waiteth for the manifestation of the sons of God. (20) For <u>the</u> <u>creature</u> was <u>made subject to vanity,</u> not willingly, but by reason of him who hath <u>subjected</u> the same <u>in hope,</u> (21) <u>Because the</u> <u>creature itself also shall be delivered from the bondage of</u>*

corruption into the glorious liberty of the children of God. (22) For we know that the whole creation groaneth and travaileth in pain together until now. (23) And not only they, but ourselves also, which have the firstfruits of the Spirit, even we ourselves groan within ourselves, waiting for the adoption, to wit, the redemption of our body." (KJV)

Ephesians 3:9–10 *"(9) And to make all men see what is the fellowship of the mystery, which from the beginning of the world hath been hid in God, who created all things by Jesus Christ: (10) To the extent that now unto the principalities and powers in heavenly places might be known by the church the manifold wisdom of God" (KJV)*

John 10:14–16 *"(14) I am the good shepherd, and know my sheep, and am known of mine. (15) As the Father knoweth me, even so know I the Father: and I lay down my life for the sheep. (16) And other sheep I have, which are not of this fold: them also I must bring, and they shall hear my voice; and there shall be one fold, and one shepherd.*

Matthew 18:11–14 *"(11) For the Son of man is come to save that which was lost. (12) How think ye? if a man have an hundred sheep, and one of them be gone astray, doth he not leave the ninety and nine, and goeth into the mountains, and seeketh that which is gone astray? (13) And if so be that he find it, verily I say unto you, he rejoiceth more of that sheep, than of the ninety and nine which went not astray. (14)Even so it is not the will of your Father which is in heaven, that one of these little ones should perish." (KJV)*

Can you see the reference here in **Mat.18** to the parable of the "Prodigal Son" in **Luke 15:11–72**? There you will read of the joy and forgiveness of the Father. And this reveals the joy of God for the return to faith in Jesus of earth's lost sons. In scripture, we are told of all the angels in Heaven who shout for joy for each person who accepts Jesus as their savior.

The Gentiles are the first host of believers (sheep) in Jesus (converted by the Hebrew apostils), and they have spread the Gospel to the earth. Most Jews hated Jesus and killed him; they are the lost souls **1 Pet.2:8–10.** But remember, the Jews are blinded by God **(John 12:40)** until the 144,000 Jewish missionaries of **Rev.7,** who will spread the Gospel to the earth, especially to the Jews. Here is revealed the lost sheepfold is earth, and Jesus has found his lost sheep of earth, both Jews and Gentiles. *Therefore, the other sheepfold is the 99 other planets God created who have remained righteous.* We will all come together into one fellowship, one body, and one fold. **(1 Cor.12)**

> **1 Corinthians 12:12–14** *"(12) For as the <u>body is one, and hath many members, and all the members of that one body, being many, are one body so also</u> is Christ. (13) For by one Spirit are we all baptized into one body, whether* we be *Jews or Gentiles, whether* we be *bond or free; and have been all made to drink into one Spirit. (14) <u>For the body is not one member, but many.</u>"* *(KJV)*

The Time of the Gentiles is that time the Church is tasked to bring the Gospel of Jesus to the lost goats of earth. But In **Revelation 7**, the 144,000 Jewish missionaries convert all the Jews to Jesus during the seven years of The Great Tribulation *(1st Harvest)*. Therefore, the converted Jews and Gentiles are Jesus' fold of sheep he came to save. Jesus' death was performed here on earth; therefore, this fold must again be earthlings. The *"other sheep I have"* is the living creatures from the other 99 planets. This concept is supported by the fellowship foretold in **Eph.3.**

> **Ephesians 3:9** *"(9) <u>And to make all</u> men <u>see what is the fellowship of the mystery,</u> which <u>from the beginning of the world</u> hath been hid in God, who created all things by Jesus Christ: (10) To the intent that now unto the <u>principalities and powers in heavenly</u> places might be known by the church the manifold*

wisdom of God, (11) <u>According to the eternal purpose which he purposed in Christ Jesus our Lord:</u>" (KJV)

We know very little about what makes up this fellowship. And God has kept it secret. When we read the word "*heavenly places,*" we generally think of our final destination after death, but the exact location and these creatures are unknown. The Bible gives us some clues which are not really clear today but appear general in meaning.

We Christians have so much to look forward to in Heaven. This fellowship **(Eph.3:9–11)** with the other 99 planets' populations will be phenomenal. Will there be multi-races as there as on earth? What will they: eat, drink, games, clothes, transportation, music, customs, courtesies, and so much to enjoy with them? They will have so much knowledge because they were not cursed with different languages? Without language confusion, God said, "*nothing will be restrained for them*" to accomplish **(Gen.11:6).** They have had 6,000 years of unrestraint. Just look at what the earth has accomplished from 1900 to 1969 (the Moon landing), even with the language confusion. Plus, we have Satan interfering with our growth progress.

Satan wants us to think all space aliens are evil, and the earthlings will need to kill them. This is partially true, as demons can appear as aliens. Do you remember **Isa14:12–16**? Satan and all his demons (evil angels) are cast to earth! But when Jesus returns, there will be no doubt who is righteous and who is evil **(Mat.25:31–33, Rev.1:7**and **Rev.19).**

> **Revelation 1:7** *"Behold, he cometh with clouds; and <u>every eye</u> shall see him, and <u>they </u>also <u>which pierced him: and all kindreds of the earth</u> shall wail because of him. Even so, Amen." (KJV)*

> **Matthew 24:27** *"For as the lightning cometh out of the east, and shineth even unto the west; so shall also the coming of the Son of man be." (KJV)*

Notice in **Rev. 1:7**, every eye shall see him. That means every eye, both those dead, *"which pierced him"*; and those alive. Think of all the: good angels (thousands times ten of thousand), all individuals born from Adam to the present (billions, if not trillions), aliens from the other 99 planets, and all wearing white robes of rightness and with the light of Jesus reflecting off these robes. This is an event that cannot be misinterpreted. *Does this sound like a "thief in the night"?* –– **NO!** The *thief* is about the Rapture. The question of righteous space aliens comes back to mind. So let us return to **Mat.24:31**. **Chapter 24** is that time the apostles asked about the end times.

> **Matthew 24:31** *"and he shall send his angels with a great sound of a trumpet, and they shall gather together <u>his elect</u> from the four <u>winds; from one <u>end of heaven to the other</u>."</u> (KJV)*

Here we read of two places Jesus' angels will collect God's elect (righteous souls). Therefore, one collection is from the earth (4 winds). This collection reveals all saved souls over the complete time man is on the planet and includes: Old Testament Saints, New Testament Saints (Church), and the Tribulation Saints. Next, we read *"<u>from one end of heaven to the other</u>."* This collection, for sure, includes all righteous angels. But what of those Living Creatures waiting for all the sons of God to be revealed? **(Rom. 8).** Yes, them too.

> **Romans 8:19** *"<u>For the earnest expectation of the creature waiteth for the manifestation of the sons of God.</u>"* (KJV)

Satan knows this event will come to fruition but has done his best to minimize the number of earthlings for Jesus. We can see this occurring by our entertainment companies, who have created this illusion and contradiction of the Bible and with all sorts of star wars and hideous monsters that need to be killed. Also, science wants God's creation to fit science theory; and not science theory to fit God's creation. We have been so hardened up with gore and destruction to toughen up earthlings for the up and coming War of Armageddon!

We Christians have a most wonderful time coming into the near future. We should thank God and Jesus for preparing this treasure of the Rapture and all events we, in Heaven, will see happening on earth. God's wonderful grace will have a glorious home just waiting for us to enjoy forever. We will see these events happening on earth but without excessive remorse for those experiencing the wrath of God. For we will be in total agreement with God's perfect justice; for then, we will understand the perfect judgment of God is due to the unrighteous earthlings. We will also see the Tribulation Saints performing deeds for God and will take pride in what God is doing with and for them. Their results around the world will be utterly fantastic. They will be instrumental in saving all of the Hebrew people. And we are told that all the angels shout for joy for the single person who accepts Jesus. We, too, will also be joyful for those who are saved from corruption and The Lake of Fire.

Also, our bodies will be incorruptible and immortal. No more physical or mental problems; blind will see, the deaf will hear, no crying, no pain, no worries, entirely energetic, no weakness but strength, friends, family, love ones; and boredom will be unknown. Joy and happiness will be our constant companions. Again, this time is spoken of in **Rom.8.**

> **Romans 8:18** *"For I reckon that the sufferings of this present time are not worthy to be compared <u>with the glory which shall be revealed in us."</u> (KJV)*

THE INHERITANCE MYSTERY

Jesus called himself the *"son of man,"* but he was also the *son of God* as Mary was a virgin and Jesus was (**Mat.1:20–25**) conceived by God. Jesus is identifying himself as a man through his conception in Mary, the daughter of man. Therefore, both names are valid of Jesus, *the Son of Man,* and *the Son of God.* Jesus must identify himself with man to prove his family fellowship with man for any shared inheritance. The name *"Sons of God"* is also necessary to establish his direct inheritance from God. But the principal reason is to declare that Jesus is both Man and God in one. Notice, God speaks of a fellowship in this mystery. One part of this mystery is revealed in **Eph.3.**

> **Ephesians 3:4–6** *"(4) Whereby, when ye read, ye may understand my knowledge in the <u>mystery of Christ</u> (5) <u>Which in other ages was not made known unto the sons of men,</u> as it is now revealed unto his holy apostles and prophets by the Spirit; (6)<u>That the Gentiles should be fellow heirs, and of the same body, and partakers of his promise in Christ by the gospel.</u>" (KJV):*

Verse 6, which states (*"of the same body"*) agrees with my assessment that the *earth is the lost sheepfold* and will have inheritance rights. By Hebrew law, the firstborn son was the inheritor of his father's property. So if we are to inherit, then we must be adopted into the Hebrew family. Therefore, if we are in Jesus and Jesus is God's son, we are in God's family. But the 99 other sheepfolds appear not to be inheritors, as there is no scripture revealing this.

First, I would like you to notice the two different references to the class distension of created beings. First is **verse 5** with *"sons of men"*; and secondly in **verse 6,** *"the Gentiles."* Sons of men take us back to **Gen.6,** where there is also an additional inference to a group of individuals *"the sons of God."* Son of men and sons of God remember they appear to be two distinct groups. Gentiles are a group within the group of the sons of man. Gentiles were named to separate them from the Hebrews (God's chosen people). The Hebrew people were to bring the knowledge of the one true God (Jehovah) to the nations. And it is the Gentiles through the Hebrews apostils that are to bring the knowledge of the triune God (Jesus, the Holy Spirit, and God) to the world. And this knowledge contains a great inference to *Jesus as the Hebrew's Messiah.*

The Hebrew nation was taught that this Messiah would conquer the world; they saw this or desired this to happen in their misery under the conquering Roman Emperors. They failed to realize this would not occur until Daniels Empire prophecies came true, well into the future. At the time of the scripture writings (1AD—100AD), which included Daniel's prophecies of both Roman Empires (6 and 8), which were yet to come, after Daniel. One prophecy was the demise of the 2nd Roman Empire (#6), and another of the revivals of the 3rd Roman Empire (#8) **(Dan.7, 8,** and **9).**

God conceived this inheritance mystery in his plan for man (Sons of God), even before the time of creation. God knew that we would fall into sin at the beginning of his plan. He made way for us to escape the eternal Death that we deserved; through a simple act of faith in Jesus. We deserved The Lake of Fire for our sins, but God not only sent salvation to us, but God gave us rewards and treasures for our acts of love to our fellow man. One such reward or treasure is our inheritance of all God possesses and the Rapture.

Ephesians 1:11 *"In whom also <u>we</u> have obtained an inheritance, <u>being predestinated</u> according to the purpose of him who worketh all things after the counsel of his own will." (KJV)*

The *"we"* mentioned here is for both Hebrews and Gentiles. Because the writer Paul was a Hebrew but sent by God to the Gentiles. Notice the word *"predestined."* It refers to God's plan, which was determined before creation. We have a powerful and intelligent God that can plan and know all events into the future for every human being—and knowing ahead of time what they would do and the corrections God would insert for every human frailty and failure. God gave everyone the right to exercise their self-will *(a prime directive)* without his interference. God will attempt to influence our actions, *but it is our responsibility to perform to his will.* God records all the deeds we have ever perform, be it words or actions. And we will make an account to either Jesus (Christians) **2 Cor.5:10,** or God (Lost Souls) **Rev.20:11–15**

What a blessing it is to be before Jesus and accounting for our sins instead of before God. Even though we deserve the Lake of Fire, we are not only set free of sin by Jesus but are rewarded for our efforts on earth. Our efforts are rewarded by our treasures that will be stored up in Heaven and our efforts to exercise God's will here on earth.

Revelation 20:4 *"And I saw thrones, and they sat upon them, and <u>judgment was given unto them</u>* (Church) *and I saw the <u>souls of</u>*

them that were beheaded for the witness of Jesus, (Tribulation Saints) *and for the word of God, and which had not worshipped the beast, neither his image, neither had received* his *mark upon their foreheads, or in their hands; and they lived and reigned with Christ a thousand years." (KJV)*

Revelation 21:7 *"He that overcometh shall inherit all things; and I will be his God, and he shall be my son."(KJV)*

In **Rev. 20:4,** please notice that these words cover many years by *"and judgment was given unto them,"* which refers to the Church Saints from Jesus resurrection to the Tribulation Saints (*1st Harvest*) by the words *"beheaded for the witness of Jesus."* This statement pertains to the Tribulation Saints of end times. The Tribulation Saints are the 144,000 Hebrew Missionaries of **Rev. 7** and all their converts during the Great Tribulation seven years. This event will occur just before and during Jesus' permanent return to earth to establish his 1,000- year Kingdom. And **Rev. 21:7** reveals the results of all persons that overcome evil. Remember, all these individuals were predestined to perform their assignment (deeds) to achieve their success.

We are predestined, but we must make an effort to overcome the testing (evil desires inserted into our bodies) to become the Sons of God and to learn of God's righteous ways. And we are to exercise those Godly principles in our daily life. Also, to help others to discover truths and accept Jesus as Lord.

These two above scriptures reveal a time of wonderful rewards, which places the Bride of Christ and the Tribulation Saints in positions of great responsibility of judging others. It is that characteristic of self-control, which is needed for correct actions in judging others.

1 Corinthians 6:2--3 *"(2) Do ye not know that the saints shall judge the world? and if the world shall be judged by you, are ye unworthy to judge the smallest matters? (3) Know ye not that we shall judge angels? how much more things that pertain to this life?" (KJV)*

Note

Let me pause here for a word on Saints. Please notice from this scripture; that Saints are you, the Bride of Christ! Paul was writing to all the Christians in the Corinthian Church. So you need to understand that all Christians are Saints. We are chosen by God and not by some committee. Many other scriptures confirm this. Now back to judgments.

In Revelation, we read all the lost will be judged by all the books God will open in **Rev.20:12.** We, too (Church), will be required to answer for our sins before the Judgment Seat of Christ **(2 Cor.5:10).** Which book will Jesus use? Answer: The Bible, God's Word, is one book that reveals our sins and just punishments for those sins. Therefore, we will be judged by God's word; so if we use God's word to judge, we are not judging but repeating God's judgment on that action. But, if we interject a non-God-directed judgment, then we are judging. For example: if you say that a person with blue eyes is going to Hell, you are judging, as that is not found in the Bible. Another most essential book is the Book of Life. *And you will defiantly want your name in this book!*

So we see only some marvels found in this Mystery of Gentiles being heirs that have been hidden in God, and it started at the beginning of the world before Jesus' 1st coming onto the earth. You and I and all mankind are to see this mystery develop. Be it from both the inside (Heaven) or outside (Hell). This process started with Jesus and will end with the 144,000 Hebrew Missionaries and their converts. All the Hebrew people will see and realize there is something they did not understand. But there will be a revealing (gospel) of this mystery by the Church to created beings in heaven (space) and earth. **(Romans 8:19–23** and **Eph. 3:9–10)**

The Hebrews will also be given this knowledge of Jesus in clarity and power by the 144,000 Hebrew Missionaries of **Revelation Chapter 7**. During times of tribulation, these 144,000 will help the Holy Spirit convert all Hebrews to Jesus. This event will complete the family (Sheep of the earth) of God, Jews, and Gentiles; brothers through Jesus' sacrifice. And as brothers, we will inherit with Jesus and Jews as God determines.

To inherit is a wonderful word for the inherence recipients. This word in Greek means:

> **"Kay-ron-om'-os** *(in its original sense of partitioning, i.e. [reflex.] getting by apportionment); a sharer by lot, i.e.an inheritor (lit. or fig.); by impl. a possessor; -beir[2]."*

Notice the word pertains to *"partitioning,"* but we read in scripture in the Old and New Testament of inheritance of great magnitude. One can be found in **Rev. 21.**

> **Revelation 21:7 *"He that overcometh shall <u>inherit all things</u>; and I will be his God, and he shall be my son" (KJV).***

This inheritance of <u>*"all things"*</u> will never fade or be expended, and it will remain with us for eternity. Peter understood the timelessness of the inheritance, waiting for you through Jesus. In **1 Peter 1,** you will read of this timeless inheritance; and incorruptible.

> **1 Peter 1:3–5" *(3) Blessed* be *the God and Father of our Lord Jesus Christ, which according to his abundant mercy hath <u>begotten us again</u> unto a lively hope by the resurrection of Jesus Christ from the dead, (4) <u>To an inheritance incorruptible</u>, and <u>undefiled,</u> and <u>that fadeth not away,</u> reserved in heaven for you, (5) Who are kept by the power of God through faith unto <u>salvation ready to be revealed in the last time.</u>" (KJV)***

It appears to me; there is such a magnitude of unfathomable blessings waiting for Christians, which words are incapable of explaining. Anything for us that lasts forever; is incomprehensible.

ADAM AND EVE'S FALL MYSTERY

THE FIRST TEST OF FAITH!

Here, we see where a tradition has been around for many years. And it is; *"that God told Adam and Eve not to eat from the Tree of Knowledge of Good and Evil."* Let us see what the Bible says about this event. So is this truth or tradition?   TRADITION!

Genesis 3 starts with Eve's temptation by the serpent that leads to Adam's early failure and man's downfall. And these words reveal the craftiness of the serpent (Satan). It is interesting why Satan deceived Eve first, and this bears some understanding. Satan could not attack Adam because he was present when God gave Adam this commandment of not to eat from the Tree of Knowledge of Good and Evil. So Adam would know Satan was wrong. But Eve was not created yet to be at this event; Satan *could create doubt in Eve's mind* to challenge Adam's words. When Satan said, *"Yea, hath God* (really) *said, Ye shall not eat of every tree of the garden?"* Notice the question was centered on Eve's *(Ye)* knowledge. Is Eve not permitted to eat from the Tree of Knowledge? Satan was not challenging God's words but Adam's words. If Eve had been there when God told Adam not to eat, she would not have fallen for this deception. But, Eve must have seen the Tree of Knowledge in the center of the Garden and would have wondered, motivated by her female characteristics. Satan played on the knowledge of Eve's initial motivations

We know that men and women have different motivational brain functions. Science knows the left brain and right brain functions, which influence *our initial reactions*. It has nothing to do with intelligence but with initial motivational responses. Men are initially motivated by logic or judgment, and women are more initially motivated by beauty, carefulness, or welfare for her and those she loves.

For example, 1) when my wife and I were driving on a very narrow country winding roads here in the Tennessee Mountains, and another car comes around a narrow blind curve towards us. I notice my wife grab a door handhold because she initially perceives a wreck is about to happen. But, I have already computed, initially in my brain, that there is enough room to pass safely by pulling closer to my side of the road. And I recognize the other car is doing the same to his side of the road. 2) When she is driving her car, she carries food for stray animals; and I do not. If she sees a stray that is abandoned, she will pick it up and care for it. Our best dog came to us this way. So God created us with these traits, so together, we make a whole.

Now Satan uses Eve's natural desires and in **Gen.3:6** tempts Eve through her initial motivations. Now Adam is not deceived by Satan; he just watches as this conversation develops.

> **I Timothy 2:4** *"And Adam was not deceived, but the woman being deceived was in the transgression." (KJV)*

So a mystery arises – why? Why did Adam not speak or do anything? This question has been around for centuries. And like when Jesus wrote in the sand with the adulteress women in **John 8:3–11**. What did he write? I think Jesus wrote, *"where is the man."* Some mysteries will continue until we meet Jesus. But we can speculate on some of the meanings. This question is an excellent question to ask in a mixed class. Divide the men and woman. Ask for a generalized answer from each group.

> **Genesis 1:1** *"Now the <u>serpent</u> was more subtil than any beast of the field which the LORD God had made. And he said unto the woman, Yea,<u> hath God said,</u> Ye shall not eat of every tree of the garden?"* *(KJV)*

Note

Language is present from the beginning. No grunting and pointing as science portray; also, an animal speaks to Eve and Eve to the animal. Wonder what science says about animals speaking? We read this again in **Num. 22:28–30.**

First, let us look at the serpent. This creature is Satan himself. **Rev. 12:9** specifically identifies the Serpent as Satan and the Dragon. Notice in God's

84

creation the serpent speaks to Eve and not to Adam. Satan does not specifically identify the Tree of Knowledge of Good and Evil but includes all trees in the garden from which they could eat. Satan lets Eve identify the Tree of Knowledge for herself. Satan lays the questionable foundation that all trees were eatable, which creates the doubt seed for deception to Eve. Why not this tree? Adam and Eve apparently had little knowledge of death. Also, Eve was not privileged to be with Adam when God spoke the words *"not to eat"* to Adam. Here we see the initial deception revealed to Eve; as *not a challenge to God but Adam's words*, as Adam had told Eve. Eve was not even created when God told Adam *"not to eat."* So Adam was the first missionary for God's Words and the first look at future ministers' first challenge. Keep in mind the woman's initial reactions to these events. Next, Eve expands on her knowledge given to her by Adam in **Gen. 1**.

Genesis 3:2–3 (2) *"And the woman said unto the serpent, <u>We may eat of the fruit of the trees</u> of the garden: (3) But of the fruit of <u>the tree which *is* in the midst of the garden</u>, God hath said, <u>Ye shall not eat of it</u>, <u>neither shall ye touch it, lest ye die"</u>.(KJV)*

The Tree of Knowledge of Good and Evil is in the center of the garden, but why mention this? Also, notice that the Tree of Knowledge is not mentioned here. Here we see Eve, including all trees in the Garden but making an exception for the trees in the midst of the garden. But Eve does not name the tree as the Tree of Knowledge of Good and Evil. Now Satan has her mentally focused on that particular tree, which Satan is about to attack. *Why that tree in particular when you can eat fruit from all trees?* Eve continues to explain in interesting terms using 1st person and 2nd person. Notice she says *"we can eat"* relating to all trees, but notice when it comes to the Tree of Knowledge, she changes to *"Ye shall not eat" (Ye is you)*. This statement tends to reveal she is not identifying herself (*Ye*) specifically in this command. Remember, Eve was not yet created when God told Adam; he cannot eat of this tree's fruit. It appeared when Adam told Eve he used this very word for "you." Also, notice the addition of *"neither shall ye touch it."* Where did this come from? Did Eve add this, or did Adam? Then next Eve says, *"lest ye* (you) *die."* Not me or we, but you. She is half right. But notice if Adam did not eat; Eve would still be saved by childbearing if they continue in *faith, charity,* and *holiness.* Here WE see the first use of *FAITH.*

I'm not sure Adam and Eve fully comprehended the ramifications of death. But here, Satan is using her lack of knowledge of death. Now Satan has Eve leaning towards the doubts of Adam. This disobedience is also initially supported by the fact; Eve did not die after eating *the fruit.* This lack of God's action (death) must have caused doubts in Adam's mind too. But Satan knew this would happen and plan this doubt against Adam.

Genesis 3:4 *"And the serpent said unto the woman, Ye* [you Eve] *shall not surely die." (KJV)*

Here we see the lie (deceptive half-truth) that is not provable to Eve or Adam as it is only provably after the fact; when he eats the fruit. This experience is likened to today's drugs. One does not know how dependent they will be until after the drug is taken. They, too, have not experienced death for Adam and Eve to know this is true or false. Eve must trust Adam's words. Also, this is a half-truth as Eve did not die when she ate. Adam and Eve think death would be instantaneous rather than long-term.

Eve must decide who told her this; God or Adam? This event is a direct challenge to Adam's words and not God's because God never told her. Why does Adam not speak out opposing Satan? We have seen he was not deceived, so why his silence? Adam was not deceived **(1Tim.2:14)** but was not fully aware of the fullness of death. When *Eve ate and did not die, this had to cause some doubts in Adam. <u>This disobedience is the first test of faith</u>.* We face the same problem today. God and Jesus tell us things that we cannot comprehend (faith), but we are still required to perform. It would need Adam and Eve to have to experience death just to start to understand its fullness and finality. They, too, had the motivations of the immediacy of an event as we do today. Satan knew Eve would not die immediately, thereby confusing Adam.

There were other pressures and influences affecting Adam as it does men today. How much influence do you think a wife has on her husband? If the truth be known, she is very influential. The Bible tells us that when a man and woman get married, they become one. How deep can a relationship become between the two? Remember, Adam was alone before Eve, and we today know how loneness affects us. Also, after a sexual relationship begins, desires grow in magnitude. We try to please each other; heartache is a very agonizing pain. Men are not emotional creatures, generally. We try to avoid emotional situations except for sex and sports. Now Adam was not knowledgeable about sports, but sex was a powerful influence. Remember, Adam and Eve were commanded to have a lot of sex (replenish the earth). Child birthing was initially not painful for women until after this fall and the curses. And it is unknown how long they were together, being naked before their fall and experiencing sex.

Now Satan has created doubts; in both Eve first and then Adam. Now Satan drives the nail into the coffin.

Genesis 3:5 *"For God doth know that in the day ye eat thereof, then your <u>eyes shall be opened,</u> and <u>ye shall be as gods,</u> <u>knowing good and evil."</u> (KJV)*

Satan hits the nail on the head with a half-truth. He tells the truth for once! Deception is best served with an iota of truth. Will their eyes be opened? ---- Yes! They saw they were naked. Will they be like gods? ----- Yes! We will be Kings, Lords, and Priest, eventually. --- Will they know good from evil? ---- Yes! We do, and we are required to do good. With this deception, Satan has captured Adam and Eve into their future coffin.

The second half, which Satan avoided, is the truth of death. Death is ready to enter the earth. Now Satan has set the stage for Eve to unwilling deceive her husband Adam, and together (one) sin entered the world. But, Adam is the responsible one for the failure as the command was given only to Adam.

Genesis 3:6 *"And when the woman saw that the <u>tree</u> was <u>good for</u> <u>food,</u> and that it* <u>was</u> <u>pleasant to the eyes,</u> *and a tree to be desired to* <u>make</u> *one* <u>wise,</u> *she took of the fruit thereof, and <u>did eat,</u> and <u>gave also</u> <u>unto her husband with her; and he did eat.</u>" (KJV)*

Eve now reveals her initial motivations of good food, beauty, and intelligence. It is important to understand that Eve ate of the tree first, and *nothing happened immediately!* Satan knew this would occur and would add to the deception of Adam. I can only imagine how good that fruit tasted initially. So Adam sees Eve eat from the Tree of Knowledge, and she did not die. If she did not die, then why couldn't he eat of the tree? Visual deception can confuse a person as this is the main deception of magic. Adam probably failed to recognize the command was to him and not to Eve. So Eve gave the fruit of the tree to Adam, and he ate. *<u>It is essential that you realize that nothing happens to either Adam or Eve until after Adam ate the fruit from the tree</u>.* That old *lust of the flesh* and *lust of the eyes* blossomed in Adam, and he ate. Lack of faith in God when all Adam had to do was be obedient to God. It was then that both Adam and Eve's eyes were opened; they became wise and intelligent from their experience and realized they were naked. So Satan was correct. Remember, the Bible tells us that sin and death came into the world by one man Adam. And sin and death will be conquered by one man Jesus.

Satan's schemes against God starts--------, and Satan laughed.

Romans 5:12 *"Wherefore, as by one man sin entered into the world, and death by sin; and so death passed upon all men, for that all have sinned": (KJV)*

1 Corinthians 15:21–22 *"(21) For since by man* came *death, by man* came *also the resurrection of the dead. (22) For as in Adam all die, even so in Christ shall all be made alive." (KJV)*

I would like you to consider the lack of faith of both; Adam to his God and Eve in her husband. Had they both exercised their faith, our world would be a different place.

Or would it?

Do you think God did not know Adam would eat of the tree? Is it possible God planned this event? Remember, God is the potter, and we are the clay!

1. Did not God establish both Good and Evil?
2. Did not God give us his directions for life (Bible)?
3. Did not God create angels
4. Did not God create Satan?
5. Did not God create Demons?
6. Did not God create vessels of mercy and destruction?
7. Did God create Satan for a purpose?
8. Did not God create the Universe for Jesus?
9. Did not God create all the natural laws?
10. Did not God create Heaven, Hell, and the Lake of Fire?
11. Did not God create the Flood?
12. Did not God create you and me?
13. Did not God give us gifts to use in his gospel mission?
14. Did not God create Salvation?
15. Did not God create the Rapture?
16. Did not God create Armageddon to destroy all evil?
17. Did not God create the Judgment seat of Christ?
18. Did not God create the Great White Throne Judgment?
19. Did not God create a New Universe and a New Earth?
20. Did not God create the Lake of Fire?

It seems to me a plan is revealed here!

Everything God created is by his design. It has a purpose and a time to be placed on this earth. God is not limited by time that he created, as he can go forward and back in time. *God's plan for his creation is massive and complete.* Every individual God created has a perfect plan for their life. He knew we would go astray, and God has a second plan to correct the situation. God's prime directive is, *he will allow us to exercise our self-will,* and he will try to influence us to do good. If we chose evil, God will use this as a learning exercise for us who are repentant of our evil deeds. No one, and I mean no one, will escape his judgment for his or her evil deeds. Praise God that God sent Jesus to pay for our evil deeds (sins); for those who believe in Jesus. *This faith in Jesus is the crowning moment for God's plan for every person. And it has been revealed at the beginning of Man.* God also created an unimaginable place of punishment for those who reject Jesus. And will create an unfathomable existence of pleasures for those who maintain their trust and faith in Jesus.

Therefore, will not God create a New Heaven and New Earth? ---YES! All remnants of evil's results: death, innocent blood, war's destruction, war materials, evil individuals, Satan, demons, sins, and our memory of our evil deeds; *will be removed.*

THE CURSES OF THE FALL

Genesis 3:13–15 *"(13) And the LORD God said unto the woman, What* is *this that thou hast done? And the woman said, The serpent beguiled me, and I did eat. (14) And the LORD God said unto the <u>serpent,</u> Because thou hast done this, thou art cursed above all cattle, and above every beast of the field; upon thy belly shalt thou go, and dust shalt thou eat all the days of thy life: (15) And I will put <u>enmity between thee and the woman,</u> and between thy seed and her seed; it shall bruise thy head, and thou shalt bruise his heel." (KJV)*

Please notice that Satan's curse is individualized, where the curse of Adam and Eve is for them and their future children. This is the location in time of the beginning of Inherited Sin and Satan becoming Jesus' nemesis.

THE SERPENT'S CURSE

This curse for the Serpent has been a thorn in my side. It is only Satan's curse, but in the Bible, the curse says Satan is to eat dust? The only thoughts that come to my mind are: we are made of dust **(Gen.2:7),** and the Satanic False Religion's leader is created by the False Prophet who comes from dust. The

Beast of the earth **(Rev.13:11)**. Both of these events are the destruction of many humans (dust). And Satan has eaten much dust since his curse. Enmity is a deep-seated unfriendliness or hostility; because Satan knows the woman, Mary, will give birth to Jesus. And Jesus will cast Satan into the abyss for 1,000 years. But Satan's army (after the 1,000 years) will eventually be destroyed by God **(Rev.20:10)** and He cast all evil into the Lake of Fire.

I have a question for women. *Why would God curse women knowing Jesus' mother would be a woman?*

THE CURSE OF WOMAN

Genesis 3:16 *"Unto the woman he said, I will greatly <u>multiply thy sorrow and thy conception</u>; in <u>sorrow, thou shalt bring forth children;</u> and thy desire* shall be *to <u>thy husband, and he shall rule over thee.</u> <u>(KJV)</u>*

This verse has been difficult for Pastors to teach as many women get offended by these words and directions. These words are the curse for <u>women only,</u> and they can and so often fight against it, but to their risk. *This is the woman's punishment and not the man's.* God has seen fit to create men at the top of the pecking order, so to speak. This is the rule of order and condition for man to rule as Jesus ruled, and His rule is of love and unselfishness. This rule does not appear installed in the workplace but at home. As many women in the Bible held high positions, one was Deborah in **Jud.4** and **5.** She was a Judge of Israel and a prophet. This curse appears to place a lot of emphasis on the value of a woman displaying the Beatitudes of **Matthew 5, 6,** and **7**; to their husband. Most men need this softcore to counter our hardcore. Men toughen women, and women soften up men, and together they become one. If Christian women do not accept this curse and live within God's conditions, their relationship with their husbands may become difficult. A woman can become afraid of a dominating and brutal husband, but **God does not permit brutality by either**.

Some women become very tough due to abuse, be it sexual, physical, or mental. Therefore, they become protective (rightly so) of themselves, becoming the opposite of God's desires. Women, this abuse is not God's desire for you; seek help in your Church first. If your husband is a true Christian, he will stop and will seek your forgiveness. *Abuse is not to be tolerated by the Church.*

Pride can raise its ugly head, too, as a woman may want more out of life, also. Many see the glass ceiling and consider it a challenge. And many women in the Bible were given very high positions in their society. But remember, children need their Moms in the early stages of their life. It seems to be God's plan as men do not have breasts for babies to suckle for nutrients. But, the children need their Dad's influence more from early teens to adulthood. Women face a dilemma; to take care of their child at the early stages of their life or for a career.

A career would necessitate her, giving her God-given responsibility to a stranger. Over time, the child may learn to love the stranger more than the mother. Her God-given breasts reveal the best and simple answer.

The curse *"in <u>sorrow thou shalt bring forth children</u>."* Failure to accept God's plan for the woman and the child can lead to lost opportunities to create fond memories, salvation for the child, help during old age, and many other Treasures. At the end of a Christian woman's life is the joy of her children. The career woman will have memories of events in her career, which cannot compare to memories of her children and their continued love. Careers will end, but love from a child will never end. *"All is vanity and vexation of spirit"* **(Ecc.1:14).** To live to an old age without love is a travesty!

Men, too, must understand a woman's curse. One is the *"bring forth children."* It is not just the pain of giving birth, but the care of her child during each child's entire life. She has been given emotions for care, education, health, safety, mental development, social abilities, religious salvation, and many more traits. To fight against God's curses is permitted by God, but she will double her curses by accepting man's curses. Men have some of these same traits and concerns for his children, *but this is not God's curse for man.* Both Husband and wife must recognize we are created with different levels of emotions and not expect the other should feel or act as they do in different situations. Also, the man, too, can accept the woman's curses, thereby doubling his curses. These are permanent curses, and we cannot force them to just go away. Women remember this; you were God's last creation on earth, beautiful, desirable even to the Sons of God. Woman is the only provider of life within her. A woman (not Man) was the provider of the life in Jesus. Your curse can also be your blessing.

THE CURSE OF MAN

> **Genesis 3:17–19** *"(17) And <u>unto Adam</u> he said, Because thou hast <u>hearkened unto the voice of thy wife</u>, and hast eaten of the tree, of which <u>I commanded thee</u>, saying, Thou shalt not eat of it: cursed is the ground for thy sake; <u>in sorrow shalt thou eat</u> of <u>it all the days of thy life</u>; (18) Thorns also and thistles shall it bring forth to thee; and thou shalt eat the herb of the field; (19) In the <u>sweat of thy face shalt thou eat bread,</u> till thou return unto the ground; for out of it wast thou taken: for dust thou art, and unto dust shalt thou return." (KJV)*

God's first statement reveals Adam's choice to believe Eve rather than God. This submission should prove the power woman has over man. If this does make woman fear their use of evil influences, they should. And man must be aware of any influence from anyone that will affect their relationship with God. As you can see in **verse 17** that God says he gave this command to Adam and not Eve. In **1 John 4,** we are told to test the spirit of everyone. We do this by studying God's word and, when not sure, by faith in Jesus. If you are uncomfortable with what you are told, pray for clarity, and study!

Man, through Adam's sin, will be cursed all of his life with work. This curse includes man's commitment to work. This work is outside the home as God has man working in the fields for herbs. Here we see the man is to be the primary provider of the family and not the wife. All of the proceeds man will bring home will be very burdensome and will take all of his day and days. *By the sweat of his face* is a <u>clue</u> that he may not have time to prepare food. These curses seem to reveal that raising children requires two individuals, husband and wife. *And this requires different roles to accomplish all the tasks but also the sharing of these tasks.* A woman cannot get up every 2 hours at night to feed or change a diaper. Men share in this role. Today these roles are misunderstood, and under conflicts and marriages are suffering.

Man is also to maintain the home in good sound condition. Fill the coffers for future expenditures, such as medical, fire damage, transportation, tools for both man and wife, a school for children, teach the children of God and Jesus. Train children to take care of themselves, teach them a trade, and be an example to their children.

If a problem arises, work it out maturely with love for your wife. Both must remember **Jam.1:9,** *be quick to listen, slow to speak, and slow to anger.* Do not exaggerate because it is a lie and will only infuriate; plus, lying is a sin; we are never to sin. *Men leave work anger at work!*

Both Man and Woman must live by attempting to do the Beatitudes of **Mathew chapters 5, 6,** and **7.** Pride must be: smothered with humility, anger stifled with patience, unrighteous overcome with righteousness, selfishness corrected with charity, depression overcome with hope, anxiety with thrust in Jesus, unrest overcome with knowledge of the future, and peace in the assurance that nothing can separate you from God, *except yourself.*

These thoughts also reflect the necessity for the Church. God desires the bride to be under Jesus' leadership. *And we men must be under Jesus' leadership and act as Jesus would acts.* Men remember women are cursed by for desires to their husband. Do not abuse this or take advantage of this curse. Trust must never be destroyed as it can seldom be regained. Both men and women must remember to: *"be quick to listen, slow to speak, and slow to anger."* And *"speak softly but carry a big ~~stick~~,"* correction, *Bible.*

MYSTERY #5 CREATION OF MAN

T hen God created life on Day 5 and 6; He created life with blood in the body. But several scriptures make a mystery in themselves. For example, in Psalms, we read **Psalm 139.**

Psalms 139:13–16 *"(13) "For thou hast possessed my reins: thou hast covered me in my mother's womb. (14) I will praise thee; for I am fearfully and wonderfully made: marvellous are thy works; and that my soul knoweth right well. (15) My substance was not hid from thee, when I was made in secret, and curiously wrought in the lowest parts of the earth. (16) Thine eyes did see my substance, yet being unperfect; and in thy book all my members were written, which in continuance were fashioned, when as yet there was none of them." (KJV)*

These verses are hard to understand in old English but let's see if I can simplify them. *"You possessed my rains"* is using the rider of a horse who directs the direction, the gate, and speed of the horse. So God is directing the construction of our complete Body, Soul, and Spirit. Your soul and spirit were created before your natural body, i.e., *"as yet there was none of them."*

"Covered me in my mother's womb" is that time God chooses to start your birthing process. This is the time your soul and spirit will be wrapped into a human body. God has planned this time for you to be presented on earth. His plan for every human was created before the process of creating the universe. In Genesis, God has woven you into the fabric of God's plan for this specific moment in time and has a plan for your life.

"I am fearfully and wonderfully made" If you ever get the chance to study the human body in detail, you will be amazed at all the intricacies in construction and functionality of all the parts of the body. The eyes are awesome to convert light to depth and color.

"That my soul knoweth right well." In these words, David is interjecting his assurances that he knows these things are true. It is not just his spirit but also his soul, both Mortal and spiritual.

Here we see our soul and spirit, which has already been created before our body; so God knows where our soul and spirit was made in a *"secret, and curiously wrought in the lowest parts of the earth."*

The question comes to mind, *"where?"* It is a secret! But it is someplace in the lowest parts of the earth[A].

It appears the center of the earth is a busy place. We find Old Testament Saints in Paradise, Old and New Testament unrighteous in Torment, Church Saints (before Rapture) in Paradise, the Tribulation Saints under the Alter, the Abyss for fallen angels (demons), Apollyon (king of the Abyss **Rev.9:11**), and Satan for a 1,000 years, the secret place we are created, and possible the holding place awaiting our placement into God's plan for each person on earth.

"Yet being unperfect" This verse shows our imperfection of our substance (Soul and Spirit) having inherited sin nature from Adam. But God still wrote in his Book the days ordained for you and me. This event occurred before your body was formed in your mother's womb. Just as Jeremiah was sanctified before he was formed in his mother's womb. **(Jeremiah 1:4–5)** So we see that God has a plan for you even before you were created. If we sin or deviate from his plan for us, he will have an alternate plan. But his primary plan is for your salvation, and it will always be present during your life on earth.

> **Romans 8:18** *"For I reckon that the sufferings of this present time* are *not worthy* to be compared *with the glory which shall be revealed in us." (KJV)*

This verse speaks of the future "eternity." There we will see all our treasures God has in store for us. And we will be utterly amazed with immense joy of those treasures. But keep in mind when God created Man, he also created both Jew and Gentiles on this earth. And God created us to be with him for eternity. **(1 Tim.2)**

1 Timothy 2:3–4 "*(3) For this* is *good and acceptable in the sight of God our Saviour; (4) <u>Who will have all men to be saved, and to come unto the knowledge of the truth. (KJV)</u>*

Keep this verse in mind as you read through this book; because this earth is a complete unit; with Jews and Gentiles. There is no more human life classification on this earth. So Jesus came to earth to perform God's desires for all men, Jews, and Gentiles. Also, notice the Tree of Knowledge of Good and Evil is to bring the initial truth to man. We have the truth in us, and only we must find it and bring it out for others who are not searching for that truth given to man. But with the help of the Holy Spirit, this complete truth will come to fruition. For the Son of Man will come to earth and claim back his title to earth. And all saved souls will receive all of their just rewards.

Matthew 16:27 "*For the Son of man shall come in the glory of his Father with his angels; and then he shall reward every man <u>according to his works.</u>*" *(KJV)*

You who are in Jesus are blessed beyond your wildest imaginations. Let your light shine to all the lost, and do what you can do for Jesus' Kingdom. Jesus yolk is easy, and his burden is light.

Mathew 5:16"Let your light so shine before men, that they may see your good works, and glorify your Father which is in heaven." (KJV)

THE AGE OF ACCOUNTABILITY MYSTERY

A question of inherited sin in children has been asked over the centuries. If children have inherited sin nature from Adam and they die, where do they go, Heaven or Hell? The Bible does not explicitly address this question, but it gives us enough information to deduce the correct answer.

First, let us read a statement about Jesus by **Isa. 7** about the sign of Immanuel.

Isaiah 7:14–16 "(14) *Therefore the Lord himself shall give you a sign; Behold, a virgin shall conceive, and bear a son, and shall call his name Immanuel. (15) Butter and honey shall he eat, that he may know to refuse the evil, and choose the good. (16) <u>For before the child shall know to refuse the evil, and choose the good,</u> the land that thou abhorrest shall be forsaken of both her kings."* (KJV)

Isaiah makes a statement about Jesus' time of lack of knowledge for good and evil. And it would be true for all children of all time. At some time in his life, Jesus gained the knowledge of both good and evil and chose good. Jesus experienced that period of time of innocence until he reached the Age of Accountability. So would not this same time be given to babies and young children, too?

Then let us look at God's desires for the man who reaches The Age of Accountability; in **1st Tim.2**

1 Timothy 2:3–4 "*(3) For this* is *good and acceptable in the sight of God our Saviour; (4) <u>Who will have all men to be saved,</u> and to <u>come unto the knowledge of the truth:</u> *(KJV)*

Here we read God wants all men, which includes children, to be saved. Next, God wants man and children *to come to the knowledge of truth.* This knowledge is a process that will take all of our lives to learn the truth. *But this truth starts at the realization of what sin is; and who can save us from our sins.* Therefore, a child just born has our sin nature in him or her, but they are unknowing of what constitutes sin and who Jesus is. Their minds must develop for them to be able to process language and concepts. In **Romans 2:12–13,** Paul addresses this period of innocence.

Romans 2: 12–13 "*For as many as have sinned without law shall also perish without law: and as many as have sinned in the law shall be judged by the law;"* (KJV)

This verse is fascinating. Notice to perish without the law; they cannot be held accountable to the law. How can they be accountable when there is no law to be responsible? The law spells out the punishment for breaking a law (sin), but how can one be liable when they have not been given the knowledge of what sin is? But those without the law will still perish without the law. Meaning they will be judged by their good deeds and condition of their heart.

The old Testament Saints before Moses had only one negative law. Do not eat the fruit of the Tree of Knowledge of Good and Evil, but that tree was removed from them early in history. So now they had to live by performing GOOD deeds. Also, God did not command Adam and Eve to do good. This doing is the beginning test of God for applying all individuals' use of their self-will. We are given the consciousness of good versus evil by the Tree of Knowledge. And God wants us to choose good over evil. But, without knowing what is evil (sin), how can God eternally save man? Answer; *by their hearts desires to do good!*

This is the Period of Innocence as they were without the law but knew good. Those individuals who heart strived to do good are saved by God's Grace and are in a location called Paradise in the center of the earth. These are the Old Testament Saints. Those who chose evil are in a place called Torments or Hell. We see this in **1st Peter 3.**

> **1 Peter 3:19–20 *"(19) By which also he*** (Jesus) ***went and <u>preached unto the spirits in prison</u>; (20) Which sometime were disobedient, when once the longsuffering of God waited in the days of Noah, while the ark was a preparing, wherein few, that is, eight souls were saved by water"***. ***(KJV)***

These in prison are those individuals who, through their self-will, chose evil over good. However, in verse 2, Peter makes a curious statement, *"Which sometimes were disobedient."* Not all the time, but only sometimes. Does this not sound like some humans today? Good people helping people, obeying man's law most of the time, but sinning only sometimes. They appear as wonderful people, but secretly, have ignored Jesus. Their fate is revealed in the last six words; only *"eight souls were saved by water."*

But those righteous individuals who tried to do good are in a place called Paradise in the heart of the earth. So God's grace saved them from Torment. And if God shared his grace on humans that knew right from wrong, would he not share his grace for children that have no understanding of the choice between good and evil. The most unambiguous indication of God's grace for these babies and children in death; can be found in **Mat.19.**

> **Matthew 19:13–14** *"(13) Then were there brought unto him little children, that he should put* his *hands on them, and pray: and <u>the disciples rebuked them. (14) But Jesus said, Suffer little children, and forbid them not,</u> to come unto me: <u>for of such is the kingdom of heaven."</u> (KJV)*

The most revealing words in these verses are *"for of such is the kingdom of heaven."* How much clearer can you get that these children are a great multitude in Heaven. In the past, so many children died from birth problems, illness, wars, evil individuals sacrificing them to false gods, and today the ultimate sin of abortion --- murder. So children have no responsibility for their lives until they reach the Age of Accountability. When they know what sin is and the punishment for those sins. Then, they become responsible for exercising their self-will to choose good or evil, salvation, or damnation

Note

Remember, we just looked at our creation of our Soul and Spirit, created before we were placed into our mother's womb. So in an abortion, they have killed (murdered) a Soul and a Spirit. As they have been denied their sanctification, God prepared for that human from God for some wonderful task.

Keep in mind the woman is alive, and her egg is alive. The male is alive, and his sperm is alive. These four living items have created a new living life.

There is no specific age mentioned in the Bible, as it depends on each individual child. Some children with mental defects will never reach the Age of Accountability, and they are saved. Others have learning problems and may not reach that age until later in life than other children. So God wants all humans to be saved, which includes children too. And **Mathew 19:13–14** is proof of God's love for the children and finds them *unaccountable for sin.* Until they know what sin is and their responsibility to choose Jesus for the forgiveness of their sins. It is the parent's, especially the father's, responsibility to teach his children of sin and forgiveness by Jesus.

THE MYSTERY OF PARADISE, TORMENT, and ABYSS

In the Bible, there are words used to reveal locations where individuals have been sent. We need to take these words at face value, or we can spiritualize them into oblivion. God has seen fit to have created places or locations in his creation to provide space to house souls. Just as God did in the beginning, when he created all individuals, He will place on this earth in the future. When death occurs, where do the different people go, and when will they go there? We usually think of Heaven and Hell, but there appears to be a holding place for souls awaiting the final judgments until a particular event occurs.

In the English language, we are limited to words for a given situation. For example, the word LOVE covers a multitude of meanings. The Hebrew and Greek have words for a particular type of love. One is agape, a Godly love. Another is Phalli, which is brotherly love. There are many more words that express different types of love.

And you will see Greek words that in English, the interpreters use Hell for many places of punishment. Hell is used so often as the final place for the lost souls, Demons, and Satan. In **Rev. 20:14,** we read that death and Hell are cast into the Lake of fire. Therefore, the final destination for all lost souls is the Lake of Fire and not Hell. So, where is Hell?

The Bible speaks of places in the center of the earth where all souls are sent after death in **Mat. 12:40** and **Luk. 23:43**.

Here are some of the Greek words translated into Hell[3]:

1. **"Sheh-ole** = **(Deu 32:22)** the world of the dead or subterranean retreat. Includes accessories and inmates. (Grave, Hell, pit) Notice this, and Hades are just places of the dead, be they good or evil.
2. **Hah-dace** (Hades) = **(Mat. 11:2)** place of departed souls, grave, or pit.
3. **Gheh-en-nah** = **(Mat. 5:22)** place or state of everlasting punishment, grave, Hell. This Hell is not the **Lake of Fire.**
4. **Tartaroo** = **(2 Pet. 2:4)** the deepest abyss of Hades, eternal torment, cast down to Hell. This is the place reserved for sinful or fallen angels.
5. **Lake of Fire** = is the final eternal destination for all lost souls".
   Please notice that almost all the words in English mean Hell. Our language falls short on specific words for a particular place. And they do not correctly identify the correct location. Notice Shehole is the place of the dead, including good or evil persons as well as Hadace. But Ghehennah identifies a specific place of punishment, Hell. But, the Bible identifies the final place of every lasting punish; as the **Lake of Fire.**

Now let us attempt to put these places into perspective. First, let us look at the primary location of these places. In **Mat. 12,** we can read of this location.

> **Matthew 12:39–40 *"(39) But he*** (Jesus) ***answered and said unto them, An evil and adulterous generation seeketh after a sign; and there shall no sign be given to it, but the sign of the prophet Jonas: (40) For as Jonas was three days and three nights in the whale's belly; so shall the Son of man be three days and three nights in the heart of the earth". (KJV)***

Here we read the first clue of Jesus' location just after his crucifixion. It is clear Jesus went to the center of the earth to a location call Sheh-ole or Hades. And while there, Jesus preached to the Preflood Captives. **(1Pet.).**

> **1 Peter 3:18–19** "*(18)For Christ also hath <u>once suffered for sins,</u> the just for the unjust, that he might bring us to God, being put to death in the flesh, but quickened by the Spirit:(19) <u>By which also he went and preached unto the spirits in prison;</u> (20) Which sometime were disobedient, when once the longsuffering of <u>God</u> <u>waited in the days of Noah,</u> while the ark was a preparing, wherein few, that is, eight souls were saved by water*". *(KJV)*

These verses are clear that Jesus went to Shehole (place of the dead) to preach to the dead who chose evil over good. These people lived during the time of Noah building the ark. Jesus went there (center of earth) to prove to those who chose evil; they received their righteous punishment. And those who chose good have received their wonderful rewards (Paradise).

First, let us look at Jesus' statement in **Luke 23**; to the thief on the cross next to Jesus, condemned to death, too.

> **Luke 23:43.** "*(42) And he* [thief] *said unto <u>Jesus, Lord,</u> remember me when thou comest into thy kingdom. (43) And Jesus said unto him, Verily I say unto thee, <u>To day shalt thou be with me in paradise</u>*". *(KJV)*

Now we have the name of where Jesus will be after his death, and this is also where Jesus preaches to those of Noah's time. Therefore, **Paradise must be in the heart of the earth (Mat. 12:39–40).** Paradise is another location revealed in the parable of Lazarus and the rich man in **Luk.16.**

> **Luke 16:19–28** "*(19) There was a certain rich man, which was clothed in purple and fine linen, and fared sumptuously every day: (20) And there was a certain beggar named Lazarus, which was laid at his gate, full of sores, (21) And desiring to be fed with the crumbs which fell from the rich man's table: moreover the dogs came and licked his sores. (22) And it came to pass, that the <u>beggar died, and was carried by the angels into Abraham's bosom: the rich man also died, and was buried; (23) And in <u>hell</u>* [Hades]*he lift up his eyes, <u>being in torments,</u>*

and seeth Abraham afar off, and Lazarus in his bosom. (24) And he cried and said, Father Abraham, have mercy on me, and send Lazarus, that he may dip the tip of his finger in water, and cool my tongue; for I am tormented in this flame. (25) But Abraham said, Son, remember that thou in thy lifetime receivedst thy good things, and likewise Lazarus evil things: but now he is comforted, and thou art tormented. (26) And beside all this, between us and you there is a great gulf fixed: so that they which would pass from hence to you cannot; neither can they pass to us, that would come from thence. (27Then he said, I pray thee therefore, father, that thou wouldest send him to my father's house: (28) For I have five brethren; that he may testify unto them, lest they also come into this place of torment". (KJV)

The rich man is in Hades (the Greek word for the place of the dead), which is reapedly called **Torments**. Remember, Jesus was preaching to the lost souls while he was in Paradise (**Luke 23: 43**). So it would appear that **Paradise and Torments are in the heart of the earth.** And there is a fixed gulf between these two locations that cannot be crossed. But notice, they can see and talk to each other. This tells us this place is a temporary place, for we know in **Rev. 20:14–15** that death and hell (Hades) are cast into the Lake of Fire. This Lake of Fire is a different location from Torments (Hell). It is the final destination for Satan, Demons, and lost souls. But, there is a prison for the worst Demons in the heart of the earth, called the **Abyss or bottomless pit.**

The Abyss is a location that fallen angels (demons) will be held prisoners until released (**Rev. 17:8**), but they too are cast into the Lake of Fire. See **Jud. 6.**

> **Jude 6** *"And the angels which kept not their first estate, but left their own habitation, he hath reserved in everlasting chains under darkness unto the judgment of the great day." (KJV)*

Here we read that these fallen Angels are keep chained down in darkness until their judgment day. Their judgment will take place at the Great White Throne judgment (**Rev.20:11 – 15**). But, where is this location these fallen angels are kept? It is in the great Abyss in the center of the earth also. In **Rev. 9:1–11**, it is revealed that Jesus gives the key to the **Bottomless Pit,** to Satan; and the King of the Abyss (in Hebrew is "Abaddon" or in Greek is "Apollyon") is released. He is so evil Jesus had to be kept in chains until the final days of the Lord. **Rev. 9**

> **Revelation 9:1–15** *"(11) And they had a king over them,* which is *the angel of the bottomless pit, whose name in the Hebrew tongue* is *Abaddon, but in the Greek tongue hath* his *name Apollyon. (12) One woe is past; and, behold, there come two woes more hereafter. (13) And the sixth angel sounded, and I heard a voice from the four horns of the golden altar which is before God, (14) Saying to the sixth angel which had the trumpet, Loose the four angels which are bound in the great river Euphrates. (15) And the four angels were loosed, which were prepared for <u>an hour,</u> and <u>a day,</u> and <u>a month,</u> and <u>a year,</u> for to slay <u>the third part of men</u>". (KJV)*

This evil fallen angel (King of the bottomless pit) must have become so bad; he needed to be locked up in the Abyss. But when he is released, he will gather a large army to fight Jesus. The sixth good angel tells the four good angels are waiting; to destroy 1/3 of mankind. In today's census, that is 2.3 Billion. But those seeing this punishment still did not repent of their: murders, sorceries, thievery, and fornications.

Note

Here you see the words; *"heard a voice from the four horns of the golden altar which is before God,"* These four horns are the voices of the power and majesty of the four voices of Gospels of Jesus: Mathews [Lion = King], Mark [Ox = Servant], Luke [Eagle = Savior] and John [Man = Son of Man]. Also, notice they come from the Alter before God. The Alter is where the sacrificial blood was spread, and it is the stored location of the murdered Tribulation Saints and the Prayers of all Saints of all time.

Imagine all these places in the heart of the earth. Then see our planet as ball-shaped, place Paradise on the inside right half and Torment on the inside left half. Then visualize a small gulf between the two that no one can cross over. And then across the lower one-third-bottom side, below Paradise and Torment, is the Abyss. You may ask how do these sections function? And a good question it is too.

These places in the heart of the earth house both the dead and evil persons. First, let us look at the simplest area. See attachment B

1. **The Abyss** (Bottom) Bad
   - At some time in the past, God locked up Apollyon in the abyss as he was extremely brutal. Also, some demons, fallen angels, have been cast out of the earth by exorcism by earthlings. Jesus, apostles, pastors, and priests have performed exorcisms to send evil demons to the Abyss. Apollyon will be released during the seven years of the Great Tribulation to do the work of Satan. Apollyon will be cast into the Lake of Fire along with the Antichrist and the False Prophet after the war of Armageddon.
2. **Torments** (Left) Bad
   - God created this place for the deaths of the evil people before the Law came to Moses.
   - Noah's linage must have righteous people that taught Noah and called on God's name. However, as time moved forward, more and more individuals turn away from God to evil. These evil people went to Torment (Hell). All evil individuals who died before and in the Flood are being held in Torment (Hell) until the Great White Throne Judgment of God. Their judgment will occur just before the New Heaven, and New Earth are created (Heaven).
   - Other people tried to live righteous lives along with Noah. But the last one died (Methuselah) the year of the Flood but before the Flood. After the Flood, Noah's prodigy that died, up until Jesus, where some were righteous, like Moses, Joseph, Jacob, and many

of the prophets, went to Paradise. The unrighteous individuals went to and kept in the place of Torment **(Rev. 20:7–15)**.

• Torment (Hell) is the location for all the lost souls. They are imprisoned there (Hell) to be tormented by the heat from the Lake of Fire. But not in the Lake. They will constantly see and feel their final home for eternity. Here they will remain until after the 1,000-year Kingdom of Jesus. When God instantly burns up Satan's rebuilt army; then comes the Great White Throne Judgment of GOD. After the Judgment, they will be cast into the Lake of Fire from eternity.

3.Paradise (Right) Good

• First, there are two Paradises, one in Heaven and one in the heart of the earth. Before Jesus, there was one Paradise in the heart of the earth. **(Mat.12:40 / Luk.16:19-31)**

• This location is for Old Testament individuals who are saved by God's Grace. They are the saved people from Adam to Jesus' start of his Church mission. It also includes those who died believing in Jesus before Jesus' resurrection. Those saved by faith in Jesus during his mission on earth are also held there. After Jesus' resurrection, those Church Saints go with Jesus into Heaven's Paradise. Again, those that die during the Church age will go directly to the Heavenly Paradise. Jesus said, *"where I am, there ye will be also."* And Jesus is at the right hand of God. **Mark 16:19**

• In Earth's Paradise remains the location for those Old Testament Saints. And the Pew Sitter Saints (saved by faith with no deeds) who die before the Rapture return of Jesus. Both will remain in earth's Paradise until the 1st Harvest, just near the end of The Great Tribulation. This time is when Jesus will return to claim his planet and ignite Armageddon.

• This 1st Harvest is for the Tribulation Saints and Old Testament Saints. It will occur just before the end of the seven years of the Great Tribulation but after the wedding of the Church (the Bride of Christ) to Jesus. This Wedding between Jesus and the Bride of

Christ should be the most attended ceremony ever. **God's uniting with his Church Saints.** The entire saved individuals from the (righteous creatures?); the Angels, the Bride, Jesus, and God himself will be there. **WOW.** However, the Tribulation Saints will not be allowed into this wedding **Mat 25:1–12.**

Note

Here I have placed Paradise and Torment locations, revealed by scriptures: **Mat. 25:33, John. 21:6** and especially **Ecc. 10:2.**

The place of Paradise in the center of the earth will be removed after the 1st Harvests. And Torments (Hell) will be moved to the Lake of Fire after GOD burns up the Army of Satan after the 1,000-year Kingdom of Jesus. This is also when God collects (2nd Harvest) all the lost souls for judgment (the Great White Throne) and casts them into the **Lake of Fire.** And then creates our new home, a New Heaven and New Earth; and everything will be forgotten become new.

MYSTERY OF SPEAKING IN TONGUES

This concept has caused some disagreements in righteous circles and needs to be studied to find the truth. The 1st time we read about this event occurring is at Pentecost. Jesus told the apostles of the coming of the Holy Spirit to them in **Acts** 1.

Acts 1:6–8 *"(6) when they therefore were come together, they asked of him, saying, Lord, wilt thou at this time restore again the kingdom to Israel? (7) And he said unto them, It is not for you to know the times or the seasons, which the Father hath put in his own power. (8) But ye <u>shall receive power, after that the Holy Ghost is</u> come upon you: <u>and ye shall be witnesses unto me both in Jerusalem, and in all Judaea, and in Samaria, and unto the uttermost part of the earth"</u>. <u>(KJV)</u>*

From these verses, we see the gift of the Holy Spirit to come to Jesus' apostles. This is a foreshadowing of the Holy Spirit coming on believers in Jesus. This is the beginning of the great commission for the Church. Its task is to spread the Gospel of Jesus throughout the world. This task was performed 1st by the apostles and then by the Church members. How are these tongues possible due to all the different languages around the world? In **Acts 2,** we read of the events at Pentecost that answers this question. God provides the apostles with the ability to speak to people in their own language.

This event, too, is a great mystery. There are 12 apostles present and 18 different languages present. They spoke one at a time, but 18 languages were heard from this one apostle speaking. It would seem God caused all the different people present *to hear* who was speaking in their own language. But **verse 4** says the apostles spoke in other tongues. In **Acts 2,** we read of all the different languages that are present at the Day of Pentecost.

> **Act 2:6–12** *"(6) Now when this was noised abroad, the multitude came together, <u>and were confounded, because that every man heard them speak in his own language.</u> (7) And they were all amazed and marvelled, saying one to another, <u>Behold, are not all these which speak Galilaeans? (8) And how hear we every man in our own tongue, wherein we were born?</u> (9) Parthians, and Medes, and Elamites, and the dwellers in Mesopotamia, and in Judaea, and Cappadocia, in Pontus, and Asia, (10) Phrygia, and Pamphylia, in Egypt, and in the parts of Libya about Cyrene, and strangers of Rome, Jews and proselytes, (11) Cretes and Arabians, we do hear them speak in our tongues the wonderful works of God. (12) And they were all amazed, and were in doubt, saying one to another, What meaneth this?"* (KJV)

This was an amazing event, and it confused the people there for all to hear all the words of one apostle, at the same time, each man in his own language. This is amazing <u>that all 18 languages were heard at the same time, listening in different languages</u>. All the apostles did not speak at once, but each in his time. **(1 Cor.14:27)** So the Holy Spirit of God solved the language differences at that time. These tongues were a sign for the Hebrew people, but many thought these apostles were drunk. They had forgotten or did not know the prophecy of **Joel 2:28.** But, Peter explained they were not drunk. In the future, missionaries will need to learn the people's language to whom they will be sent.

The Bible tells us that God is not the God of confusion **(1 Cor.14:33).** What good would it do to speak to English peasants in Latin? The uneducated would not understand a word that was said. Confusion would cause people to leave and not be interested in gibberish. They need an interpreter. It appears the Holy Spirit was the interpreter for the 18 languages present.

Now I know there are denominations that practice tongues in their worship service. And many claim it is the language of the angels. However, remember this; angels are visiting earth unaware to us. They speak our language, know our customs, know government, our society, to fit in where we are located without our knowledge. But tongues are a tool for Christians; however, their use cannot cause confusion in their use. This is spoken of in **1 Cor.13.**

> **1 Corinthians 13:1** *"Though I speak with the tongues of men and of angels, and have not charity, I am become as sounding brass, or a tinkling cymbal. " (KJV)*

So we read here of the language of angels, but also a restriction. If you do not have charity, your speaking in tongues is worthless. Charity is an English form of the Greek word of Love

Chapter 14 of **1 Corinthians** speaks many words about tongues and their use. For those individuals who practice speaking in tongues, I recommend the study of this chapter. Especially in **verses 27–28** where it says;

> **1 Corinthians 14:27–28** *"(27) If any man speak in an* unknown ***tongue,*** *let it be by two, or at the most by three, and* that ***by course*** (one a time)*; and* ***let one interpret.*** *(28) But if there be* ***no interpreter, let him keep silence*** *in the church; and let him speak to himself, and to God". (KJV)*

These verses are clear, that one cannot speak in an unknown tongue in the Church; <u>unless they have an interpreter</u> who can explain what that person just said. If there is no interpreter, I suggest you depart this group; it is questionable about their dedication to the Bible's truths. Also, in **1 Cor.14: 21–32,** we read the purpose of Tongues is not for believers; but for the unbeliever among you. But without an interpreter, they will think you who speak are mad **(1 Cor 14:23).**

From 1570 to 1962AD, the Catholic Church's Mass was preached in Latin. And some celebrations are still held in Latin. Only the wealthy, who could afford a Latin teacher, could understand them. Catholic parishioners were not permitted to read the Bible and test the spirit as required in **1 John 4:1.** Also, there were no Latin interpreters used as required in scriptures. The priest's Latin words (gibberish) were all the parishioners had. They were not permitted to read the Bible until recently in history. An ex-pastor of mine was raised in a Catholic Greece Church and was caught reading a Bible. His Parish Priest saw him (circa 1930). The priest took his Bible and was very hostile to my Pastor (as a boy) and told him if he ever saw him reading or carrying a Bible, he would dig up his grandparents and cast them out of the parish's sacred burial ground. I'm not sure what that meant, but it apparently was not a good thing.

THE MYSTERY OF PREDESTINED

A question came to light in my Bible class in my prison ministry, and it pertained to PREDESTINATION. So I decided to include this in this book. From the Strong's Concordance, the Greek meaning for this word is:

Predestine = *"4309 **Prŏ-or-id'.zo;** from 4253 and 3724; to limit in advance, i.e. (fig) **predetermination;--determine before, ordain, predestinate²."*

This predetermination occurred before or during God's creation. The webwork of his plan for humanity includes the best voyage and a unique destination for each person God will ever create. Along with predetermination is man's exclusive right to exercise his or her self-will. It appears this self-will is very important to God, and he will allow humans to exercise their will over God's will. And just because you are predestined does not mean you will attain God's predetermination desire for your life.

This predestine is God's desire and is in his plan for each human, but *not a guarantee for achievement*. God knows you and all your emotions, desires, likes, weaknesses, strengths, and dislikes. God desires you to learn how to control your self-will, grace, patience, mercies, love, and righteousness. God will allow you to exercise your self-will over God's. He will attempt to influence your decision through the Holy Spirit, but *it is your decision completely.* You can reject Jesus if you want to, but the consequences are horrible. Remember, for every action; there is an opposite and equal reaction. Meaning: doing good reaps rewards, but doing evil reaps punishment. The person or child, who is injured, will receive rewards, even in death. And the disobedient person will receive his or her consequences for their disobedience, even though it may take years.

It has become commonplace for people to blame God for allowing a human-directed catastrophe. If God is all-knowing and all-powerful, how could he permit a catastrophe? This thought pattern has been around for years and years. *If God is all-powerful, all-knowledgeable, and loving, he should protect his children from evil situations.* We fail to see that we are connected in some way into a catastrophe. God's protection is foremost for his children and *for their eternal salvation.* It is God's decision to prevent or permit an event to occur. In his wisdom, he has granted each individual his right to exercise his righteous or unrighteous behavior. God has given the Holy Spirit the job of trying to influence a person to do righteous behavior. And in so doing, can see the heart of that person who creates the catastrophe and the heart of the one who receives that event. For righteous acts, one will receive eternal rewards, and for continual unrighteous deeds, there is eternal punishment.

It appears that God has lessons for us, his children, to experience to deepen our faith in Jesus and God. We must have the faith that God is in control of all situations, and he will take care of the perpetrator and the victims. There is a chapter in **Rom. 9** that speaks of God's absolute control over his plan for man. But here I have included the main point. But please read the complete chapter.

> **Romans 9:21–24** *"Hath not the potter power over the clay, of the same lump to make <u>one vessel unto honour, and another unto dishonour?</u> (22) What if God, willing to shew his wrath, and to <u>make his power known</u>, endured with much longsuffering the vessels of wrath fitted to destruction: (23) And that he might make known the riches of his glory on the vessels of mercy, <u>which he had afore prepared unto glory, (24) Even us, whom he hath called, not of the Jews only, but also of the Gentiles?"</u> (KJV)*

These scriptures have been misunderstood for many eons. They can be interpreted in different ways. Here I am presenting one for your consideration. It hinges on the presents of aliens and is supported by scriptures.

<u>First,</u> I would have you notice the distinction in verse 21, *"one vessel unto honour, and another unto dishonour?"* Here God is telling us that He is making some humans for honor and some to dishonor. Also, this is not a statement but a question to solve. How think ye?

<u>Second,</u> God reveals in verse 22, and God makes a distinction of *"the vessels of wrath fitted to destruction:"* Is God saying he has created some entities for the Lake of Fire? It appears so! God has created Satan and the fallen angels, but does this also include humans. Another confusion is found here. How could God make a person for the Lake of Fire when that person is doing what God created him or her to do. This idea appears fallible.

<u>The third</u> is verse 23, where God is making known his mercy. *"on the vessels of mercy, which he had afore prepared unto glory."* These are all saved souls from the old Testament Saints, New Testament Saints, and the Tribulation Saints.

These words in Romans create a very in-depth concept. If you return to the *"Sheep Fold Mystery,"* we discussed 100 planets God created, and 99 planets were righteous. These are those designed for honor. They have remained faithful and obedient to God and Jesus. They were made to be righteous.

But the earth was to be created in dishonor. Why? To make known God's mercy *"on the vessels of mercy, which he afore prepared unto glory."* In God's plan, He created righteous individuals before creation. We looked at this concept in *"The Creation of Man"* and *"The Mystery of Predestined."*

God is the potter, and we are the clay. He has made some of us for honor (good) and some for dishonor (evil). We Christians are the vessels of his mercy for honor before we were created and predestine for his mercy. God also created those for destruction, so Christians will have confrontations with evil to improve our knowledge and make known God's riches of his glory or magnitude of his mercy on you and me.

This plan for man is like a play. There is a play write, a director, a manuscript with villains and victims. The author (God) develops the play, the playwright (God and Jesus) develops the timeline of events (Bible), and the Director (Holy Spirit) directs the scenes and actor's actions. The words (Manuscript) for actors are developed from events (Bible) by the team (God, Jesus, and Holy Spirit), actors (humans), and roles are selected (victims and villains). This play has a beginning and an ending. Parts are played at selective times. New actors are introduced at proper times, and the closing of this play is absolutely spectacular.

The actors play fascinating parts. The villains are to bring all sorts of evil against the victims. And the victims are to bring the knowledge of their wrongdoings, forgiveness, and salvation to these actors of villainy. It is through the victims LOVE and concern for the villains that motivates them. Some villains will convert from their evil ways, but many will not. The converts will be rewarded with unspeakable wonderful treasures, but the villains will receive their just punishments.

Our faith in God and Jesus that they are in control of everything that will happen to us will be permitted by God for our education and good. We must hold onto this faith during times of hurt, distress, confusion, feeling of helplessness, and anger against God for letting this happen. Remember **Rom. 8**,

> **Romans 8:18** *"For I reckon that the sufferings of this present time are not worthy* to be compared *with the glory which shall be revealed in us." (KJV)*

PRAISE GOD and KEEP THE FAITH!

MYSTERY--OUTSIDE THE CITY

Near the end of Revelation, there is a verse in **Rev.22** that has created questions for me in the past and present.

> **Revelation 22:14–15** *"(14) Blessed* are *they that do his commandments, that they may have right to the tree of life, and may enter in through the gates into the city. (15) For without* are *dogs, and sorcerers, and whoremongers, and murderers, and idolaters, and whosoever loveth and maketh a lie".* *(KJV)*

Notice the first words we read are about Deeds. Pew Sitter, please, please notice the words *"do his commandments."* These words mean all of his commands. The Tree of life is in the eternal Heaven.

The **Tree of Life** and the **City** are *clues* that point to the final **City of GOD (Rev.21)** on earth. The sequence of events reveals time after the New Heaven and New Earth have been created. And after all evil has been sent to the **Lake of Fire**. This period is after the New Jerusalem is on earth. **(Rev.21:10–27).** This city is a majestic city extremely large: 1,400 miles wide, 1,400 miles deep, and 1,400 miles high. God and Jesus are the light of the city. The four walls around the city are 200 feet high. There are three gates on each side (12 total gates) made of pearl.

But not all individuals will be permitted into the City. Near the end of the city's description, God adds just who will and will not be allowed into this city **(Rev.21).**

> **Revelation 21:24** *"And the <u>nations of them which are saved</u> shall walk in the light of it: and the kings of the earth do bring their glory and <u>honour into it:"</u> (KJV)*

This verse is self-explanatory that only the saved **(Rev.22:14–15)** souls will be allowed <u>into the great city</u>. Notice the Kings (Church) of the New Earth will bring their glory and honor into the city. But in **Rev. 21:27,** we read of those souls who will not be allowed into the city as their names are not in the Book of Life.

> **Revelation 21:27** *"And there shall in no wise enter into it anything that defileth, neither whatsoever worketh abomination, nor* maketh *a lie: but they which are written in the <u>Lamb's book of life.</u>" (KJV)*

Notice the last underlined words. These four words refer to the Great White Throne Judgment by God, where all evil is cast into the Lake of Fire. Therefore, **Rev.22:15** is speaking of the lost souls. In **Rev.22:14–15,** we further read similar verses.

So we see saved individuals can come and go into the city. But the unsaved cannot go into the city. One good reason is they cannot enter is because they are outside *locked in the eternal Lake of Fire, never to leave.* And this Lake of Fire; will be far removed from the New Jerusalem.

Alternate possibility

Another possibility is this occurs during the 1,000-year Kingdom of Jesus. Adam's sinful nature will still be present through the righteous survivors of the Great Tribulation and Armageddon's War. And *those who become unrighteous* during the 1,000 year Kingdom will not be allowed into the City of God. Again *a weeping and gnashing of teeth.*

John finishes Revelation with a warning.

> **Revelation 22:16–21 "(16)** *I Jesus have sent mine angel to <u>testify unto you these things in the churches.</u> I am the root and the offspring of David,* and *the bright and morning star. (17) <u>And the Spirit and the bride say, Come.</u> And let him that heareth say, Come. And let him that is athirst come. And whosoever will, let him take the water of life freely. (18) For I testify unto every man that heareth the words of the prophecy of this book, <u>If any man shall add unto these things, God shall add unto him the plagues that are written in this book: (19) And if any man shall take away from the words of the book of this prophecy, God shall take away his part out of the book of life,</u> and out of the holy city, and* <u>from t</u>*<u>he things which are written in this book.</u> (20) He which testifieth these things saith, surely I come quickly. Amen. Even so, come, Lord Jesus. (21) <u>The grace</u> of our Lord Jesus Christ* be *with you all. Amen.***"

This statement has caused fear for individuals not to speak or not to teach the Book of Revelation. How does one determine if a teacher is adding or subtracting from this book? If it is not taught, we are taking away from the text from the people God wants to give knowledge. <u>And to teach this text, is it adding to this book</u>? Seems like a **Catch 22**. *"Cursed if you do and cursed if you don't."*

No other book in the Bible has this warning. And it is a frightful concept. As a teacher and an author, I am also concerned as I do not want to give erroneous information, nor do I want to justify erroneous information.

However, God tells us in his Love Letter: the education in righteous ways of conduct and truths we bring to all nations **(Mat.28:18).** *How can we bring the full Gospel of Jesus unless we share the entire understanding of all the words* *of God?* And this includes the Book of Revelation. Remember to know to do good and not to do good is the sin of omission.

No human knows the complete message of the Bible. No Pastor, no Priest, no Pope, no Bishop, no Elder, no Deacon, no Layman, no Teacher, <u>*no one*</u>. It is the intent of their hearts to attempt to bring the truth as they understand it from the Bible and the Holy Spirit. *Therefore, it is also the reader's responsibility to test the spirit of those words given to them.*

> **1 John 4:1** *"Beloved, believe not every spirit, but try the spirits whether they are of God: because many false prophets are gone out into the world." (KJV)*

Hopefully, with both teacher and learner seeking the truth, errors can be minimized, and more truth will come forth. *This ominous warning is for those individuals who desire to use the words in the book of Revelation for their personal benefit or bring another Gospel, not from Jesus.* I pray the pastors or teacher that presents any part of the Bible as not understandable, as they are taking away from the Book of Revelation.

It is also for those Pastors who do not teach this book to His congregation in fear he will upset his flock, and they leave his Church.

UNIFORMITARIANISM MYSTERY

Many people and scientist think that all items created were from mater or seeds. But, stars and planets did not start as seeded material, as the Sun, Moon, and planets were to give signs to Adam. Also, Adam would need food when he was created.

The scientist uses a theory call Uniformitarianism: where an object changes at the same rate, under the same environment. And it is beneficial in our daily life. When cooking a meal, the different food items take different times for cooking to be cooked properly. They change at a rate for that particular item. If we want to paint pressure-treated wood, we must wait 90 days for the chemicals to dry so the paint will adhere to the wood's surface. This is Uniformitarism as we are looking forward to the completion of the drying item. Here I am revealing to you a simple explanation of the theory of Uniformitarianism.

Uniformitarianism is the procedure looking forward, but it also applies in reverse. Science uses this in determining how old an object is by using present-day uniformity in reverse. For example: if you went into a cave in the year 2000 AD; and see a stalactite, and you measured it at 10 inches long. And after ten years (2010), you return and measure the same stalactite again, and it is 20 inches long. Therefore, you deduce that a 10-inch growth in 10 years yields a growth rate of 1 inch per year. So what is the year of the stalactite birth? Being it is 20 inches long at the year 2010, then compute backward 20 years from 2010, and we find the birth year of the stalactite at 1990. And to check this figure, you can deduct 10 years off the 2000 measurement to compute 1990.

The problem with this theory is; when God created, he created different items at <u>DIFFERENT MATURITY LEVELS.</u>

Consider this. How old was Adam when he was created? Was he a helpless baby? No, he was not. He <u>walked </u>and <u>talked</u> with God in the garden. It did not take Adam 9 months to learn to walk or years to talk. Where was the nipple for baby Adam to suckle for milk? Adam was most likely created as a teenager, able to care for himself. Some studies place Adam at 13–16 years of age. Jews celebrate manhood at 15 years old (Bar Mitzvah). So if we performed a biopsy on Adam, how old would we find his internal organs? Fifteen years old. But, he has only been present on earth for 1 second. So if we used Uniformitarism, we would determine earth was 15 years old; but it is only four days old. (Day 3 to Day 6)

Now let us look at the Tree of Knowledge of Good and Evil. It already has fruit on the tree for Adam to be told *"not to eat."* (Day 3) But consider how long it would take a tree to produce fruit from seed. Fruit trees take about 8–10 years to produce fruit from seed. So you would compute earth age at 8—10 years old, but it is present on earth at 1 second old on Day 3. Also, if you cut down that tree, you would see 8—10 tree rings. *To have no tree rings would be a created lie, and God hates lies.* When God created, he made all items correct in their different mature states, with the appearance and correct functionality, as all of Mother Nature's laws (God's laws) are built into that item.

Next, let us consider a rock from the mountains. How long does it take to form a rock? Many, many years! But this rock is only 1 second old on Day 3.

Scientists use carbon dating to date the item's age as carbon dissipates at a generally consistent rate. But, scientists fail to realize their measurements are based on the age God created it to be for Adam's time. So from Adam's time to now, there have been approximately 6,000 years, but these rocks appear to be billions of years old; when in fact, they are only 1 second old on Day 3.

Scientist also uses other measurements to determine the life of the bodies in space based on the Big Bang theory. But we read in **Genesis 1:14–18** that God placed all the universal bodies in place at one time to: divide the day from night for dating: seasons, days, night, signs, and years. This event occurred before God created Adam. The Universe is complete on Day 4. Light from these bodies are present on earth at its creation. The properties of light were created on Day 1, and when bodies in space were created on Day 4, their light was present everywhere throughout the universe. Otherwise, Adam would not have starlight for four years from our closest star. Billions of years would be necessary for us to see the light from stars at a great distance; if the Big Bang is correct. However, God created these distant stars at locations that will not be seen until their light travels to the earth. They appear to be billions of years old by uniformitarianism in reverse. If we are now 6,000 years old, and a distance stars light reaching the earth today, it was created at a location so their light would reach the earth in 6,000 years.

There are so many unanswered questions about the universe and its creation that science has created theories that appear as fact. Today these theories are traditions that all universities and schools of higher learning use without question. Science has answered many questions over the years but has ruled out the Creation Postulation.   (More on this later)

TIME OF FORGIVENESS MYSTERY

We humans have become impatient and expect things to happen in short order. We are the NOW generation. But God does not work that way. He knows the best way and the best time to give us what we need or most likely what we *WANT*. When we hear of the forgiveness of our sins, we want it immediately after our repentance. But, when is the forgetfulness for those sins? First, let us look at forgiven in **Rom.4,**

> **Romans 4:7** "Saying, *Blessed are they whose <u>iniquities are forgiven,</u> and whose <u>sins are covered." (KJV)</u>*

Notice that sins are forgiven but no mention of forgotten. They are covered up or hidden. We read of Jesus speaking to this very covered up, which will be uncovered and revealed. **(Luk.12:2–3)**

> **Luke 12:2–3** "*(2) <u>For there is nothing covered up,</u> that shall not be revealed; neither <u>hid, that shall be known.</u> (3) Therefore, what ye have <u>spoken in darkness</u> shall <u>be heard in</u> <u>light</u>; and that spoken which <u>in the ear in closets</u> shall be proclaimed upon the housetops.*" **(KJV)**

Here Luke is speaking mainly to the Pharisees and lost souls. We will later read that we Christians will have to give account to Jesus of <u>everything we have done or said</u>. And this is long after the forgiveness of our sins. We find this in **2 Cor.5.**

2 Corinthians 5:10 *"For we must all appear before the Judgment <u>Seat of Christ</u>; <u>that everyone may receive the things done</u> in his body, according to that he <u>hath done,</u> whether <u>it be good or bad.</u>" (KJV)*

This is the *"Judgment Seat of Christ"* for all Christians of the Church and Tribulation Saints. And as you can see, it covers everything we have said or done. This judgment is not something to be frightened about. Our personal time with Christ is where he will reveal all he has done for us even though we were sinners. However, it will be very embarrassing to see how selfish, unintelligent, despicable, hateful, greedy, unfriendly, liars, lazy, proud, and all things Jesus abhors. But he will also see the faith, loving acts, worship of God, care for strangers and family, singing, teaching his Gospel, our contriteness, humility, souls we have helped to save, attitudes of our heart, and other good qualities of our heart. Then you will hear, *"well done my good and faithful servant.* **WOW!**

This *"Judgment Seat of Christ"* does not appear to be immediately after being forgiven; but sometime into the future. You may ask; when might this be? Good question and the exact time is unknown, but some verses address this, and one is in **Heb. 9.**

Hebrews 9:27 *"And as it is appointed unto men once to die, but after this the judgment." (KJV)*

How think ye? Is this immediately after death or later? This is the $64,000 question (from an old TV game show). Three thoughts come to mind: corporately, individually, or both.

1. **<u>CORPORATELY.</u>** When we Christians die, we go to Paradise in Heaven (*"where I am there ye will be also"),* but it appears we

must put on incorruption and immorality first **(1 Cor. 15:50–54)**. Some see these verses as pertaining to the Rapture. But, to swallow up death in victory, this cannot occur until all the saved are with Jesus and God. This event will occur at the 1st Harvest **(Rev. 14:13–16** and **1 Cor.15:54)**. So to accomplish this task by Jesus, it would appear he must judge us first. If you remember Jesus' resurrection story, Jesus told Mary Magdalene not to touch him. For he had not yet put on incorruption by his father. Jesus was still corrupted for paying for our sins. Another verse of scripture informs us that we are to confess our sins before the Brothers. **(Jam.5:16)** But be careful who you confess to. And it may be possible that we all will meet Jesus together at the Judgment Seat of Christ.

Can you imagine the magnitude of individuals borne and died since Adam? Can you imagine all the righteous angels and possible aliens there to see and hear what is said and confessed? Just imagine; you are there now, and it is your turn to be judged and to justify all you have said and done over your entire life. ***Fearful?*** --- *NO!* Because *Jesus died to pay for your sins.* **Embarrassing?** *Immensely so!* But you will hear, *"well done, good faithful servant;"* **(Mat.25:23).** And that entire audience will break out in jubilation over your salvation. **Luk.15:10**

2. <u>**INDIVIDUALLY.**</u> Then there is this possibility for us to consider. And that is, that at the time of our death, we are taken to Jesus in Heaven, judged and made incorrupt. This would be necessary to become the Bride of Christ. Then we are placed in a place of rest (RIP) like the five prepared virgins until the Bridegroom (Jesus) comes for us to go to the wedding; at the Rapture of the Church. The wedding should occur during The Great Tribulation and before the *1st Harvest* (Tribulation Saints and Old Testament Saints Harvest). They are not at the wedding as they represent the five unprepared virgins of **Mat.25**, who also were not permitted into the wedding. One other verse to consider here is **Rev.22:12**

Revelation 22:12 *"And behold, I come quickly; and my reward is with me, to give every <u>man according as his work shall be.</u>"* **(KJV)**

> This then is when Jesus returns to destroy all evil on the earth just before his 1,000 year Kingdom or during the early stages of his kingdom.
>
> 3 **BOTH.** There could also be possibilities of combinations of both of these concepts mentioned above. Remember, millions of people have died since Adam's day. The Old Testament Saints, which are righteous, are held in PARADISE, and the unrighteous are held in TORMENT (Hell). Therefore, some form of judgment was required to place them in these locations. Those in Paradise (Old Testament and Tribulation Saints) are harvested in the 1st Harvest to Jesus. Those in Torment will be harvested in the 2nd Harvest to God.

The Church Saints in Paradise and alive, are Raptured to Jesus in Paradise in Heaven, and they must be in Jesus Judgment Seat of Christ to be in Heaven's Paradise with God. Over 2,000 years, all who have died at different times would appear to cause that day corporately to be judged.

But that is based on human intellect and not God's intellect.

But probably the best time for forgetting all our sins is found in **Rev.21:4–5.** Verse 4 says, *"former things are passed away,"* and **verse 5** says, *"Behold I make all things new."* To support the concept of sins are not forgotten; is the fact that for every sin, there is a consequence. Some consequences last a long time, and God has not forgotten even after forgiving that sin. Example: God has punished the Hebrews for many years for their rejecting Jesus. David and Bathsheba sin punishment continued by God until the death of David's favorite son. Saul's sins followed him all his life. The Jews repeated sins were remembered by God, and he is now awaiting their final repentance. If God had forgotten the Jews' sins after they repented, he would not have remembered their continued falling away. But, **Heb. 8** makes a true statement of when God will forget our sins.

Now some people quote **Heb. 8:12** to prove God will not remember our sins, .and that is true, but this verse pertains to the Hebrews time of repentance by the 144,000 at the end of this earth.

> **Hebrews 8:12** *"For I will be merciful to their unrighteousness, and their sins and their iniquities will I remember no more." (KJV)*

But when will God forget our sins? Look at **verse 10** as to what this covenant contains.

> **Hebrews 8:10** *"For this is the covenant that I will make with the house of Israel after those days, saith the Lord; I will put my laws into their mind, and write them in their hearts: and I will be to them a God, and they shall be to me a people:" (KJV)*

What is *"after those days"*? To determine this, we must read all of **Hebrews 8**. This chapter centers on the new covenant with God. This event will occur after the *1st Harvest* **(Rev. 14)**. This is the harvest of all Hebrews converted to Jesus by the 144,000 Hebrew Missionaries of **Rev. 7**. This is just before the War of Armageddon, the end of the *1st Harvest*. But look at **Heb.8: 12**.

> **Hebrews 8:12** *"For I will be merciful to their unrighteousness, and their sins and their iniquities will I remember no more." (KJV)*

God will put into our (Hebrew and Gentile) minds and hearts his Laws, most likely during the *corruption to incorruption process* **(Rom.8:21)**. The Church today knows we are to use God's laws. Because it reveals what sin is. Our government has humanized God's Laws. It is no more victim repay crimes, but government repay laws. Then the victim must pay for the perpetrator's incarceration by paying taxes. Also, the Bible has many books to which God will use when judging. One is the Book of Remembrances; another the Book of Laws, but the most essential book is the Book of Life. *If a person's name is* *not found in this book, that person is going to the Lake of Fire.* And remember, when we meet Jesus, we will have to account for every *word* and *deed,* be it good or bad, we have committed, so our sins are remembered until **Rev.21:4–5! Verse 4** says, *"former things are passed away."*

I know some think this is for the Hebrews only, but remember we, too, are to inherit with the Hebrews from God. To inherit, in Hebrew law, one has to be a family member. Therefore, Christians are included into the Hebrew family. Remember, Jesus came for his flock, both Jews and Gentiles. And we Gentiles will inherit with the Hebrews.

BLASPHEME THE HOLY GHOST MYSTERY

First, I would like to express to you that this is not a composition on the Holy Ghost's total functions. That would require God himself to reveal the magnitude of all the Holy Ghost has and will do for mankind. This is only a very simple but dangerous look at one facet of the Holy Ghost. And that is the *blaspheming of the Holy Ghost.*

The Holy Ghost is an extremely important entity in the Bible and appears to have covert operations in our lives. One of his hidden jobs is to bring salvation to man. Christians cannot save; Pope cannot save, Pastor's cannot save, Mary cannot save, Mohammed cannot save; we can only help the *Holy Ghost save* by bringing the knowledge of the gospel to man. But, there is an unforgivable sin, which is **blaspheming the Holy Ghost (Mark 3).**

> **Mark 3:28–29 "(28) Verily I say unto you, All sins shall be forgiven unto the sons of men, and blasphemies wherewith soever they shall blaspheme: (29) But he that shall <u>blaspheme against the Holy Ghost hath never forgiveness, but is in danger of eternal damnation</u>." (KJV)**

This idea has been a very controversial subject for many years. So let us look into the meaning of this word. First, what does this word blaspheme mean to us today, and secondly, what did it mean in Jesus's day (Hebrew & Greek)?

Today

> 1. Funk and Wagnall's – "Blaspheme = to speak in an impious manner of (God or sacred things).2. To speak ill of; malign – v.i. 3. To utter blasphemy. [OF < LL Gk] blasphemous <u>evil-speaking</u>[3]."

Hebrew (O.T.)

> 2. Strong Concordance = "**5006** *naw-ats';* a prime root; to *scorn;* or by interch. **5132**, to *bloom:*--abhor, (occasion to blaspheme, contem. <u>Despise</u>, flourish, X great, provoke[2]."

Greek (N.T.)

> 3. "988 blasphēmia, *blas-fay-me'-ah*; from *989*; *vilification* (espec. Against God): --blasphemy, evil speaking, railing[2]."
> 4. "989 blasphēmŏs, *blas'-fay-mos*; from a der. of 984 and 5345; *scurrilous,* i.e. *calumnious* (against man), or (espc.) *impious* (against God):--blasphemer (mous), railing[2]."

As you can see, there are some subtle differences between the Hebrew and Greek meanings to the English meaning. In English, we read *evil speaking against God of sacred things*. A person, who speaks evil against God, Jesus, or the Holy Spirit, reveals the evil or apathy that resides in that person's heart. One might call this vanity or pride. Unless their hearts change to Love for Jesus and repentance for evil *words* and *deeds*, there is no hope for eternal life for them. They are dead in their sins.

For someone to speak evil of the almighty God, Jesus, and the Holy Ghost, they must be very secure and trust in his or her logical position of their disbelief. This could be because they do not believe there is life after death or some other doctrine such as reincarnation. It is also possible they think it is not worth looking into God, Jesus, and Holy Ghost presents, as it is stupid and or unbelievable. They require empirical evidence or facts to prove a truth. Why should they have faith in something unprovable? Especially if Jesus' commands interfere with their current lifestyle. Also, ghosts don't exist, except in the movies. Here too, we see the condition of their hearts, which is very secure, without a doubt, to their erroneous way of thinking.

Now **verse 29** makes a very harmful statement. To blaspheme, the Holy Ghost is unforgivable. **WOW!** Blaspheming against God and Jesus is forgivable, but against the Holy Ghost, it is not forgivable. So we had better look at this with renewed interest.

First, let us look at our bodies' makeup. In **Job 31:15,** we read we all are fashioned in the womb, and **Psalm 139:13–16** adds more information to this fashioning.

> **Psalm 139:13–16** *"(13) For thou hast <u>possessed my reins</u>: thou hast <u>covered me in my mother's womb</u>. (14) I will praise thee; for I am fearfully and wonderfully made: marvellous are thy works; and that my soul knoweth right well. (15) from My <u>substance was not hid from thee, when I was made in secret, and curiously wrought in the lowest parts of the earth</u>. (16) <u>Thine eyes did see my substance</u>, yet being unperfect; and in thy book all my members were written, which in continuance were fashioned, <u>when as yet there was none of them</u>."* *(KJV)*

In **verse 13,** we read God possessed our reins. The reins are used to control a horse. So God is in control of how he will create each of us. It is also referring to being covered (our carnal body) while in the womb. **Verse 15** reveals our substance, which is both soul and spirit. But we were created in "Secret" in the <u>lowest parts of the earth</u>. **Verse 16** tells us we are unperfect; this relates to our sinful nature during our fertilization while in the egg. All of our members are written down in a book, most likely the Book of Remembrances. But notice our eyes did see God's substance before we were formed in the womb. But, we were in fellowship with God during our waiting room experience.

So before we were born, we were soul (which is our eternal body); and spirit (which makes up our eternal spiritual life), both were waiting to be placed in our mother's womb. At birth, we received our carnal body, and now we are body, soul, and spirit. Spirit is difficult to explain as it is the essence of our being. It houses many facets of our being. Such as love, hate, apathy, concerns, desires, likes, dislikes, wants, needs, expectations, etc. The soul is the eternal body vessel that contains the spirit. We see this in the scriptures with Jesus on the walk to Emmaus **(Luk 24:13--31),** where the men did not recognize Jesus until he spoke and revealed his spirit. His eternal body (soul) was recognized by both the men to Emmaus and Jesus' apostles. They saw the scares of the puncher mark in his side and in his hands and in his feet as they were visible **(Luk 24:36–53).**

But the spirit is not as readily recognized as it is internal and hidden from sight, much like a ghost (Holy Ghost). But those who have the Holy Spirit can recognize those who also have the Holy Spirit in a short period of time. So it is the Holy Spirit that works with and through our spirit to lead us into righteous ways. One way is our conscience.

> Funk and Wagnall describe *conscience* as: "1.The faculty by which distinctions are made between moral right and wrong. 2 Conformity in conduct to the prescribed moral standard. – in (all) conscience 1. In truth; in reason, and honesty. 2. Certainly; assuredly. [< OF < L *conscire* to know inwardly][3]."

We were given the Knowledge of Good and Evil through Adam. And we all have experienced the dilemma in our spirit between choosing between doing the right thing or doing the wrong thing. For Christians, this is the Holy Spirit working with your spirit to impress you to do good, and God has recorded the consequences, be they good or bad. And remember, to know to do good and not to do good is the Sin of Omission.

For the non-Christians, the Holy Spirit works in their life to bring them to that point of accepting Jesus. Here is where Christians come into play. For humans are more motivated (sensitive) by human contact than by spiritual contact. We are to use this human contact to share the gospel with the lost to improve their knowledge of good. Remember, Jesus had to come to earth to make this human contact and pay for sins. For the seeker of truth, this Christian contact will help break through their spiritual callousness over the years of disobedience. But the longer we delay in sharing or delay in their decision, the more callous they will become and eventually will not feel the Holy Ghost's working. After Jesus' mission to earth, we read in the Book of Acts the sharing of the Gospel of the first Christians and the results.

The Book of Acts is full of references to the Holy Ghost; one, in particular, is found in **Acts 2.**

> **Acts 2:38** *"Then Peter said unto them, Repent, and be baptized every one of you in the name of Jesus Christ for the remission of sins, and ye shall receive the gift of the Holy Ghost"* *(KJV)*

> **(See also 1 John 2:3–6)**

Peter was also the receiver of the Holy Spirit at Pentecost. How much clearer can you get? *Everyone who repents and is baptized will receive God's gift of the Holy Ghost.* These words were written to the Christian (Church), and we see the beginning of this gift at Pentecost **(Acts 2).** It reveals the Holy Ghost's permanent placement into all the Church (True believers in Jesus). But the Holy Spirit was given to specific individuals in the Old Testament for a certain period of time. In **Gen.41:38,** we read that the Pharaoh recognized Joseph had God's spirit in him. There are many more events that the Spirit was present for individuals for some time **(see Acts).** But for the true Church, the Holy Spirit is present until he is removed. This taken away is revealed in **2 Thess.2.**

> **2 Thessalonians 2:7–8** *"(7) For the mystery of iniquity doth already work: only he who now letteth will let, until he be taken out of the way. (8) And then shall that Wicked be revealed, whom the Lord shall consume with the spirit of his mouth, and shall destroy with the brightness of his coming"* *(KJV):*

These verses are pertaining to the Holy Spirit being taken away. This has the earmarks of the Rapture. The Holy Spirit is in a Christians' body, and Christians are Raptured before starting the seven years of tribulation. For Christians are not appointed to wrath **(1 Thes.5:9).** This wicked revealing of Satan; will be consummated midway through The Great Tribulation of seven years. This is the time Satan will take command of the Antichrist Beast (government). Satan declares he is King and God; and will rule the earth for the last 3½ years. He thinks he is now god; as this, he has always desired. But, notice the last sentence, *"the brightness of his coming,"* refers to Jesus' 3rd, and final, coming to earth to destroy all evil (*1st Harvest*--Armageddon).

So what is this unforgivable sin of blaspheming (evil speaking) the Holy Ghost? This evil speaking is rejecting (denying scriptures), which implies: God is lying, God is not all knowledgeable, God is not all-powerful, God is not the Alpha and Omega, God is deceptive, God cannot create the Universe or the earth, God cannot create the elements of the Universe, God cannot create you and me, God cannot create the Lake of Fire, Jesus did not come to pay for our sins, Jesus cannot save us, God did not create the earth in all its complexities (Natural Laws), Jesus will not come again, and on and on and on! But, the most important of all is ***God and Jesus did not love us, as they do not exist.*** *But look at **Mark 3:29**.*

Mark 3:29 "*but is in danger of eternal damnation:*" *(KJV)*

This is a curious statement by God. Notice *"they are in danger of eternal damnation."* *"In danger of"* appears to reveal they are not yet in eternal damnation. Is this because God is writing to people that are alive, but when they die, they will be in eternal damnation? God will not give them any consideration then of his grace. Or is it a warning to them to give serious consideration to their plight and its consequences? Or is it a warning to future individuals about the Holy Ghost's eternal importance?

This is for you to decide. Choose well, my friend.

By blaspheming the Holy Spirit, we are, in effect, rejecting the Triune God (God, Jesus, and Holy Ghost) and the personage of the one whose mission is to save us, Jesus. Blaspheming is the utter disrespect for his death on the cross and his paying for the blasphemer's salvation.

This rejection of Jesus is blasphemy. However, after Jesus' death, the Christians are to sow the seeds (the Gospel) and water the seed (teach). **B**ut it is the Holy Ghost's job to make that seed grow and to accept Jesus as their Lord and Savior.

One more thought on forgiveness can be found in **Mat. 6**.

> **Matthew 6:13–15** *"(14) For if ye forgive men their trespasses, your heavenly Father will also forgive you: (15) But if ye forgive not men their trespasses, neither will your Father forgive your trespasses." (KJV)*

There are two (2) areas to consider here. One is mortal, and one is spiritual. God gave us both mortal Laws and Spiritual Laws in one Law. The most important is the spiritual law. The mortal law requires the mortal punishment for a broken law on the earth, *which requires earthly punishment, found in the Torah* (Bible).

The spiritual law requires continuous eternal punishment in the *Lake of Fire*. *This is the most crucial forgiveness for Christians.* Jesus on the cross said, *"Father forgive them for they know not what they do."* **(Luk23:34)** Jesus wants forgiveness for their eternal sins, which he was dying to pay. And this spiritual death will require eternal Death in the Lake of Fire.

Christians are to forgive the eternal sin; however, earthly (mortal sin) may still need earthly punishment. This earthly punishment must be by God's Law administered with truth, love, mercy, and justice. Payment for crimes is a necessary event in a carnal world. Keep in mind, Jesus will rule with a rod of iron in his kingdom.

To support this concept, read Jesus' statement on the cross in **Luke 23:4–44**. There Jesus asks God to forgive the thief of his spiritual sin. So God forgave his spiritual (eternal) sin, and the thief was in Paradise with Jesus, but the thief died on the cross to pay for his mortal sin.

But before the thief's request, Jesus asked God to forgive them *"for they know not what they do"* **Luke 23:34.** This request of Jesus was also for their eternal sin of murder. However, we are not aware of the mortal punishments they may have suffered.

Forgiveness is also for our peace of mind. If we truly understand the consequences of sin and its horrible pain. We should hope that no one should go into the Lake of Fire. We should exercise mercy, charity, and grace as God has given to us. Let God sort it out.

> **1 Peter4:7–8 *"(7) But the end of all things is at hand: be ye therefore sober, and watch unto prayer. (8) And above all things have fervent charity among yourselves:* for charity shall cover the multitude of sins."* (KJV)**

Do not harbor ill feelings towards others, as this reveals an unforgiving heart. Plus, you will continue to wrestle with distress, which will affect your health. When encountering a distressful situation, handle it as Jesus would. *"be quick to listen, slow to speak and slow to anger."* But best of all, capture peace in knowing ***"GOD IS IN CONTROL."***

SO THE

ONLY

UNFORGIVABLE

SIN IS?

REJECTING THE HOLY GHOST CALLING TO ACCEPT JESUS AS YOUR LORD AND SAVIOR!

BATTLE BETWEEN DEEDS AND FAITH

PREAMBLE

Salvation has and will always be *by God's grace* towards his children. And this book intends *to help clarify his plan of his Grace for man's redemption and give us that information for our knowledge.* God's strategy appears to have been adjusted over the years, much like his adjustment to the Hebrews' culinary laws, *but his grace is primary and unchangeable.* God laid down rules about which creatures the Hebrews could eat and ones that they could not eat. But, later, God adjusted that law to remove those restrictions. And this same type of adjustment may have occurred with actions pertaining to Salvation (not grace). Please keep in mind that man has known right from wrong since Adam ate from the Tree of Knowledge of Good and Evil. And most of Adam's children chose evil rather than good. This evil is confirmed by the Great Flood, which destroyed all evil souls. So let us start at the beginning and follow the requirement for deeds that initially were required for Salvation.

CONTENTS

1. PRE-FLOOD ---- 137
2. AFTER FLOOD ---- 142
3. LAW to JESUS ---- 145
4. LAW from JESUS to Resurrection ---- 162
5. 1ST RESURRECTION ---- 165
6. RAPTURE ---- 166
7. HARVESTS ---- 169
8. 1ST HARVEST ---- 170
9. UNKNOWN FRUIT ---- 184
10. 2nd HARVEST ---- 189
11. DEEDS REQUIRED ---- 196
12. GRAPEVINE ---- 203
13. WAR TO END ALL WARS ---- 211
14. THREE PASSOVERS ---- 213

PRE--FLOOD MYSTERY

We must return to the Book of Genesis to see what laws God laid down for Adam to follow. Here are the first indications of some forms of restriction that were initially in effect. (**Gen.2**)

Genesis 2:9 *"And out of the ground made the LORD God to grow every tree that is pleasant to the sight, and good for food; the tree of life also in the midst of the garden, and the tree of knowledge of good and evil"* *(KJV)*

It appears God has some future purpose in God's plan for man by inserting this Tree of Knowledge of Good and Evil as well as the Tree of Life. On the surface, it could seem as the Tree of Knowledge would give us needed knowledge, and the Tree of Life would grant eternal life. Overtly this is true, but covertly it has a greater purpose. As we will see later, the fruit from the Tree of Knowledge was not to be eaten *(a required deed)*. But, God knew Adam would eat that fruit; and the knowledge of Good and Evil would be spread to all earthlings.

This information was covert to Adam, as many more repercussions would surface. But it appears this knowledge will lead to The True Church in God's plan for man. Man initially was to use his knowledge of good and not evil during the early days to grow in goodness as a part of man's exercise in man's use of his self-will. And to know those individuals who will choose evil. This concept has been passed down through the ages, even to us today. Today I call this *Operation of Self-Will.* This operation is a function for obedience, our personal selection of good over evil. For this operation to have merit, man must know the difference between the two choices. But, he is given only the punishment for disobedience and not the reward for obedience. To compensate, God gave man (Adam) a conscience.

But it is in this transition that man failed quickly. However, God was not surprised!

Here begins the long trail of righteous education for earthlings. First is Adam's failure with God's simple law, do not eat the fruit from the Tree of Knowledge with its consequence for disobedience. But not just for Adam, but his children's children. Adam most likely did not know the severe consequences of death and had to rely on God, faith. Same with us today. We face decisional situations every day, not knowing the two or more results. But God has increased our knowledge, too, to help us, with the help of our conscience.

To make it more complicated, God creates his and our nemesis, Satan. Why? Life is tough enough without Satan. It appears God wants his children to face and learn all the evil manipulations that will challenge our self-will, resolve to do good (right).

We will also see Satan's initial emergence, the evil side, and later Jesus the righteous side. In creation, God created in darkness as first came Sunset (unrighteous) then later came Sunrise (righteous); as this schedule is revealed in **Gen.1.** Interestingly, God chose to create during six periods of darkness. And darkness is the metaphor for evil or unrighteousness, and six is the number for man. God is telling us (man) our life will be created in darkness, but we are to choose the light (righteousness).

It is evident one of God's Prime Directives, in this plan, is not to override Man's decisions. Adams descendants were given their self-will to exercise for good or evil. This choice is the same self-will that is given to man and angels even today. God has given his children the right to exercise good over evil and learn from their success or failure, hoping that their moral character for good is developed. God will aid us in Man's quest by later giving us written guidance (Bible) as to righteous and unrighteous actions by giving us instructions through his laws. But God must first reveal, to later generations, his displeasure with pre-flood punishment for unrighteous behavior and for not choosing good over evil. Thus proving that man is inherently evil and right must be stressed for man to see the benefit of righteousness. God's first laws were not egregious, and man is most capable of living by those laws. The first law God laid down was a positive law that is found in **Genesis 1.**

> **Genesis 1:27–28 "***(27) <u>so God created man in his</u> own <u>image,</u> in the image of God created he him; male and female created he them. (28) And God blessed them, and God said unto them, <u>Be fruitful, and multiply,</u> and <u>replenish</u> the earth, and <u>subdue it</u>: and <u>have dominion</u> over the fish of the sea, and over the fowl of the air, and over every living thing that moveth upon the earth.***" (KJV)*

Notice the three favorable laws: 1) have lots of babies (painlessness in births, 2) subdue the earth to your desires, 3) have dominion over all the creatures of the planet.

1. God has given Adam and Eve the right and ability to have as many children as they desire. Keep in mind that this is before the curse of Eve to bear children in pain. God has created such a powerful sexual experience between man and woman that still exists today. It is one of the most desirable sins for many people. It can be a tool for some individuals and addiction for others.

2. Subdue means to *"overcome, bring under control[3]"* of the earth. God gives man the ability and tools to perform these tasks. Man has developed inventions to help in controlling undesired elements of nature and give man a helping hand. Subdue is also the ingenuity to use nature's elements to man's benefit and pleasure, such as clothing, food, and drink. It also gives man the knowledge of how to eliminate undesirable aspects such as weeds and pests.

3. Dominion means to have *"sovereignty or ultimate control.3"* over. Man has learned to train many animals to help the man with the tasks at hand. Horses, mules, and cows have been trained to pull carts, wagons, plows,

carry packs, soldiers, Knights, etc. And carrier pigeons have been trained to carry messages; dogs warn of invaders and cats to remove rodents.

All animals have been created at this time; man had to have some ability to subdue and control these wild animals. It is in God's natural laws that animals were given a certain respect or fear of man. If not, how could Adam survive the dinosaurs, lions, tigers, bears, and flying creatures? I think we see this same respect in animals even today with their fear of man unless: they are protecting their young, starving, or trying to defend their territory. Some animals today have lost their fear of man by men feeding, training, and domesticating them. Some are amenable to domestication and training for man's use, but some are not. Some animals are territorial and cannot be trained. Much like Alpha dogs that are the leader of the pack and are very difficult to train, some are impossible. But still, man has some manner of dominion over the wild beast.

We see this innate respect for man today. Deer runs from hunters and non-hunters; birds are especially respectful of man and many other animals. But we have affected this respect by feeding wild animals or trying to socialize with their pack. This socialization has occurred by scientists studying Gorillas, Monkeys, and other family or pack animals. Once the animals lose that respect for man, man loses his dominion over animals. There is a saying in the military that says *"familiarity breeds contempt"* and is especially true with some animals.

The movie industry and schools have projected dinosaurs as voracious animals to man. Jurassic Park and other entertainment venues have made movies by projecting dinosaurs' violence, especially the carnivorous ones. There were no predatory creatures as **Gen. 1:30** says, *"I have given ever green herb for meat."* These entertainment companies have invented _traditions of untruths_ that we assume to be true. However, they may have become carnivores, as did man.

But if Adam did not have dominion over dinosaurs Adam and Eve's family could not survive carnivores. Scientists tell us that early man grunted and performed visual communications. However, the Bible is clear that Adam walked and talked with God. The Serpent spoke to Eve and Eve to the serpent. Verbal communications were built into Adam and Eve. Scientists also tell us that man-fought animals with rock-headed spears and rock knives. True, they learn to make them into fairly sharp tools, but do you think a sharp rock-tipped spear could penetrate an elephant's tough hide or a dinosaur's scaled hide? Bows and arrows, which came later, were more successful in bigger animals. The Crossbow was very successful against metal armor. So the Garden had to be perfect and safe before Adam and Eve's fall. The Garden was perfect and safe.

Adam's earth was perfect, and God's beauty in creation is magnificent. Woman, God's last creation is beautiful, so beautiful the Son of God later took all the wives they desired **(Gen.6:1–2).** But this also occurred after Adam's fall and their ejection from the Garden of Eden. But Adam and Eve still had dominion over the animals.

So the man had virtually free reign over his world, and from Genesis, we know how evil man became without some guidelines. However, there were individuals during this decline in morality that called on the name of the Lord. But, over time, fewer and fewer men called on God. Much like today. But Noe's (Noah) family line seems to have taught their children about God. Noe' and his immediate family were the only ones remaining true; among billions that were alive on the earth at that time of the Great Flood.

It was Noe's family that did the deeds that found favor in God's eyes. Noe' preached for over 120 years about God and the punishing Flood that is to come. But the people refused to believe him, and they continued in their knowledge of evil. This condition is much like today. *So good deeds were required by God,* and for those individuals to escape God's wrath and if you will permit Salvation. They, too, were to choose to do the deeds of righteousness and not evil. However, humanity refused and died in the Great Flood. This same concept is alive today as God's servants are warning humankind of the up and coming destruction of the earth through war (Armageddon) and fire **(Rev. 21)**. And for the Old Testament Saints, salvation was through *deeds of doing good and one's heart condition (love) towards God.*

AFTER THE FLOOD MYSTERY

After the Great Flood, Noah continued to teach his family about God, and they in-turn continued this task to their children. Therefore, righteous men can be found before and after the Great Flood. This same task was in effect after the Laws were given to Moses some years later. In this later period, we have learned about these righteous men such as Abraham, Isaac, David, Joseph, and Moses. But I'm sure there were other righteous men not mentioned in the Bible during this time. During this Post-Flood time, the Hebrew tribes grew and started to migrate to other locations. And in doing so, they carried with them their history to these other locations. Babylon (Babel) was the Biblical starting point for this mass migration. Here we see the results of the one language and the attempt to reach God on their own efforts (Tower of Babel). Remember, they still are living for many years producing many children, and starting the expansion of all the different tribes due to the different languages.

It is at this expansion in Hebrew history, where all the people spoke the same language. But, God saw the need to separate their languages, and those who spoke the same new language gathered together and spread even farther into other lands. We know this dispersal event today with all the different languages across the earth. Keep in mind all of these people had the same stories in the Hebrew language, which they wrote down in their own new language. You can read this today in the many writings about the flood by many writers of different tongues. Whose stories originated with Noah's family before the Tower of Babel in Babylon **(Genesis 11).** These written stories in other languages are very similar and can be found in different clay tablets worldwide, and there are very many. But this language confusion has been solved today by computer software for the interpretation of the different languages.

In his perfect timing, God gave Moses the guiding Laws for the Hebrew people to share with all the Hebrew people and later the whole world. God now gives all Hebrew people his specific laws to eliminate any human-made laws that the kings usually created. God's law was to standardize justice among all the earth people, and God used the Hebrew people and later Christians to reveal God's perfect justice for humanity. These laws show the perfectness of Jesus, as no one could keep God's law perfectly except Jesus. Jesus said in **Mat.5:17.**

> **Matthew 5:17** *"(17) Think not that I am come to destroy the law, or the prophets: I am not come to destroy, but to fulfil. (18) For verily I say unto you, <u>Till heaven and earth pass</u>, one jot or one tittle shall in no wise pass from the law, till all be fulfilled".* *(KJV)*

Jesus fulfilled all the law by the reflected light of his life. The law required a person to be perfect, sinless to live in eternity with God. Jesus was sinless as he is not only a prodigy of man but of God. For it was not Eve that caused inherited sin but Adam.

Note

A quick note; *"Till heaven and earth pass"* reveals that God's laws will be in effect until **Rev.21:1.** This time will include the time during Jesus' 1,000-year Kingdom and even for today. However, it is speaking of the revealing of sin and its punishment.

In **Gen. 2:16–17.** God tells only Adam (man) not to eat of the Tree of Knowledge of Good and Evil.

> **Genesis 2:16--17** *"(16) And the LORD <u>God commanded the man,</u> saying, Of every tree of the garden thou mayest freely eat: (17) But of <u>the tree of the knowledge</u> of good and evil, <u>thou shalt</u>*

143

> *not eat of it: for in the day that thou eatest thereof thou shalt surely die". KJV)*

Adam was commanded and not Eve! Eve was not created until after Adam named all the beast, fowl, and cattle. Further proof of this is by the fact that both Adam and Eve's eyes were not opened when Eve ate the fruit. But, it was after Adam ate the fruit of the tree **(Gen.3:7)**. Eve gave Adam the fruit, and he ate; it was then both their eyes were opened. Also, in **Rom.5**, we see the same proof.

> **Romans 5:12** *"Wherefore, as by one man sin entered into the world, and death by sin; and so death passed upon all men, for that all have sinned:" (KJV)*

> **Romans 5:19** *"For as by on man's disobedience many were made sinners, so by the obedience of one shall many be made righteous."(KJV)*

So Satan was not challenging God's word but Adam's word. Adam must have shared God's words with Eve. Adam was the First Missionary to earth.

This disobedience of Adam did not surprise God; it is in his plan for man. Apparently, God wants the people on earth to know good from evil. He is thereby creating a need for man to exercise his self-will to do good, just as God does. This period is the beginning of the teachings of all earthlings of God's mysteries, revealing the perfect way to live. Here establishes the measuring stick for us to follow, but only Jesus can measure up to and live a perfect life.

These words are pointing to the beginning of a very special time on earth. It is laying the foundation by which a condition must exist for salvation for man. That condition is perfection. God reveals that to be with God in Heaven, each human must be faultless, pure, without evil, selflessness, humble, without pride, dedicated to good, and so many other traits of God. Those that refuse God were and will be punished.

After the flood, the people still had the same laws given to Adam, except the Tree of Knowledge of Good and Evil. The two trees were most likely not available before the Flood because the guardian Angel of Eden kept man out of Eden. In any case, the two trees were not available. I have wondered if the olive leaf the bird brought back to Noah on the Ark; was the leaf from the Tree of Life?

Before Jesus' birth onto the earth, God must explain what laws man must live by and be accountable for salvation. But God knew no human, with Adams sin in them, <u>could</u> live in perfection. Therefore, God must provide a new way for man's Salvation. But until Jesus' resurrection, God's grace would be applied to those pre and post Flood; who loved God and attempted to follow his laws. These I call the Old Testament Saints. The law has revealed to man, which he was unable to keep, and the need for a different way for salvation will be needed. And this secret was revealed in Abraham's sacrifice of Isaac.

THE LAW TO JESUS

Eccl. 12, written around 977 BC, is a clear verse of scripture that expresses the need for deeds to the Old Testament and New Testament Saints.

Ecclesiastes 12:14 *"For God shall bring every <u>work</u> into <u>judgment</u>, with every secret thing, whether it be good, or whether it be evil." (KJV)*

These verses can stand all by themselves. But, for additional information, please read the remaining words of Deeds versus Faith. I have placed it here so you can keep it in mind as I build information for your more in-depth understanding. So I will start with the time Jesus is subject to God's Law of Moses.

These are the laws God himself deemed necessary for the society of earth's survival. And it appears God adds more details (Torah) about those laws that the people could understand. This is much like today with a new Christian.

God begins our education with the simple fact of salvation. The 10 Commandments came to Moses on Mount Sinai. These 10 Commandment Laws are general in nature, but more specific laws came later in the Torah (first five books of the Bible). But the initial laws (10 Commandments) were specific enough for that time for the Hebrew people. More detailed requirements came later to gives us more enlightenment through the study of his Word and the practice of his Word. It took many years for the Torah and the prophet's words to be written down by the scribes. These detailed laws and their judgment for breaking the law were focused on deeds. For example, *"Thou shall not steal."* Law required the deed or effort not to steal. But after the act, will follow the judgment (repercussions) for stealing. It was required by law for the perpetrator to pay back the victim four times the stolen property's value. Even if it meant the selling of all of the property that thief owned. If his property (including wife and children) did not cover the stolen item's value, then that thief became an indentured slave until the value was paid off through his labors for the victim.

It appears God needed to inform the world of his specific laws for society to survive over evil. God now intensifies the deeds required for the Hebrew Nation to reveal these same Laws to the world. Moses was chosen to bring God's Laws to his people that were camping near Mount Sinai. Moses went up the mountain where God wrote his ten commandments in stone. We know stone lasts until the recreation of New Earth and the New Universe. These are the deeds that all humans must keep for God's grace to save them. God knew they could not keep these laws but knew Jesus could and would. These expanded laws also carried with them the punishment God thinks necessary for society to survive. It is in the effort of the everyday person's attempt to keep these laws and sacrifice a sheep once a year to atone for their law broken sins; which God graciously forgives their sins.

In the Pre-Law and the Law periods, deeds were required for salvation as part of God's grace. But Jesus revealed a new covenant between God and man. But this new covenant was foretold in the faith of Abram's (Abraham's) faith in

God. It was Adam's failure; because of his lack of faith in God's words. It was Abraham's revealing the importance of faith through his incomplete sacrifice of his son Isaac. But Jesus (the perfect complete sacrifice) brought more profound meaning to this concept of *faith alone* for salvation. Here Jesus reveals the Law is to bring us knowledge of what is sin. And we are not to sin. But this effort requires deeds in following the Law. So a dilemma seems to appear, which is it *saved by deeds or saved by faith?*

Now appears the doctrine of <u>faith for salvation</u> and <u>deeds for Treasures</u>. *<u>Once saved, always saved,</u>* but *<u>Treasures are by deeds.</u>* Jesus gave us deeds to perform, especially in **Matthew Chapters 5, 6, and 7, and Matthew 28**

> **Matthew 28:18–20 *"(18) And Jesus came and spake unto them, saying, All power is given unto me in heaven and in earth. (19) <u>Go ye therefore,</u> and <u>teach all nations,</u> <u>baptizing</u> them in the name of the Father, and of the Son, and of the Holy Ghost: (20) Teaching <u>them to observe all things whatsoever I have commanded you:</u> and, lo, I am with you always, even unto the end of the world. Amen". (KJV)***

These verses require actions and efforts (deeds) in each Christian's life. **This is not a request but a command**; to perform this command requires acts. Deeds were required in the past, but Jesus brings *Salvation by Faith and Treasures by deeds.* Jesus himself performed deeds during his ministry here on earth. Death on the Cross was the final and most painful deed Jesus had to perform. And Jesus left with us his last command to spread his gospel (deeds) for treasures. We see this truth also in **Mat. 6**.

> **Matthew 6:19–20 *"(19) Lay not up for yourselves treasures upon earth, where moth and rust doth corrupt, and where thieves break through and steal: (20) <u>But lay up for yourselves treasures in heaven,</u> where neither moth nor rust doth corrupt, and where thieves do not break through nor steal:" (KJV)***

How does one lays up Treasures, if not by deeds? Therefore, it appears God, through Jesus, is revealing (over the ages) to us his mystery that is a very special time in human history,

THE CHURCH AGE!

The Church (true believers in Jesus for salvation) will be the fulfillment for the Apostles. The Apostles were tasked with laying the Church's foundation and bringing the Gospel to many different peoples. The Church is a continuation of the deeds of the Apostles. And we read this in **Mat. 6.**

> **Matthew 6:14–15 *"(14) for if ye forgive men their trespasses, your heavenly Father will also forgive you: (15) But if ye forgive not men their trespasses, neither will your Father forgive your trespasses." (KJV)***

This forgiveness is an act many people are unable or unwilling to perform. Hatred is a powerful emotion to control. Hatred is not a sin as <u>God hated the deeds</u> of the Nicolaitanes **(Rev.2:6)**, but not the Nicolaitanes. It is what we do with that hatred that matters. So deeds continue to be required, but how about Faith?

Forgiveness is for a person's eternal sin, but some sins require earthly consequences in the Law. Jesus said on the cross, *"Forgive them, Father, for they know not what they do."* Jesus was praying to the Father for him to forgive their eternal sin. For Laws to be effective, mortal punishment must follow. Therefore, we must ask God to forgive their eternal punishment for those who sin against us. Jesus was clear on this subject in **Luk.23** and **Mat.6.**

> **Luke 23:34 *"Then said Jesus, Father, forgive them; for they know not what they do. And they parted his raiment, and cast lots." (KJV)***

> **Matthew 6:14–15 "(***14***) *For if ye forgive men their trespasses, your heavenly Father will also forgive you: (15) But if ye forgive not men their trespasses, neither will your Father forgive your trespasses." (KJV)***

This last verse is very clear about eternal forgiveness. However, this does not necessarily mean the removal of earthly punish. A genuinely repentant soul's earthly punishment needs to be given serious thoughts. Jesus forgave the Samaritan woman at the well, the woman caught in sexual sin, and the thief on the cross. It was their faith and God's grace that was given to them through Jesus. But God has a horrible punishment for those individuals who continue to sin by breaking God's Laws. The repentant soul who has faith in Jesus is forgiven of all sins.

Faith in the Church period is paramount. We read in **Romans 3** that Salvation is by faith alone.

> **Romans 3:28 "*Therefore we conclude that a <u>man is justified by faith without the deeds of the law</u>." (KJV)***

But in **Acts 26,** we see what appears to be a conflicting message, requiring deeds.

> **Acts 26:20 *"But shewed first unto them of Damascus, and at Jerusalem, and throughout all the coasts of Judaea, and <u>then to the Gentiles, that they should repent and turn to God, and do works meet for repentance</u>." (KJV)***

However, these are not contradictive statements! They are clarifying statements. If a person is truly faithful to Jesus, his attitude would be one of immense sorry for their sins; and desire to be obedient to Jesus' and God's will. Please notice this statement was made to the Gentiles, as God will blind the eyes of the Hebrew people. So this is to you and me, the Church then and today.

The Church period is the only period in God's plan, where man is saved by faith alone. Deeds for salvation were required in Per-flood, Pre-Law, and Law periods. But Faith is for that special period, the time of Jesus and the Church. The final days (1,000 years) of God's plan will require deeds again, as the Faith alone period has ended with the Church at the Rapture of the Church. The Rapture will bring proof to the world that Jesus is the Son of God. It is also proof that the Bible is truth. So as with Doubting Thomas **(John 20:29),** *"blessed are those that believe without seeing"* (The Church). So it is clear those who believe but do not do the deeds will miss this Treasure of the Rapture. And will now go into the Great Tribulation and need to do the acts during the most troubling times in earth's history. Luke tells us of this occurrence in **Luk.8:5–15** (parable of the sower), especially **verse 15**. Those Church individuals who have perished without deeds before the Rapture are saved by faith, but they are without Treasures. We read this Treasure in **1st Thes. 4.**

> **1 Thessalonians 4:13–17 "(13)** *But I would not have you to be ignorant, brethren, concerning them which are asleep, that ye sorrow not, even as others which have no hope. (14) For if we believe that Jesus died and rose again, even so them also which sleep in Jesus will God bring with him. (15) For this we say unto you by the word of the Lord, that we which are alive* and *remain unto the coming of the Lord shall not prevent them which are asleep. (16) For the Lord himself shall descend from heaven with a shout, with the voice of the archangel, and with the trump of God: and the dead in Christ shall rise first: (17) Then we which are alive* and *remain shall be caught up together with them in the clouds, to meet the Lord in the air: and so shall we ever be with the Lord" (KJV).*

You might ask, why are the dead in Christ with no or little Treasures (deeds) Raptured? And a good question it is too. Those that have died in Christ (faith only) have completed their life journey, and there are no more deeds for them to perform on earth to build up their Treasures. They have run their race and have received their reward through Faith. After the Rapture, those alive on earth are still in the race and can and will store up Treasures. Their race will be all uphill with many obstacles and perils. They will experience Hell on earth caused by Satan and his Demons. They will be like the people in Noah's day. They will know good and evil and have to do good (righteous Deeds) just as did Noah. *They (Tribulation Saints) are saved by their faith, but they will need to go through the Great Tribulation to prove their loyalty in deeds and faith to Christ.*

But you ask, *"are not these saved by faith too?"* Yes, but remember, here is the Great Tribulation time that God requires these individuals *to choose Jesus or Satan.* There will be no other choice! Those that choose Jesus will exercise their faith and deeds. And those that fall away from Jesus will exercise their belief in Satan. There will be no gray area here, no exceptions. Jesus made this very clear in **Mat.12.**

>**Matthew 12:30** *"He that is not with me is against me; and he that gathereth not with me scattereth abroad." (KJV)*

We see this also in **2 Thes 2.**

>**2 Thessalonians 2:3.** *"Let no man deceive you by any means: for that day shall not come, except there come a <u>falling away</u> first, and that man of sin be revealed, the son of perdition;' (KJV)*

Here is a very <u>special</u> *clue* for us to consider. Falling away are those individuals that accept the Mark of the Beast. Fear of mortal death and lack of total faith in Jesus; which reveals their lack of knowing Jesus, God, and the Holy Ghost. And also shows their lack of commitment to the Gospel of Jesus. These are possibly the weak pew sitters! They know the triune God, but their heart is not into doing his works. God has revealed the necessity for deed throughout the Bible and the benefit of performing the deeds. This was revealed in the

Passover. So we must watch for this falling away, which will lay the foundational opportunity for the Antichrist #1, the son of perdition [Satan], to start his empire against man and God.

The Flood and the Hebrew Passover are points in time showing deeds required for Treasures gained. Noe' preaching to the people of his day and building the Ark; was the deed for his passing over the Flood. It was the deed of the Hebrew people, in Moses day, putting sheep's blood around their door (works) that gave them the Treasure of protection of their firstborn son and animal from the Death Angel. This event is called the Passover and is celebrated every year by the Hebrew people. They escaped death by the deed of spreading the sheep's blood around their doors. The door in the Bible is represented several times as the passage to a person's heart. So if you spread Jesus' blood around your heart, you too will be spared from eternal death. Those Hebrew people who performed that deed survived the Death Angel, and their firstborn remained on earth after the Passover. What do you think would have happened to the Hebrews who did not do the deed of spreading the blood?

We need to understand that mortal and spiritual death has two finalities. Human death is the end of life as we know it. Spiritual death is the eternal Death of our soul and being captive in the Lake of Fire. You will not come back to earth as another person, creature, or vegetation, and there is no pardon. After mortal death, we all will be judged, and with judgment come rewards, be they for good or evil. This is also revealed in **Hebrews 9.**

> **Hebrews 9:27–28** *"(17) And as it is appointed unto men once to die, but after this the judgment: (28) <u>So Christ was once offered to bear the sins of many; and unto them that look for him</u> shall <u>he appear the second time</u> without sin unto salvation." (KJV)*

Here we see that after death comes judgment. For those saved by Jesus' blood, this judgment is at the Judgment Seat of Jesus Christ and not God's Great White Throne Judgment seat. Notice also the statement *"he appears the second time,"* which reveals the Rapture. Jesus will come to earth three times. Christ Judgment Seat **(Rom. 14:10 / 2 Cor. 5:10)** is for all Christians for what <u>they have said</u> and *done* while on this earth, be it <u>good or bad.</u>

> **2 Corinthians 5:10** *"For we must all appear before the judgment seat of Christ; that every one <u>may</u> receive <u>the things</u> <u>**done**</u> in his <u>body,</u> according to that <u>he hath done</u>, whether it be good or bad." (KJV)*

Notice that twice God reveals the judgment for deeds done. Christians cannot ignore this statement. Christians will be judged by deeds. So those who have died and did very little or no deeds are already saved and judged. But, this is not so for those alive when Jesus returns to Rapture the Church. Those left behind ½ christians alive and remain on earth; can still store up Treasures during the Great Tribulation. <u>*Deeds for Satan or God*</u> *will now be required to sustain life on earth or sustain eternal life in Heaven.* I call those individuals who choose Heaven; the *Tribulation Saints.*

But please notice the underlined words **(Heb. 9:28)** that point to *Jesus' 2nd Return*. These returns could be difficult to understand as Jesus has three times he will be present on or near the earth. The <u>*first time*</u> he came to earth as our Saviour. The <u>*second time*</u> he comes in the air to Rapture his Church. And his <u>*third time*</u> to earth is to destroy all evil (Armageddon) and establish his 1,000-year Kingdom. So it appears his appearance, number 2, is <u>*the clue*</u> for the Rapture as he will not touch the earth. Jesus was corrupted for our sins and had to put on incorruption to go into Heaven **(1 Cor. 15)**

> **1 Corinthians 15:51–54** *"(5) Behold, <u>I shew you a mystery;</u> We shall not all sleep, but we shall all be changed, (52) In a moment, in the twinkling of an eye, at the last trump: for the trumpet shall sound, and <u>the dead shall be raised incorruptible,</u> and we shall be changed. (53) For this corruptible must put on incorruption, and this mortal must put on immortality. (54) So when this corruptible shall have put on incorruption, and this mortal shall have put on*

immortality, then shall be brought to pass the saying that is written, <u>Death is swallowed up in victory</u>". (KJV)

Jesus put on this incorruption when he went to God in Heaven after his death (the 1st Resurrection). His and our corruption must be changed to incorruption to have immortality. If we live in Jesus, we share in his incorruption (Perfection). This same ability continues during The Great Wrath of God during the tribulation period of seven years. But God's Word and Jesus' salvation will still be taught during that time by 144.000 Hebrew missionaries. **(Rev. 7)**

This group of 144,000 Hebrew individuals **(Rev. 7)** will complete the Great Commission during the Great Tribulation period. These individuals will go into all nations and convert the entire Hebrew individuals to Jesus and some gentiles. This time will require enormous deeds on their part and the ones also that help the Holy Spirit save those lost from their spiritual death. You will read of these saved Hebrews that have been killed (beheaded), and they are kept under the altar in **Rev. 20:4.** These (unsealed) individuals boldly preached the gospel, knowing there was a death sentence awaiting them from Satan.

In **Rev.14,** we read of the works that follow these individuals.

Revelation 14:12–13 *"(12) Here is the patience of the saints: here* are *they that <u>keep the commandments of God</u>* (deeds)*, and the <u>faith of Jesus.</u> (13) And I heard a voice from heaven saying unto me, Write, <u>Blessed</u> are <u>the dead which die in the Lord from henceforth:</u> Yea, saith the Spirit, that they may rest from their <u>labours; and their works do follow them".</u>(KJV)*

If works (deeds) are not necessary, why would God give us this verse of scripture? Jesus came to perform acts to pay for our sins. Missionaries have sacrificed their lives for the Gospel. The Pre-flood individuals were given the knowledge of good to follow. During the Law period, individuals were given

Laws to follow and perform. The *Tribulation Saints* will finish the requirement of deeds and the Great ~~Commission~~ Command.

Today the Church has fallen into the itchy ear syndrome (sweet words) and very resistant to hearing any unpleasant cold hard truths. Any pastor who preaches any unpleasant but truthful sermons will eventually lose his job from the spiritually weak parishioners. We can see this in the Church of Laodicea in **Rev.3.** It appears that they, too, have forgotten the words in the Book of James.

> **James 2:17–20** *"(17) Even so faith, if it hath not works, is dead, being alone. (18) Yea, a man may say, Thou hast faith, and I have works: shew me thy faith without thy works, and I will shew thee my faith by my works. (19) Thou believest that there is one God; thou doest well: the devils also believe, and tremble.(20) But wilt thou know, O vain man, that faith without works is dead?"* *(KJV)*

Who is James relating to in the above verses? Is it curious they believe there is a God but not **in** the works (Jesus' Gospel) from God? This condition is supported by the next statement that Satan and demons know there is a God. These people believe there is a single God and not the Triune God. Also, this is true to the Hebrew nation and even to the non-Jesus believing individuals. Why would a non-believing person do the works of Jesus when they have no faith in Jesus? But they believe there is a God. Here again, we read of these individual religious leaders (**Mat.23:23–36**): Scribes and Pharisees.

However, consider the pew setters in these verses. The one verse we looked at said we are saved without Deeds. But, James said, *"faith without deeds is dead."* These two statements appear to be contradicting each other. The pew setters are not performing required deeds but are saved; however, their Treasures are nonexistent (dead). There are no words in the Bible to explain what a Treasure is to God or Jesus. The pavement in Heaven is made of pure Gold. The foundation and walls of our new home are made of precious Gems. The high gates to our new home are made of a single Pearl. God will create a New Heaven and a New Earth for our home. To us humans, these are financial treasures, but not to God or Jesus. Our personal dedication to God's moral character, our agape Love for God, Jesus, and fellow man, our desire to help others, our humility, self-control, and the Beatitudes of **Mat. 5, 6and 7**; we will acquire Treasures from God! Heaven will be a most wonderful place, and our Treasures will always be with us to enjoy. What they will be is not clear, but they will be fantastic. And they will come by our deeds, and they will never be boring.

How many times have you heard a sermon on works? Those words are not an itchy ear subject. It will create an uncomfortable feeling in those who are not involved in Jesus' works. As deeds have some cold hard truths, we must face in our lives and our Church. Jesus spoke of truth to the religious leaders in his time on earth. **(Mat. 23)** Here is just a portion of Jesus' statement explaining who these individuals are.

Matthew 23:23—28 *"(23) Woe unto you, <u>scribes and Pharisees, hypocrites</u>! <u>for ye pay</u> <u>tithe</u> of mint and anise and cummin, <u>and have omitted the weightier matters</u> of the <u>law, judgment, mercy, and faith</u>: these ought ye to have done, and not to leave the other undone. (24) <u>Ye blind guides</u>, which strain at a gnat, and swallow a camel. (25) Woe unto you, scribes and Pharisees, hypocrites! for ye make clean the outside of the cup and of the platter, <u>but within they are full of extortion and excess.</u> (26) Thou blind Pharisee, cleanse first that which is within the cup and platter, that the outside of them may be clean also. (27) Woe unto you, scribes and Pharisees, hypocrites! <u>for ye are like unto whited sepulchres,</u> which indeed appear beautiful outward, but are within <u>full of dead</u> men's <u>bones, and of all uncleanness.</u> (28) Even so ye also <u>outwardly appear righteous unto men, but within ye are full of hypocrisy and iniquity</u>". (KJV)*

WOW! These are not *"itchy ear"* words! These words from Jesus appear to be hateful. But, truth and not *"itchy ear"* words are what they needed to hear, and we also. Jesus loved these individuals enough to die for them. *And hard love is necessary at times.* Pay particular attention to who these individuals are; they are the Scribes and Pharisees. The scribes are the individuals who have written down the Word's God gave to the Priest and Prophets. They had to know the truth, being they were privileged in writing down those truths. But they appear not to believe or to consider the meaning of those words. We can equate these individuals to the religious press of today. Bibles and Biblical studies are printed today, and some of those printers appear not interested in what they print. It can also be the writers of *"itchy ear"* doctrine are only interested in sales and not necessarily the truth. They desire people to desire what they write ($).

The Pharisees were the middle to upper class, and their beliefs were closer to Jesus' teachings than the Sadducees. But the Pharisees believed that traditions were very important too. Since the Pharisees were on the correct doctrinal course, God particularly chose them in these verses because they were close but not putting into practice what they believed. *Does this sound much like the Church of today?* If one does not practice what one preaches, he or she is a hypocrite. Jesus uses strong words and not *"itchy ear"* words. See Jesus' truthful words in **Mat. 23**.

> **Matthew 23:27** *"**Woe unto you, scribes and Pharisees, hypocrites! for ye are like unto whited sepulchres, which indeed appear beautiful outward, but are within full of dead** men's **bones, and of all uncleanness". (KJV)**

Do you think these words of truth inspired Love for Jesus by the scribes and Pharisees? Sometimes the truth hurts, but the hurt is better here on earth than in the Lake of Fire. Remember, God loves those he chastises, and if no chastisement, no son of God **(Heb.12:6–8).**

The message mentioned in **verse 23** *"omitted the weightier matters of law, judgment, and faith."* Apparently, these men have placed more concern on *traditional deeds and personal gain* rather than *"the weightier matters of law,* *judgment and faith."* Laws require proof; Jesus provided that proof. Judgments require mercy; and proper punishment for the offense. But Jesus' punishment was not correct, as there was no proof of Jesus' crime. Even Pilot knew this. Judgment by Hebrew Law says that a Court of Law could not be conducted at night, but the court of Jesus was at night! And therefore, was illegal according to God's Law. So we can see the evil fruit **(Mat. 7:15–20)** produced by these evil men in this unlawful court. And these men were religious leaders and teachers, *and how dare Jesus, a lowly carpenter, question their knowledge or righteousness.*

Arises -- Pride and Vanity ---Satan smiles.

The concept of faith was not entirely new for the Hebrew elite as they knew the faith exhibited by Abraham in his command to sacrifice his son. But the words of faith in Jesus were <u>considered *blasphemous by legal tradition;* therefore required the death penalty</u>. Nowhere is truth in the Law deserving of death. But without reliable witnesses, no death sentence could be determined.

Jesus displayed mercies for us, with the Samaritan woman at the well who was a sinner **(John. 4:6–19).** Her punishment by law was death, but Jesus provided mercy. Also, the woman (only) who Scribes and Pharisees had caught <u>in the act of adultery</u> was shown mercy by Jesus, as only she and not the man was brought to Jesus. But Jesus said, let him without sin cast the first stone. The only person present without sin was Jesus. A question comes to mind: what would have happened if the witnesses had remained? Would Jesus need to cast the first stone? But Jesus wrote something in the sand that was convicting to the Scribes' and Pharisees' hearts. Possibly, *"where is that man caught in adultery?"* For the man, too, was guilty under the Law of a capital sin. **(John 8)** So these men were not reliable witnesses, so they departed.

So it appears we face a dilemma; one to obedience to the Law and one to Faith. If we go to **Mat.28,** we see a commandment on Law.

Matthew 28:19–20 *"(19) <u>Go ye</u> therefore, and <u>teach</u> all nations, <u>baptizing</u> them in the name of the Father, and of the Son, and of*

the Holy Ghost: (20) Teaching them to observe all things whatsoever I have commanded you: and, lo, I am with you alway, even *unto the end of the world. Amen". (KJV)*

Please notice this is not a request but a command. Jesus commands you and me to do the deeds of teaching and baptizing humans into Jesus, God, and the Holy Ghost. This is not a mystery but simple, straightforward words we can understand. Some people try to weaken these words but to their peril. But we know those who are elderly and with infirmities cannot go to foreign countries, but some can do some things. Such as writing letters to missionaries to encourage them and the people within their congregation about Jesus and his Love. Send books, papers explaining different parts of the Christian doctrine with the missionary's approval. Start prayer chains or pay it forward gifts chains.

Help in the Prison Ministry; research helps inmates be released for potential jobs, housing, and other items to help change their direction in their lives. Help for their families during their incarceration. *This field is indeed ripe for harvest of lost souls, and **very few Christians are committed.***

Help for those individuals who have lost everything "The Homeless." They have lost all hope for a secure future. Many are abandoned by their family and friends. Survival is paramount to their daily life. They feel hated, unwanted, and worthless. Some have mental sickness, others deficient education and no trade skills. How can they understand the gospel of Jesus without the basic necessities for life? *Jesus died for them also.*

Jesus' salvation and aid came for the Hebrew people first, as is proven by the Canaanite (non-Hebrew) woman that asked Jesus to heal her daughter of demon possession. **(Mat.15:22–28)** Jesus saw the faith of this gentile and healed her daughter of demon possession. This event reveals to us that our first responsibility is to our family to teach them the gospel of Jesus and then to the world. If every parent taught his or her children the gospel of Jesus, we would not need many missionaries. But Satan has been successful in many countries, and strange religions have been entrenched into their lives. And politics and false religions are the most challenging concepts to overcome with the truth. Even with the miracles Jesus performed, the religious leaders would not accept Jesus; but they wanted him dead. Even after Jesus' resurrection, these leaders would not believe. And there were over 500 witnesses to Jesus' resurrection. **(1 Cor.15)**

> **1 Corinthians 15:4–6** *"(4) And that* **he** (Jesus) **was** *buried, and that he rose again the third day according to the scriptures: (5) And that he was seen of Cephas* (Peter), *then of the twelve: (6) After that, he was seen of <u>above five hundred brethren at once;</u> of whom the greater part remain unto this present, but some are fallen asleep". (KJV)*

How could the Religious leaders disbelieve this resurrection event with over 500 witnesses? Along with these words of the witnesses, we are given **Mat.27:52–53**, which states other Saints were resurrected with Jesus and went into Jerusalem with Jesus. They also were seen by many people. If 500 witnesses saw Jesus, it appears these Saints were also seen with Jesus.

Satan had his foothold on these religious leaders. We, too, must test the spirits of everyone who claims to be a spiritual leader. The Bible is clear on this concept **(1 John 4)** is clear that we are to test the spirit.

> **1 John 4:1** *"Beloved, believe not every spirit, but try the spirits whether they are of God: because many false prophets are gone out into the world." (KJV)*

The best way to test a spirit is by relying on God's Word and the Holy Spirit. We have the Knowledge of Good and Evil in us through Adam, so if something is said that does not seem correct, you go to God's Word and do research for the truth.

Jesus brought the new covenant for salvation to the earth, and the religious leaders rejected him and his new covenant from God. We, too, are subject to this entrenchment in traditions or wrong or incomplete knowledge. We do not have the mine of God, and His ways are not our ways. But God is patient with us and provides us knowledge as we can understand it in our own time. Some people are smarter than normal, and some are less smart, but God works with all to help us learn of him and his ways. It is incumbent on us to be patient with our fellow man when sharing Jesus with them. Remember, we are to plant the seeds, and others are to water, and others are to harvest **(1 Cor.3:5–9)**. We may never see our results on this earth, but we will know when we meet Jesus. Therefore, we must watch for Jesus' return and not lose our treasures. (Luke 21)

Luke 21:34–36 *"(34) And <u>take heed to yourselves,</u> lest at any time your hearts be overcharged with surfeiting, and drunkenness, and cares of this life, and* so *that day come upon you unawares. (35) <u>For as a snare shall it come on all them that dwell on the face of the whole </u>earth. (36) Watch ye therefore, and pray always, that ye may be accounted worthy to escape all these things that shall come to pass, and to stand before the Son of man." (KJV)*

Surfeiting means = in excess

<u>*"Take Heed to yourself"*</u> are very powerful words of caution. <u>*Do not deceive yourself with false justifications*</u>. Just because someone else does it, does not mean we can do it. It is a reminder that we need to examine ourselves regularly and not just before Communion only. Our lust of the flesh and lust of our eyes can cause us to slide down that slippery slope into sin without knowing it; unless we keep watch on our own motives and actions **(1 John 2:3–6)**. Pray for yourself that the Holy Spirit reveals your nearness to sinning and gives you the strength to overcome your sinful desires. Trust in **1 Cor.10.**

1 Corinthians 10:13 *"There hath no temptation taken you but such as is common to man: but God* is *faithful, who will not suffer you to be tempted above that ye are able; but will with the*

temptation also make a way to escape, that ye may be able to bear it." (KJV)

Be strong look for the way of escape from the temptations.

THE MYSTERY OF THE LAW

We read in the Bible many places where Jesus' earthly Kingdom is prophesied or inferred. In **Rev.20,** we see the word one *thousand years used six times,* and the word *works used two times.* The word works are used about judgments of deeds performed on earth. This word works should make it clear that deeds are essential to God. He requires deeds from Adam to the final days of Jesus' 1,000-year Kingdom on Earth. All the individuals that have ever lived will be judged by faith and works in Jesus, God's laws, God's mercy, and grace.

Throne Judgment, which is reserved for all the lost souls. To the non-faithful individual, when they are at The Great White Throne, they will receive judgment based on all of their recorded words and deeds that individual performed during their lifetime. Many books are used in judgments mentioned in the Bible, and two stand out in their importance. One is the Book of Law, and the other is the Book of Life. The Book of Life is the most important. If a person's name is missing in the Book of Life, their punishment is the Lake of Fire forever.

This Book of Life has every person's name that has accepted Jesus as their Lord and Savior or has found God's grace for those individuals before Jesus time on earth. All those saved will go before the *Judgment Seat of Christ* **(Rom.14)** but *not the Great White*

Romans 14:9–12 *"(12) For to this end Christ both died, and rose, and revived, that he might be <u>Lord both of the dead and living.</u> (10) But why dost thou judge thy brother? or why dost thou set at nought thy brother? <u>for we shall all stand before the judgment seat</u>*

<u>of Christ</u>. (11) For it is written, As I live, saith the Lord, every knee shall bow to me, and every tongue shall confess to God. (12) <u>So then every one of us shall give account of himself to God</u>. (KJV)

In **Luke 12,** we read that nothing will be hidden, and everything we have said or done will be revealed.

Luke 12:2–3 *"(2) For there is nothing covered, that shall not be revealed; neither hid, that shall not be known. (3) Therefore whatsoever ye have spoken in darkness shall be heard in the light; and that which ye have spoken in the ear in closets shall be proclaimed upon the housetops". (KJV)*

Every deed Christians have done, and every word spoken, be it good or bad, will be judged by Jesus. And the Bible is clear that the best results will be with the Judgment Seat of Christ. And that the Judgment Seat of Christ is only for the saved individuals. So what kind of person should we be?

In **John 5,** we read of the results of those that have done right versus those who have done evil.

John 5:28--29 *"(28) Marvel not at this: for the hour is coming, in the which all that are in the graves shall hear his voice, (29) And shall come forth; <u>they that have done good, unto the resurrection of life;</u> and they that have done evil, unto the resurrection of damnation". (KJV)*

These two verses of scriptures cover three periods of time. The <u>first occurrence is the Rapture,</u> when the dead in Christ will rise first, followed by the living deed-full and faithful Christians. The <u>second time</u> this will occur is at the *1st Harvest* **(Rev.14:14–16),** the collection of the Tribulation Saints under the Alter, Old Testament Saints, Hebrews, and Gentile converts. The <u>third occurrence</u> is *2nd Harvest* **(Rev. 14:17–20)** for all those evil souls that are the fruit of the false religion and for the entire past individuals who rejected Jesus and those who chose evil before Jesus. They will go to the Great Wine–Press of the Wrath of God. The Great White Throne Judgment comes after Jesus' 1,000-year Kingdom when Satan is released from the abyss and again gathers an army to destroy Jesus. But, God intervenes and destroys Satan and his army. Then Satan, his Army, all lost souls, and his demons are cast into the Lake of Fire forever.

END OF EVIL

Note

It appears that Jesus' 1,000-year Kingdom is to prove we are an evil bent people in sin, as sin will still occur during Jesus' Kingdom. How can sin appear in a perfect kingdom? There will be perfect government, fantastic weather, excellent food, pure water, loving worship, perfect health, no homeless, and many more perfections. But living sinful human nature will still occur in the Tribulation survivors. We read of this and also the length of life for sinners in **Isa 65.**

Isaiah 65:20 *"There shall be no more thence an infant of days, nor an old man that hath not filled his days: for the <u>child shall die an hundred years old</u>; but the sinner* being *an hundred years old shall be accursed."(KJV)*

These deaths will occur during Jesus' 1,000-year Kingdom as death cannot happen in eternity. <u>**Isa. 65**</u> covers many years from **verse 2** of Noah's day to **verse 4.** This period is when swine were not permitted to be eaten. **Verse 9** speaks of Jesus' seed (his birth), and **verse 12** takes us to the War of Armageddon and Jesus' Kingdom. **Verse 17** reveals the future creation of a New Heaven and New Earth. Then **verse 20** tells the length of life for a child, followed by **verse 22,** which speaks of a sinful adults' life span in the Kingdom. But **verses 21–25** reveal the conditions of Jesus' 1,000-year Kingdom. These individuals in Jesus' Kingdom will be those who survived the Great

Tribulation saved by faith in Jesus, those resurrected, and the Bride of Christ. So let us look at the different resurrections.

FIRST RESURRECTION MYSTERY

The Resurrections and Harvest mentioned can be a little confusing. For simplicity, I will take some liberties with the scriptures to understand the different Resurrections.

In **Mat.27:52,** at Jesus' Resurrection, many of Jesus' converts, from Jesus' time on earth, their graves were opened, and they came forth with Jesus and went into the city with Jesus. Over 500 people saw them in the city, and this is supported by Jesus' statement of *"where I am there ye will be also."* This statement reveals a need to resurrect those who believed in Jesus and died during his three and one half year mission on earth. Jesus was going to Heaven by way of Paradise in the heart of the planet. And in doing so, must take his converts with Him (the Church). Here is the beginning of the First Resurrection of the dead of both Jesus and the first of his New Testament Church Saints. This 1st Resurrection shows up again in **Rev.20:4–5.** Here the Tribulation Saints are being included in the 1st Resurrection. And is supported by, *"they had not worshipped the Beast"* nor *"received his mark upon their forehead or hans."* They also will be with Jesus when harvested. Those words also relate to **Rev.14:1,** but **Rev. 20:9–10** is the opposite; *for those who had received the Mark of the Beast have rejected Jesus.* So we see a distinction between those individuals who accepted and those who had not taken the Mark.

God includes the Tribulation Saints as they too have faith and are in Jesus just as we are in Jesus and protected by his body. Therefore, the Tribulation Saints are 1) Hebrews converts, 2) Gentile converts, 3) Old Testament Saints, and 4) the now the deed-full Pew Sitters. All four will be raised from the dead. Both groups of Saints (Church and Tribulation) are worthy of the 1st Resurrection as Jesus comes for them and is their harvester. Between the Jesus Resurrection and the 1st Harvest comes a most important event to Christians; The Rapture.

THE RAPTURE OF THE CHURCH SAINTS

***Here I see the parable of the separation of sheep from the goats** and also
the **parable of the Prodigal Son***

We are venturing into a difficult section to describe, as it is a tying together and, at the same time, separating apart the different times of the Rapture, from the 1st Harvest and 2nd Harvest. But the first eleven verses of **Thessalonians 4** lay the general period information followed by more specific information during that time. So I will start with: 1) the Rapture, 2) the 1st Harvest, and 3) the 2nd Harvest.

You might ask, why is there a Rapture? We know God is perfect, and his judgments are perfect. And we who claim Jesus as our savior believe: that he is the son of God, died to pay for our sins, rose from the grave, and will come again to take us to Heaven to be with him forever. We are perfectly sinless and pure in God's eyes, as we are *sinless in* Jesus. Therefore, we do not deserve retribution. **1Thes.5:9,** it is clear that those who believe in Jesus will not suffer God's wrath. That includes either eternal Death or God's Great Tribulation of Wrath on earth.

**1 Thessalonians 5:9 "*For <u>God hath not appointed us to wrath</u>, but
to <u>obtain salvation</u> by our Lord Jesus Christ,*" (KJV)**

We find the scripture for the Rapture in **1 Thes. 4.** The Rapture time is just before the seven years of God's Great Tribulation coming on the earth. These seven years are the remaining seven years of God's 490 years of the Hebrew's punishment. **(Dan.9)**

The verses in **1ˢᵗ Thes.4** explain God's grace to spare the believers unjust pain. We are in Jesus, then our sins are hidden in Jesus, and we are perfectly sinless. Therefore, we meet God's requirement for perfection to be with him in eternity.

1 Thessalonians 4:13–17 *"(13) But <u>I would not have you to be ignorant</u>, brethren, concerning them which are asleep, that ye sorrow not, even as others which have no hope. (14) For if we believe that Jesus died and rose again, even <u>so them also which sleep in Jesus will God bring with him.</u> (15) For this we say unto you by the word of the Lord, that we which are alive and remain unto the <u>coming of the Lord shall not prevent them which are asleep.</u> (16) For the Lord himself shall descend from heaven with a shout, with the voice of the archangel, and with the trump of God: <u>and the dead in Christ shall rise first: (17) Then we which are alive</u> and <u>remain shall be caught up together with them in the clouds, to meet the Lord in the air: and so shall we ever be with the Lord."</u> (KJV)*

In Strong's Concordance, the meaning for Caught is:

*"**Har-pad-zo**; from a der. of 138; to seize (in various applications):- catch (away, up), pluck, pull, take (by force)[2]."*

This Rapture will include both the dead and living souls who have accepted Jesus by faith and performed the deeds for Christ. The acts such as found in **Mat.5, 6, 7,** and **Mat.28:18–20** are to name a few scriptures. Those individuals (Christians) are perfect in God's eyes due to Jesus paying the price for all their sins. We also are in Jesus, and Jesus did not sin; therefore, we do not deserve God's wrath.

But there are those saved in the Church, but those individuals will go through the Great Tribulations as they do not have this treasure; for lack of deeds. They are saved (once saved, always saved) but will have to go through the Great Tribulations to gain Treasures and do the most challenging of deeds. Those believing Pew Sitters that have died without deeds before the Rapture will be in Heaven with Jesus (saved by faith); but will be without some or all of God's treasures.

This Rapture is where both the alive and dead Church Saints will go to where Jesus is located; this is revealed as the 1st Resurrection in **Rev.20:4–5**. Here God tells both the Church Saints and Tribulation Saints will reign with Christ for 1,000 years (Jesus Kingdom). But notice **Rev.20:5,** says the *rest of the dead live not again until after the 1,000 years.* But I would like to share comforting verses of scripture for those not Raptured (Tribulation Saints) found in **Rev. 14**.

> **Revelation 14:12–13** *"(12) <u>Here is the patience of the saints:</u> here* are *<u>they that keep</u> the <u>commandments of God, and the faith of Jesus</u> (13) And I heard a voice from heaven saying unto me, Write, Blessed* are *the dead which die in the Lord from henceforth: Yea, saith the Spirit, that they may rest from their labours; <u>and their works do follow them</u>". (KJV)*

> **Romans 8:18** *"For I reckon that the sufferings of this present time* are *not worthy to be compared with the glory which shall be revealed in us." (KJV)*

During this time of tribulations, all the Jews and some Gentiles will be converted to Jesus. It is by their faith in Jesus that God's grace saves both the Jews and some Gentiles. However, some of these Tribulations Saints (Pew Sitters) are there as they missed the Rapture treasure, but they will be harvested with these Jews and Gentiles in the *1st Harvest*, assuming they do not fall away. The Jews have required proof, and they will get proof by fulfilled prophecies, miracles, and signs. They will face death (beheadings **Rev.20:4)** daily, and those who are killed, their souls will be placed under the Alter in God's Temple in Heaven.

> **Revelation 6:9–11** *"(9) And when he had opened the fifth seal, I saw <u>under the altar</u> the souls of them that were <u>slain for the word of God,</u> and for the <u>testimony</u> which they held: (10) And they cried with a loud voice, saying, How long, O Lord, holy and true, dost thou not judge and avenge our blood on them that dwell on the*

*earth? (11) **And white robes** were given unto every one of them; and it was said unto them, that they should rest yet for a little season, **until their fellow servants also** and **their brethren,** that should be killed as they** were, **should be fulfilled". (KJV)*

This event is God assuring those dead under the Alter that they have only a short time, and they too will be blessed by their deeds which will follow them. Here, again, we see the testimony they (*Tribulation Saints*) held during the Great Tribulation before Satan killed them. They are given white robes, which represent the righteousness of the Saints **(Rev.19:8)**. *The white robes place these souls in the Tribulation Saints' time and separate them from the dead individuals outside the Church period. These Tribulation Saints will be taken to be with Jesus, his Queen, and Old Testament Saints in the 1st Harvest. Remember, the Harvests are dead, but the Rapture is of both the living and dead.*

HARVESTS MYSTERIES (See ATTACHMENT C)

The word Harvest in Greek is:

*2326"**ther-id-zo**; from 2330 (in the sense of the crop); to harvest: - reap[2]."*

To the Hebrew nation, the harvest is a time to collect their fruit and sell it to pay off any debts. Also, just as with crops today, the harvest is not an instant collection but takes time and care not to miss any or damage the fruit. But, the Rapture is a relatively quick collection of his Bride.

When I was a boy helping my Grandfather harvest cotton on his farm, it took us (with several people) almost a week to pick all the cotton and take it to the cotton gin. But for wine, the time to collect all the grapes, squash the juice out, filter out the solid waste, collect the juice into wineskins, then start on the next batch. In the end, properly stack skins and allow the grape juice fermentation into wine; it takes a long time.

I see in these harvest three parables. One is the *Rapture*, the separation of the Sheep and Goats parable in **Mat.25:31–46,** where the Bride (sheep) is Raptured and separated from the Goats (Tribulation Saints and Pew Sitters).

The second parable is the Prodigal Son **(Luk.15:11–32).** There, the son wants and receives his inheritance and leaves the Father. But after many sins, hunger, and disparity, the son wants to return to his father as a hired servant. This parable fits the Tribulation Saints and Pew Sitters. They want to go back to the Father. And they will succeed in the *1st Harvest.*

The third parable is the Wheat separated from the Tares **(Mat.13–30/36–43).** There is where an enemy of the owner has spread Tares in the owner's field. The worker asks if the owner wants them to pull up the Tares, but the answer is no, wait until the harvest. And then separate the Wheat from the Tares. And throw the Tares into a fire.

THE RAPTURE

The Rapture is the separation of the Sheep from the Goats. Both animals are acceptable for the annual Day of Atonement. But the sheep are a more desired animal. While it could be considered a harvest but it is different. The Rapture is quicker than a harvest as the righteous dead Saints go first to Jesus, followed by the living Saints. But the harvest is only of the deceased.

THE FIRST HARVEST

The *1st Harvest* is the timely collection of those left behind and those converted to Jesus by the Two Witnesses (1st half) and 144,000 Hebrew Missionaries during the Great Tribulation. And, most likely, this death harvest will increase during the *last half* of the seven years. *Here the converted Hebrews and Pew Sitters will be killed for not wearing the Mark of the Beast and not worshipping Satan.* They will be harvested to Jesus just before or during Jesus' *3 Return* to earth. They will be included in War #1 of Armageddon along with the Old Testament Saints. This harvest is of the righteous dead (Jew and Gentile) converted in the Great Tribulation period.

Revelation 14:13–16 First Harvest

Revelation 14:13–16 *"(14) I looked, and behold a white cloud, and upon the* <u>cloud</u> *one sat like unto the Son of man, having on his head a golden crown, and in his hand a sharp sickle. (15) And another angel came out of the temple, crying with a loud voice to him that sat on the cloud, Thrust in thy sickle, and reap: for the* <u>*time is come for thee to reap;*</u> *for the harvest of the earth is ripe. (16) And he that sat on the cloud thrust in his sickle on the earth; and the earth was reaped.*

First, I would like you to realize this is not the Rapture where the sheep (dead and alive) and Goats (Dead and live) are separated. But these two harvests are of the dead only. Notice in this next verse of scripture the relationship between the approved sacrifices. There were two, Sheep and Goats. I see the parable of the Sheep and Goats separation revealed in these verses of scriptures **(Mat.25:31–46).** The goats were also righteous to use in the Day of Atonement's sacrifice to pay for that year's sins. **(Lev.3)**

Leviticus 3:12–13 *"(12) and if his* <u>*offering*</u> *be* <u>*a goat,*</u> *then he* <u>*shall offer it before the LORD.*</u> *(13) And he shall lay his hand upon the head of it, and kill it before the tabernacle of the congregation: and the sons of Aaron shall sprinkle the blood thereof upon the altar round about." (KJV)*

We read here that a goat was an acceptable righteous animal for sacrifice in the Temple. But, the preferred sacrifice was sheep. For me, this points to two acceptable individuals into the future. One is those *in Jesus' (Sheep) and doing deeds,* and the others, *are in Jesus (goats) doing little or no deeds.* The Pew Sitters (goats) are saved by faith but are without treasures (Rapture). This Rapture is the dead and alive Sheep (Christians). The separation is the live Goats from the Raptured sheep. The dead Goats (Pew-Sitters before the Rapture) remain in Paradise with the O.T. Saints until the 1 Harvest. And this separation is also revealed in the parable of the unprofitable servant **Mat.25:23–46.**

But **verse 23** reveals the profitable servant's reward.

Matthew 25:23, *"His lord said unto him. Well done, good and faithful servant; thou hast been faithful over a few things, I will make thee ruler over many things: <u>enter thou into the joy of the lord.</u>"*

To enter into the Joy of the Lord reveals to be with the Lord. This joy is God's joy for the righteous souls He wanted with him in Heaven from the beginning of time. God's plan for man is coming to fruition. But what of those that have disappointed the lord? We read of them in **Mat.25,** too.

Where the alive goats will be left behind **(verse 30)** to go through The Great Tribulation, **w**e find this separation's opposite condition in **verse 30.** Here is revealed the <u>*clue*</u> to the Pew Sitter's location during the Great Tribulation.

Matthew 25:30 *"And cast ye the <u>unprofitable servant</u> into outer darkness: where there shall be <u>weeping and gnashing of teeth.</u>"*

It appears the unprofitable servant is the Pew Sitters. They declared Jesus as their Lord and Savior but have not produced any souls for the Holy Spirit to attempt to save. These individuals were given one talent but failed to use it for Jesus. They also have not done any good deeds for humanity either. *But, they will be given a second chance in the Great Tribulation.* The <u>*clue*</u> here is the words **"weeping and gnashing of teeth."** These words reveal the Great Tribulation, as the Lake of Fire will be well beyond a weeping and gnashing of teeth. Then God's word shows the condition and punishment for the unprofitable **(Verse 30)** and those who have also done nothing for Jesus. Also, **verse 31** reveals the coming of Jesus. His coming is after the profit period, which is the 2nd Coming of Jesus. And His coming is after the Great Tribulation.

Note

Please note the different situations mentioned between these two events. The first was for-profit, and the second is for deeds for humanity. Profit is the increase of saved souls for Jesus' Kingdom, where the love and care for Jesus' Kingdom are deeds for humanity.

The results of those of verses.

Matthew 25:45–46 *"(45) Then shall I answer him, saying, Verily I say upon you. Inasmuch as ye did it not to one of the least of these, ye did it not for me. (46) And these shall go away into everlasting punishment: but the righteous into life eternal."*

LAST CHANCE

Revelation 14:12–14 *"(12) here is the <u>patience of the saints;</u> here* are *they that <u>keep the commandments of God, and the</u>* faith *of <u>Jesus.</u> (13) And I heard a voice from heaven saying unto me, Write, Blessed* are *<u>the dead which die in</u> the Lord from henceforth: Yea, saith the Spirit, that they may <u>rest from their labours; and their works do follow them. (KJV)</u>*

Notice the *<u>clue</u>* that the Holy Spirit is in Heaven *("voice from heaven"* and *"saith the spirit")*. Therefore, the Holy Spirit is in Heaven, and this happened during the Rapture. First, we see in **verse 12** to whom the following words pertain. It is to the <u>Saints that are obedient in *faith and labors*</u>. This is justified by *"keep the commandments of God."* These Saints have patiently been waiting for Jesus' 3rd Return, but **verse 12** reveals the requirement for both Church and Tribulation Saints.

Before Jesus' return, some events must occur first. One is the Rapture, and another is removing the Tribulation Saints from under the Alter (*1st Harvest*). In **verse 13,** notice the clues: *1) "die in the Lord (saved),"* 2) *"they may <u>rest from their labours,</u>* and 3) *"<u>their works do follow them."</u>* These are the

Tribulation Saints and Pew Sitters as many will die during The Great Tribulation, and they are to be blessed from henceforth.

Henceforth starts after the Rapture and most intensely after the midpoint (Woe, Woe, Woe) of the Great Tribulation. The Two Witnesses of **Rev.11** are murdered. At the halfway point. But they have laid the foundation for the 144,000 Hebrew missionaries **(Rev.7)** during the last half. Just as Jesus had 3½ years to convert the Gentiles, the 144,000 will also have three years to convert the Hebrews. This *1st Harvest* will run to the completion of The Great Tribulation. ***This is the last chance for salvation of the Hebrews, Pew Sitters, and converts.***

But, we see Jesus rejecting the unfaithful in **Mat.25:41** due to their lack of righteous acts (deeds). Some pew sitters will fall away. God is now preparing to completely separate the Goats (now sheep) from all evil persons. **(Mat.25:31–46)**

This separating is also revealed in **Joel 3**. See also **verses 1–8**.

Joel 3:9–21 *"(9) Proclaim ye this among the Gentiles; <u>Prepare war, wake up the mighty men, let all the</u> <u>men of war</u> *draw near; let them come up: (10) Beat your plowshares into swords, and your pruning hooks into spears: let the weak say, I* am *strong. (11) Assemble yourselves, and <u>come, all ye heathen, and gather yourselves together</u> round about: thither cause <u>thy mighty ones to come down, O LORD. (12) Let the heathen be wakened, and come up to the valley of Jehoshaphat: for there will I sit to judge all the heathen round about. (13) Put ye in the sickle, for the harvest is ripe:</u> come, get you down; for <u>the press is full, the fats overflow; for their wickedness</u> is <u>great. (14) Multitudes, multitudes in the valley of decision:</u> for the day of the LORD is near in the valley of decision. (15) The sun and the moon shall be darkened, and the stars shall withdraw their shining. (16) The LORD also shall <u>roar out of Zion, and utter <u>his voice from Jerusalem;</u> and the heavens and the earth* *shall shake: but the LORD will be the hope of his people, and the strength of the children of Israel. (17) So shall ye know that I am the LORD your <u>God dwelling in Zion</u>, my holy mountain: then shall Jerusalem be holy, and <u>there shall no strangers pass through her any more</u>. (18) And it shall come to pass in that day, that the mountains shall drop down new wine, and the hills shall flow with milk, and all the rivers of Judah shall flow with waters, and a <u>fountain shall come forth of the house of the LORD, and shall water the valley of Shittim</u>. (19) Egypt shall be a desolation, and Edom shall be a desolate wilderness, for the violence against the children of Judah because they have shed innocent blood in their land. (20) <u>But Judah shall dwell for ever, and Jerusalem from generation to generation. (21) For I will cleanse their blood that I have not cleansed: for the LORD dwelleth in Zion</u>.*

Please notice **verse 13** wording is almost the same wording at the end of **Rev.14:18**

These verses of scripture reveal the War #1[C] of Armageddon, and it will be the *end of the 1st Harvest* and the beginning of the *2nd Harvest.* Notice the <u>clue</u> the Lord roars out of Zion and Jerusalem. This is the location of *Jesus' 3rd Return.* War #1 is the start of the 2nd Harvest of lost souls that will be *"cast into the great winepress of God."* This *2nd Harvest* will end after War #2C when God sends down fire to destroy Satan, after his release from the Abyss, and Just before the Great White Throne Judgment. This action is revealed as the parable of the separation of the *Wheat from the Tares **Mat.13:24–30.***

Matthew 13:28–30 *"(28) He said unto them, An enemy hath done this. The servants said unto him, Wilt thou then that we go and gather them up? (29) But he said, Nay; lest while ye gather up the tares, ye root up also the wheat with them. (30) Let both grow together <u>until the harvest</u>: and in the <u>time of</u> [2nd] <u>harvest</u> I will*

say to the reapers, Gather ye together <u>first the tares, and bind them</u> <u>in bundles to burn them</u>: but gather the wheat into my barn." **(KJV)**

I have shortened to the last three verses as this is where *clues* are for your evaluation. Notice the *1st clue* is in **verse 25;** the *men* slept but also in **verse 27,** these same men are called *servants.* Apparently, these servants did not watch to protect the wheat from the evil weed sower in the night. These servants represent the Tribulation Saints and Pew Sitters who are not performing this task of being watchful (lazy). The *2nd clue* is the lesson of not being intimately watchful as small weeds came up with the wheat, eventually choking out some wheat grain production. Here is a *clue* about Jesus' 1,000-year Kingdom.

People in the Kingdom feel so secure; they become complacent. The survivors (of War #1) will have children with the sinful nature from Adam. And for whatever reason, they will reject Jesus as their savior.

"If good men do nothing, evil will grow."

Then the servant wanted to know should they pull out the weeds. The *3rd clue* is the owner (Jesus) of the field said, no, let them grow together. This is the time of Jesus' 1,000-year Kingdom. Sin will still be present in the Armageddon saviors and their children's children. These words appear to be revealing sin will still be present during Jesus' 1,000 Kingdom. Those evil ones who die will go to Torment (Hell), and all in Torment (Hell) will be harvested to the Great White Thorne Judgment.

This *2nd Harvest* will be much more punishing in the tares' harvest (War#2). They will go to the Great White Throne Judgment and end in the Lake of Fire.

Note

We have looked into these Harvest, but here I am relating the Harvests to other parables. Please be patient with some repeats.

Revelation 14:13–16 First Harvest

Revelation 14:13–16 *(14) I looked, and behold a white cloud, and upon the* <u>cloud</u> *one sat like unto the Son of man, having on his head a golden crown, and in his hand a sharp sickle. (15) And another angel came out of the temple, crying with a loud voice to him that sat on the cloud, Thrust in thy sickle, and reap: for the* <u>*time is come for thee to reap;*</u> *for the harvest of the earth is ripe. (16) And he that sat on the cloud thrust in his sickle on the earth; and the earth was reaped.*

First, I would like you to realize this is not the Rapture where the sheep (dead and alive) and Goats (Dead and live) are separated. But these two harvests are of the dead only. Notice in this next verse of scripture the relationship between the approved sacrifices. There were two, Sheep and Goats. I see the parable of the Sheep and Goats separation revealed in these verses of scriptures **(Mat.25:31–46).** The goats were also righteous to use in the Day of Atonement's sacrifice to pay for that year's sins. **(Lev.3)**

Leviticus 3:12–13 *"(12) and if his* <u>*offering*</u> be <u>*a goat,*</u> *then he* <u>*shall offer it before the LORD.*</u> *(13) And he shall lay his hand upon the head of it, and kill it before the tabernacle of the congregation: and the sons of Aaron shall sprinkle the blood thereof upon the altar round about." (KJV)*

We read here that a goat was an acceptable righteous animal for sacrifice in the Temple. But, the preferred sacrifice was sheep. For me, this points to two acceptable individuals into the future. One is those *in Jesus' (Sheep) and doing deeds,* and the others, *are in Jesus (goats) doing little or no deeds.* The Pew Sitters (goats) are saved by faith but are without treasures (Rapture). This Rapture is the dead and alive Sheep (Christians). The separation is the live Goats from the Raptured sheep. The Goats (Pew-Sitters before the Rapture) remain in Paradise with the O.T. Saints until the 1 Harvest. And the separation revealed in the parable of **Mat.25:23–46.** The Sheep will go in the Rapture **(verse 23).**

> **Matthew 25:23, *"His lord said unto him. Well done, good and faithful servant; thou hast been faithful over a few things, I will make thee ruler over many things: <u>enter thou into the joy of the lord.</u>"***

To enter into the Joy of the Lord reveals to be with the Lord. This joy is God's joy for the righteous souls He wanted with him in Heaven from the beginning of time. God's plan for man is coming to fruition. But what of those that have disappointed the lord? We read of them in Mat.25, too.

Where the alive goats will be left behind **(verse 30)** to go through The Great Tribulation, **w**e find this separation's opposite condition in **verse 30.** Here is revealed the *clue* to the Pew Sitter's location during the Great Tribulation.

> **Matthew 25:30 *"And cast ye the <u>unprofitable servant</u> into outer darkness: where there shall be <u>weeping and gnashing of teeth.</u>"***

It appears the unprofitable servant is the Pew Sitters. They declared Jesus as their Lord and Savior but have not produced any souls for the Holy Spirit to attempt to save. These individuals were given one talent, failed to use it for Jesus. They also have not done any good deeds for humanity either. But, they will be given a second chance in the Great Tribulation. The *clue* here is the words **"weeping and gnashing of teeth."** These words reveal the Great Tribulation, as the Lake of Fire will be well beyond a weeping and gnashing of teeth. Then God's word shows the condition and punishment for the unprofitable **(Verse 30)** and those who have also done nothing for Jesus. Also,

verse 31 reveals the coming of Jesus. His coming is after the profit period, which is the 2^(nd) Coming of Jesus. And His coming is after the Great Tribulation.

Note

Please note the different situations mentioned between these two events. The first was for-profit, and the second is for deeds for humanity. Profit is the increase of saved souls for Jesus' Kingdom, where the love and care for Jesus' Kingdom are deeds for humanity.

The results of those of verses.

Matthew 25:45–46 *"(45) Then shall I answer him, saying. Verily I say upon you. Inasmuch as ye did it not to one of the least of these, ye did it not for me. (46) And these shall go away into everlasting punishment: but the righteous into life eternal."*

1^(ST) HARVEST END

Revelation 14:14–16 *"(14) And I looked, and behold a <u>white cloud,</u> and upon the <u>cloud</u> one <u>sat like unto the Son of man,</u> having on his head a golden crown, and in his hand a sharp sickle. (15) And another angel came out of the temple, crying with a loud voice to him that sat on the cloud, Thrust in thy sickle, and reap: for the time is come for thee to <u>reap; for the harvest of the earth is ripe.</u> (16) And he that sat on the cloud thrust in his sickle on the earth; and the earth was reaped."* **(KJV)**

We can read in **Mat. 26:64** *"Jesus saith unto him, Thou hast said: nevertheless I say unto you, <u>Hereafter shall ye see the Son of man sitting on the right hand of power, and coming in the clouds of heaven." (KJV)</u>*

This event is the *1st Harvest of the Tribulation Saints, the Hebrew Saints, Old Testament Saints, Gentile converts, and the Pew Sitter Saints.* This is the completion of the parable of the separation of the Sheep and the Goats **(Mat. 25).** The beginning of this separation is at the Church's Rapture (sheep), separated from the Tribulation Saints (goats). This *1st Harvest* is of the redeemed dead goats and will take seven years to accomplish. So we see the Rapture is the separation of the Sheep and the Goats, but the *1st Harvest is the future collection of the dead Goat (who have become Wheat).*

Leviticus 3:12 "***And if his offering*** be ***a goat, then he shall offer it before the LORD.*** " ***(KJV)***

Yes, but there is a subtle difference. The Goats primarily represent Israel, who, at present, do not have faith in Jesus but are God's elect. However, they will be converted to Jesus during The Great Tribulation. Also included is the believing but lazy Pew Sitters. These are saved by faith but did not store up treasures in heaven. Plus, some Gentile converts will be converted due to the 144,000 protected Hebrew missionaries during the seven years of The Great Tribulation. These individuals missed the Rapture but will be in the *1st Harvest* (also 1st Resurrection) as they have mended their relations with God through Jesus. Remember, anyone that believes in Jesus is in Jesus.

This *1st Harvest* reveals to be included in the 1st Resurrection **(Rev.20:4--6),** and it pertains to those who have faith in Jesus and resurrected <u>*in Jesus*</u>. These sheep are the first fruits of the Church. The 1st New Testament converts were resurrected with Jesus and seen by many people in Jerusalem **(Mat.27:51–53).** The Old Testament Saints are those saved by God's Grace by their deeds and attitudes of their heart. They are those like Noah, Moses, and Abraham, to name a few. Also, the Tribulation Saints will be added to God's elect and called Wheat.

This *1st Harvest* is not the Rapture, which is for the sheep. The *1st Harvest* is the collection of all the dead Tribulation Saints (goats). The Christian Pew Sitters saved by FAITH, but without works, they will miss the Rapture. With future righteous deeds, they will be harvested in the 1st Harvest, but those without future righteous deeds will be in the *2nd Harvest.* This Rapture treasure will also elude the converted Jews too. The individuals who are not Raptured still have to face the tribulation with their faith God will still save them by Faith and Deeds. Here **Rev.20:4–6** reveals their conduct until completion of the *1st Harvest* of **Rev. 14.**

TRIBULATION ---- LAST CHANCE !!!

Revelation 14:12–14 *"(12) here is the <u>patience of the saints: here</u> are <u>they that</u> <u>keep the commandments of God, and the</u> faith <u>of Jesus.</u> (13) And I heard a voice from heaven saying unto me, Write, <u>Blessed</u> are <u>the dead which die in the Lord from henceforth: Yea, saith the Spirit,</u> that they may <u>rest from their labours; and their works do follow them. (KJV)*

Notice the <u>clue</u> that the Holy Spirit is in Heaven *("voice from heaven"* and *"saith the spirit"*). Therefore, the Holy Spirit is in Heaven, and this happened during the Rapture. First, we see in **verse 12** to whom the following words pertain. It is to the <u>Saints that are obedient in</u> *faith and labors*. This is justified by *"keep the commandments of God."* These Saints have patiently been waiting for Jesus' 3rd Return, but **verse 12** reveals the requirement for both Church and Tribulation Saints.

Before Jesus' return, some events must occur first. One is the Rapture, and another is removing the Tribulation Saints from under the Alter *(1st Harvest)*. In **verse 13,** notice the clues: *1) "die in the Lord* (saved)," 2) *"they may <u>rest</u> from their labours,* and 3) *"their **works** do follow them."* These are the Tribulation Saints and Pew Sitters as many will die during The Great Tribulation, and they are to be blessed from henceforth.

Henceforth starts after the Rapture and most intensely after the midpoint (Woe, Woe, Woe) of the Great Tribulation. The two witnesses of **Rev.7**, who will have laid the foundation for the 144,000 Hebrew missionaries during the last half, are murdered. Just as Jesus had 3½ years to convert the Gentiles, the 144,000 will also have 3½ years to convert the Hebrews. This *1st Harvest* will run to the completion of The Great Tribulation. This duration is for the salvation of the Hebrews, Pew Sitters, and converts. But, we see Jesus rejecting the unfaithful in **Mat.25:41** due to their lack of righteous acts (deeds). Some pew sitters will fall away. God is now preparing to completely separate the Goats (now sheep) from all evil persons. **(Mat.25:31–46)**

This separating is also revealed in **Joel 3.** See also **verses 1–8.**

Joel 3:9–21 *"(9) Proclaim ye this among the Gentiles; <u>Prepare war,</u> wake up the mighty men, let all the* <u>men of war</u> *draw near; let them come up: (10) Beat your plowshares into swords, and your pruning hooks into spears: let the weak say, I* am *strong. (11) Assemble yourselves, and <u>come, all ye heathen, and gather yourselves together</u> round about: thither cause <u>thy mighty ones to come down, O LORD. (12) Let the heathen be wakened, and come up to the valley of Jehoshaphat: for there will I sit to judge all the heathen round about. (13) Put ye in the sickle, for the harvest is ripe:</u> come, get you down; for <u>the press is full, the fats overflow; for their wickedness</u> is <u>great. (14) Multitudes, multitudes in the valley of decision:</u> for the day of the LORD is near in the valley of decision. (15) The sun and the moon shall be darkened, and the stars shall withdraw their shining. (16) The LORD also shall <u>roar out of Zion, and utter his voice from Jerusalem;</u> and the heavens and the earth shall shake: but the LORD* will be *the hope of his people, and the strength of the children of Israel. (17) So shall ye know that I* am *the LORD your <u>God dwelling in Zion,</u> my holy mountain: then shall Jerusalem be holy, and <u>there shall no strangers pass through her any more.</u> (18) And it shall come to pass in that day,* that *the mountains shall drop down new wine, and the hills shall flow with milk, and all the rivers of Judah shall flow with waters, and a <u>fountain shall come forth of</u> the house <u>of the LORD,</u>*

and shall water the valley of Shittim. (19) Egypt shall be a desolation, and Edom shall be a desolate wilderness, for the violence against the children of Judah because they have shed innocent blood in their land. (20) But Judah shall dwell for ever, and Jerusalem from generation to generation. (21) For I will cleanse their blood that I have not cleansed: for the LORD dwelleth in Zion.

Please notice **verse 13** wording is almost the same wording at the end of **Rev.14:18**

These verses of scripture reveal the War #1[C] of Armageddon, and it will be the *end of the 1st Harvest* and the beginning of the *2nd Harvest.* Notice the *clue* the Lord roars out of Zion and Jerusalem. This is the location of *Jesus' 3rd Return.* War #1 is the start of the 2nd Harvest of lost souls that will be *"cast into the great winepress of God."* This *2nd Harvest* will end after War #2C when God sends down fire to destroy Satan, after his release from the Abyss, and Just before the Great White Throne Judgment. This action is revealed as the parable of the separation of the *Wheat from the Tares* **Mat.13:24–30.**

SECOND HARVEST

Matthew 13:28–30 "(28) *He said unto them, An enemy hath done this. The servants said unto him, Wilt thou then that we go and gather them up? (29) But he said, Nay; lest while ye gather up the tares, ye root up also the wheat with them. (30) Let both grow together until the harvest: and in the time of* [2nd] *harvest I will say to the reapers, Gather ye together first the tares, and bind them in bundles to burn them: but gather the wheat into my barn."* *(KJV)*

I have shortened to the last three verses as this is where *clues* are for your evaluation. Notice the *1st clue* is in **verse 25;** the *men* slept but also in **verse 27,** these same men are called *servants.* Apparently, these servants did not watch to protect the wheat from the evil weed sower in the night. These servants represent the Pew Sitters who are not performing this DEED of being watchful (lazy). The *2nd clue* is the lesson of not being intimately watchful as small weeds came up with the wheat, eventually choking out some wheat grain production. Here is a *clue* about Jesus' 1,000-year Kingdom.

People in the Kingdom feel so secure; they become complacent. The survivors (of War #1) will still have their sinful nature. And they have children with the sinful nature from Adam. And for whatever reason, they will reject Jesus as their King. Disobedience follows.

"If good men do nothing, evil will grow."

Then the servant wanted to know should they pull out the weeds. The *3rd clue* is the owner (Jesus) of the field said, no, let them grow together. This is the time of Jesus' 1,000-year Kingdom. Sin will still be present in the Armageddon saviors and their children's children. These words reveal sin will still be present during Jesus' 1,000 Kingdom. Those evil ones who die will go to Torment (Hell), and all in Torment (Hell) will be harvested to the Great White Thorne Judgment.

This *2nd Harvest* will be much more punishing in the tares' harvest (War#2). They will go to the Great White Throne Judgment and end in the Lake of Fire.

THE UNKNOWN FRUIT MYSTERY

This mystery is of good fruit (or good grapes or wheat) being harvested; therefore, the *1st Harvest* is of the Tribulation Saints. While some, not all, of the Tribulation Saints have been killed and placed under the Alter **(Rev. 6).** Those alive Tribulation Saints will go into Jesus' 1,000-year Kingdom as mortals.

Revelation 6:9–11 *"(9) And when he had opened the fifth seal, I saw <u>under the altar the souls of them that were slain for the word</u>*

of God, and for the testimony which they held: (10) And they cried with a loud voice, saying, How long, O Lord, holy and true, dost thou not judge and avenge our blood __on them that dwell on the earth?__ (11) And white robes were given unto every one of them; and it was said unto them, that __they should rest yet for a little season, until their fellow servants also and their brethren, that should be killed as they__ were, should be fulfilled".(KJV)

The time of these verses of scriptures is during The Great Tribulation, the Wrath of God. These Tribulation Saints (Hebrew converts and deed-full Pew Sitters) must wait until near the end of the seven years when the last of God's chosen Tribulation Saints are beheaded, as were they. **(Rev. 20:4)**

This other angel is most likely the Holy Ghost crying, *"Thrust in your sickle and reap"* and *"the harvest of the earth is ripe."* But notice there is no mention of what kind of crop is to be harvested. But since the *2nd Harvest* is grapes, we naturally assume this Harvest is of grapes also. However, let us look at another scripture in **Genesis 1:31,** where God said that everything that he had made was very good. So there is no good or evil mentioned. But the 2nd Harvest is of rotten fruit, we can safely assume, but the 1st Harvest is the opposite, good. Fruit   Very little is said here to prove this *1st Harvest* is of the Tribulation Saints. The exception is found in **Rev. 20:4–6;** particular **verse 6** calls them blessed and Holy. This silence of this fruit is interesting in its self. Therefore, God has created another mystery.

Interestingly, God does not reveal the fruit that is to be in this *1st Harvest*. There is no mention if it is good or bad fruit or what type of fruit it is. It may be made up of different fruit: Old Testament Saints, Tribulation Saints, Pew Sitters, and aliens. We also know that this angel will know a good tree by its fruit because a bad tree cannot produce good fruit **(Mat. 7).**

Matthew 7:16–20 "(16) __Ye shall know them by their fruits.__ Do men gather grapes of thorns, or figs of thistles? (17) Even so __every good tree bringeth forth good fruit__; but a corrupt tree bringeth forth evil

*fruit. (18) **A good tree cannot bring forth evil fruit,** neither can a corrupt tree bring forth good fruit. (19) Every tree that bringeth not forth good fruit is hewn down, and cast into the fire. (20) Wherefore by their fruits ye shall know them." (KJV)*

These dead Saints (good fruit) are taken to meet *Jesus and his Bride* (not the wedding) with the angels to return to earth to destroy all evil (War #1 of Armageddon). Any living Tribulation Saints that remain on the earth; will see and possibly humanly participate in War #1 of Armageddon.

Boy, does Jesus know how to throw a Honeymoon or what?

In **Rev. 20,** we read the results of Armageddon; for those beheaded Tribulation Saints under the Alter.

Revelation 20:4–6 *"(4) And I saw thrones, and they sat upon them, and judgment was given unto them: and* I saw *the souls of **them that were beheaded for the witness of Jesus, and for the word of God, and which had not worshipped the beast, neither his image, neither had received his mark upon their foreheads, or in their hands; and they lived and reigned with Christ a thousand years.** (5) But the rest of the dead lived not again until the thousand years were finished. **This** is **the first resurrection. (6)** Blessed and holy* is *he that hath part in the first resurrection: on such the second death hath no power, but they shall be priests of God and of Christ, and shall reign with him a thousand years." (KJV)*

These verses from **Rev.20:4–6** identify these events are in the 1st Resurrection as was Jesus. Here God is pointing out that all who maintain faithfulness in Jesus will be included in God's elect. The eternal righteous ones are now complete. Because our faith in Jesus will place us in Jesus, and the Jews will have faith in Jesus due to the 144,000 Hebrew missionaries during The Great Tribulation period. Plus, these Hebrews will spread the gospel to the Hebrew people. And the left behind Pew Sitters has seen the need to performed righteous acts, which they have done with enthusiasm.

Another <u>clue</u> is *"**which had not worshipped the beast, neither his image, neither had received his mark upon their foreheads, or in their hands;**"* This proves these individuals did not fall away during The Great Tribulation. And the next words, *"and they lived and reigned with Christ a thousand years."* also confirm they are the Tribulation Saints who will rule with Christ during the 1,000 Kingdom. Therefore this *clue, 1,000-year Kingdom,* proves the timing for the end of the First Harvest and the 1st Resurrection completion. But what of the Old Testament Saints?

They, too, deserve to be with God and Jesus as they have found grace and mercies from God. They were saved by their deeds in trying to do good and obeyed the Law. But the Church (New Testament Saints) are protected by faith in Jesus, and Jesus said to them, *"Where I am, there you will be also."* Jesus 1st went to Paradise in the heart of the earth and then into Paradise in Heaven. During his 1st Resurrection, the dead in Christ (early Church) was also included in Jesus' Resurrection. But we read in **Rev.14** that the *1st Harvest* is for the Tribulation Saints, and they, too, are resurrected. This event comes just before War #1 of Armageddon, and the Old Testament scriptures **(Mal. 4)** reveal that Old Testament Saints will also be included on Jesus' side.

Malachi 4:1–3 *"**(1)** For, behold, the day cometh, that shall burn as an oven; and all the proud, yea, and all that do wickedly, shall be stubble: and the day that cometh shall burn them up, saith the LORD of hosts, that it shall leave them neither root nor branch. **(2)** But unto <u>you that fear my name</u> shall the <u>Sun of righteousness arise with healing in his wings,</u> and ye shall go forth, and grow up as calves of the stall. **(3)** <u>And ye shall tread down the wicked; for they shall be ashes under the soles of your feet in the day that I shall do this,</u> saith the LORD of hosts." (KJV)*

These verses of scripture appear to pertain to the final destruction (War #2) of Satan and his army after the 1,000-year Kingdom of Jesus. The *clue* in **verse 3**,*"ye shall tread down the wicked,"* makes it clear this is War #1 as in War#2 God consumes all wicked with fire, and there will be nothing left to bury.

Verse 3 creates some confusion. The words *"will be ashes under your feet" appears to speak of War #2 as "God destroys evil with fire"* from heaven. Here there is no mention of help from any source, just God by himself. Also, in **Mal.4:4–6,** we see time moving to Jesus' 1,000-year Kingdom.

Also, in **Mal.4:4–5, we** read of a future for these verses:

Malachi 4:4–5 *"Remember ye the Law of Moses, I will send you Elijah the prophet before the coming of the great and dreadful day of the Lord: I come and smite the earth with a curse. Behold, I will send you Elijah the prophet before the coming of the great and dreadful day of the LORD.*

Another *clue* is *"the Law of Moses."* The Law will be enforced during Jesus' Kingdom after Armageddon. We know this because of what Jesus said in **Mat. 5.**

Matthew 5:18 *"For verily I say unto you, Till heaven and earth pass, one jot or one tittle shall in no wise pass from the law, till all be fulfilled." (KJV)*

The next *clue* is found in **2 Kings 2:15,** as Elisha is not Elijah, as Elijah and Enoch have yet to die. Some individuals see John the Baptists as Elijah due to Jesus' statement in **Mat.11:14.** But this is Elias and not Elijah. So the two witnesses in **Rev. 11:4–12** are Elijah and Enoch during the 1st half of the Great Tribulation.

Also, these verses were written to the Old Testament Saints *("you that fear my name").* Remember, the Old Testament Hebrew people feared God's name so much, they would skip a letter of his name when they wrote JEHOVAH; it would be (JHVH). The *"smite the earth with a curse";* is The Great Tribulation. But the first three verses show the results of this curse. Therefore, the Old Testament Saints must be in War #1 of Armageddon. (See **Isa.65**) Notice in **verse 3,** *"ye shall tread down the wicked."* This verse stipulates that we shall be involved in the destruction of the wicked. This verse is completely different from **Rev.20:9,** where God quickly destroys both paroled Satan and his final army; with no apparent help.

Armageddon will start at the end of The Great Tribulation of seven years. The dead Tribulation Saints will be under the Altar, and Old Testament Saints will be in Paradise in the center of the earth until the end of the 7th year. Still, those fallen away from Jesus will be included in the *2nd Harvest,* which starts after Armageddon and ends at War#2.

In **(Isa.65)** is scripture pointing to the time of Jesus' Kingdom. The survivors of The Great Tribulation and their children's children will still have inherited earthly sin from Adam in their bodies. So sins will continue until the 1,000 years is complete. These living Tribulation Saints will be required to do the deeds of God's law or Satan's law during the tribulation's seven years.

I hope you can see the <u>good fruit</u> pointed out here in the 1st Harvest words. The 2nd Harvest <u>is not</u> of good fruit!

2nd HARVEST (Wheat from the Tares)

Revelation 14:17–19 "(17) and another angel came out of the temple which is in heaven, he also having a sharp sickle. (18) And another angel came out <u>from the altar, which had power over fire;</u> and cried with a loud cry to him that had the sharp sickle, saying, Thrust in thy sharp sickle, <u>and gather the clusters of the vine</u> of the earth; for her grapes are fully ripe. (19) And the angel thrust in his sickle into the earth, and gathered the vine of the earth, and <u>cast</u> it <u>into the great winepress of the wrath of God. (20) And the</u>

winepress was trodden without the city, and blood came out of the winepress, even unto the horse bridles, by the space of a thousand and six hundred furlongs. (KJV)

I see a resemblance here with the parable of the Tares in **Mat. 13.** It appears both the Church Saints (Sheep) and Tribulation Saints are the Goats (acceptable for sacrifice). Still, as the goats repent and do the necessary deeds (refusing to worship Satan), they become righteous as the *Wheat* and the lost souls as the *Tares,* respectively. The Rapture separated the sheep (Faith and Deeds) from the Goats (Faith only). But during The Great Tribulation and both Jews and Pew Sitter (both with faith) must now do deeds to become righteous. Doing this, it will make them righteous (the Wheat). Those that fall away and worship Satan are the unrighteous (Tares).

Matthew 13:24–30 *"(24) Another parable put he forth unto them, saying, <u>The kingdom of heaven is likened</u> unto a man which sowed good seed in his field (25) But while men slept, his enemy came and sowed tares unto among the wheat, and went his way. (26) But when the blade was sprung up, and brought forth fruit, then appeared the tares also. (27) So the servants of the householder came and said him, Sir, didst not thou sow good seed in thy field? from whence then hath it tares? (28) He said unto them, <u>An enemy hath done this.</u> The servants said unto him, Wilt thou then that we go and gather them up? (29) But he said, Nay; lest while ye gather up the tares, ye root up also the wheat with them. (30) <u>Let both grow together until the harvest:</u> and in the time of harvest I will say to the reapers, <u>Gather ye together first the tares, and bind them in bundles to burn them: but gather the wheat into my barn.</u>" (KJV)*

This parable appears to pertain to the entire time of God's plan for the earth. Therefore, it has to pertain to the time of The Great Tribulation, too. Obviously, the enemy is Satan, and his demons have been spreading the evil seeds from

Eve to the present. The wheat seed sown; represent the seeds of righteousness sown by the Apostles and Saints. The weed seeds are unrighteous and have been sown on earth since Adam's failure. These weeds will be allowed to grow by God until the end of the 1,000-year Kingdom of Jesus. Therefore, the *2nd Harvest* starts after War #1 of Armageddon and ends at War #2 with God **(Rev.20:7–20)**. War #2 will occur at the end of Jesus' 1,000-year Kingdom. Very little is said about God's War as it is final and quick **(Rev.20:7–10);** and ushers in The Great White Thorne Judgment for all lost souls (**Rev.20:11–15**) and the creation of the New Earth and New Universe **(Rev. 21).**

Here the scriptures speak of the end of the *1st* Harvest (First *Resurrection*), and the *2nd Harvest* is at the end of the 1,000-year Kingdom of Jesus. The proof is that **"they lived and reigned with Christ a thousand years,"** and these are the: Church Saints, Tribulation Saints, Old Testament Saints, Pew Sitters Saints, Hebrew, and Gentile converted Saints. Sin will continue during the 1,000-year Kingdom **(Isa.65:20),** and sinners will be punished by War #2 with God **(Rev.20:8--10)**; and the Great White Throne final Judgment begins.

This *2nd Harvest* collects dead sinners during Jesus' Earthly Kingdom and War#2.

Note

I recommend you read **Joel 2 and 3** before continuing. Joel includes more information on the *2nd Harvest* than that found in **Rev. 14.**

Revelation 14:19–20 "*(19) and the angel thrust in his <u>sickle into the earth,</u> and gathered the <u>vine of the earth,</u> <u>and cast</u> it <u>into the great winepress of the wrath of God.</u> (20) And the winepress was trodden without the city, <u>and blood came out of the winepress, even unto the horse bridles, by the space of a thousand</u> and <u>six hundred furlongs</u>". (KJV)*

I have underlined *"<u>the great winepress of the wrath of God</u>"* to reveal the *2nd Harvest* is beginning at the start of Jesus' 1,000-year Kingdom. See **Isaiah 2** for a lengthy look at the beginning of the 1,000-year Kingdom. But **Isaiah 2:4** and the same message as in **Joel 2, 3** and **Micah 4**.

These grapes *("vine of the earth")* are the humans (dust) who believe in the False Religion of the Beast of the Earth **(Rev 13:11–17)**. The results are the evil deeds of the Satanic Religion's converts *("vine of the earth")*. Included in this vine; are the pew sitters who have fallen away **(Mat.25:31–46)** from Jesus and have worshiped Satan. It also tells us in **Rev.14:20** of the carnage of this *2nd Harvest carnage*: blood up to 4 to 5 feet deep (horse's bridle) and 180 miles long (1600 furlongs).

This event is spoken of in **Revelation 19,** where several events will occur after the Rapture but before War #1 of Armageddon.
1. Marriage of the Lamb (Jesus) to the Bride (Church).
2. The judgment of the Whore's fornications (worship of Satan).
3. The 24 Elders (Church), the four beasts (4 Gospels), and a great multitude of loud voices (Bride, angels, O.T. Saints and Tribulation Saints) worshiping God and Jesus.
4. Blessed are those that are called to Jesus' wedding.
5. Heaven is opened, and Jesus on a white horse judges and makes war (Armageddon) against all evil.
6. The army that follows Jesus is clothed in white linen (<u>righteous acts [deeds]</u> of the saints).
7. The Beast and Kings of the earth war against Jesus but lose.
8. The Antichrist and the False Prophet are cast into the Lake of Fire.
9. And the evil remnant (all evil persons "Tares"); are slain and cast into Torment.
10. And Satan is chained up in the Abyss for 1,000 years.

This second angel coming from the Temple in Heaven; is the Death Angel of **Exo. 12.** This Death Angel killed the entire first borne of Egypt but spared the Hebrews that put the lamb's blood around their door.

This death is to harvest the *"grapes of the wrath"* (humans), and we have dealt with the grape subject previously. However, notice here is revealed the same type of fruit, grapes but not good grapes but sour grapes. And grapes were used in the parable parallel lesson about what happens to a branch that does not produce fruit. Fruit represents humans that have produced deeds that are performed for good or evil. So these verses appear to talk about unrighteous acts (evil deeds). But **Rev. 14:19–20** clarifies that these grapes are the end product of the False Religion spread by Satan and especially his False Prophet. This evil vine's produce is the *2nd Harvest* of **Rev. 14**.

In **Rev.13:11–17,** you will read of the False Prophet (out of the earth), who brings forth, onto the earth, a very large false religion, which appears to be like Islam. In **2 Tim.3,** you can read the conditions of these religious leaders.

> **2 Tim. 3:1–5 *"(1) This know also, that <u>in the last days perilous times shall come.</u> (2) For men shall be lovers of their own selves, covetous, boasters, proud, blasphemers, disobedient to parents, unthankful, unholy, (3) Without natural affection, trucebreakers, false accusers, incontinent, fierce, despisers of those that are good, (4) Traitors, heady, highminded, lovers of pleasures more than lovers of God; (5) <u>Having a form of godliness, but denying the power thereof: from such</u> turn <u>away.</u> " (KJV)***

This religion will initially require worship of a false god, but later on of Satan himself. These unrighteous grapes are fully ripe, well beyond sweet. These are evil humans who deserve the *"winepress of the wrath of God"* **(Rev.14:19–20).** These grapes collected are put into a wine press to press out the juice and leave the skin behind. The juice is the evil spirit, and the skin is the human body. This reveals the survival of the evil spirit, which will be internally in— the 1st death caused by War #1 of Armageddon. In **verse 20**, you will read of the amount of blood that comes from this winepress of wrath.

This wine is bad fruit (evil spirits) of the False Prophet; the coming <u>False Satanic Worship World Religion</u>. And many humans will fall away from Jesus and join Satan. In **2 Thess.2:3–4,** we read of this falling away. But remember that the Antichrist must be revealed first. Keep In mind **verse 5,** *"Having a form of godliness, but denying the power thereof: from such turn away."* Islam leaders and teachers do not believe in Jesus being the son of God. Nor do they believe Jehovah is God. They believe only Allah is god. They do not believe in the power of Jesus or Jehovah. Allah's Quran teaches the destruction of Israel and infidels (unbelievers in Allah). So Christians are told to turn away from this religion. Jehovah has made many covenants with the Hebrew people, and Jehovah is a covenant-keeping God. Therefore, why would Jehovah break his covenant with Israel and tell Islam to destroy Israel?

God said I will bless those who bless Israel and curse those who curse Israel.

Remember **Mat.12:30,** *"He that is not with me is against me; and he that gathereth not with me scattereth abroad. (KJV)*

Allah is not the Christian's God!

ADDITIONAL INFORMATION

Many Islamic missionaries have successfully converted some Americans into the Islamic religion with many false concepts. Hopefully, these are the uninformed individuals and not weak ½ christians. This deception is foreseen in **2 Thes. 2.**

2 Thess. 2:1–4 "*(1) Now we beseech you, brethren, by the coming of our Lord Jesus Christ, and by our gathering together unto him, (2) That ye be not soon shaken in mind, or be troubled, neither by spirit, nor by word, nor by letter as from us, as that the day of Christ is at hand. (3) Let no man deceive you by any means: for that day shall not come, **except there come a falling away first, and that man of sin be revealed, the son of perdition; (4) Who opposeth and exalteth himself above all that is called God, or that is worshipped;***

so that <u>he as God sitteth in the temple of God</u>, shewing himself <u>that he is God</u>". (KJV)

Do you see the *three clues* for us to be looking for to reveal *Jesus' 2nd Return*? And they are 1) a falling away, from God and Jesus, weak ½ christians, 2) The man of sin (Antichrist) must be revealed, 3) Satan statue erected in the rebuilt Temple. *This revealing cannot happen to those who are **not** looking for the Antichrist.* Remember, Jesus will come like a thief in the night! This is the Rapture. His *3rd Return* will be: in total light, Jesus' massive army in white and multitudes making noise. This is not like a thief in the night!

This deceiving man is initially Antichrist #1, and perdition is his father (Satan). This Antichrist #1 will be the leader of the government (the Beast) and will become very powerful worldwide, in short order. In the first 3½ years, there will be two witnesses (Elijah and Enoch) in Jerusalem, and they will speak against Antichrist #1. But at the end of the first 3½ years, they will be killed by the beast from the bottomless pit **(Rev.11:7–12)**. Antichrist #1 and False Prophet will control most of the earth. And Satan will eventually place himself in the Antichrist #1 body **(Rev.13:3–14 / dragon)** and have a speaking statue of himself placed in the <u>rebuilt Jewish Temple of God</u>. These events will occur at the start of the last 3½ years of the seven years of the Great Tribulation. This statue is the *"Abomination of Desolation"* spoken of in **Mat 24:15** and **Dan.9:27**; that will be placed in God's rebuilt Temple in Jerusalem. And the world will be required, by Satan (Antichrist #2) and the False Prophet, to worship Satan or be killed. Here is where some pew sitters will fall away. This statue abomination is the trigger for God's anger and wrath on all evil. Satan being worship in God's Temple is the ultimate insult to God **(Exo. 20:3–5)**. It ends in War #1 of Armageddon; at Jesus *3rd Return* to earth. But, just before War #1 of Armageddon; comes the *1st Harvest.*

After Armageddon, where these lost souls who are killed will join all the lost dead of history; in a place called Torment (Hell). No righteous soul will be in this start of the final *2nd Harvest.* This *2nd Harvest* is the collection of lost souls of 2 wars; 1) Armageddon and 2) when God destroys Satan's and all his army; after the 1,000 Kingdom **(Rev.20:7–14)**. This *2nd Harvest* will include those evil souls who have died before and during the 1,000-year Kingdom. This harvest is the completion of the *2nd Harvest* of all lost souls (tares) from Jesus' Kingdom. This War #2 is the completed separation of the Wheat from the Tares **(Mat.13:24–38)**, collected for the Great White Throne Judgment.

Here we see the separation of the wheat from the tares. Jesus' Kingdom is the good seed (wheat) being separated from these lost souls (tares) of all times, and the tares will be pulled up and burned. They will be judged at God's Great White Throne Judgment **(Rev.20:7–15)**. And all these lost souls will be cast into the Lake of Fire, along with Antichrist #2, False Prophet, demons, fallen pew sitters, fallen angels, and Satan. But, the righteous Church Saints and Tribulation Saints will have ruled, with Christ, during His 1,000-year Kingdom.

> **Rev. 20:4–5 *"(4) And I saw thrones, and they sat upon them, and judgment was given unto them: and* I saw *the souls of <u>them that were beheaded</u> for the witness of Jesus, and for the word of God, and which had not worshipped the beast, neither his image, neither had received* his *mark upon their foreheads, or in their hands; and <u>they lived and reigned with Christ a thousand years.</u> (5) But the <u>rest of the dead lived not again</u> until the thousand years were finished. This* is *the <u>first resurrection"</u>. (KJV)***

These verses of scripture are clear proof that all individuals in Christ Jesus are in the *1st Resurrection,* including the *1st Harvest.*

DEEDS ARE REQUIRED MYSTERY!

I would like to start with verses of scripture that you can test your attitude towards deeds. And it is found in the book of tests, **1 John 2**.

1 John 2:3–6 *"(3) And hereby we do know that <u>we know him, if we keep his commandments.</u> (4) He that saith, I know him, and keepeth not his commandments, <u>is a liar</u>, and the truth is not in him. (5) But whoso keepeth his word, in him verily is the love of God perfected: <u>hereby know we that we are in him.</u> (6) He that saith he abideth in him ought himself also so to walk, even as he walked." (KJV)*

Deeds have always been required in the Old Testament and the New Testament. Here is a simple list of deeds for man during different times.

1. Pre-flood / Pre-Law --- Do not eat from the Tree of Knowledge and do good. The tree of knowledge established good.
2. Law Period--- Keep the Laws and do Good in the Law.
3. Church Period --- Be obedient to Jesus' commands and do good.
4. The Great Tribulation Period --- Do not take the Mark of the Beast and do good (convert Israel).
5. Jesus Kingdom Period --- keep faith in the King, be obedient to the King's Law, and do sound judgments.

I hope you can see that works/deeds have always been required because of the tree of knowledge to do good. Doing good is covertly required due to knowledge given to man from the Tree of Knowledge.

Remember, if you know to do good and do not do the good, it is the Sin of Omission.

As you study the Bible, I hope you become aware of the verses of scriptures that show both *Faith* and *Works* will be used in Judgement of all souls, saved and lost. The Book of James is an excellent book to read about Faith and Works. Matthew's chapters 5, 6, and 7 are excellent starting points for learning the Good to do.

JESUS DID GOOD ON EARTH FOR OUR EXAMPLE.

Even during Jesus' time on this earth, he was required to perform deeds. Jesus performed many miracles during his visitation to earth. He brought a new covenant to the world in his gospel, which would remove most religious leaders' powers. It appeared to be opposed to the Torah; for the less studious individual. His final deed Jesus performed on earth was his crucifixion. It must have been a very painful task to control himself during his excruciating pain. Jesus could have called angels of large numbers to destroy the Roman soldiers and evil priests, but he did not. He endured that crucifixion for you, me, and them. Otherwise, we would still be dead in our sins. Now we read in **Luk.22**, Jesus wished not to go through the pain and embarrassment; but Jesus was willing to do his father's will.

> **Luke.22:41–43** "(41) *And he was withdrawn from them about a stone's cast, and kneeled down, and prayed, (42) Saying, <u>Father, if thou be willing, remove this cup from me: nevertheless not my will, but thine, be done.</u> (43) And there appeared an angel unto him from heaven, strengthening him*". *(KJV)*

So we see it is not that critical (but desirable) that you desire not to do something for God; but that you do what God wills you to do (obedient). <u>*What is important is that your heart wants to do God's will.*</u> And Jesus' heart wanted to do God's will even if it meant an undesirable, painful death. Our brothers and sisters that must go through the Great Tribulation period must have this strength because they too will be put to the ultimate test of receiving or not, the Mark of the Beast. To receive the Mark is eternal life in The Lake of Fire. For a person to not receive the Mark of the Beast means carnal death on earth, but eternal life with Jesus and God. But remember, we all are spiritually immortal, and *you choose* where you desire to live spiritually; Heaven or the Lake of Fire.

Satan will require evil deeds to be performed by all humans. One *such evil act is the worship of Satan through his talking statue erected in the rebuilt Jewish Temple of God.* <u>Therefore, the Tribulation Saints will have to perform</u>

righteous deeds <u>of not worshiping Satan.</u> But also remember, the Great ~~Commission~~ Command is still required during the Great Tribulation.

Notice in **verse 43,** an angel is strengthening Jesus. Believe God will do the same for his people approaching death. We have very little information about the events in death, except body functions. But, will God reduce the pain we think is associated with man's death? I have often wondered why God has revealed two deaths. One is death (mortal), and the other one is Death (spiritual). We know that people have experienced painful times before death, but there may be the release of that pain at death itself. God loves his children and understands the events in death. And for me, as we want for our children, the absents of pain and so does our Father. And a Christian transition will be from pain to no pain.

However, for those who know not Jesus or God, their transition from life to Death is from pain to more intensive pain.

Now comes the question; *when is this transition point?*

Jesus' miracles and deeds confused the religious leaders of his day. They were still hung up on the importance of doing the Law's deeds *and especially the "Traditions of the Elders"* as explained by the Priests and Rabbis. The lesson of the Faith of Abram had eluded most of them. Jesus, for the most part, could not break down the wall of lethargy. We see this in our Churches even today *"Well, we have always done it this way."* New ideas must be a challenge for some people. Change can be uncomfortable for people. I find myself uncomfortable with a new Smart Phone system. But the Bible is very deep with information, and no person knows all that is in the Bible. New or more in-depth information will come to light, and we must give serious study to get to the truth. And many times, it changes our understanding of scripture. There have been times I am reading the Bible, and I say, *"who put that in there"* or *"Oh, that's what that means."*

The Holy Spirit is working and smiles!

Jesus brought new information about the meaning of scriptures, but leaders saw it as blasphemy, but mostly a challenge to their authority. Jesus did the deed of preaching to the people, and it is in this deed that Jesus saved many people during his ministry. But not only to the mass of people but also to his apostles. He spent time (deeds) teaching them so they too could eventually go to their own ministry and perform deeds of healing and expulsion (exorcism) of demons. The apostles did the deeds of letter writing, which we now call scriptures. They all (except John) went to their hideous death preaching the gospel. The apostle Peter was the rock by whom the early Church is founded.

The Church is all true believers in Jesus and not a particular denomination. This is the Church Jesus started. Jesus brought the new doctrine of saved by FAITH alone. What a different concept for the Hebrew people and leaders, who were locked in the Law and traditions. The average person was so entrenched in traditions, as were the leaders, they could not see the deeper truths in the Law. This blindness is still holding true in Israel and the Jews of today. Some of the common folk saw the truth Jesus preached and believed in Jesus. Without Jesus preaching and sacrifice, no one will have been saved. Jesus completed his deeds on earth for our benefit and left us the Great ~~Commission~~ Command **(Mat 28:18–20)** to finish his work. Jesus also left us this verse of scripture, too. And it is unmistakably clear.

> **Mat. 12:30** ***"He that is not with me is against me; and he that gathereth not with me scattereth abroad." (KJV)***

So we clearly see that Christians are REQUIRED to do the deeds of the Great ~~Commission~~ Command and not just the pastors. Also, in **Matthew 5, 6,** and **7,** we see the deeds of the Beatitudes. The Church has done the Great Command by supporting foreign missionaries. But why are the individual Church members not spreading the gospel here in America? Are they gathering or scattering? Are they missionaries to their kids, parents, friends, and neighbors? It is clear many are not, as Christianity is suffering more today than never before in modern times. God is being removed from America. No public prayers. No mention of Jesus in schools or workplaces. Courthouses of judgment based on man's Laws must remove the 10 Commandments from the building. Crosses being taken down, removing Jesus' sacrifice from view.

Christians are being exterminated in Africa; and other Islamic countries without a cry from America, except for a few. Our government leaders have gone to the highest bidder, from bribers of special interest groups. Our government leaders are making laws they themselves are not required to follow. Congress is making for themselves: special health programs, free lunch program, free trips, and several specials freebies for our government leaders at the ordinary taxpayer's expense. The Knowledge of Evil has prevailed over Good just as it was in Noah's day. We have all most removed God from America. And God will leave us to our own evil unless Christians get active in preaching the Gospel of Jesus. But I fear we have started down that slippery slope of no return. We read of these evil persons in **2 Tim.3.**

> **2 Tim.3:1–7** *"(1) This know also, that in the last days perilous times shall come. (2) For men shall be lovers of their own selves, covetous, boasters, proud, blasphemers, disobedient to parents, unthankful, unholy, (3) Without natural affection, trucebreakers, false accusers, incontinent, fierce, despisers of those that are good, (4) Traitors, heady, highminded, lovers of pleasures more than lovers of God; (5) <u>Having a form of godliness, but denying the power thereof</u>: from such turn away. (6) For of this sort are they which creep into houses, and lead captive silly women laden with sins, led away with divers lusts, (7) <u>Ever learning, and never able to come</u> to the knowledge of the truth". (KJV)*

Can you see all the evil deeds these supposedly righteous persons are doing? *"Ever learning and never able to come to the knowledge of truth."* This tells us they come from Church and Sunday school but cannot or will not grasp the truth for their life. Today, we see this in our Church with Catholic Priest sexually abusing young boys and the Diocese protecting that Priest. They appear to believe in Jesus but do as they will in secret places. They appear to care not for the children abused.

This statement also could be pertaining to the Hebrew race as they have been blinded by God. **(John 12:39–40)** But, these unfaithful will be destroyed by Jesus on his *3rd Return* to earth. We read of this event in **2 Thess.1**

> **2 Thessalonians 1:6–10** *"(6)Seeing* it is *a righteous thing with God to recompense tribulation to them that trouble you; (7) And to you who are troubled rest with us, when the Lord Jesus shall be revealed from heaven with his mighty angels, (8) In flaming fire taking vengeance on them that know not God, and <u>that obey not the gospel of our Lord Jesus Christ: (9) Who shall be punished with everlasting destruction from the presence of the Lord, and from the glory of his power;</u> (10) When he shall come to be glorified in his saints, and to be admired in all them that believe (because our testimony among you was believed) in that day".* *(KJV)*

Other scriptures supporting Jesus' destruction of all evil persons are found in **Rev. 19**. This Army that returns with Jesus is all the saved souls from Adam to 1st Harvest, believing souls. This doctrine is further mentioned in **Mal. 4.**

> **Malachi 4:1-4** *"(1) For, behold, the day cometh, that shall burn as an oven; and all the proud, yea, and <u>all that do wickedly, shall be stubble:</u> and the day that cometh shall burn them up, saith the* LORD of **hosts**, *<u>that it shall leave them neither root nor branch. (2) But unto you to that fear my name shall the Sun of righteousness arise</u> with healing in his wings; and ye shall go forth, and grow up as calves of the stall. (3<u>) And ye shall tread down the wicked; for they shall be ashes under the soles of your feet in</u> the day that I shall do* this, *saith the* LORD of **hosts**. *(4) <u>Remember ye the law of Moses my servant,</u> which I commanded*

unto him in Horeb for all Israel, with *the statutes and judgments".* *(KJV)*

Do you remember in **Gen. 2:1, "all the host,"** the army waiting for battle? Here we read of the event the *host*s have been waiting for, Armageddon.

Verse 4 makes a statement, *"Remember ye the Law of Moses, my servant,"* which we have not seriously considered in our past. This statement tells us that the Laws given to Moses will again be in effect in Jesus' 1,000-year Kingdom. Also, notice included in this verse of scripture, **Mal.4:4**, is the additional statement, **"with** *the statutes and judgments."* This statement makes it clear that sin will continue through Jesus' 1,000-year Kingdom. And the Judgments for those sins committed will be in accordance with the Law given to Moses, as the Law demands. The Bible verifies that evil will be present because Satan will be released from the Abyss after 1,000 years to gather an army to destroy Jesus **Rev.20:7–10.** But, God destroys Satan and his evil army forever. The proof God's Law will continue can be found in **Mat. 5:18.**

Matthew. 5:18 "For verily I say unto you, <u>Till heaven and earth pass,</u> one jot or one tittle shall in no wise pass from the law, till all be fulfilled."

"Till heaven and earth pass" refers to **Rev.21**, when the New Heaven and New Earth are created and eternity begins. Remember, Jesus died to fulfill the law to pay for all sins committed by all men to the end of the earth **(Rev.21).** During eternity we will have the mind of Christ, and therefore, it appears obedience will be effortless, normal, and desirable.

Remember, *"Jesus will rule with an iron rod."*

THE GRAPEVINE MYSTERY

In **John 15,** Jesus gives his disciples the parable of the grapevine. This parable is Jesus' attempt to teach his disciples of an inner parallel truth that would deepen their knowledge of God's provision; and rewards for applying his provisions for the benefit of man. Jesus uses a known agricultural truth to reveal a parallel spiritual truth.

John 15:1–6 "(1) <u>I am the true vine, and my Father is the husbandman.</u> (2) <u>Every branch in me</u> that <u>beareth not fruit</u> he <u>taketh away:</u> and every branch *that beareth fruit, he purgeth it, that it may bring forth more fruit. (3) <u>Now ye are clean</u> through the word which I have spoken unto you. (4) Abide in me, and I in you. As the branch cannot* <u>bear fruit</u> *of itself, except it abide in the vine; no more can ye, <u>except ye abide in me.</u> (5) I am the vine, ye* are *the branches: <u>He that abideth in me,</u> and I in him, the same bringeth forth much fruit: for without me ye can do nothing. (6) <u>If a man abide not in me,</u> he is cast forth as a branch, and is withered; and men gather them, and cast* them *into the fire, and they are burned". (KJV)*

First, let us look at the grapevine today and what we know about the growing and harvesting of grapes. Remember, there are three types of branches: 1) is the dying or sick branch, 2) a non-producing grape branch, and 3) a fruit-producing branch.

- ❖ The trunk or main vertical vine has roots and collects the nutrients and water to feed all the vines.
  - • This is the supply of God through Jesus and the Holy Spirit of knowledge for us to grow and mature in spiritual matters.
- ❖ Normally the trunk is grown vertical to the most upper vine's desired height to the horizontal support wire.
  - • Here is Jesus supplying this knowledge to all those who have faith in Jesus and are in Jesus. This supply is given through the Holy Spirit. It is to help us grow in knowledge, understanding, and wisdom.
- ❖ There at the top, the vines are trained into two branches traveling opposite each other. So they will spread horizontally on the support wires, and they appear as a **"T."**

- Here we see the vines' separation in opposite directions as we are to take this knowledge to the entire world (Hebrews and Gentiles).
- Through the Holy Spirit's power, we are to make disciples of all individuals with the knowledge of Jesus' mission on earth. The Gospel!

❖ God prunes these branches towards the light of the sun for better production of the fruit vines.

- This pruning represents Jesus testing, teaching, and corrections for us.

❖ These larger vines now produce the smaller vines, which in turn produce the grapes. They are in the end of the supply line of the nutrients for these grapes.

- The larger vine is Jesus and the Holy Spirit, which save and directs new Christian in their daily walk.

❖ These smaller vines can be producers of grapes or not. During the vines' growth, those that appear to be dying are pruned off. This pruning helps the trunk vine eliminate any possible disease and the robbing nutrients from the main vine.

- This event is our self-will to act for Jesus or not. Those rejecting Jesus are sick and dying; those working for Jesus will produce fruit (souls) for Jesus
- At the early stage of the grape buds, the budding branches are pruned back to a new bud to help the new branch grow more into the sun and produce more grapes.
- As we grow in Jesus, we will be pruned to remove ignorance and be given more knowledge to grow into wisdom. (Chastisements)

❖ The non-budding branch is pruned back to the main vine and cast away.

- We cannot produce good fruit without the Holy Spirit. If the person is not in Jesus, he or she cannot or will not tell the world about Jesus. And at some point, will be cast into The Lake of Fire.

- The Bible says some will plant, some water, some harvest, but the Holy Spirit saves.

❖ After the grapes are harvested, all branches are pruned as necessary for next year's crop. But all the pruned-off items are thrown into a fire to be burned up; including the wine grape skins, some seeds, and small twigs holding those grapes together.

- This fire represents Judgments. And saved and/or lost souls will both be judged.
- One is the Judgment Seat of Christ for Christians.
- The second is the Great White Throne Judgment of all the lost souls, demons, and Satan.

The apostle John records a parable of Jesus, and it needs some clarification. In **John 15:1–6,** Jesus uses the grape as the parable's principal object, as most individuals at that time had knowledge of grapevines and how to care for them for maximum production for wines. Therefore, the apostles could gather a deeper spiritual meaning of scripture. One such scripture is in **Mat. 7.**

> **Matthew 7:17–20** "*(17) Even so <u>every good tree bringeth forth good fruit; but a corrupt tree bringeth forth evil fruit.</u> (18) A good tree cannot bring forth evil fruit, neither* can *a corrupt tree bring forth good fruit. (19) Every tree that <u>bringeth not forth good fruit is hewn down, and <u>cast into the fire.</u> (20) Wherefore by their fruits ye shall know them*". *(KJV)*

These verses are a covert but not a difficult parable to understand. If you know how Christians are to act. The fruit results from the Christian's work of moving the nutrients from the ground (God and Jesus) to produce fruit (souls). What they are to do for people, how they are to treat people, how to Love, and other visual aids from God that people are to use to evaluate Christians. Then you can see the fruits they produce by their efforts and the effects they make on others. But also know that *if no good fruits are produced*, these people are cast into the fire. Fire in the Bible can mean judgment. Judgment comes after death. **(Heb. 9:27)**

> **Hebrews 9:27** *and as it is appointed unto men once to die, but after this the judgment:" (KJV)*

Now with these two concepts, let us look at the grapevine verses in **Joh.15.**

> **John 15:1-6** "(1) *I am the true vine and my Father is the husbandman. (2) Every branch in me that beareth not fruit he taketh away: and every* branch *that beareth fruit, he purgeth it, that it may bring forth more fruit. (3) Now ye are clean through the word which I have spoken unto you. (4) Abide in me, and I in you. As the branch cannot bear fruit of itself, except it abide in the vine; no more can ye, except ye abide in me. (5) I am the vine, ye are the branches: He that abideth in me, and I in him, the same bringeth forth much fruit: for without me ye can do nothing. (6) If a man abide not in me, he is cast forth as a branch, and is withered; and men gather them, and cast them into the fire, and they are burned".* (KJV)*

Verse 1, Jesus starts by revealing he is the trunk of the vine, and God is the director of operations for the roots. And Jesus is doing the works (deeds) of God. And it is Jesus who provides the necessary nutrients for our physical and spiritual success.

Verse 2, Jesus explains that every branch in him that does not produce fruit is taken away. Now notice the statement *"in him,"* which are those individuals that have accepted Jesus as their savior; and are to produce fruit (deeds). Those that do nothing (no deeds) are not producing good fruit. Notice these branches are *taken away*, pruned off the vine from which they received nutrients. These are the pew sitters in Christ, and some will eventually repent and do the deeds. And they will be in the *1st Harvest*. They who perform no deeds will be eventually be thrown into the fire (judgment of God). Those burned are the pew setters of **verse 6,** as those are the fallen away (lost) not remaining in Jesus. Their final judgment will be affected by their lack of deeds during the Great Tribulation and wearing the Mark of the Beast. They are going to the Lake of Fire.

Verse 3 Jesus explains we are cleaned of all our sins by his words of salvation and our faith in Jesus. One of these works (deeds) is the Great Commission in Mathew 28:18—20, But we cannot perform works unless we remain Jesus, the vine trunk. If we are not abiding in Jesus, we will become numb to the Holy Spirit's leading and be spiritually detached from Jesus. And the slacker will be saved but will receive no treasures.

Verse 4 is so specific. If we remain in Christ, we must: pray, study God's word, tell about Jesus to the lost, aid the sick, care for the homeless, teach your children of Jesus, fellowship with brothers in Christ, be charitable to your enemy, do not think better of yourself than others, and more **(Beatitudes Mat.5,6 and 7).** These are how we remain in Jesus. And if we do not stay in Jesus, we can do nothing for Jesus' kingdom.

Verse 5 tells us that you and I are the branches which are to bring forth the fruit. But to do the work correctly, we must remain in Christ and follow the scriptures. And it is Jesus' nutrients (sustenance that will help us produce good fruit (followers).

Verse 6 now appears a fearful statement from Jesus. This verse speaks to the lost or weak. And it says **IF**. This **if** is a conditional word (If you do or if you don't), and there is no gray area here. Jesus was speaking to those that *DON'T* abide in Christ. Now notice the word *ABIDE*. This word infers that they were once in Jesus, but they chose to be passive to Jesus' leading, or fall back, into a sinful or sedentary life.

Also, there are those I call the transition christians, who have accepted Jesus to please someone else: a spouse, a potential spouse, a friend, a recent tragedy, an immediate fear, hurtful experience, or any event that creates a selfish desire for relief and not a sincere repentant attitude. These are the dying branches. They have received the nutrients from the roots (God) but did not accept them or became diseased (sin), and they will be pruned off the vine *(2nd Harvest)* and cast into the fire and **are burned.** Fire is judgment, and burned is eternal punishment.

This last statement needs to be looked into. Fire in the Bible can refer to judgment. We know everyone will be cast into the fire of judgment. To the saved children of God and Jesus, we will meet at the *Judgment Seat of Christ* **(Rom.14:10–12 and 2 Cor.5:10)** to answer for every word and deed we have ever performed or neglected to do. It will be embarrassing but not fearful. And we will not be burned in the Lake of Fire.

But for the Pew Sitters, who repent and do the deeds during the Great Tribulation, they will be removed *(1st Harvest)* from the vine but will not be burned, meaning not going to the Lake of Fire (See **Rom. 4).** However, the pew setters that fall away will be judged at the Great White Thorne of God.

> **Roman 4:5** *"But to him that worketh not, but believeth on him that justifieth the ungodly, his faith is counted for righteousness." (KJV)*

So we see salvation is by faith alone, but those that do not perform the deeds will miss the treasures they could have had, such as the Rapture.

> **Matthew 6:19–21** *"(19) Lay not up for yourselves treasures upon earth, where moth and rust doth corrupt, and where thieves break through and steal:(20) But lay up for yourselves treasures in heaven, where neither moth nor rust doth corrupt, and where thieves do not break through nor steal:(21) For where your treasure is, there will your heart be also:" (KJV)*

These pew setters will miss the Rapture treasure and go through the Great Tribulation (7 years), but they will be saved. They will go through terrible trials and will perform painful righteous deeds. *One deed is not receiving the Mark of the Beast.* Not receiving this mark means that you reject Satan, and painful punishment will occur by Satan or even death on earth. These are the Jews and some Gentile Tribulation Saints who are beheaded and are under the Temple Alter in **Rev. 6:9–11**

> **Rev. 6:9–11 "(9) *And when he had opened the fifth seal, I saw under the altar the souls of them that were slain for the word of God, and for the testimony which they held (10) And they cried with a loud voice, saying, How long, O Lord, holy and true, dost thou not judge and avenge our blood on them that dwell on the earth? (11) And white robes* (the righteousness of the Saints) *were given unto every one of them; and it was said unto them, that they should rest yet for a little season, until their fellowservant also and their brethren, that should be killed as they* were (beheaded), *should be fulfilled.***

Notice those that abide in Christ are given white robes and to wait for their brothers who will be killed (beheaded) as they. This statement proves that both Harvests will occur over a period of time and not a one-time event. All those souls that have rejected God, Jesus, and the Holy Spirit, their Judgment is at God's Great White Throne **(Rev. 20:11–15).** And the terror and sadness will be such a powerful stench. As they now know their sins and their future eternal home (The Lake of Fire) and boss (Satan). And this represents the dying branch of the vine and not the nonproducing vine.

Eventually, all branches will be pruned for the next year's crop and burned (judgments by Christ's or God's). All lost will be burned in the Lake of Fire for eternity. But there is additional information about the grapevine in **Rev.14:14–19.** Go back to the Harvest section if you need more information for the Harvests.

WAR TO END ALL WARS MYSTERY

In the Bible, this war is called *"the Day of the Lord."* And this *occurs after Jesus' 1,000-year Kingdom*. But, no evil person will enter into this 1,000 Kingdom (**1 Cor.15).** But sin will continue after Armageddon and in Jesus' Kingdom.

**1 Cor.15:53–54 "*(53) For this corruptible must put on incorruption, and this mortal* must *put on immortality. (54) So when this corruptible shall have put on incorruption, and this mortal shall have put on immortality, then shall be brought to pass the saying that is written, Death is swallowed up in victory".(KJV)*

This *"swallowed up"* event will occur to the Bride and all Saints on their removal from earth to Heaven (Rapture and later the *1st Harvest*). Death no longer affects their lives. This is immortality. But those Saints who live through the Great Tribulation must do deeds, and they will still be mortals. The **significant deed they will have to perform is the rejection of the Mark of the Beast and not to worship Satan**. To accept the Mark is an eternity in the Lake of Fire. However, many will take the Mark of the Beast and continue to sin even more.

Sin will still be present during the 1,000-year Kingdom of Jesus; due to the mortals who survive the tribulation on earth. They and their new offspring still have a sinful nature. The living Tribulation Saints will live a normal long life as did our Genesis forefathers who lived hundreds of years. But death will follow them. This death is spoken of in **Isaiah 65:20.** In **Isaiah 65** is a prophecy of Jesus' 1,000-year Kingdom, where the remnants (Tribulation Saints) are saved but will eventually die. This death occurs in Jesus' Kingdom because there will be no Death in Eternity!

**Isaiah 65:20 "*(20) There shall be no more thence an infant of days, nor an old man that hath not filled his days: for the child shall die* *an hundred years old; but the sinner being an hundred years old shall be accursed". (KJV)*

These individuals who are accursed; will be the Army of the paroled Satan; establish to fight Jesus *after* his 1,000-year Kingdom. These are the people that have lived in the 1,000 years of Jesus' perfect Kingdom. Satan has deceived them for the need to destroy Jesus and make Satan King. This event can be found in **Rev. 20.**

Revelation 20:7–10 *"(7) And when the thousand years are expired, Satan shall be loosed out of his prison, (8) And shall go out to deceive the nations which are in the four quarters of the earth, Gog and Magog, to gather them together to battle: the number of whom is as the sand of the sea. (9) And they went up on the breadth of the earth, and compassed the camp of the saints about, and the beloved city: and fire came down from God out of heaven, and devoured them. (10) And the devil that deceived them was cast into the lake of fire and brimstone, where the beast and the false prophet are, and shall be tormented day and night for ever and ever". (KJV)*

It has always been a mystery to me how these people who have lived in a perfect 1,000-year Kingdom could turn against Jesus. How could Satan trick them to fight Jesus? Satan has had a thousand years to plan this event. This plan will bring the *2nd Harvest* to completion. Next comes that period of God's Great White Throne Judgment for all the lost souls from Adam's time to the present time in **Rev.20.**

THE FINAL JUDGMENT

Revelation.20:11–15 (11) And I saw a great white throne, and him that sat on it, from whose face the earth and the heaven fled away; and there was found no place for them. (12) And I (John) *saw the dead, small and great, stand before God; and the books* *were opened: and another book was opened, which is <u>the book of</u> <u>life:</u> and the dead were judged out of those things which were written in the books, <u>according to their works.</u> (13) And the sea gave up the dead which were in it; <u>and death and hell delivered</u> <u>up the dead which were in them:</u> and they were judged every man <u>according to their works.-(14) And death and hell were cast into</u> <u>the lake of fire.</u> This is the second death. (15) And whosoever <u>was</u> not found written in the book of life was cast into the lake of <u>fire</u>". (KJV)*

War #2 occurs after Jesus' 1,000-year <u>earthly Kingdom</u> **(Rev.20:7–10).** Satan has been released from the abyss and has created a massive army to fight Jesus. However, all the things God wants for his children to experience have come to fruition; and the last lesson begins. This lesson is proof that we are infested with sin. And we will die and be cast into the Lake of Fire **unless** *someone pays our debt of sins.* That someone is Jesus, who died to pay for our debt of sins. And even in a perfect environment, Man could not obey the Law.

Even though we are evil, God loved us enough to remove our sins and rewarded us for our attempts to please God. God will also war on our behalf to remove the deceiver and Death. **(Rev. 20:7–15)** The defeat of Death can only occur before the New Heaven and New Earth!

THE PASSOVERS MYSTERIES

When we think of Passover, we think of the time Moses wanted the Pharaoh to let the Hebrew people go back to their land to worship JEHOVAH. **(Exo. 3–14)** This Passover is but one overt Passover, but I see more than one. So, let us consider the possibility of multiple covert Passovers.

The Jewish's definition of Passover is: "6453 **peh'-sakh**; from 6452; *pretermission*, i.e., *exemption;* used only tech. of the Jewish *Passover* (the festival or the victim): Passover (offering)[2]."

MOSES' PASSOVER

Interestingly, several appear to be covert Passovers in the Bible, without actually calling them a Passovers. This Passover was when the Hebrew people were captives in Egypt (symbol of unrighteousness), and God told Moses that he was to go to the Pharaoh to seek their release to worship God outside the city. Moses went to the Pharaoh many times only to be refused, and God punished the Egyptian people; each time the Pharaoh refused, the punishment increased. The last time Moses went to the Pharaoh, the Pharaoh activated his own sentence by threatening to kill all the Hebrew's firstborn. So this was to be the Pharaoh's punishment, too **(Exo.7–Exo. 12).**

This is the time God, through Moses, instituted the Passover incident **(Exo.12)** as given to him by God. It is so special of a celebration that it changed the calendar the Hebrews used to mark time. This will be the first day of the new month of the year. And there are specific tasks that will be accomplished, and they are:

1. On the tenth day of the new month, a perfect male lamb is taken into the house.
2. Keep the lamb in the house until the 14th day.
3. The lamb is to be killed the evening (start) of the 14th day.
4. The lamb's blood is to be placed around the entry door.
5. Roast the animal and eat all of it that night.
6. Unleavened (no yeast) bread and bitter herbs are to be eaten.
7. Anything remaining must be burned up before morning.
8. Place the blood of the lamb around their doorpost and lintel.

During that night, the death angel will go throughout Egypt and kill all the firstborn men and animals who do not have the blood around their entry door. This was the final punishment and a crushing blow for the Pharaoh, as his firstborn son died. So the Pharaoh let Moses' people go.

There are many metaphors revealed in this event. Interestingly, God gave such specific instructions on just how to celebrate or eat a Passover animal. First, to change the date, 1st month, and a new year, this must have a *clue* for us to decipher. It appears this is a tremendously important event *to start afresh* a new calendar monthly dating; and starting a new point for the year too. *This Passover is the release of God's people into freedom from captivity.* Isn't this precisely what Jesus did with his death? Jesus paid our sin debt and freed us from God's Great White Thorne Judgment and the Lake of Fire.

Do we not put Jesus' blood around the door to our hearts? Do we not take Jesus into our home (our Body) during Communion? Did we not kill Jesus with our sins? Do we not eat his flesh and drink his blood at Communion? Was not Jesus' illegal trial performed in the dark (evil) of the night? Did not Jesus rise again after three days and three nights, becoming the bright morning light? Was not Jesus the start of a new day of salvation by Faith? Is it possible God wants the Hebrews to celebrate Jesus' death and resurrection for their and our salvation? Do you see a hidden mystery here?

Keep in mind that this is a new start for the Hebrew people and eventually all people of earth. It seems appropriate for God to give the Hebrews and us a *clue* as to Jesus' salvation. The old covenant will be superseded by their Messiah at Jesus Resurrection (a new day). There are over 300 prophecies in the Old Testament which points to Jesus, which the Priest missed or ignored. Even today, some denominations fail to recognize how important Jesus is to knowledge, understanding, wisdom, and especially Salvation!

Next, you will see a graph revealing the hidden meaning of this Passover process. It represents the 3½ days and 3½ nights Jesus was in the grave.

HEBREW DAY STARTS AT SUNSET, ENDS AT THE NEXT SUNSET.

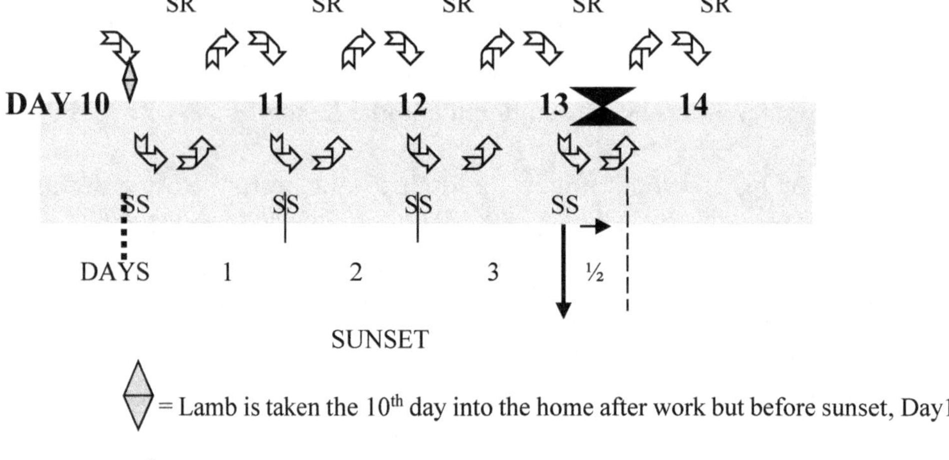

= Lamb is taken the 10th day into the home after work but before sunset, Day11.

13 =   End of the 12th Day / Beginning of 13th Day. (3 **Days**)

= Lamb is killed, cooked, and eaten after sunset on the 13th day, and left-overs burned before sunrise.

This chart assumes the father brings the sheep into the house at the end of the workday—the end of the 10th day. And before the 10th-day sunset. At the beginning (sunset) of the 13th day, the father kills, and the family eats the lamb that evening. And if not entirely consumed, it must be totally burned up before sunrise, the 14th day. Here is the metaphor of taking the lamb into our bodies. This appears to be a celebration of Jesus' future mission and death on earth. The sheep will no longer (in the future) need to be killed in the Temple Sacrifice to atone for sin. As Jesus will become the perfect sacrifice. Also, the darkness represents unrighteousness and points to the time. Jesus' sacrifice will usher in complete righteousness at daylight on Day 14. Remember, Jesus said to the lost that he would come like a thief in the night. But for Christians, Jesus said, be prepared and watch for his return. So it is possible daylight brings Jesus Kingdom of Day 7 creation; where there will be no *"even and morning of the 7th day"*, as his Kingdom will be forever.

Jesus' overt mission was 3½ years in our home, earth. This symbolizes the start of a new covenant with man, which Jesus will bring. Jesus' resurrection will restart the salvation by Faith process for the future; a new month or new period to time. At the end of Jesus' 3½ years, Jesus is to be killed by our forefathers. Jesus will be three days and three nights in the heart of the earth (our home) preaching to the pre-flood (darkness) victims. **(Mat.12:40 and 1 Pet. 3:19–20)**

NOAH'S PASSOVER

The Bible does not call this a Passover; however, it has all the earmarks of a Passover. Noah was informed of the flood that would occur, and God gave Noah 120 years to build the Ark. Moses also told the people to place blood around their doors (heart). Noah was given the instructions of building the Ark, and Moses was instructed what and how to celebrate Passover. Moses was required to perform the deed of collecting, caring, killing, cleaning, butchering, cooking, and eating (taking into their bodies) the lamb. Noah and his step-sons needed to build the Ark.

And the most obvious clues are Moses' Passover of the death angel, while Noah and his family passed over the deadly flood. These two Passovers point to the most significant Passover yet to come. Noah and his sons-in-Law had to do the deed of building a massive wooden vessel, which took them approximately 120 years to build. Without this deed, Noah and his family would have perished

God's wrath for Noah's Passover was for all evil beings on earth and collateral damage to all animals, not on the ark. But with Moses' Passover, it was limited to the firstborn of man and animal of the Egyptians. The Flood is to destroy all living creatures on earth; here is a metaphor for the final War #2. There God is to destroy all evil as did the Flood.

It has been a mystery to me why God's wrath, caused by evil man, was also punished for innocent babies and animals. But we see in each Passover a reduction of animals to be destroyed. The third Passover does not explicitly say animals are to be destroyed but might infer their demise by **Rev. 21:1** and **2 Pet.3:10** and **12.**

2 Peter.3:10. *"But the day of the Lord will come as a thief in the night; in which the heavens shall pass away with a great noise, and the elements shall melt with fervent heat, the earth also <u>and the works that are therein shall be burned up.</u>" (KJV)*

So what is this third and final Passover? Remember, all Passovers are initiated because of God's coming wrath. The greatest wrath yet to be expended on earth is The Great Tribulation that will last for seven years. And if Jesus does not return, no life will survive. This wrath of God has been reserved for the total destruction of earth and all evil.

THE RAPTURE PASSOVER

We find the words on the Rapture in **1 Thess. 4**

I Thessalonians 4: 13–17 *"(13) But I would not have you to be ignorant, brethren, concerning them which are asleep, that ye sorrow not, even as others which have no hope. (14) For if we believe that Jesus died and rose again, even so them also which sleep in Jesus will God bring with him. (15) For this we say unto you by the word of the Lord, that we which are alive* and *remain unto the coming of the Lord: and the dead in Christ shall rise first: shall not prevent them which are asleep. (16) For the Lord himself shall descend from heaven with a shout, with the voice of the archangel, and with the trump of God (17) Then we which are alive* and *remain shall be <u>caught up together</u> with them in the clouds, to meet the Lord in the air: and so shall we ever be with the Lord.*

Here too, this Rapture also has all the earmarks of a Passover. This Rapture is told to us by Jesus through his apostles. The specific words come to us from Paul in **1 Thes.4:13–17.** And this event is supported in **1 Thes. 5.**

1 Thessalonians. 5:9 *"For God hath not appointed us to wrath, but to obtain salvation by our Lord Jesus Christ," (KJV*

If we (Christians) are not appointed to God's wrath, then we must be removed from this earth, as God's Great Tribulation of his wrath will include all of the planet with its death and destruction. As with Noah's Passover, God informed Noah before God sent the flood and Moses before the Death Angel. And likewise, God has told us through his scriptures of his coming wrath. God has kept his words of telling us before it would happen **(Isa.42).**

Isaiah. 42:9 *"Behold, the former things are come to pass, and new things do I declare: before they spring forth I tell you of them."* *(KJV)*

God is faithful to his promises to the children of this earth and has always been so. Therefore, this Rapture (Passover) will occur before the Great Tribulation punishment of the earth's human beings. Jesus will return (2nd) to take us home, both those dead in Christ first, then we which are alive. So what do we need to do to receive this blessing (treasure)?

Jesus has given us the things we must do to achieve this treasure. Noah had to build the Ark to be saved from the flood; Moses people must place the Lamb's blood around their door to escape the Death Angel; and the Raptured Saints requires *faith and good deeds*, revealed in the Law and the New Testament teachings. We must do deeds to build up our treasures. *We are saved by faith in Jesus but receive treasures by loving deeds to humankind.* So this Passover is to remove us from earth and the hate from Satan; and God's destruction of evil human life.

Jesus' Kingdom will come, and God's destruction of all evil for all eternity will occur later at the War to End All Wars #2. This treasure, the Passover (Rapture), you do not want to miss.

For far, too, long, well-meaning Pastors have reassured their Church members that we cannot work our way into salvation, and that is half true. But in speaking it so frequently, they have unintentionally inferred, we do not need to do any physical deeds. *Not true!* So human nature takes the position of doing no deeds and just sit in the pews (Pew-Sitters). This half-truth needs to be corrected! The Book of James is clear that our treasures are revealed by our desire to do Jesus' and God's good deeds for humanity. God tells us that he will bless those that continue to perform righteous deeds during trials and temptations. **Jam. 1.**

James 1:12 "Blessed is *the man that endureth temptation: for when he is tried, he shall receive the crown of life, which the Lord hath promised to them that love him." (KJV)*

This verse of scripture applies to all souls ever created. But it can be a powerful encouragement to the Tribulation Saints experiencing man's and Satan's wrath during those horrible days of the Great Tribulation period. Then is when it will take deeds of rejection in **Rev. 14.**

Revelation 14:9–10 *"(9) And the third angel followed them, saying with a loud voice, If any man worship the beast and his image, and* receive **his** *mark in his forehead, or in his hand, (10) The same shall drink of the wine of the wrath of God,* (2nd Harvest) *which is poured out without mixture into the cup of his indignation; and he shall be tormented with fire and brimstone in the presence of the holy angels, and in the presence of the Lamb:" (KJV)*

Here is the scripture that reveals works for salvation, working their way to Heaven!

Notice the requirement *to not take the Mark of the Beast*. This requirement will be a monumental task (deed) for the Tribulation Saints. Satan will be in control requiring the world to accept the Mark and worship him only. Satan will use any and all types of tortures to break a person's resentence to remain in Jesus. Those who resist are the Tribulation Saints.

It appears that we are spared this horrible existence by the Rapture. The horrific scene spoken of in verse 10 is for angels and the Lamb as they will be the only ones capable of tolerating the sights and sounds of these lost souls. If we were there, we might see family members and /or close friends who might bring us pain and sorrow. And this our loving God has spared us from this pain and sorrow.

Instead, God has placed us in a place of great joy, peace, and eternal LOVE. Our treasures will be unbelievable. Crowns we will be given which we will cast before Jesus' feet. God's heavenly beauty will be breathtaking; our mansion will be magnificent; weather will be extraordinarily pleasant; food and drink the tastiest we have ever sampled; exploration of the New Universe will tingle our intellect; safety and LOVE will be ever-present. All will be made new, and then all the past sins are forgotten.

THE MYSTERIES OF THE SAINTS

PREAMBLE

This Bible mystery information appears to have been around for many years. This mystery has come to me recently, and it appears to answer many questions in the Bible. Keep in mind previous written information on Tribulation Saints. And please bear with me as I may repeat some here in this Chapter.

We have labored with the understanding that all Saints have been chosen by a committee of individuals who have chosen Saints by some act or acts by Godly humans, be they male or female. However, many verses in the Bible point to another concept; all those in Jesus are called SAINTS. The Church is called the Bride of Christ, Queen of the Universe, and is given the right to rule with Jesus in Jesus' Kingdom. These individuals are to rule from that period of Jesus' 3rd Return (Armageddon); I name them the Church Saints. The exception is David, whom God made King over the Hebrew nation forever, and the Hebrew Tribulation Saints.

But God, in His grace, has saved humans all the way back to Adam and Eve. It has been and always will be by **God's grace** for the forgiveness of sins for salvation. In Old Testament times, God gave Adam four laws: 1) was a negative law "Do not eat from the tree of knowledge, 2) was Replenish (have many babies) on the earth, 3) have dominion over every creature, and 4) subdue the earth" (**Gen.1**)

> **Genesis.1:28** *"And God blessed them, and God said unto them, <u>Be fruitful</u>, and multiply, and replenish the earth, and <u>subdue</u> it: and <u>have dominion</u> over the fish of the sea, and over the fowl of the air, and <u>over every living thing</u> that moveth upon the earth."* **(KJV)**

There were initially God-fearing people on the earth, and they were taught of God by other good people. We see the linage of Noah[E] in Genesis from Adam to Methuselah. So there were righteous men before the Flood. And they were saved after death by God's grace *except for Enoch.* Enoch never died but was taken to Heaven by God. **(Gen.5:24)** However, as time moved forward, people became separated, and God's word also disappeared into oblivion. Noah continued preaching, but his words were of no avail. Every person on earth (billions) was evil, except Noah and his family. Therefore, God destroyed all of evil humanity with the flood and all animals not on the Ark. But where are those souls of the individuals who tried to do good and taught others to do good? Noah and his family carried the sin nature into the future.

Mystery of the Saints Contents

1. SAINT CONCEPT --- 224
2. OLD TESTAMENT SAINTS ------------------------------- 225
3. CHURCH SAINTS -- 227
3. TRIBULATION SAINTS ----------------------------------- 228
4. THE 10 VIRGINS --------------------------------------- 232

SAINTS CONCEPT

To understand this concept of Saints, we need to understand *the difference between the early Church concept and God's concept of Saints.* After the apostles' time, the early Catholic Church began to recognize Saints for deeds they had done in their previous life. The Sainthood had to be documented by some form of written or verbal provable facts. But God's selection of Saints is different, as his word (Bible) specifies that all who are in Christ Jesus are Saints.

Many people have performed righteous acts with no documentation of their many wonderful deeds performed for God and Jesus. They, too, are called Saints by God. This condition is especially true with the Church Saints. [More on Church Saints later].

OLD TESTAMENT SAINTS

The time *before the flood*, many of Adam and Eve's children called on the name of the Lord. They were to be committed to good as best they could. We see this consistent justification of God for his grace in salvation. (Luk **8:14–15.)**

> **Luke 8:14–15** "*(14) And that which fell among thorns are they, which, when they have heard, go forth, and are choked with cares and riches and pleasures of this life, and bring no fruit to perfection. (15) But that on the good ground are they, which in an honest and <u>good heart,</u> having heard the word, keep it, <u>and bring forth fruit</u> with patience." (KJV)*

The only law in Adam's day was Obedience, and he failed by disobedience to God's word. But what of Adam's children that tried to be obedient? God's grace looked upon their attempt to do good and their heart's desire to please God. And in his mercy, God saved them from their sins.

However, over time, Adam's offspring spread out across the land, and God's worship and knowledge decreased. There were no scriptures yet until all that was left was their evil nature. **(Gen. 5)E**

> **Genesis 5:11–13** "*(11) The earth also was corrupt before God, and the earth was filled with violence. (12) And God looked upon the earth, and, behold, it was corrupt; <u>for all flesh had corrupted his way upon the earth.</u> (13) And God said unto Noah, The end of all flesh is come before me; for the earth is filled with violence through them; and, behold, I will destroy them with the earth." (KJV)*

So, where are these dead righteous souls in Noah's time before the Flood? They are in a place called Paradise. And we have previously read that it is in the *heart of the earth* **(Mat.12:39–40).** You can find this place in **Luke 16:19–31,** the parable of Lazarus and the Rich Man. There are two locations mentioned thereof Torment and Paradise. Abraham was in a righteous place called Paradise with Lazarus, but the unrighteous rich man was in a painful place called Torments. Now *Paradise is where Jesus went after his crucifixion with the thief.* **(Luke 23:43)** So from these verses of scripture, we see two locations; one for the dead righteous individual *Paradise*; and one for the dead unrighteous individual *Torment*. Abraham was an Old Testament Saint, as well as Lazarus, so they being saved from Torment are to be considered Old Testament Saints. God's grace saved them *by their life's deeds* and the *attitude of their hearts.* These Old Testament Saints cover the time from Adam to Jesus.

The Catholic Church (the first organized denomination) has acknowledged many of these righteous individuals they classified as Saints. And are rightly so but, what of the Saints that have no written evidence of their righteous deeds? What are the names of these believers that have died in the Roman games? Or those that were Protestants; killed during the Dark Ages by the Catholic Church? Also, the Catholics were killed in this war with the Protestants. Who were the scientists killed for being heretics because their truth was different from what the Pope declared as truth?

So many individuals were killed (millions) by the powerful unrighteous leaders of the church. And these killings occurred during the reformation period when the truth was coming forth by many righteous individuals. These are the Old Testaments Saints, before and after the Law was given to man. And how many names of these righteous individuals are not known to be selected by a committee? *But God and Jesus know, and they call them Saints.*

All the Old Testament Saints are in a location I call *earth's Paradise.* They will be there until the *1st Harvest* of **Rev.14.** Those Old Testament unrighteous dead individuals are held in *Torment (Hell).*

We see the Church committee named many Old Testament righteous people as Saints and some New Testament Saints (apostles). But what of the individuals who have performed righteous deeds, even to death, on Jesus' behalf. Do they not deserve to be called Saints? Of course, they deserve that name. But, what about the name of the righteous New Testament saved individuals, the Bride of Christ?

CHURCH SAINTS (Sheep)

We read in many verses in the New Testament of individuals called to be Saints (**Rom.1.**).

> **Romans 1:5–7** *"(5) By <u>whom we have received grace</u> and apostleship, <u>for obedience to the faith among</u> all nations, for his name: (6) <u>Among whom are ye also the called of Jesus Christ:</u> (7) <u>To all that be in Rome</u>, beloved of God, <u>called</u> to be <u>saints:</u> Grace to you and peace from God our Father, and the Lord Jesus Christ." (KJV)*

Notice in **verse 5**, they have received **grace**, the one requirement to be saved at that time. But also notice it is through their *obedience to faith*. They (all) were called to be Saints. But, being called does not mean it will be accomplished. But **verse 5** assures us these are saved individuals (Saints). However, notice **verse 6**, they are called by Jesus, which means; if you are called by Jesus and accept Jesus as Lord, King, and savior, you will be named a Saint. This is spoken to the Church (all believers in Jesus), who will become the Bride of Christ. Only those who believe in Jesus; and are obedient to Jesus commands will become the Church Saints. And this group of Saints has many unique treasures; one is the Rapture. They also will be Jesus' Bride, the Queen of Heaven, rulers with Jesus and inherit all things with Jesus.

How many righteous Church individuals have died for Jesus and performed the deeds required by Jesus? Not all are known to us. The apostles are Saints, but so are John Dow and Mary Smith. Many have served Christ and are unknown to us? But do they not deserve to be called Saints? Of course, they do! Therefore, we have another group of righteous individuals I call the Church

Saints. The Church believes in Jesus unto death and performs the deeds required by Jesus. But what of the believer who does not perform deeds?

Remember that deeds have and will always *be required* for *treasures.* For the Old Testament Saints, they first had the Tree of Knowledge of Good and Evil. God desired for them to choose good over evil. But, many chose to sin, and they had no treasures, just death. But to Noah, his treasure was the ark to escape God's tribulation on earth, the Flood. This Flood is a precursor of God's tribulation on earth at the end of time and should be celebrated as a Passover too.

Some of the Church's Pew Sitters who do not do the deeds for Jesus; will miss the treasure of the Rapture. And also the wedding feast of Jesus for his bride (The Church). They will need to do the deeds (hopefully do) of Jesus during the most perilous times (The Great Tribulation). See **Mat.25.**

If the Bride of Christ does not deserve to be called a Saint, then who does?

TRIBULATION SAINTS *(Goats)*

Please bear with me as this has some repeats.

Revelation 6:9--11 *"(9) And when he had opened the fifth seal, <u>I saw under the altar the souls of them that were slain for the word of God, and for the testimony which they held:</u> (10) And they cried with a loud voice, saying, How long, O Lord, holy and true, dost thou not judge and avenge our blood on them that dwell on the earth? (11 <u>And white robes were given</u> unto every one of them; and it was said unto them, that they should rest yet for a little season, until their <u>fellow servants also and their brethren,</u> that should be killed as they were, should be fulfilled."* *(KJV)*

These under the Temple Alter are the dead saved Tribulation Saints, converted by the protected 144,000 Hebrew missionaries, executed during The Great Tribulation. They appear to have a special place for their souls to reside different from earth's Paradise.

Here we see the Tribulation Saints found in many scriptures, but not by this name. However, it becomes more apparent as you study. In **Mat. 22,** we read about the King's son's wedding feast invitations were being rejected. This parable runs hand in hand with the Parable of **Mat.25;** the 10 Virgins.

In **Mat. 22,** we read of the marriage feast for the King's son. This parable is a metaphor referring to the marriage of Jesus to his Bride the Church. Here we see the King as God arranging the marriage for his son (Jesus). He sends his servants (Prophets) to selected individuals (Jews). They make excuses for not attending (not coming to Jesus', the King's son's celebration). The King makes another attempt to call them to the marriage feast by sending his servants (the Apostles). But evil men kill these servants (as did the Jews). Overtime (time of the Gentiles), the preparations for the feast are ready. *But the previously invited (Jews) would not be allowed to come to the marriage of his son (Jesus). This event is also the consequence mentioned in **Mat. 25** for the 5 Unprepared Virgins.* But the Hebrews have been blinded by God (King). **(John 12)**

> **John 12:39–40 "(39)** *Therefore they could not believe, because that Esaias said again, (40)* <u>*He hath blinded their eyes, and hardened their heart;*</u> *that they should not see with* their *eyes, nor understand with* their *heart, and be converted, and I should heal them." (KJV)*

Thereafter the King sent his servants to the highways to gather both the good (righteous) and the bad (Gentiles) to his son's marriage feast. These servants are the apostles, prophets, pastors, laypersons, priests, you and me, all who believe in Jesus for their salvation. They have performed the deeds of gathering the Gentiles (lost/bad) to Jesus.

These Gentiles (Christians) are gathered at the marriage Feast, but one person does not have on a wedding garment (white robe – the righteousness of the Saints), and that person is tied up and thrown out of the feast. This person represents the 5 Unprepared Virgins (goats) who were not permitted into the wedding (these are the Tribulation Saints). They are saved by faith for eternity but have not performed righteous acts (Pew Sitters). They will go through the Great Tribulation period, and they (Tribulation Saints) will meet Jesus, the Church (Bride of Christ), and the Old Testament Saints at the *1st Harvest* of **Rev. 14:14–16.** This joining will be just before War #1 of Armageddon. Jesus, the Bride, angels, Tribulation Saint, and Old Testament Saints will destroy all evil individuals. This Armageddon ending will also start the *2nd Harvest* of evil souls during the 1,000-year kingdom. And those that accepted the Mark of the Beast will be eventually condemned to the Lake of Fire. In **Mat. 25:1–13,** we read of a similar event.

Note

In **Mat.22:13,** you will read *"into outer darkness* (evil); *"there shall be weeping and gnashing of teeth,"* pain, sorry and anger. This is not Hell (Torment); it is the period of Great Tribulation of 7 years. Outer darkness represents those evil persons outside of Jerusalem, Jesus' headquarters. They are not permitted to enter Jerusalem. It is not Torment, as it is the location for dead lost souls. And it is not the Lake of Fire, as that is the final location for all lost souls. And the pain in that Lake of Fire will be well beyond the weeping and gnashing of teeth.

These individuals are those who have missed the Rapture and must go through the Great Tribulations. They are the Pew Sitter who have not performed any deeds for Jesus' Kingdom and are left behind. They will now come to their senses and realize they must not take the Mark of the Beast.

One thought for those Tribulation Saints is found in **Dan. 12.** The words there will tell them of the exact date of Jesus' *3rd Return.* Pastors and leaders for years have been telling us that no one knows when Jesus will return, and they are half-right and half-wrong, as there are still two returns remaining from today. Jesus spoke at times about our need to be watchful for his 2nd Return. And not to be caught by a thief in the night. This watching pertains to the Rapture; because trumpets will herald his 3rd Return, Angels shouting and light everywhere; with every eye seeing him. Does this sound like a thief in the night? So how can you tell what date Jesus will return (3rd) to claim back his earth? To answer this, we go to **Dan. 12.**

> **Daniel 12:11–12** *"(11) And from the time* that *the daily* sacrifice *shall be taken away, and the abomination that maketh desolate set up,* there shall be *a thousand two hundred and ninety days. (12) Blessed* is *he that waiteth, and cometh to the thousand three hundred and five and thirty days." (KJV)*

1st clue we read is the *daily sacrifice is removed.* This removal is the Jewish requirement for the morning and evening sacrifice in the rebuilt Jewish Temple of God. This taken away will occur halfway through The Great Tribulation, when Antichrist #2 (now Satan) breaks the seven-year covenant with Israel.

The *2nd clue* is the abomination is *Satan's statue set up in God's rebuilt Temple in the Holy of Holies.* All people will be required to come and worship this talking statue, receive the Mark of Satan, or be killed. (Read also **Dan. 11:31--40).** This time is for the *2nd clue; 1290* days are 3½ years in the Jewish calendar with a leap month (30 days) added. This duration is when God permits the abomination to exist in God's rebuilt Temple to test the remnant, but at the end of 1290 days, it starts War #1 of Armageddon. Here is Jesus' *3rd Return*; and will initiate the *2nd Harvest* on earth **Rev. 14:18--20.**

The *3rd clue* is the **1335 days** of **verse 12.** Both of these days have been misunderstood for centuries. *These additional 45 days is the time it will take for the earthly government of Jesu*s to be established. It will include the War, the burial of the dead, the cleanup of all the war implements, the Temple's cleansing, and many other chores for Jesus' Kingdom. And many of these tasks

231

will be performed by the Christian survivors of The Great Tribulation period. This establishment of Jesus' government with Saints, human survivors, and the selection of each ruling body, the movement to their location, and the setting up that government. This event will take some time as Jesus is dealing with survivors (humans) who still have human needs for food and rest (sleep).

THE 10 VIRGINS MYSTERY

The scriptures in **Mat.25:1–13,** we find ten virgins (faithful) waiting for the Bridegroom (Jesus). Faithful virgin is used as they have never worshiped any other god, nor had sex. Five virgins (sheep) have their lamps of righteousness (deeds) full of oil (used in righteous events) and additional oil (heart for continuous deeds) for a long wait. But the five unprepared virgins (goats) do not have extra oil for their lamps. They have set in their pews and done nothing for Jesus. The Lamp is representative of the source of our outward righteous appearance in deeds. **Mat. 5.**

> **Matthew 5:16.** *"Let your light so shine before men, that they may see your <u>good works,</u> and glorify your Father which is in heaven."*

This verse indicates that these virgins had their light shining in the past. Five virgins (sheep) have kept their lamps bright and are keeping them bright by the continuous renewal of their oil, the medium to fuel their light. Oil in the Bible is used in several ways, such as.

1. Light in Lamps
2. To prepare food.
3. Healing of sores
4. Anointing
5. Used in the Temple Altar

But, five of the virgins (goats) had become lethargic in performing visual deeds before man. They have not sought the renewal of their spiritual life by study and performance of righteous deeds or Love for the lost. They have turned their wicks (deeds) down to conserve their oil. They reveal laziness by reducing their trips to obtain oil, and their light (righteousness) is about to go out. They fear insulting, losing friends, unqualified, fired, breaking some law, or other weak excuses.

If you do a study of Judgments, you will find that judgments are based on two requirements. One is FAITH, and two is on doing DEEDS. It takes both to be acquitted and set free.

These five virgins have their lamps (weak light) but not enough oil. Their oil (righteous deeds or acts) is shallow, and their lamp is about to go out. The bridegroom delays a long time but arrives late in the night (like a thief). When the bridegroom arrived (the Rapture), the five unprepared virgins ask the five prepared virgins to give them some of their oil as their lamps have all but gone out (their righteous light). But the five refused and told them to go buy oil as they did not have enough for them both. This same type of condition occurred in the letter to the Church in Laodicea, where the Church is told to go buy gold (purity **Rev.3:18)** tried in the fire (self-judgment) for repentance of their sin of non-performance. To know to do right and not to do what is right; *is the sin of omission*. Those individuals that will not perform deeds will miss the marriage feast (Rapture) and be kept outside. These are the Tribulation Saints. Many in the Church of Laodiceans are prideful of their financial condition as they need nothing. If they want it, they go buy it. The Church of Laodicea's righteous acts (light) is about to go out. They have no need for God; just wants. This Church in **Rev.3**:19 is told:

> **Revelation 3:19** *"As many as I love, I rebuke and chasten: be zealous therefore, and repent." (KJV)*

Hopefully, the majority of Laodiceans will repent. The Tribulation Saints also will be Hebrews taught by the 144,000 Jewish missionaries of Jesus, their now Messiah. Many converts will be beheaded **(Rev. 20:4)** and placed under the Alter **(Rev. 6:9–11)** in the rebuilt Jewish Temple. These converts from these Jewish missionaries will repent and accept Jesus as their Messiah. Most of the

Tribulation Saints will be Hebrews, but some will be the Gentile Pew Sitters. But, they too will join the army of Armageddon to destroy all evil. This condition is also found in **Rev. 14:13–16** that speaks of the *1st Harvest*.

These Tribulation Saints will be required to worship Satan as god or be killed or their families. They will be tortured and made to watch their loved ones tortured hideously unto death. Unless; they accept Satan as god, and wear Satan's Mark on their hand or forehead. ***To receive this, Mark is the kiss of eternal death in the Lake of Fire. No parole!*** This temptation appears to be the greatest test by God for their faith in Jesus. The Tribulations Saints (Jews and Pew Sitters) will now understand what they were told in Church; but were apathetic to the words of deeds, which Jesus requires for treasures. *There will be a weeping and gnashing of teeth.* **Rev. 14:13** makes it clear they must produce works.

> **Revelation 14:13** *"And I heard a voice from heaven saying unto me, Write, <u>Blessed</u> are <u>the dead which die in the Lord</u> from henceforth: Yea, saith the Spirit, <u>that they may rest from their labours; and their works do follow them.</u>" (KJV)*

The Jews have always required visible proof such as a miracle to believe and then ignored the miracle when it occurred. We read in scripture that God has blinded the Hebrew people. This tribulation period will be the time God removes the blindness from the Hebrew people by 144,000 Hebrew missionaries and the previous two witnesses of **Rev. 11:3–2**. *Now the Jews know who Jesus is, the Messiah and the Son of God.* They now have their proof demanded and the tribulation punishment to test their loyalty to Jesus for their salvation.

The Pew Sitters believe in Jesus but performed no deeds. They are spiritually saved from The Lake of Fire, but physical acts will be required to reject Satan as god. Both Jews and Gentiles will be in this group. The 144,000 Jewish missionaries will convert all Jews to Jesus, and their treasure is to rule and serve Jesus. **(Rev. 7)**

These words are harsh, but God tells of his hard love in **Heb. 12**.

Hebrews 12:6–8 *"(6) For whom the Lord loveth he chasteneth, and scourgeth <u>every son whom he receiveth.</u> (7) If ye endure chastening, God dealeth with you as with sons; for what son is he whom the father chasteneth not? (8) <u>But if ye be without chastisement, whereof all are partakers, then are ye bastards, and not sons."</u> (KJV)*

Being chastised is to be reassuring of God's hard LOVE. And if he loves you, God will lead you into righteousness by any appropriate means God knows will work. Those Christians trying to please God will not receive intense chastisement; that is reserved for those who are aphetic to God's and the Holy Spirit's leading. So take heart during times of trouble. Believe there is purpose in this trouble and set your heart on **Rom. 8**.

Romans 8:15–18 *"(15) For ye have not received the spirit of bondage again to fear; but ye have received the Spirit of adoption, whereby we cry, Abba, Father. (16) The Spirit itself beareth witness with our spirit, that we are the children of God: (17) And if children, then heirs; heirs of God, and joint-heirs with Christ; if so be that we suffer with him, that we may be also glorified together." (KJV)*

(And best of all.)

(18) "For I reckon that the sufferings of this present time are *not worthy* to be compared *with the glory which shall be revealed in us" (KJV)*

Stay strong in Jesus; keep your FAITH strong; remember God and Jesus LOVE YOU. Consider that all situations will work for the good by Jesus. And Jesus will come for you in his time. Be patient, look for the good, trust Jesus, help others, speak the Gospel, and Love everyone. These trials and punishments will eventually end. We also see this punish for the Jews in the book of **Dan. 9.**

> **Daniel 9:23–27** "*(23) At the beginning of thy supplications the commandment came forth, and I am come to shew* **thee***; for thou* art *greatly beloved: therefore understand the matter, and consider the vision. (24) <u>Seventy weeks are determined upon thy people and upon thy holy city, to finish the transgression, and to make an end of sins,</u> and to make reconciliation for iniquity, and to <u>bring in everlasting righteousness,</u> and <u>to seal up the vision and prophecy,</u> and to anoint the most Holy. (25) Know therefore and understand,* <u>that *from the going forth of the commandment to restore and to build Jerusalem unto the Messiah the Prince* shall be *seven weeks, and threescore and two weeks: the street shall be built again, and the wall, even in troublous times. (26) And after threescore and two weeks shall Messiah be cut off, but not for himself: and the people of the prince that shall come shall destroy the city and the sanctuary;* and the end thereof</u> *shall be with a flood, and unto the end of the war desolations are determined. (27)And <u>he shall confirm the covenant with many for one week: and in the midst of the week he shall cause the sacrifice and the oblation to cease, and for the overspreading of abominations he shall make* it *desolate, even until the consummation, and that determined shall be poured upon the desolate.</u>" (KJV)*

In **<u>verse 24,</u>** we read 70 weeks are determined against the people (Jews) and upon Jerusalem. This 70 is 70 weeks of years or 70 x 7 = 490 years of punishment for Israel and Jerusalem. These 490 years are to *<u>"make an end to sin."</u>* This coming of Jesus, the anointed one, will bring in (start) the end of sin. Also, *<u>"Everlasting righteousness and make reconciliation for iniquity."</u>* This event can only occur at Jesus' return but completed only after God destroys Satan and his army **(Rev 20:7–9).**

Verse 25 tells us about the time of Jesus 1st coming to pay our debt of sin. The *clue* pertaining to Jesus' coming is hinged on the time of the command to restore and rebuild Jerusalem. It shall be *"seven weeks and threescore and two and two weeks."* (A score is 20) Therefore, **7 x 7**= 49 plus; 62 sevens is 62 x 7 = 434 +49 = 483 years. So if we subtract 483 years from the 490 years, we have seven years of punishment of the Hebrew people remaining.

In **verse 26,** the seven sevens (49 years) appear to be that time of restoration for Jerusalem. Several edicts were from the Roman emperor to rebuild, but only one decree included all of God's requirements. These 62 sevens (434 years) are the time from the rebuilding of Jerusalem to the Coming of the Messiah and his crucifixion *("cut off")*. Some scholars have computed Jesus' death (*cut off*) from the correct edict's date to rebuild Jerusalem to Jesus' death on --- APRIL 6, 32 A.D. After the crucifixion, in the future (70AD), Jerusalem and the Temple will be (and was) destroyed.

Then there appears an extension of time until ***"the end thereof*** shall be ***with a flood, and*** <u>***unto the end of the war desolations are***</u> ***determined.*** *"* Please notice **"of the *war* <u>*desolations*</u>"** is a plural word.

Note

> There are two wars of desolation. The first is the war of good and evil, Armageddon **(Rev.19).** The second war of desolation is when God burns up paroled Satan's army after the 1,000 years of Jesus' earthly Kingdom **(Rev.20:7–9).** The result of this final War #2 is to remove all evil from the earth. All the blood that has soaked into the earth from Adam to this last war will require God to make a New Earth and New Universe **(Rev.21).** And this is the time that all sins will be forgotten.

Verse 27 moves forward in time to the beginning of the Great Tribulation's seven years. Antichrist #1 makes a 7-year Covenant with Israel. This Covenant most likely will be for Israel's protection from Islam. After the first 3½ years, the Antichrist #2 (Satan incarnate) will break this Covenant with the Hebrew people; by stopping their sacrifices and offerings in the rebuild Jewish temple. Then Satan will set up a talking statue of himself in the temple and require all peoples of the earth to worship him through his statue. This statue is the greatest insult to God. **(Duet.5)**

> **Deuteronomy 5:7–9" (7) _Thou shalt have no other gods before me_" (8) "Thou shalt not make thee** any **graven image,** or **any likeness of any thing** that is **in _heaven above_, or that** is **in _the earth beneath_, or that** is **in the waters beneath the earth:" (9) Thou shalt not bow down thyself unto them, nor serve them: for I the LORD thy God** am **a jealous God, visiting the iniquity of the fathers upon the children unto the third and _fourth_ generation of them that hate me," (KJV)**

The graven image in Hebrew means *"peh-sel"* = *"idol carved from wood or stone[2]."*

Here we see the commandments not to create any graven images from heaven or on earth. Now Satan blatantly violates these Laws of God. Can you think of anything more significant that would anger God more than to see Satan's statue set up in God's Temple? This statue is a double insult to God. Not only is there a graven image in the Temple, but it is the image of Satan. And also have evil persons and fallen away ½ christians come to worship Satan in God's temple. God's anger will come to fruition in his 7th years of The Great Tribulation. God will rescue only the Tribulation Saints and not the fallen away pew sitters. So after the *last 3½ years* of the seven years of The Great Tribulation, Jesus returns (3rd) to destroy all evil (lost individuals); and to lock Satan up into the Abyss for 1,000 years (*2nd Harvest* starts).

You may ask, what has all this have to do with the Tribulation Saints? And it is a reasonable question. I want anyone who is not motivated to do deeds for Jesus' Church here on earth to understand The Great Tribulation of desolations and torments they may go through to prove their worth for treasures in heaven. Do we understand the magnitude of God's wrath and how it will affect the

Tribulation Saints? Pastors have emphasized salvation by faith for far too long, and you cannot work your way into salvation. And of course, this is half true, but the lack of emphases for works makes it appear as works are unnecessary. But deeds have always been required all through history. One of the last verses in the last chapter in the Bible is in **Rev.22.**

> **Revelation 22:12–14** *"(12) And, behold, I come quickly; <u>and my reward</u> is <u>with me, to give every man according as his work shall be</u>. (13) I am Alpha and Omega, the beginning and the end, the first and the last. (14) Blessed</u> are <u>they that do his commandments,</u> that they may have <u>right to the tree of life,</u> and may enter in through the gates into the city." (KJV)*

See the words <u>works</u> and <u>commands</u>? Do not be resistant to deeds but cherish them, my friends. You will not know what a blessing works can be until you try them. Jesus tells us in **Mat. 11,** his yoke is easy, and his burden is light.

> **Matthew 11:28–30** *"(28) "Come unto me, <u>all</u> ye <u>that labour</u> and are heavy laden, and I will give you rest. (29) Take my yoke upon you, and learn of me; for I am meek and lowly in heart: and ye shall find rest unto your souls. (30) <u>For my yoke</u> is <u>easy, and my burden is light."</u> (KJV)*

I taught Sunday school for many years, and my Pastor asks me to do a prison ministry at our local prison. I fought it but eventually agreed to do as he requested. I dreaded my first lesson with them. The thought of men in chains was discomforting. But, the result of my lesson was a real blessing for me. This was many years ago, and I am still doing that ministry today, but in another prison. I look forward to my next encounter with these men. Many men have given their lives over to Jesus, and what a blessing it is to have played a small part in the Holy Spirit's mission of Salvation. We are blessed.

Thank you, Jesus!

THE

THREE

CLOCKS

MYSTERIES

PREAMBLE

I taught adult Sunday school for over 30 years and, in doing so, I got involved with the Book of Revelation, which opened my eyes to many truths in the Bible. Many verses started to fit together, and I became aware of the nearness of Jesus' return to reclaim his earth. This feeling of nearness has provoked me to write about Jesus' coming; my concerns move me for my fellow Christians who are not aware of the nearness of his time. Many Churches have not been teaching unpleasant truths and have not been motivated to reveal hard love for some lost souls. Jesus' Great Commission is more appropriate today as we see a decline in Church attendance (falling away) and the increase in sins.

My concerns are for all lost souls and disobedient Christians; they have been the motivating force behind my desire to share the truth as God has provided to me. The Bible is a Love Letter to each soul and is an avenue for us to know his Love. I know God is patient, but his patience has a limit. Also, his punishments for the errant and lost will be horrendous. Therefore, we need to do the deeds we can do for these lost souls and Jesus' kingdom.

Salvation is by FAITH, but Treasures are by DEEDS.

I want all my brothers and sisters in Christ to have a multitude of Treasures in Heaven, waiting for them to enjoy for eternity. So I am trying to show you just how close is Jesus' *2nd Return. There are three clocks in the Bible for us to count down to Jesus' soon return.* If you have not been busy with Jesus' work, you may want to reconsider.

CLOCKS MYSTERY CONTENTS

1st Clock of Creation ———————————————————————————— 252
    1. Pre-Genesis ——————————————————————————— 252
    2. Day 1 Creation (plan, time, maturity and light) ——————— 267
    3. Uniformitarianism ————————————————————————— 287
    4. Day 2 Creation (waters divided) ———————————————— 293
    5. Day 3 Creation (land, seas, vegetation) ————————————— 305
    6. Day 4 Creation (Celestial bodies) ————————————————— 314
    7. Day 5 Creation (Fish, fowls) ——————————————————— 325
    8. Day 6 Creation (animals and man) –Rapture ———————— 330
    9. Day 7 Creating Completed (God rests) ——————————— 342
    10. Clock's Construction ————————————————————— 351
    11. Witness Chart ————————————————————————— 372
    12. Clock Application ————————————————————————— 373

2nd Clock of Empires ———————————— 393
    1. The Dream and Interpretation(Statue & Beasts) —————— 393
    2. Babylon ——————————————————————————————— 395
    3. Medes and Persians ————————————————————————— 396
    4. Greek Alexander the Great ————————————————————— 397
    5. Roman ——————————————————————————————— 398
    6. Revised Roman (Antichrist's) ——————————————————— 399
    7. Revised Roman (Satan's) ——————————————————————— 401
    8. Jesus' Rock Empire (1,000 years) ———————————————— 405
    9. Satan's Paroled Empire ———————————————————————— 406
    10. 4 Animal Beasts ——————————————————————————— 407

3rd Clock of Church History ————— 411
    1. Pre-clock Information ———————————————————————— 414
    2. Fruchenbaum Chart ————————————————————————— 415
    3. Ephesus ——————————————————————————————— 415
    4. Smyrna ——————————————————————————————— 415
    5. Pergamos ——————————————————————————————— 416
    6. Thyatira ——————————————————————————————— 418
    7. Sardis ———————————————————————————————— 419
    8. Laodiceans ————————————————————————————— 423
    9. Earth's End Best Clues ————————————————————————— 423
    10. Daniel's Prophecy Unsealed ——————————————————— 439
    11. Falling Away ———————————————————————————— 440
    12. Salvation ——————————————————————————————— 441

TIME THEORY

The concept of this mystery is to give the reader a *general perception* of God's timing in his plan for man and earth.

Note

> **This book is in no way an attempt to place actual and specific dates as to Jesus' *2nd Return*.**

There are three times Jesus comes to the earth. The <u>First time</u> was to bring the gospel of salvation and pay for all sins. The <u>Second time</u> Jesus comes is not on the planet but close to it, *in the air*. We call this event "The Rapture," where Jesus collects all the Church Saints to him so they can escape God's Great Tribulation of 7 years. The <u>Third time</u> Jesus comes to earth *is as King and destroyer of all evil beings* (those who are unsaved) and set up his 1,000-year kingdom.

We are told in **Mat.24:3** when Jesus was asked three questions by his disciples as they thought it would be only one event. These three questions are: *"1) When shall these things be? 2) And what shall be the sign of thy coming? 3) And of the end of the world?" (KJV)*

Jesus went into a long dissertation of events and signs that would occur before his return in **Mat. 24** and **25**. Jesus added in **Mat. 24.**

> **Mat.24:36 *"But of that day or hour knoweth no man, no not the angles of heaven, but my father only." (KJV)***

Therefore, there is a question we must ask; to which return is Jesus referring?

When Jesus spoke of an exact time (day or hour), he was referring to his 2nd Return, the Rapture. But, he also balanced that information by indicating in Mat. 24:32–33 (the fig tree) that we would know the general time of Jesus' *2nd Return*; **if** we studied the scriptures for *clues* and looked for those signs. These signs are not hard to find in the Bible. One of the best signs is located in **2nd Thes.2**.

> **2nd Thessalonians 2:2–3** *"(2) Now we beseech you, brethren, by the <u>coming of our Lord Jesus Christ</u>, and <u>by our gathering together unto him,</u> (2) That ye be not soon shaken in mind, or be troubled, neither by spirit, nor by word, nor by letter as from us, as that the day of Christ is at hand. (3) Let no man deceive you by any means: <u>for that day shall not come, except there come a falling away first,</u> <u>and that man of sin be revealed, the son of perdition;"</u> (KJV)*

Notice the *1st clue* is *"our gathering together unto him."* This *gathering together* is the Rapture. *"Unto him"* speaks of gathering *"brethren"* which, identifies those in Jesus, the Church. These next two signs will be made known to those who are watching. Pay particular attention to **verse 3.** The *2nd clue* is there will be **a falling away** of Church attendance and anti-God sentiments by many. *This <u>clue</u> is present at this writing.* Anyone who is observant can see the anti-God sentiments occurring today. Removal of prayers in public, laws of removal of Christians signs. Evil laws like abortion, keeping silent about Jesus and God, praying in silence, to mention a few. The *3rd clue* is the Antichrist mentioned as the ***man of sin,*** and ***he will be made* known.** This statement is for the Church as none believers will be uninterested in religious information. This recognition is given to the Church, so they will know how close the Rapture is to occur. *This clue is essential for the Church, especially pew-sitters, future Tribulation Saints, and Jews.* Now the Antichrist #1 is the son of perdition, SATAN. Always keep in remembrance what God said in **Amos 3.**

> **Amos 3:7** *"Surely the Lord GOD will do nothing, but he revealeth his secret unto his servants the prophets."* (KJV)

These words should give us comfort, especially for those Christians actively looking for Jesus' return. God has done everything to point us to Jesus' near Return #2 and #3; its *clues* are revealed in **Daniel 12.** There we are given everything, including the year, month, day, and watch time.

More clues abound today in the 21st century than ever before. Prophases are being fulfilled before our very eyes. Our young people turn to drugs, fornication, the murder of babies, robbery, anti-government, anti-police, disrespectable to parents, drunkards, want God out of their life and so many other evil signs our society is advocating; at Satan instigations **(2nd Tim. 3:1–7).** These verses of scripture paint a picture of our present earth. Even our government is falling into this category of sinners. But, Jesus' *2nd Return* is to rescue all these righteous Christians and activate God's wrath on evil earthlings. This is the time mentioned of his coming like a thief in the night. And seven years after that event is the *#3 Return. This Return* can be figured to the very day **(Dan. 12).** This final return will not be like a thief in the night, but with the loud noise of singing, bright light around the earth, the army of God coming to destroy all evil.

The Rapture time is unknown, but Jesus *3 Return* will be known to the very Day. But, Jesus gives us a *clue* in **Mat. 24** as to the Rapture's general time.

> **Matthew. 24:32–33** *"(32) Now learn the parable of the fig tree; When his branch is yet tender, and putteth forth leaves, ye know that summer is nigh: (33) So likewise ye, when ye shall see all these things, know that it is near even at the doors." (KJV)*

Jesus knew that his disciples were familiar with the life of the fig tree. That spring brings forth the leaves, which precedes summer's heat, which brings the fig fruit. In the same way, these events or signs must precede Jesus' *2nd Return* (Rapture). I do not claim to be a scholar or have any exceptional vision or gift. However, the Holy Spirit will give knowledge to God's people. **(1Cor.2)**

1Corinthians. 2:12–14 "**(12)** *Now we have received, not the spirit of the world, but the spirit which is of God; that we might know the things that are freely given to us of God. (13)Which things also we speak, not in the words which man's wisdom teacheth, but which the Holy Ghost teacheth; comparing spiritual things with spiritual. (14) But the natural man receiveth not the things of the Spirit of God: for they are foolishness unto him: neither can he know them, because they are spiritually discerned.*" *(KJV)*

It is God's expressed purpose to share his information with his children, you, and me. Teachers experience this desire to share information they have found as they ply their gifts in God's service. As Christians, we need to put on our thinking caps to fully understand the information presented to us and not make hasty, uninformed, or prejudicial decisions about the material's validity. Remember, this is the pit the religious leaders fell into when Jesus came. Also, we need to try all information to see if it comes from God; which we can do with the study of God's word. **(1 John 4)**

Once that material has been digested and understood, we need to determine if that information is correct and what we must do. Sometimes it requires action on our part to pass, or not, it on to others. We must also keep in mind that all righteous man's interpretations are neither entirely correct nor completely wrong. Most scientists build from a concept that ideas are not completely accurate, and it is during the study, designing, trial, and error process that faulty information is proven wrong. New information is experimented with until all that remains is the correct information. Today we have more and more truth coming to us from God.

Keep in mind that no human knows all the knowledge of the scriptures. This includes Pope, Bishops, Priests, Pastors, Elders, Deacons, and Scholars, Lay Persons or any religious leader. But, what is said needs to be seriously considered. However, those learned men and women must be respected as

God's emissary, and we should give them special attention and credibility. But if you feel an error exists, you must test the spirit. If an error exists, go one on one with the person and discuss the difference with the individual. Both may learn.

We see similar problems Jesus had when he was trying to inform the religious leaders of Jesus' day of a new and utterly different salvation concept. Priest and Rabbis were laboring under the influence of *old traditions* rather than the complete information from the Torah and prophets. This situation continues today even with good meaning Pastors and teachers as well as unreligious leaders. Blind trust has been taken advantage of by an evil individual in our past.

We Christians must understand that new and possible different information will be coming from the Holy Spirit to improve our knowledge of God's vast and complicated plan for man. We see in **Daniel 12** that God has hidden the understanding of scripture until it is needed for Christian's performance.

> **Daniel 12:9–10** *"(9) And he said, Go thy way, Daniel: for the words are closed up and sealed till the time of the end. (10) Many shall be purified, and made white, and tried; but the wicked shall do wickedly: and none of the wicked shall understand; but the wise shall understand." (KJV)*

The next verse of scripture points to a time when God will open these words enclosed and remove his official seal so that this prophecy can be revealed to man. And this has happened today! The proof is found in **Dan. 12.**

> **Daniel 12:4** *"But thou, O Daniel, shut up the words, and seal the book,* <u>even</u> *<u>to the time of the end: <u>many shall run to and fro, and knowledge shall be increased</u>." (KJV)*

THESE SEALED-UP WORDS ARE NOW UNSEALED!

Clue 1 is our knowledge has increased due to the computer software for language interpretation. The software has removed God's language curse given at the Tower of Babel **(Gen.11:4–9).** And *Clue 2* is we today can travel (run to and fro) anywhere we desire on earth, and even into space, shortly to Mars. *So, knowledge and travel have increased drastically in the last 100 years.* We did not fly aircraft until around 1900, but in 1969, we went to the Moon. That is only 69 years and mostly without computers.

This prophecy of **Dan. 12** is coming true before our very eyes today. But, Satan will make an effort to confuse man by creating diversions and deceptions. One such deception comes from our TV programs. Sin scenes are ramped, cruelty is normal, and the best is the invaders from space. These invaders' programs are poisoning our minds against Jesus' *3rd Return*. Satan is prepping man to fight Jesus (Armageddon). And Satan is propagandizing humans to defend the earth from the assumed evil aliens.

Also, our entertainment community is slowly changed our morality. It was not long ago that vile language was not permitted in radios, movies, TV, or sexual pornographic scenes. But today, it is challenging to watch entertainment without this garbage invading our minds. And sad to say, it is affecting our Church members and children too. If we see it enough times, we become hardened to filth and begin to accept it and later crave it. **Phil. 4** warns us in a roundabout way of this problem.

> **Philippians 4:8** *"Finally, brethren, whatsoever things are true, whatsoever things are honest, whatsoever things are just, whatsoever things are pure, whatsoever things are lovely, whatsoever things are of good report; if there be any virtue, and if there be any praise, think on these things." (KJV)*

Satan has used the technique of deception since he deceived Eve in the Garden of Eden. Satan deceived Eve with a trap that made her think Adam lied to her about eating from the Tree of Knowledge of Good and Evil. This tree to her was too beneficial to pass up. Lust of the flesh and lust of the eyes; reared its ugly head.

Satan smiled.

The education field knows that humans remember more by what they see; than by what they hear. However, the combination of both seeing and hearing improves retention drastically. Add to that, actual hands-on practice (simulators) and retention get close to over 90%. Today, Satan has a vast amount of tools to affect our actions for good or evil, and Satan chooses evil. For example, the computer industry has brought Satan the tools of Gaming. Now kids can hear and see the game and participate in deadly war games with no negative results, except losing the game. They eventually have no concept of extreme pain of wounds or death.

They have no feelings for those unknown aliens that die—just winning and losing and gaining more points (rewards) than other players. Aliens invasions are of evil, trying to destroy the world. Satan's attempt to harden the young boys and girls to think Jesus return to earth for Armageddon are evil aliens come to destroy mankind and take over the world. And it is a distorted truth from Satan. But if earthlings are evil, they will be correct as Jesus will come to destroy all evil beings. Satan has been preparing this assumed evil army for a long time. Kids have grown up and had kids which they buy the same types of games for them. Adults see violence so much; they commit violence at athletic events their kids are playing. Good sportsmanship is a thing of the past. God is being removed from sports, and God will leave us to our own consequences of our actions or deeds. So many people believe what they see on the internet is true. But nothing could be farther from the truth.

We must not fall into that trap of believing everything we hear or see is true. We must try the spirit to see if it is from God **(1st John 4:1).** And only study of the Bible will lead you to truth through the Holy Spirit. This verse of testing is given to us to direct our research to God's Word. How can we learn if we do not do our homework? But keep **Jam.1** in the back of your mind.

Jam.1:19–20 "(19) *Wherefore, my beloved brethren, let every man be <u>swift to hear, slow to speak, slow to wrath</u>: (20) <u>For the wrath of man worketh not the righteousness of God."</u>* **(KJV)**

We have seen evil in our own life during the government's hearing of Judge Kavanaugh's approval to the Supreme Court (Oct. 2018). In their attempt to destroy Judas Prudence (innocent until proven guilty), these actions by democrats and the MeToo movement were and are unacceptable. They were not interested in facts of innocence or guilt but the destruction of Judge Kavanaugh. These democrats were not swift to listen, as they interrupted the speaker before he could complete his sentence. Therefore, they were not slow to speak either, and anger eventually reared its ugly head. So if **James 1:20** said, *"<u>wrath of man worketh not the righteousness of God."</u>* The perpetrator of this evil attempt to anger will be held accountable. Jesus even got angry with the money changers' unrighteous actions **(John 2:14–15)** in God's Temple. Jesus even made a whip and scourged the money changers with it. There are times we Christians are to physically stand for the truth against untruth, righteousness against unrighteousness.

Also, just because we study does not mean we get it entirely right the first time. It is through the more in-depth study that clarity from the Holy Spirit will come to correctness. For my Christian friends, remember God has written the Bible, so evil cannot understand God's meanings. Therefore, it will require our dedicated study of God's words to fully understand and appreciate his knowledge and wisdom.

Now with all that being said, let us look into the central theory of this book. The main idea is **TIME PASSAGE.** So let us examine the three clocks revealed in the Bible. They are:
1. The Clock of Creation.
2. The Clock of Empires.
3. The Clock of Churches.

These clocks will reveal the passage of time on Earth. But look into the present scientific theory of Uniformitarianism. This theory is based on the fact that all elements in our Universe change at that element's natural progression depending on the same conditions exist. Science believes and supports the Big Bang theory to explain the creation of the Universe. And it also depends on Darwin's theory of evolution. ***Both are theory and not verifiable.*** However, our education system presents these two theories as proven facts and are not confirmed (a Lie). They accept these theories as fact but reject the theory of Creationism.

I will start first with The Clock of Creation.

GENESIS: THE CLOCK OF CREATION

PREAMBLE

Please keep in mind as you study Genesis that the Biblical account of creation is primarily the information that pertains to our earth. However, it is also clear it is the creation of all the elements of the Universe. These chapters reveal a clock, and the hands cover the larger and lesser passages of time.

Questions

Question: **Why would God (the great economizer) do in seven days what he could do at the twinkling of an eye?**

We know that God does nothing without purpose and does not waste time, effort, or materials. He also records nothing that is not for our benefit and education. We also know God does not explain some things in great detail. If he did, there would not be enough room on this earth to house all the volumes that could be written. So this question comes to mind. *Why would God do in seven days what he could in the twinkling of an eye?* I'm sure you remember God spoke, and the complete Universe was formed. So, this is a *big clue* to answer! Why is he taking so much time (7 Days) to create the earth and man when he did the universe in one day?

1. Is God just telling us the story of creation?

2. Is God hiding information from unrighteous inquisitors?

3. Is God revealing hidden knowledge to his children?

4. If God has a beginning; and an ending, would he not reveal his general timing to his children? So they would not be caught by the thief in the night?

5. Is it possible that the duration of creation is the duration for his creation?

The answer to all five of these questions *is yes*, and here are some reasons.

1. Is God just telling us a story of creation?

God wants his children to have information about his Great Plan for them. Part of that plan has a beginning or starting point, which we, as human beings, need to fix our life journey upon. We need to know where we came from, so we can hopefully see where we are going. You can see this natural curiosity in our children as they ask where they came from. The age of a person is asked many times during our lives. Restrictions are applied to us for different events such as driver permits, flying permits, Military service, drinking, employment, birthdays, and more. We all need a foundation of time.

Then as God reveals his master plan and we as his children ask, *"Are we there yet?"* It is a natural desire, on our part, to want to know where we fit into our Father's plan and how far along that plan we have proceeded. When we tell our children bedside stories, we share with them stories they can understand. Likewise, as with God, he will say to us about extremely complicated events in stories, visions, or concepts we can understand through parables. As with children's stories, there is also hidden information presented for us to unravel. Take, for example, "The Three Little Pigs." The underlying concept was to make an effort to build your house (body and soul) strong enough to withstand an attack. "Pinocchio" was about the problems that accompany lying, and "Little Red Riding Hood" exposed the dangers of deceptions and gullibility.

Our father does not want us ignorant of his plan. Jesus, through his parables, revealed similar covert spiritual meanings to his apostles *and us*. Jesus speaks from a known earthly concept to a parallel spiritual concept. And God hides information from those he chooses.

Matthew 13: 10–11 *"(10) And the disciples came, and said unto him, Why speakest thou unto them in parables? (11) He* (Jesus) *answered and said unto them, Because it is given unto you to <u>know the mysteries</u> of the kingdom of heaven, but <u>to them it is not given.</u>" (KJV)*

These verses are clear. Jesus is establishing the concept that God has given to his children, God's mysteries of his plan for his children. But, God has purposely created mysteries in the Bible to hide knowledge from unrighteous individuals.

The Book of Revelations is given explicitly to his children so they may know his end-time plan. If God gave us the Book of Revelation about the process of ending earth's time, wouldn't he give us a message concerning the beginning process of God's time in the Book of Genesis? Also, God has given many prophecy books and some with very specific days concerning some event to occur; for example, in **Dan. 12.**

Daniel 12:11–2 *"(11) And from the time that the daily* sacrifice *shall be taken away, and the <u>abomination that maketh desolate set up,</u> there shall be <u>a thousand two hundred and ninety days. (12) Blessed is he that waiteth, and cometh to the thousand three hundred and five and thirty days." (KJV)</u>*

Here we read that Daniel is given the <u>*clues*</u> to God's timing for Jesus' *3rd Return* at 1,290 days *(<u>clue #1</u>),* anchored on the time the abomination of Satan's statue *(<u>clue #2</u>)* is set up in the reconstructed Jewish Temple *(<u>clue #3</u>).* This Satanic statue is diametrically opposed to the 1st and 2nd Commandments *(<u>clue #4</u>);* of God's 10 Commandments found in **Exo.20.**

Exodus 20:3–5 *"(3) Thou shalt have no other gods before me"* **(4) *Thou shalt not make unto thee any <u>graven image</u>, or any likeness of anything that is <u>in heaven above</u>, or that <u>is in the earth beneath</u>, or that is in the water under the earth: (5) Thou***

shalt not bow down thyself to them, nor <u>serve</u> *them: for I the LORD thy God am a jealous God, visiting the iniquity of the fathers upon the children unto the third and fourth generation* <u>*of them that hate me*</u>*;" (KJV)*

In **Daniel 12,** next God gives us: 1,335 days *(clue #5),* which is from the end of the war of Armageddon *(clue #6),* establishing Jesus' earthly 1,000-year Kingdom *(clue #7)* with earthly survivors <u>clue #8</u> and the cleansing of the rebuilt Jewish Temple *(clue #9),* and other governmental needs. *(Clue #10)*

Daniel's seal **(Dan. 12:4)** is broken today; more and more truths of God's words are becoming apparent.

2. Is God hiding information from unrighteous inquisitors?

God has written the scriptures in such a manner that the unrighteous individual would have a difficult time understanding the true and more profound spiritual meanings of the scriptures. This does not mean that a person cannot understand the simple truth of Jesus' salvation. We just read in **Mat.13:10–11** that the mysteries of God are not given to the lost souls. Also, in **John 12,** we read, God has blinded Israel to God's words and Jesus.

John 12:30–40 *"(39) Therefore they could not believe, because that Esaias said again, (40)* <u>*He hath blinded their eyes,*</u> *and* <u>*hardened their heart;*</u> *that they should not see with their eyes, nor understand with their heart, and be converted, and I should heal them."(KJV)*

It is clear that the Jews are blinded, as they had Jesus as their teacher and Messiah. They rejected him because they were taught incorrect information from the *Traditions of the Elders*, Old Testament scriptures, and God's Law. But they so often depended on their religious traditions taught to them by their Priest and Rabbis. Some non-Jews have also rejected Jesus because of their lack of knowledge too. Remember, in **Luk 23,** Jesus' statement on the Cross.

Luke 23:34 *"Father forgive them they know what they do." (KJV)*

What and how many forgiveness are there?

Another blinding by God is when God sealed up Daniel's prophecy about the <u>clues</u> to the approaching end of time for earth and man. God is reserving Daniel's <u>clues</u> until people have enough knowledge that they could understand God's final days for man. In **Dan.12,** God tells us of a confused Daniel. With these words:

> **Daniel. 12:8–10** *"(8) And I heard, but I understood not; then said I. O my Lord, what shall be the end of these things? (9) And he said, go thy way, Daniel; <u>for the words are closed up and sealed till the time of the end.</u> (10) Many shall be purified, and made white, and tried; but the wicked shall do wickedly: and <u>none of the wicked shall understand; but the wise shall understand.</u>" (KJV)*

Notice what God said to his child Daniel: God's words are closed up to everyone and sealed until near the end of time. At some point in the future, God will reveal his plan to the end time Saints. Even Israel's (God's elect) blinded eyes will be healed **(John 12:37–40).**

Many seekers have come to know Jesus, as their personal savior, by reading God's words for truth and love. However, God reveals to his chosen ones (believer in Jesus) that we cannot expect an unbeliever to fully understand the complexities of God, his knowledge, and his plans. This misunderstanding occurred with Phillip and the Ethiopian eunuch in **Acts 8.**

> **Acts 8:30–31** *"(30) And Philip ran thither to him, and heard him read the prophet Esaias, and said, Understandest thou what thou readest? (31) And he* (eunuch) *said, "<u>How can I, except some man should guide me?</u>" And he desired Phillip that he would come up and sit with him."(KJV)*

We can read the results of Phillip's efforts to explain the scriptures about Jesus to the eunuch. The eunuch was saved and baptized! God has given us, his children, the privilege of sharing our knowledge of the scriptures with the lost, errant, or confused. He freely gives us the gift and then blesses us when we apply that gift. It's a Win, Win situation. And we all have a gift. Some are given the gift of prophecy, some pastors, some teachers, and many others are given unique gifts. But, God will reveal your gift if you look for it. Another thing God will reveal is --- up and coming prophetic events.

In Amos 4:7 *"Surely the Lord God will do nothing. But he revealeth his secret unto his servants the prophets."(KJV)*

Isaiah 42:9 *"Behold, the former things are come to pass, and new things I do declare: Before they spring forth I tell you of them."(KJV)*

All through the history of Israel, God has given his people assurance that an event would occur, and it did.

- To Adam, death would occur if he ate of the Tree of Knowledge of Good and Evil.
- To Noah, a Great Flood would occur.
- To Abraham, that he would have a son and Abraham's offspring would be like the sands of the sea.
- To Moses, he would lead his people to a land flowing with milk and honey.
- There are over 300 prophecies of Jesus and many more examples too numerous to mention here.

We are given all that God deems necessary in his words to reveal his plan to those individuals that will search for it as a treasure. To do less would cause confusion. And **1 Cor.14:33** tells us that God is not the author of confusion. Over the last few years, we have seen a proliferation of books written about the end times, and for a good reason. God is revealing to his people God's truth and his plan for the end of time. **Amos 4:7** confirms this character of God; and that he will reveal his plan to us. **Proverbs 2** also admonishes us to study God's words.

> **Proverbs 2:1–6** *"(1) My son, if thou wilt receive my words, and hide my commandments with thee; (2) So that thou incline thine ear unto wisdom, and apply thine heart to understanding; (3) Yea, if thou criest after knowledge, and liftest up thy voice for understanding; (4) If thou seekest her as silver, and searchest for her for hid treasure; (5) Then shalt thou understand the fear of the Lord, and find the knowledge of God. (6) For the Lord giveth wisdom; out of his mouth cometh knowledge and understanding."(KJV)*

It becomes clear from these words from God; we are to put forth an effort to search out the scriptures for all of God's information. He has deemed it necessary for us to receive and understand his plan for man. I know that the Old Testament foreshadows things to come, and the New and Old Testament must agree for a thing to be true. If this is the case, then we have an agreement with the information in **Jhn. 16.**

> **John 16:13** *"Howbeit, when he, the Spirit of truth, is come, <u>he will guide</u> you <u>into all truth;</u> for he shall not speak of himself; but whatsoever he shall hear, that shall he speak: <u>and he will show you things to come."</u> (KJV)*

This Spirit of Truth is the Holy Spirit that did come to earth at Pentecost, and it is the Holy Spirit that guides us to truths. For us to be guided, we must study the scriptures. God has written them in such a manner that only that person committed to serious study and discovery will receive the deeper meaning in the scriptures. In **Mat. 13,** we read:

> **Mathew 13:10–11** *"(10) And the disciples came, and said unto him, Why speakest thou unto them in parables? (11) He* (Jesus)

answered and said unto them, Because <u>it is given unto you to know the mysteries of the kingdom of heaven, but to them it is not</u> given."(KJV)

Here again, we see that He will hide information from people, but all information is available and revealed to his followers. Then it is the receiver of the information who is responsible for explaining the knowledge gained to other searching souls. All we need do is ask the Holy Spirit to reveal the hidden meaning of the scriptures to us, and in his time, he will honor that request. The early developing Church had apostles to expound on the scriptures and his sayings. It is evident in scriptures that God gave different apostles and prophets different concepts, and some apostles needed to correct some small differences in understanding **(1Cor.8:1–9).** This correction is proof of **1 John 4:1** to test the spirit. Today we have the Comforter, the Holy Spirit, to help us as he reveals God's truths from scriptures to many different people.

3. Is God revealing hidden information to his children?

Even Jesus used hidden information in his parables to his apostles **(Mat.13:3– 30** The Sower). It became necessary for Jesus to reveal what the parable elements reflected and the parallel spiritual information or theme they corporately created. Prophets, too, were used in the days before the scriptures were completed, and their words are still difficult to understand even today **(Eze.1** and **10)** Chariots of Fire.

God gave his word to the prophet, and the prophet gave it to the people. Certain prophets were given specific information on future events that would take place at the return of Jesus. Daniel has been given *specific days* for certain events to yet come true. Also, the Book of Revelation speaks of *specifics*, and they are there for our knowledge and use. What would be the Bible's purpose if it were not to give us truthful information, *both mortal and spiritual,* for us to use? If God has a master plan, why wouldn't he share it with his children? The answer is obvious. He does, he has, and he will!

In the **Book of Daniel,** God spent many words on future event times that Daniel was not privileged to understand; but it was for the future end-time Saints, who could understand **(Dan.12:8–10).**

It requires that Saints of all ages be on the alert, study the scriptures, and watch for prophetic signs. We can see in Daniel God's plans to reveal this information to some Saints at the end of time. Who will be the persons that God permits to share Daniel's message of interpretations? The Bible has revealed it will (most likely) be Saints of little renown. God has revealed to us over and over that he chooses people of little notoriety. All of the Apostles were common men, except for Paul. Even Daniel was given specific information about when Israel's captivity in Babylon would end, but Daniel had to read and study scriptures to get that knowledge **(Dan.9:2).**

4. If God has a beginning and an ending, would he not reveal this <u>general timing</u> to his children?

God has given us glimpses of his timing in various parts of the scriptures: **Jer.25:12 / Jer.29:10 / Dan 9:24–27 / Dan.12:7, 11–12,** and the **Book of Revelation,** just to name a few. In **Revelation 2 and 3,** these seven letters to the seven Churches reveals the general duration of that particular Church period in God's end of time plan. And it dovetails into his general overall timing. But that is for a later discussion. All of this should motivate us by seeing that time is short, that we need to be doing the works of Jesus. We have been given the Book of Genesis, a book of the beginning. The name Genesis in its self tells us that God created time (*"In the beginning"*). That Genesis starts God's clock on his plan for man, and what more fitting place to reveal his overall general time plan to his children.

In our everyday plans, we see that we have an initial desire to know the time it will take to perform some task. It helps us to schedule things to be accomplished. We can reveal to another person the length that it will take to achieve a task. With unfathomable precision and accuracy, God created heavenly bodies to help us tell time and help us determine where we are located within that time frame. He gave us time for knowing: when to plant seeds, when to harvest, when winter is approaching, when winter is approaching completion, time for the longest daylight, time of the shortest daylight, and on and on. In the book of Genesis, God reveals seven periods when He has performed some special event of creation. He tells us that it is a day, which we understand is a specific time. His use of Day reveals that all the periods are of equal duration of 24 hours. God took literally six days, as we know it, to create his glorious creation.

God's earth proves this 24 hour day concept with the earth's revolving around the Sun to measure a year. And the 24-hour rotation of our planet is for the measurement of one day. The movement of the subpoint of the Sun on the earth's surface; moves 15 degrees of Longitude for every hour.

Note

The subpoint is a point on the earth's surface where the line of sunlight strikes. If you connect a string to the center of the Sun and connect that string to the center of the earth, where the string intersects the earth's crust, it is called the Subpoint.

This timing is so precise it takes years to see a minuscule change. What would be the purpose of this information if it is not for our use? Our whole universe moves with such precision that celestial navigation can be performed on earth and in space travel. And this mystery of a more precise timing will be revealed in this book as to God's plan for man develops.

5. Is it possible that the duration <u>of</u> creation is the duration <u>for</u> creation?

It is my contention that God has revealed his general overall timing for the duration of his creation. This story of creation contains the foundation of God's covert time for man on this 1st earth. It is the theme for this book to give you information to consider as to that timing. I've shown you that God has a beginning and an ending. Also, Abba (father) wants his children to know him, Jesus, the Holy Spirit, and his plan for his children. I will start with Day One of the creation story and review the pertinent material. Then I will identify the key points around which this thesis is built.

One item I would like you to know is; anytime you see me mention Saints, they are those saved by God's grace; and not some individual selected by some earthly committee. There are so many verses in scriptures that support this Believer / Saint concept. There are three types of Saints: Old Testament Saints, Church Saints, and Tribulation Saints. In **1 Cor. 1**; we read of the Church Saints.

> **1 Corinthians 1:1–2 *"(1) Paul, called* to be *an apostle of Jesus Christ through the will of God, and <u>Sosthenes</u> our brother, (2) Unto the church of God which is at Corinth, to them that are <u>sanctified in Christ Jesus,</u> called to be <u>saints, with all that in every place call upon the name of Jesus Christ our Lord, both theirs and ours:"</u> (KJV)***

(Sosthens equals--So then too)

Paul reveals the *1st clue* in this passage that the brothers that are sanctified <u>*in Christ Jesus*</u> are called Saints and not only they of the Church in Corinth, *2nd clue* but onto all them, in all places, *that are in Christ Jesus* (call upon his name). All believers are sanctified (set apart) in Christ. Again we see Paul identifying the Saints: Timothy, our brothers, all members of the Church in Corinth, and surrounding the area of Achaia.

There is no mention of any organization in the Bible to choose or elect who are Saints. The Church Saints and Tribulation Saints are determined by those who have accepted Jesus Christ as their Lord and savior. Tribulation Saints are saved by God's grace in faith and late deeds. If needed, return to the chapter on SAINTS.

One other concept I would like for you to consider is God's <u>creation of all things</u>. It is every item in the universe was created during this time. We will read of the completed universe on Day 4. That will include all the Galaxies, Solar systems within those Galaxies. There are Moons and all sorts of unique phenomena that are between and within those Galaxies. There are things in the Universe we have yet to discover. Just in our Galaxy alone, the odds are that we could have over 1 million solar systems with one planet in each that could support life. Just as our lack of knowledge of all things pertaining to this earth, it is with a greater lack of knowledge of the universe and items therein. We still have so much to learn.

Note

Genesis speaks of 6 days of creation, and God's creation day is 24 hours. God could have created all instantly, but he chose seven days for a reason. Why?

Is it because God reveals to us in Genesis an overview of God's general duration for his plan for man. Each day has covert information for us to unravel. These revealing's will tell of many mysteries hidden in God's plan. One such mystery is found in **2 Pet.**

2 Peter3:4–8 *"(4) And saying, Where is the promise of his coming? for since the fathers fell asleep, all things continue as* they were *from the beginning of the creation. (5) For this they willingly are ignorant of, that by the word of God the heavens were of old, and the earth standing out of the water and in the water: (6) Whereby the world that then was, being overflowed with water, perished: (7) But the heavens and the earth, which are now, by the same word are kept in store, reserved unto fire against the day of judgment and perdition of ungodly men. (8) But, beloved, be not ignorant of this one thing, that one day is with the Lord as a thousand years, and a thousand years as one day". (KJV)*

These verses of **2 Peter 3** *are central to the concept around which this book's thesis is based. Especially that which is found in* **verse 8.** And it has been

263

misinterpreted far too long. Please read the complete chapter to get the fullness of time from creation, the flood, and the earth's destruction. This span of time covers all of God's earth's history.

Verse 5 *clue 1* speaks of the beginning of the time of creation **(Gen.1:1)**. *Clue 2* is when there was a void space *"face of the deep"* in *Day 1***(Gen.1:2)**. It also reveals *clue 3* of the division of water, earth, and atmosphere in *Day 2* **(Gen.1:7–8).**

Verse 6 *clue 4,* we read of this world overflowed by water (the Flood) that occurred 1,656 years later in **Gen.6–7,** which destroyed all creatures except Noah, his family, and animals on the Ark. Also, God gave them a sign that this flood would never happen again (*the Rainbow*). **(Gen.9:11–13)**

Verse 7 clue *5,* we read that during the 7,000 years, God will keep the earth and heavens reserved for fire (Judgment day); and the perdition (eternal punishment) of the unrighteous individuals. This *clue* covers the time from the flood to the very final Day of Judgment, The Great White Throne Judgment of God.

So you can see in these verses, and the remainder of **Chapter 3** covers *the entire life span of God's plan* for *earthlings*. We see in **Rev.21:1,** *clue 6,* where God destroys the earth and creates a New Heaven and New Earth. *This event will happen after the Great White Thorne Judgment of the unrighteous souls. And this is the end of time as we know it today.* All these <u>unrighteous individuals</u> who have ever lived will receive their just rewards; ***The Lake of Fire****. So, God gives us a concept of his planned duration for man in.***2 Peter3.**

☆ **2 Peter 3:8 *"But, beloved, be not ignorant of this one thing, that <u>one day</u> is <u>with the Lord as a thousand years, and a thousand years as one day."</u> (KJV)***

This *clue 7* in **verse 8** has been revealed by many well-meaning teachers that this verse is just to tell us what God generally thinks of measurement of apparent time. Some claim it has a spiritual inference to time and not an actual day's or years to measure time as we know it. Some doctrine claim this is revealed by the 1,000 cattle on 1,000 hills. *We really need to test that spirit.* However, let us look at what God says about the way we are to speak. (**Mat. 5**)

Matthew 5:37 *"But let your communication be, Yea, yea; Nay, nay: for whatsoever is more than these cometh of evil." (KJV)*

This verse is found in the lesson Jesus was teaching about swearing, but it also tells us about the simple truth we are to speak. If it is true for God, it is true for us, for God is truth and hates lies. Therefore, 1,000 days means 1,000 days, and 1,000 years means 1,000 years. But how is God using these days and years?

Peter is simplifying this verse in **Pet.3:8** but associates it with the completeness of God's duration of time for man. It is obvious **2 Peter 3** covers that time from the <u>*creation to the destruction of the earth.*</u> So if God said a day is like 1,000 years and 1,000 years is like a day, this is truth. And this verse is wrapped around the completeness of earth history or God's total plan for the earth. So Genesis' 7 days equal 7,000 years.

It appears entirely appropriate; God is telling us in the Genesis account that each day of creating *symbolizes* a day of 1,000 years for the maximum transitional time of earth's history. But, not to be applied to a single day of creation, as it is a proven 24 hours per day of creating. And if each day also resents 1,000 years, it must have some meaning or clues for us to decipher? For example, the six days of creation are symbolic of 6,000 years, and *day seven is symbolic of Jesus' Kingdom of 1,000-years Kingdom* (**Rev.20:2–7**) *before the final Judgment day.* And Jesus' Kingdom will last eternally after the Judgment day (end of Day 7). This agrees with **Genesis 2:1–4** as there is <u>no</u> <u>statement of</u>, *"there was evening, and there was morning of the seventh day"* as day seven is forever. For scriptures tell us Jesus' Kingdom will be forever **1**

Pet.5:11. Some newer interpretations of the Bible include this *"evening and morning"* statement in Day 7, but the original Old King James does not.

Please notice the words in **Gen.2:4,** *"these are the generations of the heavens and of the earth."* Here we see the plurality of generations of both heavens and earth. Typically a generation today covers a period from birth to the age to give birth (30 years).

Generation *"to-led-aw'*; from 3205; (plur. only) *descent,* i.e. *family*; (fig.) *history:* --birth, generations.[2]*"*

This word generation appears to support the theory that every day in creation represents a generation of 1,000 years and for God's overall timing of 7,000 years for his present earthly creation. However, a specific 12 hours (sunset to sunrise) within 24 hours; is the actual time for creating that day's items. These 24 hours were when God created the heavenly bodies; and remains the same today as it did then, proven by the earth rotation. Now let us look into each 24 hour day and God's 7,000 years in the Clock of Creation.

DAY ONE

Genesis 1:1–5 ”*(1) In the beginning God created the heaven and the earth. (2) And the earth was without form, and void; and <u>darkness was upon the face of the deep</u>. And the spirit of God moved upon the face of the waters. (3) And God said <u>Let there be light, and there was light.</u> (4) And God saw the light, that it was good; and God divided the light from the darkness. (5) And God called the light Day, and the darkness he called night. And the evening and the morning were the first day.”(KJV)*

FIRST A PLAN IS CREATED

Note

Keep in mind as you read Genesis that when God created items, he made them at <u>different maturity levels</u>. And also, He included into those items his immutable Natural Laws and their relationship to each created item. There is no earthly way we can fully grasp the magnitude of God's plan for the universe.

Before creating, God devised his plan for Heaven and Earth and all things within both of these locations. Every item made must have its immutable natural laws within them and be consistent in performance. Many items have dependencies on other items for survival and growth. For example, fruit trees must have bees to cross-pollinate their blossoms to produce fruit and seeds. Hummingbirds must have sweet nectar from the flower blossom to survive, and the flower needs the Humming Birds to cross-pollinate the flower for future blooms. God also had to build into the items its relationship with other created things. For example: if we mix Flour with milk, sugar, butter, eggs and heat it, we get a cake or a cookie. All-natural laws must be built into all items as they were created. And how they are to function together for good or bad.

They also must be kept in perfect working condition, which is God's job, but on Day 7, it becomes Jesus' job.

We read *"In the beginning"*; beginning of what? It is clear that God has a plan for man, and this plan was conceived in its completeness from beginning to end. Just think; God's planning for every item: trillions and trillions of people, animals, vegetation, angels, aliens (?), galaxies, etc. And this is over eternity and not just this earth. God would not start something that he was not intimately knowledgeable of all events that would occur, be they good or bad. And what his reactions would be. This plan also must encompass each entity ever created. This plan is not open-ended; it has an ending. **(Rev.9:15 and Rev.21:1)** Each person's life is a plan in itself, and it is woven into the larger plan for humanity. God has a time for your beginning and a time for your ending. Therefore, He has an exact date for our introduction into his plan (our birthday). And an exact time for our removal (our death) from this world. It is this duration that God has set aside for us to: improve our moral character, learn of God, surrender to Jesus, and store up our treasures in heaven.

Please understand this note.

*<u>This earth is not reality;</u> it is only a proving ground for our confrontation with evil. It is our time of testing that God has designed for each of us, and He intended to have the Church reveal God's manifold wisdom to the principalities and powers even in the heavenly realm **(Eph. 3)**.*

*Ephesians 3:8–11   "(9) And to <u>make all</u> men <u>see</u> what is **the <u>fellowship of the mystery</u>, which <u>from the beginning</u> of the world <u>hath been hid</u> in God, who created all things by Jesus Christ: (10) To the intent that now <u>unto the principalities</u> <u>and powers in heavenly</u> places might be <u>known by the church the manifold wisdom of God,</u> (11) <u>According to the eternal purpose which he purposed in Christ Jesus</u> our Lord:"(KJV)*

These verses have genuinely been a mystery to mainstream Christians for years. The <u>*1st clue*</u> is *to make all men see a fellowship* from the beginning **(Genesis 1).** But if we read the words, <u>they are clear</u>; but *covered by the fog of traditions.* God's wisdom is to be brought to the *principalities and powers in heavenly places by the Church.* The word *"by"* reveals the Church is to bring to these principalities and powers in heaven God's wisdom. And this task for humans was planned by Jesus and God; *to be performed by the Church* Saints. This task is part of the Great Commission spoken of in **Matthew 28.**

> **Matthew 28:18–20 *"(18) And Jesus came and spake unto them, saying, <u>All power is given unto me in</u> <u>heaven and in earth.</u> (19) Go ye therefore, and <u>teach all nations,</u> <u>baptizing them</u> in the name of the Father, and of the Son, and of the Holy Ghost: (20) <u>Teaching them</u> to observe all things whatsoever I have commanded you: and, lo, I am with you alway,* even *unto the end of the world. Amen." (KJV)***

This thought brings up another question for your consideration. Is this the final overall wisdom revealed from the lessons learned in the life of the Church? Or is it an individual Christian's task which comes from that period of the Church's existence? By now, the Church Saints will have the mind of Christ. Also, by the words *"teach all nations,"* we by traditions assume the word *"nations"* pertain to only to earth. But the primary word in Greek is (lah-os') for a nation is *people and "not one's own populace:-people."* Therefore, can principalities and powers also be considered people? ------ Yes

> *Please bear with me as I feel the need to repeat prior information*
> *on aliens. They also are in God's plan for eternity.*

We have been given an excellent opportunity to be included in the Fellowship Mystery **(Eph.3:8–11)** and as heirs with Jesus and become Kings, Lords, and Priests.

> "Fellowship =2842 *koy-nohn-ee'-ah*: from 2844; *partnership* i.e.
> (lit) *participation*, or (social) *intercourse*, or (pecuniary)
> *benefaction*; - (to) communicate (-ation), communion, (contri-)
> distribution, fellowship[2]."

This fellowship is defined as a partnership or social intercourse. Both indicate a very close relationship. And this fellowship has been hidden since earth's creation by God.

We know that we have been in partnership with angels as they have been involved with mankind from creation. The Bible has many examples of angels coming to earth to help or pass information to man from God. Therefore, this fellowship mentioned here must be a different mystery as it has been hidden from us until now. If these principalities are not people, then how does the *"manifold wisdom of God"* relate in. **Eph. 3:10**

> **Ephesians 3:10** *"To the intent that now unto the principalities and powers in heavenly places might be known by the church the manifold wisdom of God," (KJV)*

So is this revealing the hidden fellowship between the Church and the principalities and powers in heavenly places? It appears so. But notice, in **Eph. 3,** it is an eternal propose of God.

> **Ephesians 3:11** *"(11) According to the eternal propose which he purposed in Christ Jesus our Lord:" (KJV)*

It appears from this verse, this was in God's plan for His Church before creation, and his purpose began at creation but was purposed into Jesus' mission on earth. Is this telling us of a hidden partnership with principalities and powers in heavenly places?---Yes! But who are these principalities and powers in heavenly places? They appear to be outside our atmosphere (space).

Verse 11 reveals a great deal of information to consider. God designed for Jesus to bring God's salvation plan for man and for man to be the teachers to these principalities and powers in heavenly places. If we are to bring knowledge to these entities, they must be like us, made in God's image, with a brain. Can you imagine the enormity of this task? Where are they? How do we get there? What lesson plan do we have? What subject to start with first. Will we need training aids? And on and on. Or is it that they will be learning by watching us during the Church period of existence on earth? But remember, we will be given the mind of Christ. **(1 Cor.2:16)**

At no other time in earth's history (before Jesus or after the Church Age) have people been given this blessing of being the Bride of Christ and rule with Jesus. One exception is the Tribulations Saints that will rule forever under David's kingdom (Israel). So why do so many people miss this opportunity?

Many people fail to recognize that *Eternity is our reality; and not this short time on earth.* Heaven is the final destination for those who believe in God's son Jesus. Earth is the place we will live for just a few years. God has given us seventy (70) to eighty (80) years here on his proving ground **(Psalms 90:10).** And he has provided: experiences (test), written material (Bible), and teachers (Holy Spirit) to help us attain some measure of righteousness. The race we run is likened to the schools we have attended. In both, there is a start (1st Grade) and a finish (12 Grade). There were things for us to learn from: books, teachers, homework, and study, by practical and spiritual trial and error. We attempt to stay on the path that leads to graduation by obtaining the necessary disciplines (credits / Treasures). We will spend our lives looking for that narrow spiritual road and trying to stay on that road that Jesus tells us about in **Mat. 7.**

> **Matthew 7:13–14** *"(13) Enter ye in at the straight gate: for wide is the gate, and broad is the way, that leadth to destruction, and many there be which go in there at; (14) Because straight is the gate, and narrow is the way, which leadeth unto life, and few there be that find it."(KJV)*

It is this road we travel day after day to arrive at our final destination, Heaven. There will be bumps in this road, twists and turns, hard climbs and easy descents, good weather and bad weather. The trip is on the scenic route of great beauty, which we need to appreciate. This narrow way (one way) indicates we must be watchful and not slide off the road. But, this road is there for our guidance to our destination. God has given us a map, the Bible, to follow, which is our assurance we are on the correct path. Our arrival time is unknown to us due to our detours along this road. But, in God's plan, he has already recalculated our return route to the correct way.

Not only was this road created before the opening operation in God's plan, but also the concept of time, as we know it. The time and plan are so married together that it is impossible to separate the two.

TIME CREATED

"In the beginning," God is revealing that he created time. He is saying that he is starting his plan, and this is the point we can mark as the starting time of his plan. This plan has a start point (Genesis) and an endpoint (Revelation). With a starting point and an ending point, it would seem reasonable, less confusing, to have given duration markers between those two points. And markers to reveal one's present position within that time frame. These markers are like our watches with hours, minutes, and seconds. This duration is supported by **Revelation 9.**

> **Revelation 9:15 "*And the four angels were loosed, which were prepared for <u>an hour</u>, and <u>a day</u>, and <u>a month</u>, and <u>a year</u>, for to <u>slay the third part of men</u>." (KJV)**

It certainly appears that God has a specific duration *clue* for his plan for these angels. How much clearer can God get than 1) an hour, 2) a day, 3) a month, and 4) a year. This data is not spiritual time but actual time on earth. Jesus said we would know the time by the season in **Mat. 24.**

> **Matthew 24:32–33 "*(32) Now learn a parable of the fig tree; When his branch is yet tender, and putteth forth leaves, ye know**

that summer is *nigh: (33) So likewise ye, when ye shall see all these things, know that it is near,* even *at the doors." (KJV)*

God has hidden this duration because God knows if some people knew the time, they would postpone their decision to accept Jesus until the last moment. They forget that their life can be terminated in an instant at any moment, and their soul forfeited to Hell. There is a saying in the military that says, *"there are no atheists in fox holes."* When faced with imminent death, soldiers will pray to God for mercy. They know they are about to meet God (Tree of Knowledge) and are unsure of their destination. Please do not wait as you may not have the opportunity to accept Jesus.

The ending point of God's plan is dependent on the many objectives within God's plan. So it would seem appropriate to give some attention to what might be some (not all) of his objectives.

1.	**God wants all beings with him in heaven**. This assumption is based on the fact that God created man and that in **1 Tim 2,** God says that he wants all people to be saved.

> **1 Timothy 2:3–5 *"(3) For this is good and acceptable in the sight of God our Savior; (4) who will have all men to be saved; and come unto the knowledge of the truth. (5) For there is one God and one mediator between God and men, the man Christ Jesus ;"(KJV)***

> There is no other name for salvation but Jesus.

2. **God gives each person a certain number of years** to come unto this knowledge of truth and accept his son Jesus. We read in **Psalm 90** that our life span is 60 plus 10 years, or 80 if we are strong. (Score equals 20 years)

> **Psalm 90:9–10** *"(10) For all of our days are passed away in thy wrath: we spend our years as a tale that is told. (10) The <u>days of our years</u> are <u>threescore years and ten</u>; and if by reason of strength they be <u>fourscore years</u>, yet is their strength labour and sorrow; for it is soon cut off, and we fly away." (KJV)*

These verses are a <u>*clue*</u> that can be easily overlooked. In Adam's time, people lived hundreds of years; for example, Methuselah lived 969 and Noah lived 950 years. And after the Flood, the life expectancy decreased until not too long ago it was below 50 years of age. But today, humans are precisely in this life expectancy range mentioned in **Psa. 90.** Is this a possible <u>*clue*</u> for us to consider? ---YES!

3.   <u>**God does not want his children ignorant**</u> of his plan and its purpose? --- NO! All of the Bible, particularly Proverbs of Solomon, instructs the righteous and what God thinks is important. *Knowledge, Understanding,* and *Wisdom;* are heavily encouraged to be sought after. The Bible is full of God's knowledge that he has given to us to understand and put into use wisely. Consider *1st knowledge* as learning the alphabet, the A, B, and C, etc. Next is the *understanding* of putting together letters to form words: CAT, BOY, GIRL, etc. But *wisdom* is placing the truthful, wise words into meaningful wise righteous sentences.

> **1 Timothy 3:16–17** *"(16) All scripture is given by inspiration of God, and is profitable for <u>doctrine</u>, for <u>reproof</u>, for <u>correction, for instruction in righteousness.</u> (17) That the man of God may be perfect, <u>thoroughly furnished</u> unto <u>good works."(KJV)</u>* [Deeds]

What good are these words if we do not apply what we have been given to share with the lost? When God gives, he expects a return. **(Mat.25:14–30)** These verses in **1 Tim 3** confirm that we are to study and use what we have learned or become like the servant that buried his talent in the ground in Mat.25:14–30 and cast into outer darkness.

4. **God has a time and proposes for everything** under the sun. In His wisdom, he has placed events in a particular place in time during our past, present, and future. These events are devised for each person ever borne. It is an overview for each of us of the events we might encounter in God's plan for our lives. These words are to prepare us and reassure us; these are everyday events to expect. And not to be discouraged but strengthened. In **Ecc.3,** you will read:

Ecclesiastes 3:1–8 *"(1) To every <u>thing there is a season, and a time to every propose</u> under the heavens: <u>(2) A time to be born, and a time to die;</u> a time to plant, and a time to pluck up that which is planted; (3) A time to kill, (4) A time to weep, and a time to laugh; a time to mourn, and a time to dance; (5) A time to cast away stones, and a time to gather stones together; a time to embrace, and a time to refrain from embracing; (6) A time to get, and a time to lose; a time to keep, and a time to cast away; (7) A time to rend, and a time to sew; a time to keep silence, and a time to speak; (8) A time to love, and a time to hate; a time of war, and a time of peace."(KJV)*

Each of these events mentioned here has a more in-depth understanding for us to consider in our walk with Jesus. It appears a good thing for us to take these events as real things that will happen in our lives. And not be disturbed when they visit us.

5. **God wills his earthly plan to be permanent**. His plan cannot be added to, nor can anything be subtracted from it. It has been in place in the past and will continue to the very end of time. God's earthly plan is fixed and unchangeable; *<u>therefore, it must have a specific duration. But God has an eternal plan that will never end.</u>*

Ecclesiastes 3:14–15 *"(14) I know that, whatsoever God doeth, it <u>shall be forever</u>: <u>nothing can be put to it, nor any thing taken from it</u>: and God doeth it, <u>that men should fear before him</u>. (15) That which <u>hath been is now</u>; <u>and that which is to be hath already been</u>; and God requireth that which is past."(KJV)*

As you can see, nothing can be added or subtracted from God's plan. But, also notice **verse 15,** which speaks to past generations' sins, are present in our generation. *And that has been is now*; reveals that Satan's successes and failures have also been in the past. Satan's tactics are the same now as they were yesterday.

These verses prove God can move to any ant location in time. God can move into the past and the future, as he is not limited by time or space. And also, nothing is new in Satan's plan against God. Satan's goal is the same year after year; only the sin names and faces change. However, Satan will make his final move against God after the last half of the Great Tribulation of seven years. God will require the recognition and payment of each human's past deeds, be they good or bad.

God will permit us to apply our self-will above that of God's will but at a heavy cost. God could stop atrocities we see in our daily lives, but *he reluctantly permits it to happen*. For example: if you were so depressed that you want to commit suicide by jumping off the Empire State Building in N.Y. city, God would send someone, or the Holy Spirit, to try to convince you that suicide is a sin. But you jump anyway. Suicide is a SIN; it is one you cannot ask for forgiveness after the fact.

But, on your way down, you decide you have made a grave mistake; and you ask God for forgiveness. Will he forgive you? --- DEPENDS! --- But, will he change your outcome? --- MOST LIKELY NOT! ---Will God save you after impact? --- DEPENDS! This word DEPENDS, is on your righteous relationship to Jesus and God's plan for your life. If you are seeking avoidance of the results from impact --- NO!!!!!

We must keep in mind that there is a consequence for every action, be it for good or evil. The Holy Spirit works through our knowledge of good or corruption due to the sin of Adam. We are given that consequence through the Tree of Knowledge of Good or Evil. And God wants us to exercise our self-will based on good.

Therefore, the innocent that are abused are cared for by God, as they are blameless for causing the evil action. But, the perpetrator of evil will have a very painful consequence for his or her actions.

It is impossible for us to intimately understand the complexities of God's plan for his creation because his ways are not our ways. But, he will reveal to us through the Holy Spirit as much as he thinks necessary for our edification and use. God is not surprised when we deviate from his perfect plan for our lives. He knew each of us would deviate, and he has already created another (less ideal) plan for each of us. But we must search for it as we would search for a treasure. **Mat. 7** says this:

> **Matthew 7:7–8** *"(7) Ask, and it shall be given you; seek, and ye shall find; knock, and it shall be opened unto you: (8) For every one that asketh receiveth; and he that seeketh findeth; and to him that knocketh it shall be opened." (KJV)*

This Scripture is pertaining to all things. It includes human carnal needs as well as spiritual needs and the mysteries of God. See **Col. 2.**

> **Colossians 2:2–3** *"(2) That their hearts might be comforted, being knit together in love, and unto all riches of the <u>full assurance of understanding</u>, to the acknowledgement of <u>the mystery of God</u>, and of the Father, and of Christ; (3) <u>In whom are hid all the treasures of wisdom and knowledge</u>." (KJV)*

These verses were written by Paul to the Colossians and the Laodiceans. It is valid for all believers also. God has given us this information, and it is in his

Love Letter, the Bible, to all believers in Jesus. All information is there, but you must: ask, seek (study), and God will reveal his information to you at the proper time. *Be patient!*

If you received a Love Letter from a special person you loved very much, would you not read it over and over to place those precious words in your memory and heart? Men, would you not smell the letter for the familiar scent of her perfume to bring her closer to you? Would you not save those love letters to read again, into the future, to warm your heart? *God loved us so much that he gave his only Son to die and pay for our sins* (**John 3:16**). God's Love Letter to us is the most fabulous Love Letter you will ever receive. Please read it and cherish it. Now the foundation has been laid, let us return to Genesis

LIGHT CREATED

> **Genesis 1:2** *"And the earth was without form, and void; and <u>darkness was upon the face of the deep</u>. And the spirit of the Lord moved upon the face of the waters. (3) And God said let there be light; and <u>there was light</u>." (KJV)*

First, there was darkness, and then God divides darkness and light. But, notice this darkness *"is upon the face of the deep."* Darkness has no depth to our eyes. Complete darkness is smothering to some people as they see no depth. Spelunker's experience this in dark caves when they turn off their source of light. This *"face of the deep"* is space with no source of light.

The concept of light is very complicated. For example: how would you explain light to a person that is blind from birth? How would you describe the color Red? Impossible! Light has many properties that we take for granted daily. When I say light, I am **not** speaking of a source that creates the light but of the light's properties in its self. You will notice God created our natural source of light on Day 4. So light *(Jesus)* is present before a natural source is made. This sentence has a more profound inference to Jesus, *"the light of the world."* One other aspect of creation we must remember is that during the creation of the different elements, God also developed and put into action his natural laws for these elements; and their relationship between affects and effects. That all of the properties within that created object is complete and present at its creation.

For example, the Garden of Edom was complete. It did not take years and years for all the plants to grow as food from seeds, as it was present three days before Adams's creation for his necessities. [More on this later].

Let's take a look at a few properties of light, which are:

1. <u>The light must be reflected to been seen.</u> When we look into outer space, we see large areas of darkness and then a planet, stars, or other heavenly bodies. The darkness here is because there are no solids or gaseous particles in space for the light to hit and be reflected. We see the moon because the moon is reflecting the sun's light rays. Our night is the result of the earth shadowing when the sun is on the opposite side of the planet. In our atmosphere, we have all sorts of solids and gases floating around in the air, reflecting the sun's light rays even at night. That is partially why we have a blue sky and beautiful sunsets, instead of a black sky

   In our daily Christian walk on this earth, we are seen by reflecting light off of our bodies. Whatever we do, we are seen and judged by those reflected actions. Therefore, it behooves us to be examples of non-believers, as well as our brothers and sisters in Christ. We are under scrutiny by those looking for truth, trying to justify their godlessness, or searching for a secure foundation. Some of these individuals know that there is more to life than their shallow existence.

2. <u>Light has a visual and invisible spectrum.</u> One of the properties of light is that some frequencies of light are not visible to the naked eye. Ultra Violet light cannot be seen by the naked eye, but it can be felt. Have you ever been at a swimming pool or beach when the sun is hidden by clouds? Most of us in our youth have been sunburned this way because

the ultraviolet sun rays can penetrate the clouds and damage the skin. This same ultraviolet light is also beneficial in destroying harmful elements such as germs, bacteria, and others.

3. <u>Light can be helpful, as well as harmful.</u> Today we have the means to harness light for good as well as evil. Our medical field has learned to apply light to perform surgery through the use of Lasers. Lasers have made a tremendous difference in the success of certain surgeries.

Some of our movie and TV industry has used light in evil ways. The camera captures the reflected light from the actors and places those images on a material that holds those images. That material can be a movie film, videotape, compact disk, thumb drives, and new devices. Then at a selected time, those images can be seen on a screen. The results are the storage and transmission of light.

Light is also necessary for our health and wellbeing. Have you ever noticed how you feel after many days of cloud coverage? We get vitamin D from sunlight through our eyes. Some people need a lot of light for a healthy mental attitude. Some people even need high-intensity light treatments to stay healthy.

Sunlight intensity can be harmful as it can get items so hot they can catch fire or explode. In **Mal. 4,** we read of the utter destruction of those who have rejected Jesus.

> **Malachi. 4:1–3** *"(1) For, behold, the day cometh, that shall burn as an oven; and all the proud, yea, and <u>all that do wickedly,</u> shall be stubble: and the day that cometh shall burn them up, saith the LORD of hosts, that it shall leave them neither root nor branch. (2) But unto you that fear my name shall the Sun of righteousness arise with healing in his wings; and ye shall go forth, and grow up as calves of the stall. (3) <u>And ye shall tread down the wicked; for they shall be ashes under</u>*

<u>*the soles of your feet*</u> *in the day that I shall do this, saith the LORD of hosts." (KJV)*

4.   <u>Light travels very fast</u> at <u>approximately</u> 186,000 miles a second; 11,160,000 miles a minute; 669,600,000 miles an hour; 16,070,400,000 miles in a day; and 5,865,696,000,000 miles in a year. Our closest star is approximately <u>4 light-years</u> or about 23,462,784,000,000 miles away. When God created light, he created it in place and ready for a source. Light from some stars and other heavenly sources of light were present on earth and did not need to travel from the source to earth. Otherwise, Adam would not have a star for at least four years, and there would have been light gaps in creation. So when the source of light was created on Day 4, light was available immediately everywhere, within certain parameters.

5.   After creation, any visual events that have occurred in space will have to travel the distance to earth (See note below). However, the light will also have its maturity level. That light from many bodies will be present on Day 4. All light sources will be at the correct distance from the earth at creation. New light sources formed will be present to earthlings at some point during the 7,000 years. Most lights are present at man's creation, some to 7,000 years out. But not 2 billion light-years to travel to earth.

Note

> I am using 2 billion light-years just as an example of a maximum distance at Day 4's creation. And the light at a greater distance from earth, the scientists will discover it in the future. At creation, below, the visual stars are mature within the 2 billion Light years from earth. Those outside of this distance will eventually show their light at the light-years they were created from earth. In the below example, the lower stars light will be appearing sometime from Creation to the future 7,000 years.

281

LIGHT YEARS (L.Y.) AT CREATION

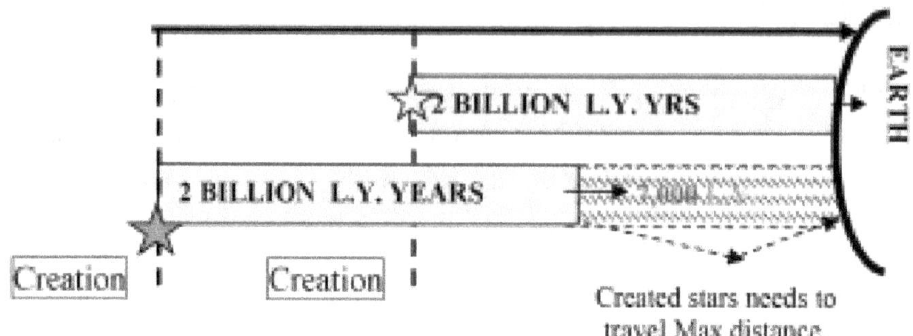

6. <u>The sun is our source of light</u>. It gives us light, on average, for 12 hours and darkness for 12 hours. God has seen fit to limit the duration of intense light. God is reminding us daily that the light he has created for this earth also has a limit. Jesus was and is the light of the world during his ministry here on earth and will be again.

7. The light of the Moon (Genisus1:16–18 to rule the night) is the Church's period of reflecting the light of the righteousness of Jesus in unrighteous dark times. The Moon's period in darkness is a lesser light foretelling of the evil times when darkness (evil) will be on the earth. This spiritual darkness came at Adam's failure and will last until Jesus' birth (the Full Moon). Then darkness returned at Jesus' death. The Church is to be the lesser light of Jesus until his *3rd Return (full Moon)* to claim his earth. The Great Tribulation will be one of the darkest of spiritual times ever on earth and is reflected by the <u>*Moon's period of total darkness*</u>. However, the sunlight will come again. This cycle occurs over and over; as a monthly reminder of Jesus' and the bride's life's journey on this earth. Also, there is a time both the sun and moon can be seen together. This is the sign of the Rapture and wedding of the bride (Church) in heaven. Remember God said he would make signs in heaven. **(Gen.1:14)**

8. <u>The Moon</u> is the mirror of the Church. In Old Testament times, the moon was the revealing Jesus' light coming on earth in the different stages. Jesus' mission was revealed in the Moon cycle. The cycle starts in darkness and grows brighter to the full Moon (Jesus on earth), then starts its fading light until darkness when the Church is removed (the Rapture). But Jesus' light continues to shine, but it is hidden by the evil earth (The Great Tribulation). But this story cycle begins again at sunrise.

We depend on the sunrise every day. The sunset is dependable too, and it reveals that darkness (evil) is coming to this earth in the end times. The sun's life-giving rays will end, and a new light (Jesus) will provide the perfect light and life more desirable than the sun.

8. <u>Also, the eclipse</u> is revealing the Tribulation Saints (Goats) are in Heaven. The Moon is reflecting Jesus' light back to Jesus. Showing Jesus they (Tribulation Saints) have performed the deeds he requires. On our side, we see the dark side revealing the evil of their past lack of deeds.

9. <u>The sun is time-limited.</u> Scientists know that the sun will expand significantly at some time in the distant future, enveloping planets Venus and Mars. It will grow in size, heating up our earth, and melting the ice packs causing flooding for some time. And the sun will eventually explode, destroying most of our planets in our solar system. But this is foretold by God to his children. God told this to the prophet in **Isaiah 60** many years ago, and it has been preserved for our edification today.

Isaiah 60:19 *"The sun shall be no more thy light by day; neither for the brightness shall the moon give light unto thee: but the Lord shall be unto thee an everlasting light and thy God thy glory." (KJV)*

In **Revelation 21:1 & 23,** "*1) And I saw a new heaven and a new earth; for the first heaven and the first earth were passed away; and there was no more sea. (23) And the city* (New Jerusalem) *had <u>no need for the sun</u>, neither of the moon, to shine in it: <u>for the glory of the Lord did</u> <u>lighten it,</u> and the Lamb is the light thereof.*" *(KJV)*

TIME MEASUREMENT CREATED

We use the sun for our measurement of time here on earth. It is based on hours and minutes and: days, weeks, and years. Our calendar depends on the earth's complete rotation per day; our year is based on its complete revolving around the sun. These natural laws of the earth's movement with the sun are accurate and dependable; we can use it in our computer for extreme accuracy in space travel and celestial navigation. This Moon sign is a metaphor for the dependability light of Jesus.

In the Old Testament, we are told that a day to the Israelites started a sunset one-day and ended the next day at sunset.

There was darkness first, then light, and this reflects God's creation as there was first darkness, then sunrise. Darkness is a metaphor used through the Bible for unrighteousness; light is referred to as good (righteousness). This is an analogy that we are evil (in darkness) until we accept Jesus as our savior. And then we become the righteous (light), thereby being divided from darkness (evil). We Christians are commanded <u>not to walk</u> in darkness **(John12:46).** Here again, we see this concept revealed on earth. If you have seen the earth's dark side (from space), you will be amazed at the small individual lights all over the planet. If you think of those tiny lights as Christians, then you should understand how God wants us to be the dimmer light to show Jesus' light to the universe. One small light with many other small lights can become a very bright light (the Church). Isn't God brilliant to show the Church as the light to the Universe; and Jesus' reflection from the Moon (the Church) to the earth? What other chore does God have for the Moon?

The Moon is the foundation for the Jewish calendar. The Moon usually revealed itself at or after the sunsets (darkness). Being Lunar, the lesser light **(Gen. 1:16);** it is not as accurate as of the sun. And like our Leap Year, the Jews must add a month every 2 to 3 years. This division of calendars appears to be God's plan to confuse or hide the dating of events to the unbelievers. So most lunar years are 360 days, and their lunar leap year is 390 days.

Isn't it interesting that God chose to influence Israel to use the very lesser light source of the Moon, which symbolizes the very light source reflecting Jesus righteous life on earth through the Church!

Here we are told that light properties were created during darkness. And that they were divided one from the other. However, light is still present during the night (darkness). God is telling us that during dark times of trouble that his light is still there. Also, remember that the Moon's light increases and decreases over the month, and this reveals that time when Jesus' (Son) light increased and decreased after his death and darkness came on the earth **(Luk. 23:44).** Then the Moon (Holy Spirit) assumed providing Jesus' reflected light to his Church. This light of Jesus has increased in brilliance unto the Church age. But, the Church of Laodicea will have reduced its brightness to the world by its apathy **(Rev. 3).**

When we look for the Sunlight, it reassured us that Jesus is with us. God is telling us that his plan was conceived in darkness but will end in light. We are in darkness until we receive into our hearts the light of Jesus (salvation). It is then Jesus who will bring us into the Light of Life (eternity).

> **John 8:12 *"Then spake Jesus again unto them, saying, I am the light of the world: he that followeth me shall not walk in darkness, but shall have the light of life."(KJV)***

Notice as you read this account that God did all his creating in darkness. For six (6) days, God created during the *"evening to morning."* You can see this is true by reading the final part of each one of God's creative days. But, the only day that has no darkness mentioned is day seven (7). And as a matter of fact, God does not mention an evening or morning at all on Day 7. It appears he is telling us there will be no end of light for this Day7. God reveals that he is creating the Church (Bride of Christ) through these periods of darkness (evening to morning) and during the time of Satan's Kingdom. And the final day (Day 7) refers to Jesus' 1,000-year earthly Kingdom and his eternal Kingdom with his Bride (the Church). Jesus will reclaim the earth and establish his Kingdom, which will have no end. [More on this later].

Hebrews. 1:8 *"But <u>to the Son he</u> (God) <u>saith,</u> Thy <u>throne, O God</u> is for ever and ever; a scepter of righteousness is the scepter of thy kingdom." (KJV)*

Did you notice in **Heb.1:8** that God said to his Son that he also is God? And Jesus' throne will be forever the Throne of righteousness.

Revelation 22:5 "And there shall be no night there; and they need no candle, neither light of the sun; for the Lord God giveth them light: and <u>they shall reign for ever and ever.</u>" (KJV)

So it would appear that this lunar calendar is pointing to another light created in darkness. Day 7 has no morning either as Jesus will come in the night (utter unrighteousness) as he is the bright and morning star **(Rev.22:16).** This is supported by Jesus' statement where numerous times he says he will *come like a thief in the night*, the **Rapture**. In **Rev.19** and other locations that reveal Jesus' *3rd Return will be: by noise, singing, a great multitude of angels, and great light* that goes around the Earth.

This sunrise is our daily reassurance that Jesus will return to destroy all evil and establish His righteous Kingdom. But notice the last words of this verse; *"they shall reign forever and ever." "They"* is a plural word referring to God and Jesus. But many times in the Bible, we are told that those who believe in Jesus (the Church) and Tribulations Saints; will rule with Christ.

MATURITY of ELEMENTS

Uniformitarianism

Many people and scientists think that all items created were from matter or seeds. But, stars and planets did not start as seeded material, as the Sun, Moon, and planets were to give signs to Adam. Also, Adam would need food when he was created. Therefore, food plants were present before Adam's creation.

Scientists use a theory call Uniformitarianism: where all objects change at a uniform rate, under the same environment. And it is advantageous in our daily life. When cooking a meal, the different food items take different times of cooking to be cooked properly. They change at a rate for that particular item in that environment. If we want to paint pressure-treated wood, we must wait 90 days for the chemicals to dry so the paint will adhere to the wood. This is Uniformitarianism as we are looking forward to the completion of the item. But Uniformitarianism is the same in reverse to find out how old is an object.

We must understand that when God created all the items in Genesis, all the items were completed at different ages of maturity. Some mature, some young, and some in between. For example, the Garden of Eden's plants had to be in varying maturity levels as Adam had food available to him immediately. Plus, he was to tend the garden and care for its future growth. His initial food did not spring forth from seeds, as his natural body could not wait for the different vegetables to grow and produce. Likewise, fruit trees started from seed would take years to produce fruit. And it is clear that the Tree of Knowledge of Good and Evil was mature (with fruit) at its creation, as was the Tree of Life. Those two trees had to be present, and with fruit, for God to command only Adam not to eat the Tree of Knowledge fruit. Adam was obedient until later after Satan's deception of Eve.

It had to be many days before God created Eve **Gen.2:19–23,** as Adam's first lengthy job was to name all the creatures God had made. There must have been a significant number of creatures; when you consider all the different species of creatures in the sea, air, and land. I know God could have sustained Adam during seed growth periods, but that seems less efficient as he had created the vegetables and trees before Adam. So why not make a mature source of food for man and animals?

Also, God would build the natural laws that will be found in a particular item. For example, we know the natural law of trees is that every year produces, inside the trunk, a year ring. (Caveat). And if the trees inside the garden were of different ages, there would be rings present to those trees' apparent age. If that tree appeared to be very old and we cut it down, and it had no year rings, then that would be a lie. And not in keeping with the natural laws of God. And we know God hates lies and cannot perform a lie. So, keep this maturity level in mind as we continue through the creation of that particular day.

Scientists have placed a lot of trust in Carbon dating, and they also consider uniformity of growth. For example: if you go into a cave in 2000 AD and see a stalactite and record its length at 10 inches long, and you come back in 1,000 years (3000 AD), and the same stalactite is now 20 inches long. You would deduce that a stalagmite grew 10 inches or one inch per 100 years. So when is the birth year for this stalagmite? If we subtract 20 inches from 3000 AD, we deduce 1,000 AD is the birth year for this stalactite. Carbon dating should also show these same results.

The problem with this Uniformitarianism is it is based on the starting point of the Big Bang theory and not Creationism. As with the stalagmite, we were there and saw the proof, if you could live 1,000 years. So science needs to work with carbon dating to compute agent years. Creationism is based on the time God created a particular item in its apparent mature state.

Also, we know that the weather and elements can change the uniformity of its growth. Mt. Saint Helen's eruption caused a significant problem to this uniformity theory. Because the eruption did in 6 months, what the scientists have been telling students, it would take nature two million years to accomplish that event. Another problem for scientists is the Bible's words on creation.

But let us look into creation. Adam was created (most scholars believe) as a young man. For this example, I will use 15 years old. If an autopsy were performed on Adam right after his creation, all of his organs would appear as a young man of 15 years of age; BUT HE IS ONLY 1 SECOND OLD. Also, consider the Tree of Knowledge of Good and Evil. It would need to have fruit present, which Adam could not eat. It takes a fruit tree many years from seed to produce fruit. But the Tree of Life had fruit. Now, if it takes ±8 years for a tree to produce fruit from seed, scientists would compute that these two trees were ± eight years old. BUT THEY ARE ONLY 1 SECOND OLD! God cannot lie. If he made Adam at 15 years old, then his body would have needed his entire organs at the same maturity level to survive and the same for a tree *or a rock*.

We read in Genesis that God created mountains that mostly were not all that high. And Jesus tells us, from dust we came and dust we will return. Now scientists use carbon dating to determine how old a rock is. But, the problem is, when God created rocks and mountains, he would have included the same internal natural growth laws. So if a stone looks very old, then God made it at that age of maturity during his creating. So if we carbon-dated that rock, it would show thousands and thousands of years old; BUT IT IS ONLY 1 SECOND OLD. Let us also consider the creation of light.

The light was mature in its division from the darkness. But the source was not created until Day 4. For each light source created, its actual light transmitted will be directed towards all quadrants of the Universe. However, after the Universe is completed on Day 4, any new light source must follow the law of light created in that source. Namely, the light from that new source would need to travel from that new source to earth. And we know many stars or other sources of light have been seen to appear after creation. Now, if this light creation phenomenon is not valid, then Adam would have had no starlight source on earth because our closest star is four light-years from Earth. So Adam would not have its starlight for four years. And many other stars and galaxies would not be seen for a great many years. So starlight was at its correct mature distance from earth.

One of the scientist's Carbon dating techniques is based on the uniformity of change, meaning carbon changes at a uniform rate. But the fallacy of this is; they start at what they call: "The Big Bang Theory." This theory assumes all space elements were drawn into a single unit and were drawn together so tight they exploded (expanded). And then they started its change to what we have today, at the rate change of carbon, into those items. There are a lot of fallacies in this theory. One is the fallacy of age dating because God created different items at different ages of maturity.

Another problem with the Big Bang Theory is there is no wholly voided area in space. When we were kids and fired off Fire Crackers, we could see where the Fire Cracker was detonated, but there was only a little paper left in that spot. This paper was due to gravity. But, in space, there is no gravity, except close to a planet. But there were no planets. Therefore, all the items that came together to explode would expand continually, in all directions, and unrestricted into space. And no particles would be left in that location at the point of detonation. A vast void in space should be present and growing, as all items in space are expanding outwardly in space. But there is a partial less dense area in space but not an utterly void area. Being there is no resistance to space movement, they will not slow down. And if there has been billions of time since the Big Bang, the void space should be incredibly vast. Plus, if we are not in the center of the Big Bang explosion, one side should have bodies' farther out from us than the other side. Like two cars passing but heading in different directions. The space will between the two cars will exspand.

There is the partial void space but is it in the center of the Universe? Unknown at this time! There is a semi-void space in the Universe, but it still has some items within it. If the explosion occurred in a vacuum with no gravitational pulls, it should be completely void of anything. And if it is not located in the center of dispersal, it cannot be the point of origin for the Big Bang.

All the items created have a mature age God built into them. So Carbon Dating starts from God's mature produced results and not from a Big Bang.

By the way, where did those fundamental elements, floating in space, come from to cause the Big Bang? Where did the enormous magnetic or gravitation attraction come from to pull these elements together? Remember, these elements floating in space are made up of atoms: electrons, protons, and neutrons. Who made these and the laws that keep them together? And from where did the natural laws for atomic detonation come? More and more unanswered questions from science.

Scientists know they cannot create a new element. They must use elements already made and their natural laws to create a new item. For example, two elements (H) for hydrogen and (O) for oxygen create water (H^2O). God's natural laws inserted into these two elements give consistent results. These scientists believe the essential elements have always been there. It seems it is easier to accept the elements and natural laws have always been there; than to believe there is a God who has always been there to create all those elements and natural laws.

Consider the atom. So small we cannot see them. Billions make up our bodies of different types. Each having a purpose to perform some task. The smallest has one neutron, one proton, and one electron. Each has a roaming path to follow, and held together by some purposeful force. The atom has built-in natural laws. One such law is; if split it will generate a tremendous deadly force. Of what are those three particles made, and how small are they. And does this continue to infinity?

The Bible says we are made of unseen items. This also includes everything in earth and in the universe. All this by happenstance? And all natural law too. The magnitude of this creation unfathomable. Science will never figure it all out.

How think ye?

The following graph will be at the end of each day's dissertation. It is an aid for some people. They can visualize things better if they see it all together. As each day is discussed, it will be added so the graph will grow in size and complexity. It is an attempt to give you the information in a progressive way, not to be too confusing at the end.

These charts will have two periods of time represented. 1st is the 24 hours' time for actual creation, and 2nd is the overall time plan for all creation. The 2nd overall plan will be revealed later as I lay the foundation of information to understand this concept of time.

DAY 1	
ITEMS CREATED	***PLAN STARTED*** ***TIME CREATED*** SPIRIT MOVED *On WATERS* ***LIGHT & DIVIDED***
COMMENTS	Light is present without its natural source, which is created on Day 4 **Good**
PERIOD	Man's time of innocence NO LAW

DAY TWO

G**enesis 1:6–8** *"(6) And God said, Let there be a firmament in the midst of the waters, and let it divide the waters from the waters. (7) And God made the firmament, and divided the waters which were under the firmament from the waters which were above the firmament: and it was so. (8) And God called the firmament Heaven. And the evening and the morning were the second day."(KJV)*

FIRMAMENT (SKY) CREATED

What is the firmament? Strong's Concordance defines this Hebrew word as:

> **"Râqîya',** *raw-kee'-ah; from 7554; prop. An expanse, i.e. the firmament or (apparently)* <u>*visible arch of the sky*[2]</u>.*"*

So we recognize the firmament as our sky, which includes all the atmospheres above the earth's surface. Most of which contain water in mostly a gaseous state. And there are six areas: Troposphere, Stratosphere, Mesosphere, Thermosphere, Ionosphere, and Exosphere. Our sky's outer limit is the Exosphere, which is 400 miles from the earth's surface. Outside of the Exospheres is Space with no water! These spheres have the purpose of protecting the world from different types of harmful elements from reaching the earth. One thing to remember when you read of heaven is, birds are flying in heaven, and this is only in the Troposphere (our sky) where oxygen is available to birds.

This arch is the dividing point of the waters (liquid) from under the arch; to the waters (Gaseous) above the earth, which we call, the sky. Also, notice that God does not mention that he created water on either Day 1 or Day 2 or any Day. It appears to give the impression that the water was already present. This water could be a metaphor for people as water is used in the Bible for nations, tongues, and people. It may be justifying that we humans were created before any object in the Creation.

However, we know that God created water because of Paul's statement to the Church of Colossians. Water can be found in three states: liquid, gaseous, and solid (ice). The first creation is water, and it is possible (due to cold) the earth was solid water where the atmosphere was gaseous.

> **Colossian 1:16–17   *"(16) For by him* (Jesus) *were <u>all things created</u>, that are <u>in heaven</u>, and that are <u>in earth</u>, visible <u>and invisible</u>, where they be <u>thrones</u>, or <u>dominions</u>, or <u>principalities</u>, or <u>powers</u>; all things were created by him, and for him: (17) And he is before all things, and <u>by him all things consist</u>."</i> (KJV)**

Notice *"created that are in heaven."* This statement is not just about inanimate objects in space but also *"principalities and powers."* We will read of this again in: **Rom. 8:19–23 / Eph. 3:9–10 / Eph. 6:12,** and **Col. 1:15–18.**

The first underlined statement points out that *"all things created"* refers to earth and heaven. Heaven in the Bible can be our sky, space, or God's abode. But **Eph.3:9–10** appears to be referring to space. It is God who keeps all the natural laws working correctly and consistently until Day 7, where Jesus takes command.

A question comes to mind: why didn't God mention his creating water? If we read in **Rev. 22:1–2**, water is an eternal element to give life to the immortal souls, even in Heaven. Water, therefore, appears to be the sustainer of life. And we are made up of mostly water, and we have life.

Scientists are searching for life on planets in our galaxy, and they believe water is one major element necessary for life. But what is LIFE? Scholars and scientists have pondered this concept for years and cannot develop an adequate answer. The Bible mentions that God breathed the breath of life into Adam;

and that the Hebrew word means spirit. Adam already had a body and soul at creation, but now he needed a spirit.

As you can see, this concept of life and spirit goes hand in hand. And it is too complicated for this humanity to grasp at this time. It is possible God did not mention water's creation to reduce any philosophical confusion.

God may have a particular inference for dividing the waters. He wants to overshadow water's creation. We know that we are mostly water (approximately 60% of our body weight is water), and we all were created before the creation account. Now we know Jesus (also 60% water) came to divide the righteous individual (60% water) from the unrighteous individual (60% water), and God divided the unrighteous from the righteous with 100% water (the Flood). Then God created his Rainbow (gaseous water) promise to us (60% water) that this flood (100% water) would never happen again by water. And he gave us a sign in heaven, the rainbow (gaseous water), for his eternal promise. WOW, I don't think I could say that again.

Water has many functions in our lives, and we cannot survive without a regular intake of water. Water is used in so many life applications from food preparation, cleansing, cooling, medicines' creation, and crops for food and on and on. And even in the creation of man. From dust, we came, and to dust, our bodies will go (0%). And God chooses what he would make of us. **(Rom.9)**

> **Romans 9:21–23** *"(21) Hath not the potter power over the clay, of the same lump to make <u>one vessel unto</u> <u>honour, and another</u> <u>unto dishonour?</u> (22) What if God, willing to shew his wrath, and <u>to make his power</u> <u>known,</u> endured with much longsuffering the vessels of wrath fitted to destruction: (23) And that he might make known the riches of <u>his glory on the vessels of mercy,</u> <u>which he had afore prepared unto glory,</u>" (KJV)*

These are very curious verses of scripture. God is the potter, and we are the clay (dust). But to form clay into a useful vessel, one must mix clay with water and heat it with fire or a source of heat.

Wow! Does this scripture not blow your philosophical mind? Here again, we see water as an element of creation, not only of the vessel's carcass (our body); but also of the life inside that vessel. And there is a river of life flowing from the throne of God in eternity **(Rev. 22).** There again, we see trees on either side of it with fruit.

Notice it is during God creating that all entities are made, some for righteousness (honor) and some for unrighteousness (dishonor). This *1st clue* for me has been a thorn in my side, so to speak. It appears God created some people for destruction. And if he made them for destruction, would he condemn them to the Lake of Fire for doing what He made them to do. And if so, do they have a soul? This idea seems not to be the right idea as God, in perfect judgment, would not create beings for dishonor, then cast them into a punishing Hell for doing what God created them to do. *But, he did create Satan and the fallen angels who are destined for Lake of Fire.*

I AM STILL WAITING ON CLARIFICATION FROM GOD ON THIS QUESTION!

Also, notice the *2nd clue* God has exercised great patience showing how great and wonderful his mercy is with those he created for the honor. This honor is a *clue* that God is waiting patiently for Christians to come to Jesus. His patience is also directed to those created for destruction and wrath. Remember, *God's mercy and grace have always been his motivations for salvation.* Old Testament Saints were saved by God's Grace through their deeds and their heart's desires to do good. The New Testament Saints are saved by grace through faith. The Tribulation Saints are saved by grace through *faith* and *deeds*. We can see God's great patience during the many years sins were performed by those souls who will eventually be saved. Keep in mind God was present in Noah's day for 120 years until the Ark was built. It appears God created those killed (*"fitted for destruction"*) in the flood to reveal to Christians; God's power of **Rom. 9:22**. But, to what purpose?

These vessels of "honour" bring to those vessels of "dishonour" the knowledge of God and his plan of salvation. To which God is patiently waiting for their conversions over man's 7,000 years.

The *3rd clue* comes in **Rom.9:23**; God wants to reveal the riches and God's glory to be shared *with the saved* (*"vessels of mercy"*). It appears God wants us to know the two extremes of God's power and mercies. The *4th clue* pertains to the fact God created us for honor before we were created spiritually or mortally. Here is one look at God's plan for man, but is there more? *Heavens - ---- YES.*

God has another event with water that will bring these waters back together to divide the unrighteous from the righteous. We know it as The Great Flood. We know that there was no rain before the flood, so plants' watering was from underground waters. But we see in **Genesis 7:11** that God caused both the waters (gaseous) above the earth and the waters below the earth surface (liquid) to come together to cause the Great Flood. This flood (100% water) was to divide the waters to clean the earth of evil water, people; except Noah and his family. Here God divides the righteous (honorable) humans from unrighteous (dishonorable) humans. Not only the humans but of animals of every kind. What an awesome event, and the magnitude of which we cannot imagine. So horrible of an event that God promised it would never happen again in the same way. This Flood reveals God's ultimate power for the Saints to trust in God's mercies. However, God will destroy this present earth with fire and create a New Heaven and a New Earth **(2 Pet.** and **Rev.17).**

> **2 Peter 3:11 & 12** *"(11) Seeing that all the things shall be dissolved, what manner of persons ought ye to be in all holy conversation and godliness, (12) Looking for and hasting unto the coming of the day of God, wherein the heavens being on fire*

shall be dissolved, and the elements shall melt with fervent heat?" (KJV)

In **Rev.21**, please notice no more seas, but there will be a river (water) from God's Throne.

> **Revelation 21:1** *"And I saw a new heaven and new earth; for the first heaven and the first earth were passed away; and there was no more sea." (KJV)*

These same waters that had caused death in man's early existence will be joined together into a river of life. This river will originate from God's throne. It will provide water for the Tree of Life, which will be for eternal life and the healing of all nations.

> **Revelation 22:1–2** *"(1) And he showed me a pure river of water of life, clear as crystal, proceeding out of the throne of God and the Lamb. (2) In the midst of the street of it, and on either side of the river, was there the tree of life, which bare twelve manner of fruit, and yielded her fruit every month: and the leaves of the tree were for the healing of the nations." (KJV)*

Water is essential in the Bible. It was used to clean all sorts of infections, ailments, washing animal sacrifices, and Baptism. Jesus at the well with the Samaritan woman in **John 4:13–14,** Jesus used water to reveal a hidden concept; that Jesus is the way to life. To the person that accepts Jesus as savior, they will never have to continue searching for the meaning of life. And that person will be refreshed (strengthened) by Jesus' love. Just as the waters of Genesis are divided, those who refuse God's gift, Jesus, will be separated from those who have accepted Jesus as savior. The lost will not share the waters from God's throne, nor of its healing power. Jesus was there before the creation as apparently were the waters; water has a special meaning or significance for the future.

We see in **Rev.17:15** *water is also a symbol for peoples* (60% water), multitudes, nations, and tongues. And every person's souls that will ever be present on earth were created on Day 6. God created nothing after Day 6; until the time of **Rev.21.**

Revelation 17:15 *"And he saith unto me, The waters which thou sawest, where the whore sitteth, are peoples, and multitudes, and nations, and tongues." (KJV)*

Is it interesting God chose to teach us about water in his first dissertation on creation? Notice how He has taken us from Genesis to Revelations. And early in scripture, he has revealed his power and Glory.

	DAY 1	**DAY 2**
ITEMS **CREATED**	*PLAN STARTED TIME CREATED* SPIRIT MOVED *On WATERS LIGHT &DIVIDED*	*FIRMAMENT* WATERS DIVIDED 1656 AC
COMMENTS	Light is present without its natural source, which is created on Day 4 **Good**	Water symbol of the source of Life in Baptism and Flood Divides Good from evil.
PERIOD	Man's time of innocence **NO LAW**	

In the section where I say **NO LAW**, I am referring to that time before introducing Moses's Law. We, as a human species, have always had laws in our lives. God gave Adam the 1st negative law **(Gen. 2:17)** *"do not eat from the tree of knowledge of good and evil."* The 1st positive law was on Day 6, where God commands all man to multiply.

> ***Genesis 1:28** "And God blessed them, and God said unto them, Be fruitful, and multiply, and replenish the earth, and subdue it: and have dominion over the fish of the sea, and over the fowl of the air, and over every living thing that moveth upon the earth." (KJV)*

> **Dominion** means **"râdâh,** *raw-daw';* a prim. Root; to *tread* down, *.ie. Subjugate*; spec. to *crumble off.*—(come to, make to) have dominion, prevail against, reign, (bare, make to) rule, (-r over) take[2]."

Isn't it wonderful to know that God's 1st law (Replenish) was positive, and this law was the same for humans (Day 6) and was not a burden at that time? It isn't until later that birthing became painful through the curse to Eve **(Gen.3:16)**. Man had no governing laws up until the introduction of the Law of Moses.

The first negative law was to Adam only; to not eat from the Tree of Knowledge of good and evil. Man later created his own rules as he saw fit, and the results were disastrous. In today's same light, our governments are trying to return to that same system that is a proven failure. Our government is succeeding in removing God's Law and replacing it with HUMANISM. No longer are victims of crimes repaid by the criminal who perpetrated the offense (God's Law requires repayment). Instead, the crime is against the state; thus, the state prospers (fines and fees) instead of the victim. The victim must now also pay for the criminal's incarceration through taxation. There are many more injustices but beyond this treatise. But justice will come to earth with Jesus.

> **Romans 2:12–13** *"(12) For as many as have sinned without law shall also perish without law: and as many as have sinned in the law shall be judged by the law; (13) For not the hearers of*

*the law are **just before God, but the doers of the law shall be justified.**" (KJV)*

God is telling us that those righteous individuals, who lived <u>before God's Law</u> given to Moses, *will not* be eternally judged by the Laws of Moses. Many of these people knew God initially and passed down their relationship and knowledge of God. Noah preached against the people's actions in his day and was taught by a righteous father or uncles. But as the tribes grew and moved away, the knowledge of God waned. Many individuals who lived in the 1,656 years[E] before the Flood are saved by God's Grace. They had *no laws*, and the Tree of Knowledge of Good and Evil and the Tree of Life are gone. Therefore, they are not subject to legal judgments, but they still perished without the Law. But where are their souls? The Tree of Knowledge of Good and Evil gave them the knowledge of what was good and what was evil, and the majority chose evil. God gave them their freedom of self-will to choose good or evil, just as we have today. Many chose evil and became subjects to his divine punishments outside the Law by the lack of God's grace. They exercised their free will just as we today have the same right to exercise our free will. In **1 Pet. 3** we read of Jesus preaching to these post-flood souls in prison.

> **1 Peter 3:18–20** *"(18) For Christ also hath once suffered for sins, <u>the just for the unjust</u>, that he might bring us to God, being put to death in the flesh, but quickened by the Spirit:(19) <u>By which also he went and preached unto the spirits in prison;(20) Which sometime were disobedient when once the longsuffering of God waited in the days of Noah,</u> while the ark was a preparing, wherein few, that is, eight souls were saved by water." (KJV)*

Here we read of Jesus in Paradise (center of the earth) preaching to those disobedient souls, from the flood, which are in prison (Torment). Remember, *obedience has always been a requirement from God.* **Do Good.**

But today, we have the Law, which is the knowledge of what constitutes sin. They did not have that Law, so how can they be judged by a Law they did not have? But, they had knowledge of good or evil, so God's punishment was for their rejection of good. But those who had chosen good, Noah and family, were saved from God's punishment. God's grace was applied to those who tried to live a good life. Those pre-Flood righteous individuals are in Paradise[B], as with all the righteous individuals under the Law (Moses, Abraham, David, etc.). And are waiting for the *1st Harvest* **(Rev. 14).** Those who chose evil (unrighteous) are in a place called Torment[sB] (Hell) awaiting the final war **(Rev.20:7–15)** and the *2nd Harvest* to go to the Great **White Throne Judgment.**

Note

It is a curious thing that this Day 2 of creation (in my King James Version) is not initially addressed as a day in the creation of being GOOD. Is it something God is trying to tell us, or is it just a typo mistake? It is possible that I read too much into this vacancy, but I think not. This Day 2 represents a future time when God destroy His children. It is also revealing the two Wars of destruction coming into the future. All three of these total destructions are of evil being. Apparently, the 3rd time is the charm.

However, the Great Flood day is a telltale of War #1 of Armageddon's destruction day where Jesus will kill all evil children of which there were billions (by scholarly estimations). The 2nd War is also of evil beings from Jesus' Kingdom. The average person's natural death did not occur for hundreds and hundreds of years, and childbearing was also happening for the majority of those years. It would be possible for each family to have hundreds of children in their life span. Then each of those children would have hundreds of children. This slaughter of billions of humans was a horrific event where God killed his children. Not a good day for God.

So it would seem possible God does not see Day 2 as a good day. This day of the dividing of waters represents the destruction (Flood) of his children; it is a day of pain for God. Only a parent that has caused the death of one of their children can appreciate what pain God must experience in not only losing a child but being the perpetrator of their destruction.

God will be the perpetrator of the death of all his unrighteous children. The 1st time was the Great Flood of Genesis, where only eight survived. The 2nd time there will be no unrighteous survivors of War#1 of Armageddon, where Jesus returns to earth to destroy all evil. The 3rd time, War #2 **(Rev.20:7–10),** will be before the Great White Throne Judgment of the unrighteous souls of all of history. And this will occur after Jesus' 1,000 year Kingdom. Then, God destroys Satan, Gog, Magog, and the army of unrighteous souls from Jesus' Kingdom **(Rev.20:7–15).** What an enormous sight at the Great White Throne judgment as all evil entities, ever created, from the beginning of time will be there before God awaiting their judgment and eternal punishment.

Keep in mind there will be many children who will be born to survivors of War#1 of Armageddon, and they will come into Jesus' Kingdom with the inherited sin of Adam. Many of these children will grow to be adults and join Satan to defeat Jesus.

Just imagine the number of souls from 7,000 years of deaths gathered together at the final judgment seat of God. Knowing they are about to enter the Lake of Fire for all times and with no pardon available. I can only imagine that a person being there could smell the horrendous fear from these souls. If there were dogs present, their fear smell glands would be massively overpowering for those animals.

I do love my pets we have had over the years, and I, too, hope they will be in Heaven with us.

But God does say later that all the original days of creation were GOOD, even Day 2, as is verified by **Gen. 1.**

Genesis' 1:31 *"And God saw <u>every thing</u> that he had made, and, behold,* <u>it was</u> *<u>very good.</u> And the evening and the morning were the sixth day." (KJV)*

This verse will reveal that all God made is very good, even Day 2. After God had created everything and nothing will be created after Day 6 except the New Universe and New Earth.

Note

As you read further, a possible question may come to you about Day 2 revealing the dividing of water representing the Flood. Genesis is telling the story of the 24-hour day for creation. But the Flood is represented by the separation of waters (People). Here's the alternate time representing the 1,000 year day. The metaphor of Day2 is the dividing of good and evil revealed in the Flood, which occurred in 1,656 AC (After Creation). That is very close to the middle of Day 2.

DAY THREE

Genesis 1:9–13 *"(9) And God said, Let the waters <u>under the heaven</u> be gathered together unto one place, and <u>let the dry land appear</u>: and it was so. (10) And God called the <u>dry land Earth</u>; and the gathering together of the waters <u>called Seas</u>: and God saw that it was good. (11) And God said, Let the earth bring forth grass, the herb yielding seed, and the fruit <u>tree yielding fruit after his kind,</u> whose seed is in itself, upon the earth: and it was so. (12) And the earth brought forth grass, and <u>herb yielding seed</u> after his kind, and <u>the tree yielding fruit,</u> whose seed was in itself, after his kind: and God saw that it was good. (13) And the evening and the morning were the third day."(KJV)*

EARTH CREATED

God now gathers the element together under heaven (sky) and creates *dry land.* From which is the dust which man will eventually be formed. Therefore, God has created the earth; but it was somewhat of a different size than we know it today. Because God has a future plan to change the earth's surface, which is to be accomplished by his Great Flood. He has formed all the continents needed at that time, which are mostly covered by the earth's crust. The seas were much smaller, as most waters were stored under the earth's crust. At this time, God creates the natural laws pertaining to the earth's operation. One such law relates to the spinning of the world to maintain a stable platform in space orbit. Earth is a giant gyro, which has the properties (laws) of stabilization from change. This natural law of rotation (spinning) was started at creation and is the same today and will be verified later by the stars' and the sun's creation.

With this constant spinning of the earth, we have a constant time to complete a rotation. We will later also determined this spinning will take 24 hours. Here again, this will be proven by the stable position (relative to earth) in space by the Sun, which the earth will revolve around. This revolving around the sun will provide the future seasons, which we enjoy today. In the beginning, God created time just by the fact he started. It appears God is providing information about a time before we need it. Isn't that just like our wonderful loving God to provide for his children's future? This spinning and revolving is proof that a day in creation is a 24 hour period, and one revolution around the Sun is a year.

Next, God creates the first living things, *vegetation, and trees.* Please take note that this life God created at this time is *bloodless life.* In the natural event of things, God would need to provide food for his future creation of man and animals, vegetation. However, God has chosen to create vegetation (Day 3) a full day before the sun is created (Day 4). It would seem that God would have made the sun first, as the vegetation and trees will need the sun for growth and survival. So a question comes to mind.

> *Why did God create Bloodless life before its natural provision, the sun?*

Vegetation can live for a couple of days before the sun is created, but not years. So the statement of *"evening to morning"* is an actual 12 hours as we know it. This is not to be confused with the concept of *"a day to God is like a thousand years"* **(2Pet.3:8),** as this verse's statement refers to God's overall timing of his plan for man. [More on this later.] Because we know plants cannot live a thousand years without the nutrients from the sun's rays. Their seeds will not even germinate. We also know God could sustain them but to what purpose? One other *clue* I want you to see is in **verse 12.** Notice both trees and vegetation are producing seeds and fruit. So food is available to Adam on Day 3. Isn't it fascinating that the fruit of the Tree of Knowledge is Man's death, but the fruit from the Tree of Life is life for Man? This concept in its self is a mystery for another dissertation.

BLOODLESS LIFE CREATED

Here is one of the *first clues* to God's clock. This bloodless life is analogous to the Prelaw and the Law period because *the LAW could not bring life.* The blood of animals, which the Law required, was not sufficient to save mankind for all times. It was used to point to a time when the shed blood of man (Jesus Christ) would be sufficient to provide salvation for humanity. And just as the vegetation could not survive long without the provisions of the sun, neither could humanity survive long without the provisions of the SON. These days between vegetation and animals are necessary *to reveal the actual time between LAW (Moses) DEEDS and FAITH (JESUS).*

This time is needed for the construction of the clock. It is much like the distance required in an ordinary clock between the hour marks. Twenty-four equally spaced hour marks are needed to make the complete rotation of the 24-hour hand. Likewise, the Days of Creation are the equally spaced time points required for God's clock to be complete. It is essential to know that God gave Moses the written LAW in ±1,450–1,400 BC, and the LAW was abandoned in 70 A.D. This time spacing is approximately 1,500 years.

Take notice; this is the second place that God says that His creation is "good." What makes this creation's Day 3 elements, and the remaining days, worth God's recognition that they are good? It is because God is revealing to us his appreciation for all life forms. And the creation of life is worthy of God's praise. It would do well for us to have that same attitude about his products, especially his human creations. From this point on, God ends each day's creation with the words that reveal that day's creation as "good."

Next, we read the straightforward words of easy understanding; but these words house a greater understanding also; for example, in **Gen. 2.**

> **Genesis 2:5–6** *"(5) And every plant of the field before it was in the earth, and every herb of the field before it grew: for the LORD God had not caused it to rain upon the earth, and there was not a man to till the ground. (6) But there went <u>up a mist from the earth</u> and watered the whole face of the ground."(KJV)*

These words here start to shed some light on the initial conditions of the earth's created make-up. It is clear that before vegetation, there was no rain but only mist that waters the ground. While there were seas, it will appear that the bulk of the water was under the earth's surface (crust). Interestingly, the _clue_ mentioned here is easily missed. And there is a difference in mist and water. We read in **Gen.7:1** of the waters of the <u>great</u> deep was under the earth's surface. But here, there is only a mist to water the earth's surface. Therefore, this difference must have a deeper meaning, and it is also another division of water.

Note

The water above the earth's crust can be considered gaseous (mist) and below the earth's crust, liquid. I see a reference to 2 dimensions: mist is the spiritual, and water is the mortal dimension. We know these dimensions exist due to Jesus just disappeared from the men on their walk to Emmaus. Jesus visits the Apostles after his death; Jesus walked through physical doors. John was changed to spirit for his trip to Heaven, demons, angels mentioned are spiritual and other Biblical statements. *So we have two dimensions: mortal (water) and one is spiritual (mist).* If you remember, water can be represented in the Bible as nations, tongues, and people. Just a thought to consider. Now back to **Gen.7.**

Genesis 7:11 ***"In the <u>six hundredth year</u> of Noah's life, in the second month, the seventeenth day of the month, the same day were all the <u>fountains of the great deep</u> <u>broken up</u>, and the windows of heaven were opened." (KJV)***

Please notice that the great fountains of the <u>GREAT deep</u> _broke upward_. The word *deep* was used in **Gen.1:1** to reveal the large volume of space. But here, the word *great* adds emphasis to the *deep*. It appears God is telling us that the

308

radius of the earth's surface was farther out than it is today. The surface is supported by *"the fountains of the deep."* Also, notice these fountains of the deep *broken up* or upward. Broken in Strong's Concordance says:

> **Broken** *"Baqa', baw-takh'; a prim. Root; to cleave; gen. to rent, break, rip or open:-make a breach, break forth (into, out, in pieces, through, up), be ready to burst, cleave (asunder) cut out, divide, hatch, rend (asunder), rip up, tear, win²."*

It appears that the crust of the earth broke downward as the fountains of water broke upward. We read that all the high hills were covered by 15 cubits (27 feet) of water in Genesis.

> **Genesis 7:19--20 *"(19) And the waters prevailed exceedingly upon the earth; and all the high hills, that were under the whole heaven, were covered. (20) Fifteen cubits upward did the waters prevail; and the mountains were covered."(KJV)***

How is this possible? Mount Everest is 29,035 ft. above our present sea level. That is 5½ miles high! This height has been a problem for scholars for ages. For this to happen, the earth's crust must be originally farther out from the center of the planet (great deep) than it is today. And the crust was held up by a tremendous amount of water. Most continents are supported by very hard rock plates. And the crust between these continents must have been covered mostly by sandstone, a soft, weaker stone. When the water broke up from under the softer sandstone, the pressure from the sandstone's descending weight forced the water under the sandstone up with great force. This sandstone eventually found its place at the bottom of the oceans and also on our beaches. What remained above the old crust; is the water that ultimately covered the earth's mountains of solid rock, which were initially called high hills. Now this covering in Strong's Concordance means:

> "3680 *kaw-saw;* a prim root; prop. To *pump*, i.e. *fill up* hollows;
> by impl. *to cover* (for clothing or secrecy): --clad self, close,
> clothe. Conceal, cover (self), (flee to) hide, over whelm. Comp.[2]"

Here we see to *fill up* and *overwhelm*. Some of us think it is a complete covering for a specific long time uninterrupted. However, this coverage could be from Tsunami type waves of great proportions covering Mount Everest.

This event is the time of the demise of prehistoric animals, even the one's living in the waters due to the choking debris or later being stranded on dry land. The debris stirred up by the tremendously turbulent waters must have cause Tsunamis of unbelievable portions. Cities, towns, and villages were utterly destroyed. Vegetation floating on top was hampering air-breathing sea life to struggle to find air and their intake of water from huge waves crashing over their breathing hole. And huge sandstone sections, covering miles, are descending and covering many creatures below it that were unable to escape. There will be all sorts of creatures' lifeless bodies floating on the top until sinking to the bottom of these waters to be covered by the settling debris of vegetation and soil. Many sea creatures will be caught in areas where the receding waters will leave them stranded on solid ground to suffocate.

I am not a scientist, but I think this turbulent water could cause the earth's spinning axis's tilt. If the earth were perfect in its creation, I would think that its spinning would be perfect; that is, the spin axis is 90° to the solar revolution track. Adam and Eve would need vegetation for food all year. Therefore, the equator would be in line with the earth-sun revolution or orbital path. If the presser is applied to a spinning gyro, it will topple at a point 90° from the presser point and establish a new tilt angle.

But we know now that the earth's spin axis is tilted at an angle 22.1° to 24.5° from the vertical and wobbles at about 2° at the tilted poles. The spin axis (axial tilt) is fixed but makes this 23.4° (avg.) rotation cycle every 41,000 years. This axial tilt and wobble could be because of the earth's weight shift during the Flood (my assumption). Now the earth has four seasons. Water weighs approximately 8 pounds per gallon, and how many gallons do you think is in the Pacific Ocean? Mammoths have been excavated that were frozen in perfect condition with greens still in their stomachs. Mammoths are cold-weather animals, but they were quickly frozen. How?

The temperature lapse rate is roughly 2°C (3.5°F) per 1,000 ft. of altitude change. Anyone on the crust near Mount Everest at zero Sea Level (due to the larger earth circumference) before the flood may have experienced this lapse rate phenomenon. When the earth surface (Sea Level) suddenly dropped 29,000 ft. (behind a great Tsunami) to our present Sea Level. If so, this lapse rate would have produced a 2°C [(3.5°F) per 1,000 feet] drop in temperature alone over the 29,000 ft. This temperature change would create a minus -58°C (-101°F) rapid change down to the present-day Sea Level. That is enough to freeze most anything quickly. Then add in the high winds and heavy rains, which also would aid the freezing. We do not know the temperature at the crust surface before the Flood, but it would have been perfect at the equator for growing vegetation. But, as you go to the North Pole, the temperature would get colder. What about earthquakes?

Earthquakes must have assisted this water force under these waters due to Tectonic Plates shifting, creating new continents, and moving others. And we today have seen the results of earthquakes and Tsunamis. But this Flood must have had the most significant Tsunami ever to occur. This shifting of the Tectonic Plates would have caused underwater volcanic actions too, which would have added to these disastrous effects. The Tectonic Plates could have created new and taller mountains forcing more water movement and great crevasses. Some of the trenches in the oceans may be the result of these earthquakes. The trench off the coast of Japan is around 36,000 feet deep (6.8 miles).

This is the greatest recorded destruction of earth known at this time. It is not close to the final destruction of this <u>earth and the universe</u> as revealed in many books of the Bible, especially in **Rev. 21**. Now back to the Creation story.

Tree of Knowledge of Good and Evil and Tree of Life.

This Day 3 must be the day that God creates two extraordinary trees in the Garden of Eden. Interestingly, these trees precede Adam. This is proof that God has made previous plans for man! God knew Adam would fail. But God wants all individuals to understand His project will take into account all the things Satan and man will do, and God already has alternate plans. Remember, *"nothing can be added to it or subtracted from it "***(Ecc.3:14–15).** Therefore, God's plan takes into account all events, nature, or man will ever do.

Notice that Day 3 in God's clock falls after the division of water in Day2. Therefore, God is telling us that some vegetation will survive the Great Flood, and it did **(Gen. 8:11).** It makes me wonder if Noah's olive tree leaf is the representation of life? It was the olive that was the oil for the lamp's light. This Tree of Life will be seen again in Heaven **Rev. 22.**

> **Revelation 22:2 *".In the midst of the street of it, and on either side of the river,*** was there ***the tree of life, which bare twelve*** manner of ***fruits,*** and ***yielded her fruit every month: and the leaves of the tree*** were ***for the healing of the nations." (KJV)***

Isn't it interesting that this tree will have 12 different types of Fruit? Also notice, that these trees appear to be revealing time by producing their fruit every month. Make me wonder if there will be a measure of time in Heaven. It is most likely God's way of revealing a constant supply of life, giving food for eternity.

	DAY 1	**DAY 2**	**DAY 3**
ITEMS CREATED	***PLAN STARTED TIME CREATED*** SPIRIT MOVED ***On WATERS LIGHT &DIVIDED***	***FIRMAMENT*** WATERS DIVIDED	DRY LAND SEAS VEGETATION TREES
COMMENT	Light is present without its natural source, which is created on Day 4 **Good**	Water symbol of source of Life in Baptism and Flood. Divided good from evil.	**BLOODLESS LIFE CREATED** **Good**
PERIOD	Man's time of innocence **NO LAW**		**LAW** -STARTS

DAY FOUR

Genesis 1:14–19 *"(14) And God said, Let there be lights in the firmament of the heaven to divide the day from the night; and <u>let them be for signs, and for seasons, and for days, and years:</u> (15) And let them be for lights in the firmament of the heaven to give light upon the earth: and it was so. (16) And God made two great lights; the greater light to rule the day, and the lesser light to rule the night: he made the stars also. (17) <u>And God set them in the firmament of the heaven to give light upon the earth,</u> (18) And to rule over the day and over the night, and to divide the light from darkness; and God saw that it was good. (19) And the evening and the morning were the forth day."(KJV)*

UNIVERSE CREATED

Space and objects

Our textbooks of today explain that the Big Bang Theory created the heavens. But there are some holes in this theory, such as:

1. Where did the so-called matter in space come from?
2. What is its makeup of this matter, and how was it created?
3. Just how much matter will it take to form all the future items in the Universe? WOW
4. From where did the Laws of Matter of Attraction come?
5. Why are there some planets and some suns?
6. From where did the Laws of compressibility of matter to detonation or expansion come?
7. Who created the Laws for collision and explosion?
8. From where did the Laws of gravity come?
9. Where is the voided space created by the Big Bang Expansion in all directions?

10. Why are galaxies spiraling disk shapes instead of ball-shaped, like the Sun and planets?
11. From where did the Laws of matter dispersion come?
12. From where did the creation of atoms and their associated laws come?
13. What holds atoms together during their movements?
14. Why is there such a release of power when Atoms are ripped apart from their orbits?

The magnitude of the lack of scientific information on the Universe at this time is staggering but far short; more information is coming every day. The complexities are enormous. There are so many more unanswered questions.

Question number 1 is interesting as science uses the same augment as the religious concept. Namely, *"that matter has always been there,"* which is the same argument as *"God has always been there."* I believe science also says that original matter cannot be created but only changed or altered. So how did the original matter come into existence if it can't be made? It seems that it is easier to believe in a creator of intelligent design; than pure chance (evolution). Evolution must have natural laws to form, so from where did those laws come? **And, most important, why did Darwin's Theory of Evolution stop?** We have the: same sun, same elements, same food source, same temperatures, same waters, and the same natural laws. Darwin himself said if we do not find transitional evidence, his theory is wrong. ***But no transitional evidence has ever been found, and it should be abundant!*** So again, why did evolution stop? We humans have changed over the centuries in size and weight *but not into a different creature.*

The end of Day 4 is the beginning of a new period in God's timing. Day 5 will usher in the period of *Blood creation*. This is a crucial, pivotal point in history where <u>Bloodless life (Day 3 and Day 4) come together and Blood life (Day 5 and Day 6) come together; and a new covenant given to man.</u> And the new covenant is: that those who believe that Jesus is the Son of God and gives their life over to Jesus, they shall be saved from damnation in the Lake of Fire for eternity.

This concept of Darwin is a direct contradiction to God's Law given to the Jews. But God's plan is revealed in the Torah, and if the scientist had studied in earnest, they would have been aware and would have praised Jesus coming. Some scholars were aware of Jesus coming from the Torah and prophets, but those in power were only interested in retaining their social, religious position, or power. Very sad! They also missed the sign of the relationship between the sun and the moon.

The sun and moon are to have dominion (rule) over the day, and night respectively. Light is referred to in scriptures as a tool for revealing the obstacles in one's pathway. It is the light that keeps us informed of what lies ahead of our lives and helps us to avoid the pitfalls set by Satan. The Old Testament (Moon) was to guide and rule in our forefather's (times of darkness) lives to keep them safe on their trek through their life. The moon is also a light of the New Testament Church, which will reveal more righteousness to modern man and provides a clear and only way to God. Many of our forefathers were clearly in the dark to God's plan of salvation, and it was not until Jesus came and brought man out of the darkness by giving light (knowledge) as to Salvation in God's Son.

Jesus taught a very different doctrine than the High Priest, Priest, Rabbis, and scholars. But it was still anchored in God's word. Jesus revealed the *erroneous traditions* that had crept into God's word by humans in authority. *How and why did traditions take precedence over God's words?* And we see the same things happening today. Our society is more dependent on Humanism (traditions) rather than the Words of God. Satan has been successful in confusing the masses. And anyone trying to bring God's truth to man can be ridiculed and dismissed as a heretic. Today is becoming just as it was in Noah's day (**Mat.24:37–39** and **Gen.6:5**). In **Mat.24,** we read of everyday events, but with **Gen. 6** considered together with **Mat. 24**, it reveals that evil had become the normalcy. In the Dark Ages, people were not allowed to test their religious leaders' spirit under the penalty of death.

We are told in scripture to test the spirit of anyone who brings information to this world.

1 John 4:1 *"Beloved, believe not every spirit, but try the spirits whether they are of God: because many false prophets are gone out into the world." (KJV)*

To test, you must: 1) listen for full understanding, 2) study God's Word, and 3) compare the two for the truth. Be prepared to accept the fact. No one on earth knows all of God's plan or God's knowledge. We are still in the process of learning from God, Jesus, and the Holy Spirit. We are like the religious world of Jesus' time. As we, too, have many traditions that have crept into our religious doctrine. We see this in all of the different Christian religious denominations. Satan has been very fruitful in separating Christian doctrine into various factions, *"Divide and Conquer."* Our history teaches this, as there were extreme penalties for disagreeing with the religious doctrine of that day. The Dark Ages was when millions were killed for believing a different but truthful doctrine from that demanded by the religious leaders of that time.

Jesus also was killed for preaching a different gospel that opposed the Chief Priest. Even today, Satan has also created a completely different religion from the remnant of the Jewish nation. We see its starting point in the casting out **(Gen. 21)** of Hagar and Ishmael from Abraham, at Sarah's request, and from the Hebrew tribe in the desert. Hagar's and Ishmael's hatred for the Hebrews (due to Sarah) has been passed down through the Ishmaelites **(Gen.21:9–21)** to the Islamic religion, as Mohammad was an Ishmaelite. However, the Islamic Religion gives tremendous honor to Abraham, the father of Ishmael. Today Islam calls Allah the creator god to make him greater than Jehovah our Creator God. They believe Jesus is the Devil. But consider this! Our God has made many eternal covenants with the Hebrew people and nation. We also are graphed into the Hebrews and Jesus as inheritors. And God and Jesus are covenant keeping God's. So our God (Jehovah) cannot break his covenant with Israel or Christians. Jehovah also has provided written material of LOVE for all people. Our God has given us righteous laws. And one is, *thou shalt not kill (murder)*; but Islam teaches and desires the killing of the Hebrew people and any infidel not excepting Allah as their god. Where have we seen this requirement before? **(Rev. 13:15)** So it appears that our God is the God of LOVE, and the Islamic god is the god of HATE. Action-based on hate is not permitted for Christians because it is against God's Law. Hate is not a sin, as revealed in **Rev.2:6,** but the evil actions (carnal and spiritual) we take motivated by hatred is sin. To know to do good and not to do good is the sin of omission. We are to Love even those who do not believe in Jesus as we do. Christians are not permitted to revenge an act as that is God's job. He knows their hearts and life story, and we do not. But the Torah permitted revenge by the Kinsman Redeemer **(Num.35 and Jos.20)**, but Jesus is our Kinsman Redeemer. Therefore, Jesus will perform revenge on evil individuals during the War of Armageddon.

Now back to Day 4 (Gen.1:14).

Please note my underlined words are revealing lights in heaven to show seasons, days, and years. Here God is telling the spans of time for man's time on this earth. And these periods are as we know them today. If Day 4 is a 24 hour day, then Days 1—3 are equal to Day 4 and are 24 hour days. Please notice the word seasons, which reveals the four seasons with the climate changes, which means God will tilt the earth's rotational axis about 23°. Not to be confused with the 2° wobble of the earth's axis. However, both the tilt and the wobble could have been the results of the Great Flood. So God now is revealing time by the seasons too.

In **Ecclesiastes 3:1–8,** God speaks of signs being performed by celestial items. What signs do we have in the universe, and what do they mean? For an agricultural and advanced society, there are many signs, such as:

1. When to plant.

2. When to harvest.
3. When to kill and preserve meat.
4. When to celebrate the different required feasts.
5. When to collect sheep's wool.
6.   The summer solstice
7. The winter solstice.
8. Weather changes coming.
9. The Star of Bethlehem.
10. Movement of heavenly bodies for navigation.
11. Comet and asteroid impacts.
12. When and where an eclipse will occur.
     And many more I am sure you can add.

God clarifies that his time is useful for us to make decisions for proper timing, celestial knowledge, remove the fear of eclipses, the danger of heavenly bodies (Revelation events), and the Star of Bethlehem (Jesus birth). God does not give arbitrary information to his children. What would be the good in that? Here we see revealed future events as signs; some of these events occur after the Great Flood. Signs will continue until their sources are removed. The sun and moon relationship signs will survive until they are no more needed and removed by God. This time will occur in **Rev. 21**.

Revelation 21:1–5 "*(1) And I saw <u>a new heaven and a new earth</u>: for the first heaven and the <u>first earth were passed away;</u> and there was no more sea. (2) And I John saw the holy city, new Jerusalem, coming down from God out of heaven, prepared as a bride adorned for her husband. (3) And I heard a great voice out of heaven saying, Behold, <u>the tabernacle of God</u> is <u>with men,</u> and he will dwell with them, and they shall be his people, and <u>God himself shall be with them</u>, and be their God. (4) And God shall wipe away all tears from their eyes; and there shall be no more death, neither sorrow, nor crying, neither shall there be any more pain: for the former things are* *passed away. (5) And he that sat upon the throne said, <u>Behold, I make all things new.</u> And he said unto me, Write: for these words are true and faithful". (KJV)*

Another concept that will be revealed about **Day 7 is** that God labels this day as Day 7, but there is no ending mentioned this day (no "*evening to morning*"). Therefore, there must be a reference to a time but possibly not 24 hours but related somehow. Keep in mind this Day 7 is also forever. This concept will be further examined later.

Here in Day 4 God creates all the universe items and our (earth's) <u>light source (the sun)</u>. Light's properties were created on Day 1 and vegetation on Day 3. What a curious event as God created his natural laws for the operation of things he created. It would appear that God should have made the sun then the vegetation and trees per those natural laws.

God may be here revealing a time delay between the Law (Bloodless life) and Jesus (Blood life). And it is during this delay Jesus is still providing needed spiritual substance for God's elect? This light source (the Law) also refers to the light of Jesus, as Jesus broke no Laws. Jesus is with the father during all creation as we have seen from scriptures; all things were created for him and by him **Col. 1.**

Colossians 1:16–17 "(16) For by him were <u>all things</u> created, that are <u>in heaven</u>, and that are <u>in earth</u>, <u>visible</u> and <u>invisible</u>, whether they be <u>thrones, or dominions, or principalities, or powers: All things were created by him</u>, and for him: (17) And he is before all things, and <u>by him all things consist.</u>"(KJV)

These verses are another *clue* that relates to Jesus' presence at the creation on Day 4. And that Jesus will be the sustainer of the creation of all things created, and he keeps them functioning as needed. There appears to be an essential emphasis that God is placing on this day that a form of blood life is created; Jesus is the sustainer of this life form. Later in the scriptures, we see that Jesus is the only way to Eternal Life and the father. Many religions would like you to believe that there are many ways to God, but there is <u>only one way.</u> That way is narrow, and it is only through Jesus. If there were other ways to God, Jesus would not have needed to come and be crucified, but there is no other way.

> **1Timothy. 2:4–5** *"(4) Who* (God) *will have all men to be saved, and to come unto the knowledge of the truth. (5) For there is one God and <u>one mediator between God and men, the man Christ Jesus.</u>"(KJV)*

> **Acts 4:12** *"Neither is there salvation in any other: <u>for there is none other name</u> under heaven given among men, <u>whereby we must be saved.</u>"(KJV)*

The role that Jesus is to play in man's salvation is God's plan's central theme. God is to give all things to Jesus as Jesus is the inheritor of all things. **Hebrews 1** claims this to be true.

> **Hebrews 1:1–4** *"(1) God, who at sundry times and in divers manners spake in time past unto the fathers by the prophets,(2) <u>Hath in these last days spoken unto us</u> by his <u>Son, whom he hath appointed heir of all things,</u> by whom also he made the worlds; (3)Who being the brightness of his glory, and the <u>express image of his person,</u> and <u>upholding all things by the word of his power,</u> when he had by himself purged our sins, sat down on the right hand of the Majesty on high; (4) Being made so much better than the angels, as he hath by inheritance obtained a more excellent name than they." (KJV)*

Jesus must be covertly introduced into the creation story at the correct time, and that is when a bloodless life form is first created on Day 3. Jesus is to uphold all things (all natural laws), including God's Law to Moses. The Law was the first system designed for man to reach God (Eternal Life); if he (man) could live without breaking just one of the laws, perfection. But God knew this is an impossible task for an ordinary human to do (especially with inherited sin from Adam), but not for Jesus. But the religious leaders did not recognize the inability of man to fulfill God's requirement of perfection. They saw the Day of Atonement as sufficient for salvation.

Jesus was from Mary, but His father was God. Therefore, Jesus did not inherit the sin nature **(Rom. 5:12).** Man and not the woman pass down sin nature. **(Gen.3:6–7)** Otherwise, Jesus would have received the sin nature.

The awesomeness, majesty, and power of Jesus are unfathomable, and God wants us to know Jesus and be saved. Jesus did not break one of God's Laws during his entire life. And he was tempted many times in his life span. He obediently went to the cross to pay for your sins and mine. Mary didn't do it, the Pope didn't do it, Buddha didn't do it, Mohammed didn't do it, James Jones didn't do it, Joseph Smith didn't do it, and no one except Jesus has paid the cost for man's sins. Therefore, his personage is so vital that he requires a place in the creation story from Day 1 (the light of the world) to Day 7 (king of the earth).

On Day 4, God has continued the revealing of Jesus to us. Here God creates the heavenly objects for man. God says that there will be the sun for day and the moon for night to give man light (righteous).

Here God reveals two future times, 1) Jesus being present on earth for those attending to see the light he reflects, and 2) the time His light will be reflected by the moon during darkness (unrighteousness). And after Jesus' resurrection, his light is reflected by the Church (Moonlight) period.

Please notice that the Moon was to rule the night. It is during the night that God is creating. I take this to mean that God will be developing the Church during times of evil. Who among us cannot see that evil has been here on earth since Adam's disobedience. This darkness surrounding the Moon reveals the time of the rule of the Old Testament Law. This Law illuminated what Sin is and what God's punishments are against Lawbreakers. The Moon is a dim reflection of sunlight. It is the sign of the Church. It shows the coming of Jesus by the various stages of the moons travel to the full moon of reflecting the brightest light (full moon). This moon travel is the growth and demise of the Church's life. It was made in darkness (sunset to sunrise) and will return to darkness, evil.

There is an excellent time <u>to bring to attention the Christmas light</u> of so long ago. This light heralded Jesus' physical introduction into God's plan. The sign to the wise men was a star in the East, to which they followed. This same star God and Jesus created so long ago is another <u>clue</u> to us. Along with heralding Jesus' birth, it foretold his death; and the completion of his initial mission on earth as a servant. It is that mission that started the Church and the Church period on this earth. Jesus' birth was at approximately 5 BC to 4 BC, and it is his light (gospels) the world should see reflected by the Church (Moonlight). Both the sunlight in the daytime and the reflected sunlight at night; reveals the reflected light of Jesus even in darkness during the Church's period. People should see Jesus reflected through the individuals that claim Jesus as Lord of their life. (**Mat. 5**)

> *Matthew 5:16 "Let your light so shine before men, that they may see your good works, and glorify your Father which is in heaven." (KJV)*

One could also say the Church is like the moon reflecting Son's light. And that light will shine until the Church is removed, which is promised in **1 Thessalonians 4:13–17**. Here is Jesus' 2nd Return of coming in the clouds to Rapture his Bride, the Church. This event will be followed by the dark Moon (no reflected light), the Great Tribulation period.

REMEMBER THE MYSTERY IN LIGHT CREATION?

	DAY 1	DAY 2	DAY 3	DAY 4
ITEMS CREATED	*PLAN STARTED TIME CREATED* SPIRIT MOVED *WATERS LIGHT DIVIDED*	*FIRMAMENT* WATERS DIVIDED	DRY LAND SEAS VEGETATION TREE	Stars Planets Sun Moon Signs & seasons
COMMENTS	Light is present without its natural source, which is created on Day 4 **Good**	Water symbol of source of Life in Baptism and Flood. Div. good from evil.	**BLOOD LESS LIFE CREATED** **Good**	First position where days, as we know them, are mentioned **Good**
PERIOD NO LAW	Man's time of innocence		Bloodless life **LAW** period	
			ETERNAL LIFE	
			TEMPLE	

DAY FIVE (Imperfect Blood Life)

GENESIS 1:20–23 *"(20) And God said, Let the waters bring forth abundantly the moving creatures <u>that hath life,</u> <u>and fowl that may fly</u> <u>above the earth in the open firmament of heaven.</u> (21) And God created <u>great whales, and every living creature that moveth</u>, which the waters brought forth abundantly, after their kind, and every winged fowl after his kind: and God saw that it was good. (22) And God blessed them, saying, be fruitful, and multiply, and fill the waters of the sea, and let the fowls multiply in the earth. (23) And the evening and the morning were the fifth day."(KJV)*

Note

Before getting into Day 5, notice the statement that proves the firmament is the earth's atmosphere (Troposphere). The fowls are created to fly in heaven's firmament, which we know as our sky, because they need oxygen to live. Also, notice that this is the first place that the word life is used (*"that hath life"*).

CREATION OF LIFE WITH BLOOD

This is the day that God created Blood Life. We know fowls, whales, and moving creatures, have blood flowing in them to sustain their life. And Day 5 is the point in time where God reveals that blood is a requirement for life. This day is analogous to the requirement for blood to be the critical element for eternal life. We see from the Old Testament scriptures that God required blood sacrifices to atone for sin. In these sacrifices, God is foretelling us that animal blood is good only for atonement for sins, but there is a better way for forgiveness of sin to be revealed. These sacrifices point to the day Jesus will sacrifice his blood and establish a new covenant between God and man. In this new covenant, man need only believe in Jesus as the Son of God and turn the control of his life over to Jesus. Here is a stumbling stone for many people and religions as they fail to believe that Jesus was raised from the dead. This Day

5 begins the period of blood that is required starting with animals and ending with the blood of Jesus. It is interesting to note that the Law that specified the shedding of blood for the atonement of sin was given to Moses at approximately 1,450 BC.

In creation, God gives his first command, *"be fruitful and multiply."* This command is given to creatures we think as unable to understand a command such as this. This is not a simple command such as "sit, roll over, come, down, or fetch," which are learned responses. These commands are the natural Law that God is establishing within these creatures for the survival of the species. We see this impetus in the scriptures as to the fertility of the Israeli family. A woman was not respected if she could not bear children; she felt (as others) as if she was cursed by God when unable to multiply *(tradition)*. God knows the exact number of human beings that will come into this world, and he wants all to be with him in heaven **(1 Tim. 2:3–4).** As Christians, we have been given this task of being fruitful in bringing souls into the Church family. **(Mat. 28:18–20)**

We see in numerous places in scripture that we Christians are to be *"fruitful and multiply*." We will also know the children of God by their fruitfulness of helping the Holy Spirit bring souls to Jesus. But the Church must be aware of deceiving religious leaders. Jesus reveals this information in **Mat. 7**.

> **Matthew 7:15–20** *"(15) Beware of false prophets, which come to you in sheep's clothing, but inwardly they are ravening wolves. (16) Ye shall know them by their fruits. Do men gather grapes of thorns, or figs of thistles? (17) Even so every good tree bringeth forth good fruit; but a corrupt tree bringeth forth evil fruit. (18) A good tree cannot bring forth evil fruit, neither can a corrupt tree bring forth good fruit. (19) Every tree that bringeth not forth good fruit is hewn down, and cast into the fire. (20) Wherefore by their fruits ye shall know them." (KJV)*

These verses are clear Jesus is talking about people (trees). What a simple but complicated knowledge to be put to use. Some people are very good at deception. Therefore, we must watch the results of their actions. Jesus tells us that the fruit of their efforts will become known. There is a saying that comes to mind. *"Do they walk the talk?"* The truth will eventually be revealed. But we are to obey the Great Commission brought to us by Jesus; despite false prophets.

In this location in time Day 5, Israel is given the task of making known the one and only God (JEHOVAH). This task is the beginning of the revealing to the Church of God's plan for man, and it will climax with the resurrection of Jesus from the grave. The New Testament scriptures will reveal the more intimate details of God's plan for his people. Just as the Israelites were to tell of the one true God, the Church is responsible for continuing that task for Jesus. We must be fruitful in this endeavor to be called the children of God.

It is also interesting that one of the first blood creatures created during this period of creating is the fish. For many years the Christians used the fish as a secret symbol for Christians. God used a large fish to contain Jonah; the first miracle of feeding the multitude was with fishes, and even today, we still place the fish on the rear of our vehicles. I'm not sure if it means anything in God's plan, but it created an interest for me that the first mention of blood life is the same creation that would feed the lost. There is an old saying; *"to feed a man give him a fish, for man to feed himself, teach him to fish."* Jesus used a similar statement to his disciples when He said, *"I will make you fisher's of men."* So Jesus taught them to fish for men!

> **Matthew 4:19 "*And he* (Jesus) *saith unto them, Follow me, and I will make you fishers of men." (KJV)***

Another interesting fact is that Joseph and Mary used fowls for Jesus at his birth.

Matthew 2:23–24 *"(23)As it is written in the law of the Lord, Every male that openeth the womb shall be called holy to the Lord; (24) And to offer a sacrifice according to that which is said in the law of the Lord, A pair of turtledoves, or two young pigeons." (KJV)*

I find it very interesting that God would give this law to Moses some years before Jesus' birth. Jesus continues that call for all men, even today. That call began on Day 5 of creation and continues today.

DAY 1	DAY 2	DAY 3	DAY 4	DAY 5
PLAN STARTED TIME CREATED SPIRIT MOVED WATERS LIGHT DIVIDED	*FIRMAMENT* WATERS DIVIDED	DRY LAND SEAS VEGETATION TREE	Stars Planet Sun Moon Signs & seasons	Water Creatures Fowls Whales
Light is present without its natural source, which is created on Day 4 **Good**	Water symbol of source of Life in Baptism and Flood. Div. good from evil.	**BLOOD -LESS LIFE CREATED Good**	**First position where days, as we know them, are mentioned Good**	1st Command Multiply **1st Blessing Jesus' Blood life Good**
Man's innocence **NO LAW**		Bloodless life **LAW** period		**Law** fulfilled ✝
		Bloodless Spiritual LIFE		**Blood Life**
		TEMPLE		**CHURCH**

✝ Near the bottom of the chart, you will notice this sign I have included. This sign is the transition point from LAW to FAITH. Jesus in **Mat 5:17** said that he came not to destroy the LAW but to fulfill the LAW. When John the Baptist disciples asked if Jesus **(Luke 7:19–23)** was the one to come, Jesus used his miracles to substantiate that he (Jesus) was the one to come, and blessed is the person that is not offended in Jesus. This is an essential transitional point in God's covenant with Israel's Priesthood. In a few short years, Jesus is going to satisfy the LAW requirement for blood (death) for breaking any of God's Laws. Jesus broke no Laws of Man or God. It is Jesus' perfect sacrifice of his perfect life for our imperfect life, which will be the consummation of the requirement of blood foreshadowed in the Old Testament LAW. The responsibility for our righteousness has transferred from our responsibility to keep the LAW'; to Jesus' responsibility to keep the LAW. Jesus was perfect and broke none of Man's or God's LAWS, and we must live in Jesus to be protected by his perfection. To live in Jesus is a difficult concept for non-Christians to understand. It requires that each person ask Jesus to come into and lead that person's life.

In doing so, that person is asking Jesus to allow that person to live in Jesus' spiritual life, which has already paid the death debt. As an act of obedience, that person is baptized (submerged in water; buried) as a declaration that they die to themselves (their desires, wants, self-will); and is resurrected out of the water (born again and cleansed) into Jesus' a new spiritual life. They declare by this act that they want to: follow Jesus' teachings, will attempt to be obedient to Jesus' commands, place him as the Lord and King of their life. They are submitting their will to the will of Jesus.

DAY SIX [Perfect Blood Life]

Genesis 1:24–31 *"(24) And God said, Let the earth bring forth the <u>living creature</u> after his kind, cattle, and creeping thing, and beast of the earth after his kind: and it was so. (25) And God made the beast of the earth <u>after his kind,</u> and cattle after their kind and <u>every thing that creepeth upon</u> the earth after his kind: and God saw it was good. (26) And God said<u>, Let us</u> make man <u>in our image, after our likeness:</u> and let them <u>have dominion</u> over the fish of the sea, and over the fowl of the air, and over the cattle, and over all the earth, and over every creeping thing that creepeth upon the earth. (27) So God created man in his image, in the image of God created he him; male and female created he them. (28) And <u>God blessed them,</u> and God said unto them, <u>Be fruitful and multiply,</u> and replenish the earth, and subdue it: <u>and have dominion over the fish of the sea, and over the fowl of the air, and over every living thing that moveth upon the earth.</u> (29) And God said, Behold, I have given you every herb bearing seed, which is upon the face of all the earth, and every tree in the which is the fruit of a tree yielding seed; to you it shall be for meat. (30) And to every beast of the earth, and to every fowl of the air, and to every thing that creepeth upon the earth, where in there is life, I have given every green herb for meat: and it was so. (31) And God saw every thing that he had made, and, behold<u>, it was very good.</u> And the evening and the morning were the sixth day."(KJV)*

Please notice that *"the earth"* is referred to nine times in these verses of scripture. These words reveal that all of the creations mentioned are for the earth. No other single body in space is mentioned to receive something special. Therefore, God is showing the earth is unique for some purpose. And it appears he did not do it to any other planet or moon in our solar system. For me, this brings back those verses of scriptures in **Rom.8:17–23** and **Eph.3:9–10.**

On Day 6, God consummates (to make perfect) his creation of Blood Life started on Day 5. Day6 is the final day God creates, and all that is created is complete and <u>at different maturity</u> <u>levels</u>. God will not create another thing except the New Heaven and New Earth **(Rev.21).** The creature that God wants to be the primary sacrifice (sheep) for the Old Testament atonement for sin is revealed this day. The initial desirable sacrificial animal is created, the sheep that is the first creature that God wanted as a sacrifice as an atonement for sins; pointing to Jesus (Son of Man) as the final perfect sacrifice. Goats were also acceptable creatures for sacrifice **(Lev.1:10),** and they too are also created on this day. But, there is a subtle difference between sheep and goats. **(Mat. 25:31–46)**

On Day 5, we see fowls created and that fowls were permitted to be a sacrifice in place of sheep for first borne; and the poor person that could not afford a sheep. According to Moses's Law, in Luke 2:23–24, we read where Joseph and Mary used fowls (two turtledoves or two pigeons) to present Jesus to the Lord. This event was the first sacrifice for the beginning of a person's eternal life.

Next, notice that God claims that he is plural *"let **us** make man in **our** image."* The Jewish leaders have argued that God is one God, and they are blinded to the fact that God is plural with the Father, Son, and Holy Spirit, all existing in one. They use this scripture in **Deu 6** to make their point that *God is one LORD.*

> **Deuteronomy 6:4 *"Hear o Israel: The LORD our God is one LORD :" (KJV)***

Here the word for <u>one</u> used in Hebrew is:

> **"echâd, ekh-*awd'*;** a numeral form 258; prop. <u>*United,* i.e. *one;*</u> or (as an ordinal) *first*:-a, alike alone, <u>altogether,</u> and, any (-thing) apiece, a certain, [dai-] ly, each (one), +eleven, every, <u>few,</u> first, +highway, <u>a man,</u> once, ONE, only, other, <u>some, together</u>[2]".

> **"258**= âchad, *aw-khad';* perh. a prim. root; *to unify,* i.e. (fig.)
> *collect (one's thoughts):-* go one way or other[2]."

Using this word, we can see the idea is *"united,"* and if there was only one element, there could be no uniting, as it takes more than one to unite. Also, we see that the idea again is to "unify or collect" from the prime root. Here again, there must be more than one to unify or collect. However, notice that the word does indicate that the idea is that of gathering together more than one item (gathering one's thoughts) but *into one complete unit.* The Hebrew word for LORD used in **Deu.6:4** is <u>el-o-heem', which is</u> plural (<u>em'</u>) for God. The word for GOD is <u>YEH-O-VAH'</u>, the self-existent or eternal.

So we come up with a number of Gods that are alike and are collected to be united together into one God, which is the LORD (Elohim): Father, Son, and Holy Spirit.

The next thing is that God wants to make man in His image and likeness. This statement reveals that all living human creatures are created in the image and likeness of God. What do these words mean in the Old Testament language?

> **"1823 d^e mûwth,** dem-*ooth';* from 1819; *resemblance; concr.*
> *model, shape;* adv. *like:*--fashion, like (ness, as), manner,
> similitude[2]."

Here we read the meaning from Strong's Concordance. To be fashioned in God's likeness is to resemble God in shape and as our physical model. We are in the likeness in manner and similitude of God.

Here reveals that we are created in the physical and spiritual form of God. If we return to Moses' time on earth, we read in **Exo. 33**: there, Moses requests to see God's glory.

> **Exodus 33:18–23 "(18)** *And he said, I beseech thee, shew me*
> *thy glory. (19) And he* (GOD) *said, I will make all my goodness*

pass before thee, and I will proclaim the name of the LORD before thee; and will be gracious to whom I will be gracious, and will shew mercy on whom I will shew mercy. (20) And he said, <u>Thou canst not see my face</u>: for there shall no man see me, and live. (21) And the LORD said, Behold, there is a place by me, and thou shalt stand upon a rock: (22) And it shall come to pass, while my glory passeth by, that I will put thee in a clift of the rock, and will cover thee <u>with my hand</u> while <u>I pass by</u>: (23) And I will take away mine hand, and thou shalt see <u>my back parts</u>: but my <u>face shall not be seen</u>."(KJV)

Notice the similarities of God's features to our bodies. God has a face, hand, and back parts. A face would indicate eyes, nose, mouth, and ears; if made in his image and likeness. Also, God appears to Moses as God moves past. The type of locomotion is not revealed, but if we are in God's resemblance, He would have legs and feet? God <u>walked</u> in the Garden of Eden in the cool of the day **(Gen.3:8).** This verse would support the idea that God has legs and feet. Remembers Jesus too walked on Earth after his resurrection.

Can we use Jesus' physical appearance *as clues* to our future bodies? When Jesus returned to earth, he had a body very close to his earthly body. However, his locomotion was very different but also the same. He walked and talked with the men going to Emmaus **(Luke 24:13–31)** but vanished out of their sight when they recognized he was Jesus. Apparently, Jesus' body and features appear somewhat different to these men, but to the Apostles, Jesus was recognizable immediately. He showed the scars on his side and hands.

Another idea to keep in mind is the appearance of angels. In **Heb.13,** we read

Hebrews 13:2 *"Be not forgetful to entertain strangers: for thereby some have entertained angels unawares." (KJV)*

If we have entertained strangers who are angels, then their appearance must be the same as a man. Otherwise, we would not be unaware. I know that angels do appear in scripture as glorious beings that have caused powerful individuals to faint. But this verse also proves they can be as normal humans also. This condition is additional proof that all living created human entities are created in God's image too.

There are good reasons to believe we are physically like God because our bodies were originally designed to last forever. We see this in Old Testament Saints that lived for hundreds of years. Even today, we see how marvelous we are made. Minor and major injuries healed; certain parts replaced. But we are missing something that extends the life of our bodies over long periods. In the Garden was a tree called the Tree of Life. In the final Heaven, this same Tree of Life will be on either side of the river coming from the Throne of God **(Rev.22:1–2).** This Tree has some properties that will extend life, and the leaves will heal nations. The Fountain of Youth is not a spring of water but the fruit from a tree.

What one must answer is: *is this instant creation, or is it a process over a period of time?* The initial process in the creation of all items is instant for each day. Some individuals believe that each day was 1,000 years to create all those days' items. However, God declared after creating, *"it was evening and morning of* that particular *day."* These words speak of 12 hours (sunset to sunrise). After Day 6, there is no more mention of creating, only God resting. But an exception is found in **Rev. 21:1**. Also, there is no mention of *"evening and morning"* for Day 7. Therefore, Day 7 will have no end. This never-ending day is Jesus' Kingdom for eternity. But, when was each individual created? Since God performed no more creations (except New Earth and Heaven) after Day 6, it appears that all persons, over all the centuries, were physically created on Day 6. Our souls were in God's waiting room, waiting for God to place us into our Mother's womb at the right time; and place of God's choosing.

We have been blessed to be presented into this world at this time in history. No other history individuals have been blessed to be included in the Church (Bride of Christ). All our brothers and sisters from Jesus' resurrection to the

Rapture are the most blessed individuals of God's plan. We are the Church, the Bride of Christ, the Queen of Heaven, Kings, Lords, Priests of God unto the Universe, and inheritors of all God possess.

God has created within our soul the potential abilities and characteristics that are a part of God's plan. However, it will take many years to become the person God would have us to be. We start life with a mind that is opposed to God's ways, and then when the Holy Spirit saves us, he starts our mind's transformation to the mind of Christ.

Romans 12:1–2 *"(1) I Beseech you therefore, brethren, by the mercies of God, that ye present your bodies a living sacrifice, holy, acceptable unto God, which is your <u>reasonable service.</u> (2) And be not conformed to this world: but <u>be ye transformed by the renewing of your mind</u>, that ye may prove what is that good, and acceptable, and perfect, will of God."(KJV)*

This transformation process will take our entire life. The level of spiritual maturity is, in a big part, up to our efforts. God wants us to study his word and apply those lessons in our lives. If we do our part, God will do his and reveal the truths of his word.

2 Timothy 2:15 *"Study to shew thyself approved unto God, a workman that needth not be ashamed, rightly dividing the word of truth." (KJV)*

We see again **(Gen.1:28)** the command to be fruitful, multiply, replenish the earth, plus subdue it, and rule over every living creature. Only is man given the right to subdue and rule. Both days receive a blessing from God too. The man gave up his right to rule over the earth and surrendered it to Satan when Adam ate from the Tree of Knowledge of Good and Evil. Adam surrendered his dominion, earth, to the god of darkness, and it will take the God of Light to take it back. The payment for that title deed has duration; sort of like our home mortgage payments have duration. In the near future, that payment will be complete at some point in time, and Jesus will return to take possession of the earth. Since man was given the title deed to the earth, it will take a man (inheritor) to receive back that title deed to the earth. In **Revelation 5**, we see God's plan for the Son of Man to receive back the title deed (Seven-Sealed Book) to the earth; that only the "*Lion of the tribe of Judah, the Root of David*" (Jesus) can open those seals in the Book.

These two days (Day 5 & Day 6) are analogous to the Church period. Both days reveal blood as a creative element. The blood of sheep or goats started the sacrifices in god's Tabernacle, but it will end with the sacrifice of Jesus outside of God's Temple. It is the sacrifice of the blood of Jesus that covers our sins and gives us eternal life. It began at Jesus' death and Resurrection and continues after Jesus' returns to take possession of the earth. And this includes those individuals that go into and through The Great Tribulation (Goats).

We also see this revealed in the sacrifice of Isaac, Abraham's son. Isaac was the incomplete sacrifice, pointing to Jesus as the complete and perfect sacrifice. One last thing I would like to bring to your attention is **Gen. 2.**

> **Genesis2:7 *"And the LORD <u>God formed man</u> of the dust of the ground, and <u>breathed into his nostrils the breath of life</u>; and man <u>became a living soul."</u> (KJV)***

This verse is the first use of the breath of life. Notice it occurred only to Adam. The results of this breath of life breathed into Adams's nostrils is a significant event in the creation story and so easy to overlook. This point in time is God's plan where God creates a carnal living soul. This soul is tot houses our spirit. *Our spirit is what Jesus came and died to save.* Notice man became an everlasting soul, which cannot disappear from existence. We will exist eternally with God in Heaven or with Satan in the Lake of Fire.

This life appears different from the life given to the creatures that have life in them in **Gen.1:20.** This breath gave our spirit all the characteristics, talents, emotions, intellect, weakness, strength, and other abilities to possess and use in our lifetime. And God predestinated or sanctified us for some purpose in his plan for man. Through Adam, eternal life came initially, and it is through Adam, eternal death came, too. And each man is given by God his right to exercise his own will over God's will. *God will let us chose obedience or disobedience.*

DAY 1	DAY 2	DAY 3	DAY 4	DAY 5	DAY 6
Plan started Time Spirit moved Waters & Light Div.	Firmament Waters Div.	Dryland Seas Vegetation Trees	Stars Planets Sun Moon Sign & seasons	Water Creatures Fowls Whales	**Animals** Male / Female Dominion God breath of life
Light is Present without a source, which is on Day Time measurement before time elements. **GOOD**	Water symbol of the source of life, Baptism & Flood Divide evil from Good.	**Bloodless life created.** **GOOD**	First position where days, as we know them, are mentioned. Sun before vegetation. **Bloodless, Lifeless objects created**. **GOOD**	1st command to Fruitful/ multiply 1st Blessing **LIFE WITH BLOOD created.** Jesus' blood gives spiritual life. **GOOD**	2nd command to Fruitful Multiply Subdue Dominion **LIFE WITH BLOOD created.** **GOOD**
Man's time of innocence **NO LAW**		Bloodless life represents the **LAW** period. LAW could not produce eternal life. Signs of the prophets & Jesus		**Blood** life represents the **Church** period. Blood of Jesus produces eternal life. ✝	
		BLOODLESS LIFE		**BLOOD LIFE**	

THE RAPTURE

1 Thessalonians 4:13–17 *"(13) But I would not have you to be ignorant, brethren, <u>concerning them which are asleep,</u> that ye sorrow not, even as others which have no hope. (14) For if we believe that Jesus died and rose again, even so <u>those that sleep in Jesus will God bring with him.</u> (15) For this we say unto you by the word of the Lord, That we that are alive and remain unto the coming of the Lord shall not prevent them which are asleep. (16) For the Lord himself shall descend from heaven with a shout, with the voice of the archangel, and with the trump of God: <u>and the</u> <u>dead in Christ shall rise first: (17) Then we which are alive and remain shall be caught up together with them in the</u> <u>clouds, to meet the Lord in the air: and so shall we ever be with the Lord."</u> (KJV)*

Note

I have added the Rapture at the end of Day 6 to represent an escape plan by God. It is to proveide a way of escape from His wrath for the earth. Day 6 is when man is created, and those who accepted the Son of Man (in Jesus) will be removed from the world. And there is no better time to reveal in this clock; than when man is created

Jesus' birth was the beginning of the end for condemnation, by the Law, for those accepting Jesus as their savior. Jesus fulfilled the Law. He did not abolish it. The Law is still there to teach us God's character and what sin is, and we are not to sin. However, when we do sin, God will forgive us if we confess our sins.

1 John 1:9 *"If we confess our sins, he is faithful and just to forgive us our sins, and to cleans us from all unrighteousness."* *(KJV)*

1 Thessalonians 5:9 *"For God hath not appointed us to wrath, but to obtain salvation by our Lord Jesus Christ," (KJV)*

Here we read that to be forgiven, all we need to do is confess the sin we have committed. But this first requires repenting of that sin. Repentance is the attitude of being genuinely sorry and regretful for performing our sins. It also reveals the sinner knows the sin. And this is disobedience on the sinner's part. Sometimes our sins are caused by ignorance of Satan's temptations, as was the case with Eve. Eve only had the word of Adam, but we have the word of God. So Jesus tells us to test the spirit for truth **(1 John 4:1).**

To test: you must listen intently for full understanding, study God's Word, and compare the two for the truth. Be prepared to accept the fact. In **James 1,** we read some admonishing words.

James 1:19 *"Wherefore, my beloved brethren, let every man <u>be swift to hear</u>, <u>slow to speak</u>, <u>slow to wrath</u>:" (KJV)*

This verse holds true when reading scripture as well as in everyday life. And if you are in a class, we generally hold up a hand without interrupting the leader's thought process. Always discuss conflicting opinions in an adult manner. Repeated interruptions usually offend both the speaker and the class members. If one has many questions, it is best to make a personal appointment with the teacher. Most teachers will bring to the class any good questions and answers to the next class period.

Be particularly aware of traditions that can be unscriptural. Traditions have been the cause of many sinful failures of man. For Preflood Man, there was only one punishment for their disobedience, death. But Preflood Man created his own laws, which became traditions. False traditions were created to explain events caused by a lack of knowledge. Example: The Hebrews had a tradition that a childless wife was considered cursed by God for some hidden sin. The early Church created traditions by the Pope that was not based on Biblical scriptures. Example: Indulgencies; pay the Priest enough money, and he would pray you into Heaven. <u>Wrong!</u>

We are still in the process of learning from God, Jesus, and the Holy Spirit. We are like the religious world of Jesus' time; we have many traditions that have crept into our religious doctrine. We see this in all of the different Christian religious denominations. Satan has been very fruitful in separating Christian doctrine into various factions. Our history teaches us there were extreme penalties for disagreeing with the religious doctrine of that day. The Dark Ages was when millions were killed for believing a different but truthful doctrine from the standard traditions demanded by the religious leaders of that time.

Jesus also was killed for preaching a different gospel that opposed the Chief Priest. Even today, Satan has also created a completely different religion from the remnant of the Jewish religion. At Sarah's request, we see its starting point in the casting out (Gen.21) of Hagar and Ishmael from Abraham. Hagar's and Ishmael's hatred for the Hebrews (due to Sarah) has been passed down through the Ishmaelites to the Islamic religion, as Mohammad was an Ishmaelite. However, even today, the Islamic Religion gives great honor to Abraham, the father of Ishmael.

Today Islam calls Allah the creator god to make him greater than Jehovah our Creator God. But consider this! Our God has made many eternal covenants with the Hebrew people and nation. And he is a covenant-keeping God, or he lied. So our God (Jehovah) cannot break his covenant with us and Israel, as that would be a sin. Jehovah also has provided written material of LOVE for all people. Our God has given us righteous laws. And one is; thou shalt not kill (murder), but radical Islam teaches and desires the killing of the Hebrew people and any infidel not accepting Allah as their god. I am aware some Islamic individuals are not radicals, but it is their responsibility to stop the radicals within their religion and not people of other faiths. Their corporate lack of action is the same as an agreement with the radical cause. Remember, Jesus said, *"you are with me or against me."* Fear is no excuse but is a great motivator. Where have we seen this requirement before to worship only Allah? **(Rev.13:15)**

> **Revelation 13:15** *"And he (Satan) had power to give life unto the image of the beast, that the image of the beast should both speak, and cause that as many as would not worship the image of the beast should be killed" (KJV)*

So it appears that our God is the God of LOVE, and the Islamic god is the god of HATE. Action-based on hate is not permitted for Christians because it is against God's Law. Hate is not a sin, but the evil actions (carnal and spiritual) we take motivated by hatred, is sin. Also, to know to do good and not to do good, is the sin of omission. We are to Love even those who do not believe in Jesus, as we do. Christians are not permitted to revenge an act as that is God's job. He knows their hearts and their life's story, and we don't.

This brings us to the close of creating on Day 6. Nothing will be made after this day until **Rev.21**. Nothing will change God's course of action. The players are in place, awaiting their turn to be placed into the play at the proper time. These events are developing for man's salvation. It will include: scripts, costumes, stage (earth), good players, evil players, resources (Bible), teachers teaching, pastors revealing truths, trials, tribulations, success, failure, despondency, exhilaration, friends, enemies, love, hate, and HOPE. Now comes the beginning of the most fantastic day and joy for those in Jesus.

NEXT, THE DAY GOD RESTED!

This up and coming day has different but important *clues* for you to uncover. It is one of the most covert *clues* and very important to nail down an anchor point to understand God's timing.

DAY SEVEN [the Kingdom and Eternity]

Genesis 2:1–3 *"(1) Thus, the <u>heavens</u> and the <u>earth were</u> <u>finished</u>, and <u>all the host of them</u>. (2) And on the <u>seventh day</u> <u>God ended his work</u> which he had made; <u>and he rested on the</u> <u>seventh day from all his work</u> which he had made. (3) And God blessed the seventh day, and sanctified it: because that in it he had rested from all his work which God created and made."(KJV)*

> **Host** in Hebrew is – "tsᵃbâ'ah, *tseb-aw-aw'* from 6683; <u>a mass of persons</u> (or fig. things), espec. reg. <u>organized for war</u> (an *army*); by impl. <u>a *campaign*,</u> lit. or fig. (spec. *hardship, worship*):- appointed time, (+) army, (+) battle, company, host, service, solders, waiting upon, war (-fare)[2]."
>
> "6683 says - tsûwlâh, *tsoo-law';* from an unused root mean. To *sink*; an <u>*abyss*</u> (of the sea): -deep[2]."

It would appear that God is telling us that the *"host"* in **Genesis 2** is a mass of individuals that are in the army of God, and he has prepared them for a campaign for the appointed time (Armageddon). Each soldier and their weapons are waiting for the warfare to occur for them at their appointed time. These soldiers' objective is to sink their opponent into the abyss (Hell), deep in the waters of the sea (The Lake of Fire). Notice that the entire hosts are created, and there will be no more making until each of these soldiers has accomplished their mission (Armageddon). It is then that Jesus completes the *1st Harvest* for the righteous souls (**Rev.14:14–16**).

As with every army, there must be a leader. And Jesus will be the leader on his white horse **Rev.19**. This army reveals the near end of God's plan, but Genesis is the beginning. Therefore, Day 6 is advancing knowledge in Genesis (creation of earth) to the Book of Revelation (the end of the planet). Thus, this mass of soldiers appears to be a covert relationship with the time mentioned in Day7.

At the end of Creation, there are two humans on earth, Adam and Eve. So where is this *"Massive Army"?* God reveals to us he has created every person who will ever be and placed them in God's waiting room. A place where souls are held is where they will be ordained and sanctified until their time comes to be placed on earth. **(Jer. 1)**

> **Jeremiah 1:4–5 "(4)** *Then the word of the LORD came unto me, saying, (5)* *<u>Before I formed thee in the belly I knew thee; and before thou camest forth out of the womb</u> I sanctified thee, and I ordained thee a prophet unto the nations." (KJV)*

Here we read that God knew Jeremiah before he was placed in his mother's womb. Just as God knew Jesus before he was placed in Mary's womb. Notice that God also sanctified (consecrated) Jeremiah and ordained him to be a prophet before he was born. It appears from this statement; there was some form of contact while Jeremiah was in God's waiting room. It also appears you and I was in that same waiting room, awaiting our placement into the earth. God knew us and established some tasks for us. It is a blessing to be born during the Church (Bride of Christ) period and share the Gospel with the world. And for our efforts, we will receive Treasures and also an inheritance from God.

It is clear that Day 7 is eternal after all individuals are created in Day 6; nothing is made on Day 7 except the concept of rest. No other souls will be created. These earlier created souls are the start of God's Army recruitment to fight unrighteousness from all the duration of man's existence. The Holy Spirit will eventually form it with Adam and Eve's children; and placed into battle in **Rev. 19**. But many years will be needed to develop this army, and some of God's children will be deserters. Without regulations to guide these civilian soldiers, they are destined to fail.

Before the flood, the man did have only one negative regulation, *not to eat from the tree of knowledge*, which was given to Adam. But Adam's offspring did what they wanted to do or what they thought was right for themselves. There were no regulations or central leader, and man floundered and failed. Even with Noah trying to preach to them about good and evil, they depended on their own logic, feelings, traditions, or desires. The angel of death was coming for them as they continued to ignore Noah's warnings. Noah was an army of one with two earthly things to help him; family and Ark. Can the Navy say they were the first into the spiritual fray?

All of God's people are soldiers waiting for their time to be put into the battle. Many of our soldiers have performed their duty and have gone on to their rest and recuperation (R&R). We are in the battle now and should be doing our part (reasonable duty) to serve Jesus, our Commander and Chief. As in war, the Commander: selects different persons, for different objectives, for different times. The Commander also makes sure that the person is trained and equipped for the task assigned. God has chosen the time for us to be inserted into skirmishes with Satan, and God has equipped and trained us for the task. The one thing that's different in our battle is that our commander is there beside us, helping fight at every event. A time is coming **(Rev. 19)** when our commander will return with his entire army to war against and destroy all evil on this earth. We will be his army, for the Book of Revelation tells us that this is true.

> **Revelation 19:11–14** *"(11) And I saw heaven opened, and behold a white horse; and he that sat upon him was called Faithful and True, and in righteousness <u>he doth judge and make war.</u> (12) His eyes were as a flame of fire, and on his head were many crowns; and he had a name written, that no man knew, but he himself. (13) And he was clothed with a vesture dipped in blood: and <u>his name is called The Word of God. (14) And the armies</u> which were in heaven followed him upon white horses, <u>clothed in fine linen, white and clean.</u>"(KJV)*

Some people think the army is all angels; however, **Rev.19:7–8** explains that this army is the saved souls of all ages.

> **Revelation 19:7–8** *"(7) Let us be glad and rejoice, and give honor to him: for the marriage of the Lamb is come, and <u>his wife</u> hath made herself ready. (8) And to her was granted that <u>she should be arrayed</u> in fine linen, clean, and white: for the fine linen is the righteousness of saints." (KJV)*

Remember that verse of scripture says, *"where I am, there you will be also."* So the Bride of Christ will also be with Jesus. Therefore, she is also with this returning army. Notice that the Bride (Church) is ready and adorned by their righteous acts. The marriage spoken of is between Jesus and the Church. We are called the Bride of Christ numerous times in scripture, and she is the one to wear the "*fine linen, clean, and white.*" It then becomes clear that we Christians are in God's army. Once our initial task on earth is accomplished, we are taken to a rest and recuperation (R&R) location (Heaven), and once rested, called upon to return with our Commander and Chief to destroy the enemy (Satan). At that time, Satan will be thrown into the (Abyss) bottomless pit **(Rev.20:1–3).** Satan's army is cast into the Lake of Fire **(Rev.19:20–21)**.

We also read of this in **Mal. 4:1–3,** but **verse 3** captures the fact that we Christians will *"tread down the wicked"*. This statement is further proof we will be in Jesus' army of **Rev. 19.**

> **Malachi 4:1–3** *"(1) For, behold, the day cometh, that shall burn as an oven; and all the proud, yea, and all that do wickedly, shall be stubble: and the day that cometh shall burn them up, saith the <u>LORD of hosts,</u> that it shall leave them neither root nor branch. (2)But unto you that fear my name shall the Sun of righteousness arise with healing in his wings; and ye shall go forth, and grow up as calves of the stall. (3)<u>And ye shall tread down the wicked; for they shall be ashes under the soles of your</u>*

**feet in the day** **that I shall do** *this,* **saith the __LORD of hosts.__"(KJV)**

Notice in **verse 1**, _"Lord of hosts,"_ which takes us back to **Gen, 2:1–3.** So we see from Genesis that the first army failed and was destroyed, except for Noah and his family. Their initial attack by Satan was their greatest battle to lose. Casualties were humongous, and recruitment must restart. Can we learn a lesson from that flooding event? I sincerely hope so. The lesson is -- we are in the battle whether we like it or not. Satan is warring covertly for our souls, and he is quite successful in his efforts.

Question? **Why would God rest on the seventh day, when he has unlimited power and strength?**

This is a crucial question, and the answer is a significant _clue_ to God's clock's construction. And it will help establish the central concept of God's clock. To say that God needed rest would be to say that God is power limited. We know this is not true because the Bible tells us that God is all-powerful. Also, if God rested, who kept the universe functioning as needed? --- JESUS!

So why would God rest on the seventh day?

1. God is trying to tell us that this is a special day.
2. God is trying to tell us that his son (the inheritor of all things) is taking over God's duties for Day 7.
3. Why did God sanctify this day and not one of the other days?
4. God is establishing a more profound concept for these Sabbaths. The 7th day, 7th week, 7th year, and 50 year Jubilee (7 years x 7 = 49 or the 50th Jubilee).

I believe the answer to these questions is yes. As we have seen from Genesis, God's workday started at sunset and ended at the next day's sunset. During light (day time), God did not create until darkness was again present. However, notice that God breaks this consistent description on Day 7. He said each day was "*the evening and the morning was the # day.*" Here on Day 7, there is no mention of evening or morning. Because Jesus (Light) will be present, the scriptures tell us that there will be no need for the sun and moon, as Jesus will be the light of the earth. His light will never be removed again from this earth or the new earth to come; there will be no darkness ever again. Therefore, there will never be an *"evening,"* only the morning, and The Morning Star **(Rev.22:16)** will be the light.

Eternity will have arrived!

Note

I must place a caveat here. Jesus' and God's light will begin after God destroys Satan Army **(Rev.20:7–15)** after the 1,000-year Kingdom. As many individuals will survive The Great Tribulation, but they and their children will need sleep for good health during Jesus' Kingdom.

Throughout the Bible, darkness is an analogy to evil. And there will be a time <u>on this earth</u> when external evil will not be present. In **Rev.20:4–5,** we read about the dead's 1st Resurrection, which includes: Jesus, his converts, the Rapture of the Church, Old Testament Saints, and the Tribulation Saints. The Church is revealed in the statement, "*and I saw thrones*" and "*judgment was given to them.*" These are the Christians and the 144,000 Jews.

Next revealed are the Tribulation Saints by, "*and I saw the souls of them that were beheaded*" and "*did not worship the beast or his image, neither had received his mark.*" These are the Tribulation Saints. Therefore, the Church is already Raptured, and this First Resurrection *(1st Harvest, **Rev.14**)* is for the Old Testament Saints and Tribulation Saints as they, too, are now with God and in Jesus.

Revelation 20:6 "*Blessed and holy* is *he that hath part in the first resurrection: on such the second death hath no power, but*

they shall <u>be priests of God and of Christ</u>, and <u>shall reign</u> with him a thousand years. (KJV)

This verse follows **Chapter 19,** where God is telling us Jesus is in his *3rd Return* to the earth, with his army, and they will defeat evil. But immediately <u>preceding</u> Armageddon, there will be the ending of *1st Harvest.* During the Great Tribulation, as the Tribulation Saints are killed, their souls will be kept under the altar in the Heavenly temple, but they will be harvested just before Armageddon (War #1)

In the *1st Harvest* (1st Resurrection of the Tribulation Saints); God tells us this in **Rev. 20**:

Revelation 20:1–6 *"(1) And I saw an angel come down from heaven, having the key of the bottomless pit and a great chain in his hand. (2) And he laid hold on the dragon, that old serpent, which is <u>the Devil, and Satan, and bound him a thousand years,</u> (3) And cast him into the bottomless pit, and shut him up, and set a seal upon him, that he should deceive the nations no more, <u>till the thousand years should be fulfilled</u>: and that he must be loosed for a little season. (4) And I saw thrones* (Bride of Christ), *and they sat upon them, and judgment was given unto them: and <u>I saw the souls</u>* (Tribulation Saints) *<u>of them that were beheaded for the witness of Jesus,</u> and for the word of God, and which <u>had not worshipped the beast,</u> neither his image, <u>neither had received his mark</u> upon their foreheads, or in their hands; and they lived <u>and reigned with Christ a thousand years</u>* (Tribulation Saints). *(5) <u>But the rest of the dead</u>* (lost) *<u>lived not again until the thousand years were finished.</u> This is <u>the first resurrection.</u> (6) Blessed and holy is he that hath part in the first resurrection; on such the second death hath no power, but <u>they shall be priest of God</u> and of Christ and <u>shall reign with him a thousand years."</u> (KJV)*

These verses speak for themselves. This time is when Israel comes to Jesus by the 144,000 Hebrew Missionaries. Israel will reject Satan and will rule over Israel during the 1,000-year Kingdom. They will rule under Jesus, then David King of Israel **(2 Sam 7:16).**

SUMMERY

There are many places in scripture that God tells us about this thousand-year reign of Jesus after destroying all evil. *Jesus will be the King of Kings* and will rule over the works of God's creation. In a sense, God will rest. During this time, Satan will be incarcerated not to tempt the people of Jesus' Kingdom. This society in Jesus' Kingdom will have a perfect government, perfect weather, perfect food, perfect neighbors, perfect laws, perfect judges, and perfect justice. No person can blame the Devil for tempting them above what they can handle as Satan is locked up. Sin will be present for the Great Tribulation's mortal survivors. So we can see that it is *our own lust of the flesh and lust of the eyes* that is the primary cause of our sins and not Satan. The people will understand that we are evil-bent people unable to keep the laws in a perfect environment and are in need of a savior. No excuse, *"the devil made me do it,"* will remain.

The Raptured and later the 1st Harvested Saints will be given the mind of Christ and will know how to judge the actions of the surviving people during that millennium Kingdom. Most of God's plan for this earth will be revealed by this time. All that will remain is Satan's final punishment, the *2nd Harvest* of the damned, and the sinners from the 1,000-year Kingdom. God's final judgment (the Great White Thorne Judgment) verdict will be *"the Lake of Fire"* for Satan, demons, and *all the lost souls.* Then a New Heaven and New Earth will be created for God's children.

This period has got to be one of the most glorious day of creation, the day God rested.

DAY 1	DAY 2	DAY 3	DAY 4	DAY 5	DAY 6	DAY 7
Plan started Time Spirit moved Waters & Light Div.	Firmament Waters Div.	Dryland Seas Vegetation Trees	Stars Planets Sun Moon Sign & seasons	Water Creatures Fowls Whales	**Animals** Male / Female Dominion God breath of life	**God** **Rest**
Light is Present without a source, which is on Day Time measurement before time elements. GOOD	Water symbol of the source of life, Baptism & Flood Divide evil from Good.	**Bloodless life created.** GOOD	First position where days, as we know them, are mentioned. Sun before vegetation. **Bloodless, Lifeless objects created.** GOOD	1st command to Fruitful/ multiply 1st Blessing **LIFE WITH BLOOD created.** Jesus' blood gives spiritual life. GOOD	2nd command to Fruitful Multiply Subdue Dominion **LIFE WITH BLOOD created.** GOOD	Jesus takes over Final war. **Jesus' Kingdom begins** VERY GOOD
Man's time of innocence **NO LAW** (spans DAY 1–2)		Bloodless life represents the **LAW** period. LAW could not produce eternal life. Signs of the prophets & Jesus † (spans DAY 3–4)		Blood life represents the **Church** period. Blood of Jesus produces eternal life. (spans DAY 5–6)		
		BLOODLESS LIFE (spans DAY 3–4)		**BLOOD LIFE** (spans DAY 5–6)		

CLOCK OF CREATION'S CONSTRUCTION

The most crucial <u>clue</u> to the construction of God's clock starts here at Day 7 and *moves backward in time to Day 1, due to Day 7 is Jesus' 1,000-year Kingdom.* This theory is supported by the witnesses of the days of creation in themselves. There is a verse of scripture that gives us some insight into *God's estimation of time and is the <u>central consideration</u> of this thesis.* You should notice that these scriptures include the *creation of the earth, Noah's flood,* and *the earth's fiery destruction.*

2 Peter 3:3–9 *"(3) Knowing this first, that there shall <u>come in the last days scoffers</u>, walking after their own lusts, (4) And saying, Where is the promise of his coming? For since the fathers fell asleep, all things continue as they <u>were from the beginning of the creation.</u> (5) For this they <u>willing are ignorant</u> of, that by the word of God <u>the heavens were of old,</u> <u>and the earth standing out of the water and in the water:</u> (6) Whereby the world that then was, <u>being overflowed with water, perished:</u> (7) But the heavens and the earth, which are now<u>, by the same words</u> are <u>kept in store, reserved</u> unto fire against the <u>Day of Judgment and perdition of ungodly men.</u> (8) But, beloved, be <u>not ignorant of this one thing, that</u> <u>one day is with the Lord as a thousand years, and a thousand years as one day.</u> (9) The Lord is not slack concerning his promise, as some men count slackness; but is long suffering to us-ward, <u>not willing that any should perish,</u> but that all should come to repentance."(KJV)*

Notice, **<u>verse 3</u>** starts by revealing what is to follow pertains to *the last days of God's plan for the earth.* These verses of scripture **(2 Peter 3)** can be misunderstood if one does not recognize the underlying *impetus is of earth's time of existence.* People of the planet have become so insensitive to prophecies they think the world will remain as it is. But in **verse 1,** Peter says, *"I stir up your pure minds by way of remembrance,"* as Peter wants us to probe our knowledge over the past to bring knowledge of the future. *Past to present*! We can see the traditions we have been taught that these verses are not real-time values but reveal God's general value of time. Now we must decide if these mentioned times are true or untrue? Teachers use specifics from scriptures such as **John 3:16**; they believe it is a true statement. But when some numerical value is specified, they tend to spiritualize that value. This statement is especially true if they have no idea of the meaning of these scriptures. When God says a day, he means a day; as we understand, it is 24 hours. When God says 1260 days, 1290 days, 1335 days, or 144,000, he means precisely that value. We cannot pick and choose what we want to believe. Either the Bible is the complete truth. Or it is filled with lies.

Note

In 2nd Pet.1:16–21 is a warning about the foundational truths in the truths found in the Bible. Notice the words in verse in **verse 19**, *"you do well to take heed."* This warning should motivate us to reconsider the verses sincerely and not just pass them off.

<u>Verse 4</u> speaks of the *"from the beginning of the creation' (Genesis),* which is the start of God's time and plan for man. These words reflex the condition of today's man, *"Where is His coming?"* He is unwilling to study the Bible or look for knowledge of events pertaining to the end of God's plan. *"Where is the promise of his coming?"* And these words are prevalent today: as prophecies are not studied nor compared to present-day events. Pastors are taking away the Book of Revelation by not teaching it. And that is to their peril, too. **(Rev.22:19)**

<u>Verse 5</u> starts the past's remembrance process by referring back to creation with *"the heavens were of old."* This statement reveals *times past* of the universe at the beginning of Day 1. Also, *"and darkness was upon the deep"* **(Gen. 1:2).** Day 4 is the *time* when God created *all the items in space.* These words refer back to Day 2 *"as earth standing out of water and in waters."* This *time* is of the division of the waters in Day 2.

Then **verse 6** moves *time* forward to the flood *"overflowed with water perished,"* which occurred approximately 1650 years After Creation, to the *time* of Noah's Flood. **(Gen.7)**

In **verse 7,** time moved to the future for us. You will read that Heaven and Earth (world) *"are kept in store"* and *"reserved unto fire and Day of Judgment for the ungodly men."* This statement covers many years of movement as we earthling know is into our future **Rev.21:1 / Mal.4:1–3.** This is a remembrance of past prophecies of the end of earth's *time*. Lost souls will be judged at the final Great White Throne judgment of God, and the world and the universe will be destroyed by fire. For present-day earthlings, this judgment by God is held in storage until **(*"the last days"*)** time has run its course. And at the end of *time*, God will judge all evil entities living and dead **(Rev.20:12–15).**

This storage is Paradise in Heaven *for the Bride* of Jesus during the Great Tribulation period.

The storage for the *righteous* Old Testament Saints is in Paradise in the heart of the earth or Heaven. In the Old Testament, *unrighteous* individuals are stored in a place called Torment in the heart of the earth[B]. But there is a gulf between Paradise and Torment. But the dead Tribulation Saints are protected under the Alter in the temple.

Then in **verse 8**, we read a most profound statement. God here is giving us a clue to his value or *his measurement of this expanse of time.*

> **2 Peter 3:8** ***"one day is with the Lord is as a thousand years, and a thousand years as a day."* (KJV)**

This measurement is not a suggestion, approximation, generalized, or spiritualized period but an actual measurement of the earth's and man's time. If it is not valid, then God has lied, and God does not lie. He hates lies. So where does this *time* of thousand years apply?

It is associated with the *start of creation and continues to the end of time, as these previous verses reflected.* This period is what those verses in **2 Pet.3:3–9** are relating to. *This movement of time is from the beginning to the ending of God's plan.* However, we know that each day's time is 24 hours based on the earth's rotation and a period of 12 hours (Sunset to Sunrise) or half a day. So how does this Day that is a thousand years fit into creation?

Good question! God is telling us that he does not want us to be ignorant of his duration for the earth! These passages of scriptures are to give us knowledge of time. This knowledge is missing or lacking in man and is due to old traditions about the timing of Biblical events. How can we do his command to watch for Jesus' return if God does not give us information about the approximate time of Jesus' return? Our leaders have got to stop this tradition of "*we will not know the time of his return.*" Understanding this will require us to put our thinking hats on.

So let us review a few clues we have been given.

1. God rested on the 7th day of creation.
2. Jesus will return to earth to reign.
3. Jesus' earthly Kingdom will last *"a thousand years."*
4. God will rest, and Jesus will take the reins on day 7.
5. God says that a thousand years is like a day and a day like a thousand years.

Jesus' 1,000 year Kingdom* (Rev. 20) *is revealed on Day 7 by God's resting. God reveals to us that all days in creation are analogous to one *thousand years in God's clock based on Jesus' 1,000-year reign.* Therefore, God is telling us that the duration for his plan for sinful man is 7,000 years, with eternity following. Each of those seven days will reveal the presents of sin, even in Jesus' Kingdom.

It is also arguable that God could be establishing that each day during the creation process consumed 1,000 years to accomplish that day's creating. If this is so, then God's revealing *"evening to morning'* (12 hours) would not be correct. And God would be in error. But God is error-free. It is clear that each day of creating consumed one day (24 hours) as we know it. This is proven in Day 4, where God created the sun, moon, and stars. The operation of the earth around the sun was set then for a year. And the spinning of the earth was set for 24 hours each day. If I am correct in my observations, then there should be some witnesses to back up my theory, and I have some.

Witness Number One,

The Tabernacle, MOST HOLY PLACE

The first place to start is with the first Tabernacle, in which God gave Moses specific instructions for its: offerings, materials, construction, furnishings, and operations **(Exo. 25–30).** The Tabernacle has been called "*the house of symbols"* because everything in it symbolizes something about: God, Jesus, or Holy Spirit. This Tabernacle occupied time and space, and these two elements are covert symbols and need to be considered.

In **Exodus 26,** God gives Moses the wall boards' measurements based on the roof coverings that will enclose the Tabernacle. You will see that the Tabernacle will be approximately 30 cubits long, 10 cubits wide, and 10 cubits high and a volume of 3,000 cubits cubed.

The Tabernacle was divided into two rooms, The Most Holy Place (Holy of Holies) and The Holy Place. These rooms are separated by a vail. This is the curtain (or vail) in the Temple that split when Jesus died on the cross **(Mat. 27:51).** The split signaled the priesthood any priest could enter the Holy of Holies any time, instead of once a year by the Chief Priest.

One room called The **Holy of Holies (The Most Holy Place)** has in it; only the Ark of the Covenant (God's Mercy Seat) and only the Chief Priest could enter once a year under the curse of death; if not accomplished by obedience to the laws of the Tabernacle. This event is analogs to the adherence to the Old

Testament laws for the salvation of man. Man had to obey the law completely (impossible) to get to Heaven. This room was a place for God to guide the Hebrews and a seat (Ark of the Covenant) for God to sit. It is from this room that God led Israel through the wilderness. This room is 10 cubits long, 10 cubits wide, and 10 cubits high. Its volume is 1,000 cubits cubed (1,000 years). This reflects Day 7, the most Holy Day of Jesus' 1,000-year earthly Kingdom.

God is telling us that this spiritual space of the Tabernacle is analogous to a specific time of creation. On Day 7, the day God rested, symbolizes the Mercy Seat in the Holy of Holies (God's room) where God sat (rested). That room volume is 1,000 cubits cubed, which occupied time and space. This space coincides with the 1,000-year earthly Kingdom of Jesus; therefore, Day 7 is equal to 1,000 years in God's clock. Since all days of creation are similar (evening to morning), this 1,000 years period must apply to the other days of creation. This means that God's spiritual clock has a 6,000-year life span before Jesus' *2nd Return* and a total of 7,000 years for final War #2 and of the lost souls going to the Great White Throne judgment.

Witness Number Two,

The Tabernacle, HOLY PLACE

Now let's look at the Holy Place within the tabernacle. This room is located before the curtain (veil) in front of the Most Holy Place (Holy of Holies), and this room is called the Holy Place. This room is the first room the Priest would enter into the Tabernacle and before the Holy of Holies. The Holy Place furnishings are symbolic for Jesus and the Church because the Table held the Shewbread (Jesus bread of life). The Lamp Stand (Menorah) has seven lamps, which are the Seven Spirits of God **(Isa.11:2)** and the seven angels to the seven churches **(Rev.2–3).** And the Altar of Incense is the Prayers of Saints **(Rev.6:9–11 & Rev.8:3–5).** This room, all the priests could go in and out as needed; and we will be a priesthood to Jesus **(1 Pet.2:5–9)** with access to Jesus. When the curtain ripped in half at Jesus' death, it gave us access directly to God because Jesus' blood cleanses us, and we are in the Priesthood of God.

This Holy Place room measures 20 cubits long, 10 cubits wide, and 10 cubits high.

The area volume of this room is 2,000 cubits cubed. Here we see Jesus and the Church, his bride, and they will cover Day 5 and Day 6 of creation or 2,000 years. Remember that it was on Day 5 that blood life was created, and on Day 6, the perfect blood life (Son of Man) was sacrificed. Therefore, this is the Church period that will be approximately 2,000 years in length. It is that time from Jesus' 1st Resurrection to the Rapture and removal of the Holy Spirit in the future.

A word of caution seems appropriate here. These Years reflected here in the Tabernacle are not exact because there is no mention of the height for the sockets that the wallboards set upon. Also, how the corner wallboards were attached to each other could create some additional measurements to consider. I believe God left out those small measurements, so we could not find out the exact area. The rooms' approximate areas are very close and give quite usable information as to general timing. As I said before, I am not trying to set an exact date for Jesus' *2nd Return* (Rapture) but to help establish the season. We are told in scripture not to set any dates for his *2nd Return*. However, remember Jesus said in **Matthew 24,** we would know the season.

Witness Number three,

The Moses Passover

The Flood Passover

The Rapture Passover

We have covered these three Passovers previously, and they occurred at different times in God's plan for man. These 3 Passovers are (man's three deed chances) to motivate humankind to be righteous. But the third time appears to be instrumental in converting the Hebrew nation to Jesus.

1. The Flood Passover occurred around 1656 AC^E with only eight survivors. God's first chance for humankind.
2. The Lamb Passover, for Moses and the Hebrew people, occurred next around 2063AC, with millions of survivors from the Death Angel. This is God's second chance for Hebrews.
3. The Rapture Passover will occur in the future, and only the Church is included. This is God's third chance for humankind. After this Passover, all prophecies will come to fruition.

Note

The Hebrews and the Pew-Sitters will have their last chance to prove their loyalty to Jesus during The Great Tribulation.

Witness Number Four,

Jesus' Resurrection

Jesus' resurrection was after he paid for all sins that would ever be committed, and in so doing, created everlasting life for you and me. *This event is the Most Important day to Christians*; because without his Resurrection, we would still be lost in our sins. This 1st Resurrection is the visual proof that Jesus paid for our debts of sins. As Jesus was accepted into God's presents, clean and righteous, we will also be seen as righteous as we are in Jesus.

Jesus came to establish His Church (The Bride of Christ). This day will be the foundational day that Jesus gives the responsibility to spread the gospel to his disciples and therefore starts the Church Period. Argument can be established that the Church period began at Jesus' Baptism. However, it is in his Resurrection that proves Jesus' sacrifice was acceptable to God for all of humanity's sins. Therefore, Jesus can present *The Church* to God as pure and white, completely clean of sins; and we are righteous.

In the timing of God's clock, it is necessary to understand the time of Jesus' Resurrection. We know that Jesus was born approximately 5-4 BC as Herod the Great **(Mat. 2:1)** was King, and his reign ended in 4 BC according to secular historical documents. Jesus lived for approximately 33½ years. Therefore, Jesus Resurrection appears to have occurred around 28 to 30 A.D.

Witness Number Five,

The Rapture of the Church

The Church (true and practicing believers in Jesus) is righteous in God's eye because of The Blood of Jesus. Therefore, they do not deserve God's wrath but God's blessings; and **1Thess. 5** state this fact.

1 Thessalonians 5:9 *"For God <u>hath not appointed</u> us to wrath, but to obtain salvation by our Lord Jesus Christ," (KJV).*

However, for the unrighteous sinful individuals, God's wrath will be eternal and extremely painful. In the end times, God will bring his enormous wrath upon the earth's evil men. There are seven years that God has set aside to convert Israel and punish the unbelieving world.

In **Dan.9:24–27,** God has set aside 70 weeks of years for punishment for Israel. These are 70 weeks of years (70 x 7) is 490 years. And through different historical events, the 490 years is presently down to 1 week of years or 7 years, which is the time for the covenant between Satan and Israel **(Rev.9:27).** But Satan will break his covenant halfway through the seven-year agreement, or at the last 3½ year starting mark.

As Jesus said, the Church is not deserving of wrath; therefore, God will not punish the Church. It then becomes clear that God must remove his Church from his wrath to come. We see a witness to this in Exodus (Exo.12), where God sent the Death Angel to Egypt to kill the firstborn of man and beast. This event is called the Passover, which we have studied previously. The Passover has been celebrated every year since; it is a witness that God will Passover the person protected by the blood of the Lamb (Jesus). The Passover has been seen in the past with Noah as he passed over the Flood in the Ark. The Hebrew Passover (death of firstborn) occurred later in Egypt, spared by the Lamb's blood spread around their doors. And will happen to the Bride of Christ in the Rapture by the Lamb's Blood around their hearts.

> **1 Thessalonians 4:13–17** *"(13) But I would not have you to be ignorant, brethren, concerning them which are asleep, that ye sorrow not, even as others that have no hope. (14) <u>For if we believe that Jesus died and rose again,</u> even so them also which sleep in Jesus will God bring with him. (15) For this we say to you by the word of the Lord, that we which are alive and remain unto the coming of the Lord shall not prevent them which are asleep. (16) For the Lord himself shall descend from heaven with a shout, with the voice of the archangel, and with the trump of God; and the <u>dead in Christ shall rise first: (17 Then we which are alive and remain shall be caught up together with them in the clouds, to meet the Lord in the air:</u> and so shall we ever be with the Lord." (KJV)*

This Rapture (Jesus' *2nd Return*), which is for the Church, will occur at or just before the 7-year covenant is made between the Antichrist and Israel. This event will usher in the Great Tribulation from God. The Church will be in Heaven observing these events. The Church will be waiting for the Old Testament Saints and Tribulations Saints, who will join the Bride of Christ at the *1st Harvest* **(Rev.14).** This event will occur just before the coming back of Jesus to conquer Satan at Jesus' *3rd Return*.

<u>*Witness Number Six,*</u>

The Law (The Law to Jesus ±1472 year

During DAY 3 and DAY 4, we have seen that Bloodless Life was created and that the heavenly bodies were given for signs. That day represents when the LAW was given to Israel, but it gave no eternal life to God's people; except by

God's grace. This sign is the LAW. It only reveals sin, and sin can only condemn sinners. Therefore, it could not produce eternal life. The LAW required the blood of animal sacrifices as that was a way for atoning for broken LAW for that year. It also foretells a day when the Lamb's blood (Jesus) would produce eternal life. Animal blood had to be shed yearly to atone for sin, but Jesus' blood need only be shed once for all people, for all times, and all sins. The LAW is still good for Christians to use as their daily guide to their actions in this life, but the Blood of Jesus shed for all humanity that produces man's salvation from The Lake of Fire.

History tells us that the LAW was given to Moses approximately 1450 BC. When we view that backward from Jesus' Resurrection, we notice that it falls towards the middle of DAY 3 (Day of Bloodless Life). There appears to me to be a witness here that God is revealing that the 1,000-year rule will put the Law of Moses in the day that God created vegetation or Bloodless life. Just as vegetation has no Blood, the LAW also had no saving Blood

Witness Number Seven

The Signs

Along with the LAW, God sent messages to his prophets and signs to confirm its authority. While Moses was trying to get the Pharaoh to let Israel go, God sent signs to the Pharaoh in the manner of plagues, death of 1st borne, a cloud of fire, and finally the open Red Sea. All through the Old Testament, the prophets used signs to convince the people that the message or act was from God. Before the Church began, he performed many miraculous acts, which were signs of who He was. One event used the heavenly bodies for The Star of Bethlehem. This star was a sign to the wise men that a King was born. The only way for them to know about this event was by study and observation. A *clue* for us also.

Jesus performed many miraculous signs during his ministry to prove who he was. It was after the LAW was given to Moses that the prophet became a powerful tool for God. They were signs performed for Israel to convince Israel, and the world, of God's desires. Just as the heavenly bodies came after Day 4 (Planets and stars), so did many prophets come after the LAW. After Jesus' resurrection, there are several signs pointing to Jesus' coming during the end time. [See **Mat.24** and **25**].

The other meaningful sign is; the sunlight is righteousness, and darkness is unrighteousness. Revealing the moon is the sunlight reflecting (by the Church) righteousness in unrighteous darkness. The dark moon is the time of the Great Tribulation when the Church is removed from the earth. But the sunlight returns at the break of dawn. And we can see both the moon and the sun together; revealing the Church's Rapture to Jesus is complete. And there will be no darkness in eternity **(Rev.22:5).**

<u>*Witness Number Eight*</u>

Dividing of Water

Another witness can be found in DAY 2 as God tells us that he divided the waters. God put water in the atmosphere but mostly underground, so all vegetation could be watered by subsurface water (no rain), just mist. Both DAY 1 and DAY 2 speak of water. When we take the duration of the lives spoken of in Genesis, we can derive the day the Flood occurred from the beginning of the creation, which is 1,656 years AC (After Creation)D. This point falls just past the middle of DAY 2, effectively dividing Day 2's duration in half. An interesting side note is **(Gen.7:10)** that God gave Noah 7 days after he entered the ark (a type of Passover) before the waters (God Wrath) came. Note that dry land was created before vegetation, just as Noah landed on dry land after the waters divided and before the LAW was given to Moses. With what information is available at this time, we can see that it will take approximately 864 years (some studies 1039) until the LAW is given to Moses. This period was where the people were still expected to do good.

Another interesting observation is that all the patriarchs had died before the Flood. Methuselah was the last patriarch who died the same year as the Flood but just before the flood 1656 AC (After Creation[E]). Only Noah and his family remained, and his life spanned the Day 2 period as Noah was born in 1056 AC and died in 2006 AC at 950 years old.

On this attachment[E], you will see a chart of Day1 and Day 2; and within those days, these events did occur. Please notice how the flood divided Day 2 in a little over halfway. **Gen.1:7** speaks of the dividing of the waters under the firmament from waters above the firmament. There are six gaseous water atmospheres above the earth's liquid water. But notice God used the word dividing rather than separating those waters. Also, notice God joined these same waters of division together again, which divided Day 2.with the Great Flood. This division in this clock falls near the middle of Day 2.

This Great Flood appears to be a covert metaphor for two parables. But it contains more in-depth information. One is the separation of the Sheep from the Goats. Another is the separation of the Wheat from the Tares.

The first is the separation of the Sheep and the Goats. Noah was the only righteous man on earth **Gen. 6: 8** *"righteous and perfect in his generation."* But what of his three sons and their wives? If Noah was the only perfect person, are we to assume that his wife, sons, and their wives are less than perfect?

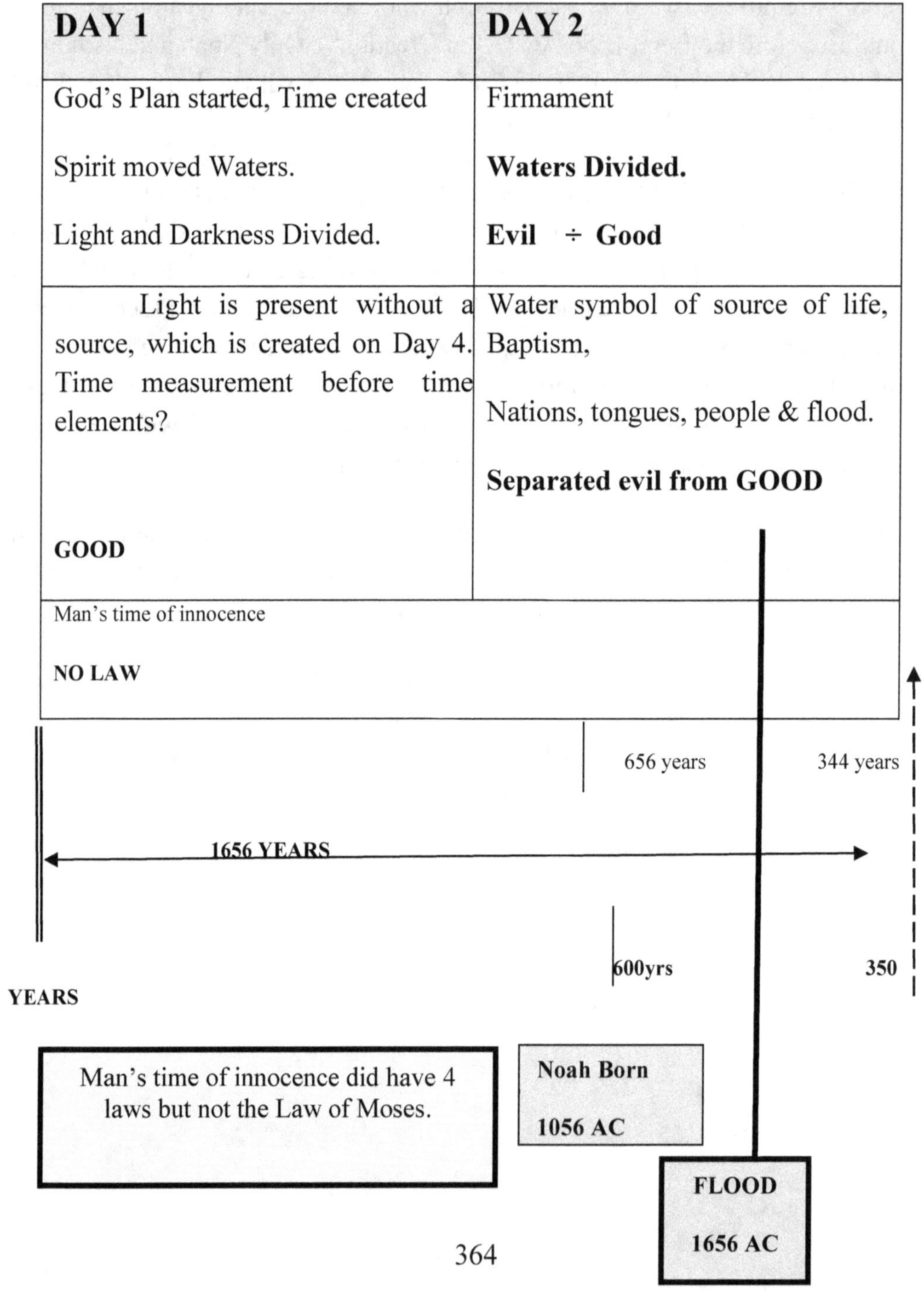
Not to scale

DAY 1
God's Plan started, Time created
Spirit moved Waters.
Light and Darkness Divided.
Light is present without a source, which is created on Day 4. Time measurement before time elements?
GOOD

DAY 2
Firmament
Waters Divided.
Evil ÷ Good
Water symbol of source of life, Baptism,
Nations, tongues, people & flood.
Separated evil from GOOD

Man's time of innocence
NO LAW

656 years
344 years
1656 YEARS
600yrs
350
YEARS

Man's time of innocence did have 4 laws but not the Law of Moses.

Noah Born
1056 AC

FLOOD
1656 AC

Witness Number Nine,

Jesus by water and blood

In **1 John 5**, we read that if we overcome this world, we are the sons of God.

> **1 John 5: 5–6** *"(5) Who is he that overcometh the world, but he that believeth that Jesus is the Son of God? (6) This is he that came by water and blood, even Jesus Christ; not by water alone, but by water and blood. And it is the Spirit that beareth witness, because the Spirit is truth."(KJV)*

Notice that not only did Jesus come by water and blood, but also all who believe (*"overcome the world"*) that Jesus is the Son of God. Here is the requirement to be saved and is for the Church and Tribulation Saints. Therefore, all of us that have accepted Jesus as our personal savior have also come by water and blood. At the least, we came by our mother's water braking and the blood of birth. Jesus also came by natural birth. But it again can be referring to our being in God's waiting room to pass over the Flood. Baptism is an excellent *clue* for water. As it is the visual representation of our death resurrection into a new life.

Water throughout the bible was used for many circumstances. It is also used as analogous to people. Remember, in the creation story that God does not mention creating water but dividing it. But we know from scripture that God created everything. There must be multi-meanings to these verses of scripture. Let's look at a few possibilities:

1. **Cleansing.** Water was used to clean all sorts of items, from people to animals.
2. **Sustenance**. Water needed to survive, and Hebrews searched for it in their travel through the desert.
3. **Purification**. Water was required to ceremonially clean individuals, and items in the Temple and Baptism.

4. **Punishment**. Water used to punish during the flood; and the crossing of the Red Sea.

5. **Healing.** Water use in the pool in the temple to heal when the angel stirred the waters. Jesus used his spit for the blind man's eyes to cure his blindness.

6. **Baptism.** Water was used to symbolize death to Resurrection, the washing away of sins, and to purify.

7. **People.** Water is used in the Bible to represent people, nations, and tongues.

As a child of God, we use the right of water Baptism as a visual representation of our death, burial, and resurrection. It is the symbol of our being reborn again into Jesus. It is a visual declaration that we claim Jesus as our savior; and that God has cleansed us from our sins. It is an act of purification. Jesus was also obedient when he was baptized (he was without sin), and the Holy Spirit came to him just as the Holy Spirit comes to each of us. It is the visual promise that God will send the Holy Spirit to all the children of God in the Church Age. Remember, when the Church is Raptured, the Holy Spirit will be removed, and evil will not be restrained.

Water also shows us the passage of time: the dividing of water, the destructive Flood-waters, the deadly waters of the Red Sea, the Jews passing through the Jordan into the promised land, the birth of Jesus (60% water), the ceremonial Baptism of Jesus and more. Jesus was present at all these events thought Israel's history.

Blood is used in many of the same ways as water:

1. **Cleansing.** Blood was required to cleanse us from our sins. God declared this with the early sacrifices of blood for atonement for sins. The Blood of a Red Heifer is required to cleanse the Jewish Temple **(Num. 19:2–10).**

2. **Sustenance.** Jesus tells us that we must eat his flesh and drink his blood, or he will have nothing to do with us **(John 6:53).** This is an analogy to the Communion Sacraments that God's children participate in regularly. We are to review our lives before we partake so as not to bring punishment **(1 Cor.11:26–29),** and we are sustained by the admitting of our sins to God so he will uphold our walk with Jesus.

3. **Heals**. Jesus' blood heals our souls and opens the way to maintain a healthy soul. Same with our physical life.

One additional thing I would have you see is; God's clock traversed those periods of water and blood. Water represents the Flood, and Blood being the time of sacrificing of animal blood. Jesus and you and I were also present, as God had created everything that would ever be by Day 6. And we all traversed those time periods as we were waiting for our time to be placed into this world. Jesus himself had to traverse those periods of water and blood to arrive at his exact time in God's plan.

These next two witnesses (10 and 11) tell us of Jesus' 1st trip to earth as Servant and Savior.

Witness Number Ten

The Three Witnesses

> **1 John 5:7–12** *"(7) For there are three that bear record <u>in heaven,</u> the <u>Father,</u> the <u>Word,</u> and the <u>Holy Ghost</u>: and these three are one. (8) And there are three that bear witness in <u>earth,</u> the <u>Spirit,</u> and the <u>water,</u> and the <u>blood</u>: and these three <u>agree</u> in one."* *(KJV)*

Here God continues to reinforce the earlier passages of scriptures with witnesses in heaven

First, God reveals the *THREE WITNESS ARE IN HEAVEN,* showing their original home. But, God is also telling us these three are the foundation of the future. God wants us to know they are the absolute power and unlimited strength to base our lives' trust and faith. For there is no other entity or entities with these virtues.

1. **<u>The Father</u>**. The creator of all things and the parent of all. The figure of authority over the entire family of earth. Adam was the father of man on earth and was at the beginning. Abraham is the father of Faith, and he was at the transitional point of Day 5 & 6. Abraham's birth was approximately ±2166 BC (*1948 AC*) and death ±1991 BC (*2123 AC*). Isaac was the son of Abraham and the incomplete sacrifice, but Jesus, the Son of God, is the completed sacrifice. Isaac's incomplete sacrifice occurred at approximately ±2051BC.

2. **<u>The Word.</u>** Threefold meaning: the <u>*scriptures,*</u> <u>*Law,*</u> and imperative are the *commands of <u>Jesus</u>*. **(John 1:1–5)**

   The *Bible* is our love letter and guidance from God. The Law is f our knowledge of sin, but *Jesus* is our Salvation for our sins of disobedience as a lawbreaker.

3. **<u>Holy Ghost</u>**. (Also the Holy Spirit) We see from scripture that God sent the *Holy Spirit to earth for a witness* and to save all individuals. Rejection of the Holy Spirit by blaspheming him and is the only unforgivable Sin. The Holy Spirit came to the earth at Pentecost **(Acts 2:2–6)** and will be removed from the earth **(2 Thes.2:1–7)** at the *time* of the Rapture.

Next, God reveals the **Three Witnesses on the Earth.**

1. **<u>Water.</u>** Here the primary witness on earth is the Flood. We can see the Flood results on our planet today with the different sediment layers uncovered around the earth. These marks refer to the period

of creation that concerns water or the first two days. We see the ancient writing around the earth in different languages (after the Tower of Babel) telling us of the same Flood. Water is used on earth for Baptism too.

2. **<u>Blood.</u>** During Israel's history, we see how God gave us this witness to point to the perfect Blood of Jesus. During this time, animals were sacrificed to fulfill the requirement of God for the Day of Atonement. These sacrifices show the beginning of the Blood requirement that started with animals and ends with Jesus' Blood. The most important thing is that He came to earth, shed His perfect blood for the payment for our sins on earth, for those who accept Jesus as their Lord. We can read and see this witness in the earthly history books, archeology, and the scriptures. This witness refers to the Period of LAW. Also, we see Jesus born as a human child. And Jesus' Blood fulfilled the Law.

3. **<u>Spirit</u>** This will be the most: prominent, unnoticed, and ignored witness. Words cannot fully explain the mission of the Holy Spirit for man. Spirit is not a seeable object, so he is also called The Holy Ghost. He is invisible to our human eyes, but he is apparent to our spirit if we listen and feel. Let us look into the makeup of our body's construction.

We are made up of body, soul, and spirit. And the interplay between these three units is very complicated. Our bodies are so wonderfully made. We know we are mostly water (60% of body weight). We bleed blood when injured. And we have a conscience given to us through the Tree of Knowledge of Good and Evil. Also, those of us in Jesus have the Holy Spirit within us. All three of these are or should be powerful witnesses to us that we are saved.

The Holy Spirit came at Pentecost and will be removed from earth with the Raptured Church. How can the world not recognize the taking away of such a significant amount of peoples? Neighbors missing, workers not showing up for work, Doctors not available to provide needed services, aircraft grounded for lack of pilots, police shortages and crimes increase, riots at prisons, government stalls for lack of people, ground transportation jammed up, and so many other events that are short of personnel.

Or could it be; that not many ½ christians will be Raptured or deserving of the Rapture? Will it be as it was in Noah's day where only eight passed over the flood out of billions of humans? Jesus spoke in Mathew that many will fall away from Jesus. If this is so, then not many will be Raptured, and very few will be missed. Is this the time of which Jesus spoke of in **Mat.24?**

> **Matthew 24:42–43 *(42) Watch therefore: for ye know not what hour your Lord doth come. (43) But know this, <u>that if</u> the goodman of the house <u>had known in what watch the thief would come</u>, he would have watched, and would not have suffered his house to be broken up. (44) Therefore be ye also ready: for in such an hour as ye think not the Son of man cometh." (KJV)***

These words *"had known"* reveal that Satan (thief) has (after the act) broken into their life. It means many ½ christians will not know the general time and *clues* of Jesus' *2nd Return* to take his Bride (sheep) to the wedding. Just as the five virgins (goats) of **Mat. 25** who did not have oil (righteousness) for their lamps. And after getting the oil, they were not allowed into Heaven and the Wedding of Jesus to his Bride (Church).

How could practicing Christians not be aware of current world events that point to Jesus' soon return? Is it due to lack of study of God's Word, Pastors not teaching their sheep of the nearness of Jesus' return, or apathy towards looking for Jesus' return? This condition is so apparent in **(Rev.3:14–22)** the letter to the Church of the Laodiceans. Their apathy and their need for nothing are paramount. They have no concept of the near return of Jesus for his Bride.

In this event, the disappearance of righteous people and the pew-sitter being left behind, it will become obvious to those who have heard the Word but have not walked the talk. They have missed Jesus' *2nd Return* (the Rapture). The Rapture should prove their need to correct their walk-in righteousness during the coming Great Wrath period. **Revelation.3.18–21** should trigger an epiphany to those left behind.

> **Revelation 3:21** *"To him that overcometh will I grant to <u>sit with me in my throne</u>, even as <u>I also overcame,</u> and am set down with my Father in his throne." (KJV)*

This verse reveals a second chance for those left behind. Notice the voices' description, which tells His opinion of those left behind. But **verse 20** is the 2nd chance for those left behind. It will require a deed to open a door (repent), thereby letting Jesus into their (door) heart. This effort, on their part, will require great loyalty to Jesus during fearful and horrendous times. This Church of Laodicea will need to go buy gold (purity = faith) just as the five unprepared virgins needed to go and buy oil (light = deeds).

Interestingly, these verses in **Revelation 3:18–22** are written immediately after the seven Churches' seven Letters and before the tribulation begins. These words come before the revealing to the left behind that all they have to do during the coming Great Tribulation is fully accept Jesus' commands. The following events are for their chastising. **(Rev.3:19)**

✝ **These Witnesses are pointing to both the *2nd Return* and *3rd Return* of Jesus to this earth as King of Kings. Whose Kingdom will last forever!**

Witness Chart Note to scale

CLOCK'S APPLICATION

First, let me make it perfectly clear that I am not trying to set a specific date or a time of our Lord's *2nd or 3rd Returns.* That would be futile, as Jesus said in **Mat.24:36,** that no man knows the day or hour of his return. But we need to know which of the two returns Jesus was referring. However, we need to balance that statement with Jesus' words in Mathew.

> **Matthew 24:42–44** "*(42) Watch therefore: for ye know not what hour your Lord doth come. (43) But know this, that if the goodman of the house <u>had known in what watch</u> the thief would come, <u>he would have watched,</u> and would not have suffered his house to be broken up. (44) <u>Therefore be ye also ready</u>: for in such an hour as ye think not the Son of Man cometh". (KJV)*

In these past tense words, *"had known"* and *"he would have watched,"* Jesus himself is referring to a pasted watch, which is for a given period of time for a specific day. This watch is usually a 4 hours period of time, 6 times a day or 3 hours 8 times a day. So Jesus is saying **if** we had known which watch (study and revealed by the Holy Spirit), we would only know which 4 or 3 hours to be vigilant but not have the exact hour, minute, and second. And this is my attempt, with this writing, to bring you to this watch. This event does not mean my timing is within 4 or 3 hours, but it makes you aware of the nearness of Jesus' *2nd Return.* In **Mat.24,** we read of the sign of his near return.

> **Matthew 24:32–34** "*(32) Now learn a parable of the fig tree; When his branch is yet tender, and putteth forth leaves, <u>ye know that summer</u> is <u>nigh</u>: (33) <u>So likewise ye,</u> when ye shall see all these things, know that it is near, <u>even at the doors.</u>" (KJV)*

Here Jesus is giving us a (future tense) *clue* of a season. It appears the *clue* is spring, as, of course, spring comes before the heat of summer. Also, look for the verses pointing to the future warning *("likewise ye");* and the verses pointing to just before the Rapture *("at the door").* One warning to the future

373

is not only **Mat.24** but also in **1Thess.5,** where we are admonished to be sober and watch for Jesus' future return.

> **1 Thessalonians 5:4–6** *"(4) <u>But ye, brethren, are not in darkness, that that day should overtake you as a thief. (5)</u> Ye are the children of light, and the children of the day: we are not of the night, nor of darkness. (6) <u>Therefore let us not sleep, as do others; but let us watch and be sober.</u>"(KJV)*

Please notice **verse 4** is a positive statement, which we are not in darkness. This statement pertains to Christians on earth who are studying God's word and earnestly looking for Jesus' return. They will know the nearness of Jesus' *2nd Return* to earth. Sleep mentioned here is not the sleep we need every night for good health, but our brain's inactivity when we are awake.

But many verses are negative, revealing many people will be caught unaware of Jesus' 2nd Return. **(1 Thes.5:2 and Rev.16:15).**

> **Revelation 16:15** *"<u>Behold, I come as a thief.</u> Blessed* is *he that watcheth, and keepeth his garments, lest he walk naked, and they see his shame." (KJV)*

Here we read again Jesus *<u>will come like a thief</u>* because few are looking or are aware of the signs of his 2nd Return. To watch for an event to occur, we must have some knowledge of the time, appearance, and indicators pointing to the approach of that event. It appears that Jesus' Rapture return will be at night too, due to the words like *"sleep" and "thief in the night" of* **1 Thess.5.**

> *1 Thes.5:2 "For yourselves know perfectly that the day of the Lord so cometh as a thief in the night." (KJV)*

Again, this verse is about his silent 2nd Return (thief in the night) compared to his bright and noisy 3rd *Return* (Armageddon) will be just the opposite of his *2nd Return*. The *3rd Return* will be: with the whole world illuminated with bright lights, thousands and thousands of angels, all those saved souls, dressed in white, from Adam time to that present time and hallelujah music. **(Rev.19)**

This 2nd Return event will take our study of God's Word and the application of the knowledge learned. The Bible has many words pointing to Jesus' returns, and it is up to us to interpret their meaning with the Holy Spirit's help. With that being said, let us see if we can apply God's clock today.

REFERENCE POINT

This application will need a point of reference common to both earth history and God's events. There are many studies as to dating events of the Bible, and they are at best approximate. To locate this common point, we must look in both directions from After Creation (AC) forward and earth history rearward (AC to BC).

In the book of Genesis, we are given the life spans of the descendants[E] of Adam. By putting them together, we can find the year of their birth and death; using <u>After Creation (AC).</u> One person we can track is Abraham. In summing up the ages mentioned in the Genesis account, we learn that **Abraham was born ≠1,948 AC[E]** (<u>A</u>fter <u>C</u>reation). When we look at the approximate date from historical studies, Abraham is given a **birth date ±2,166 BC.** This date gives us an approximate common point between AC and BC, but the movements of these times are in opposite directions. Therefore, there is a problem with determining the dating.

Doesn't God have a great sense of humor?

The reason for using Abraham is because he is the Father of FAITH. However, the proof of his faith was his obedience to sacrifice his son Isaac. Even though God prevented Isaac's sacrifice, Abraham proved his faithfulness to God in Abraham's attempt to fulfill God's command. It is at this point that God is revealing to humanity that righteousness comes by FAITH. Therefore, this position on God's clock is an essential point, and it is before the Law. But I will use Abraham's birth to find the Common Point as dates appear more accurate.

I am selecting the 2,000 AC and 2,000 BC lines as there appears to be an agreement between those two dates. History seems to be crossing each other at that mark. Isn't it interesting that this is the central point when Jesus and God are declaring Faith takes presidents over deeds for salvation? It is also Day 2 (1,000–2,000 years) that God divided the waters and represents the Flood that separated Good from Evil (1656 AC)[E.]

It is deeds that had taken precedence up to this point by the Tree of Knowledge of Good and Evil and later through God's Law given to Moses. God's grace was applied to each human's life in their attempt to keep the Law, which was impossible for man. Therefore, God is to send to earth the only human that could keep the Law and be sinless. This human is to fulfill the requirement in the law of perfection in deeds. Jesus was perfect and sinless; He did all the deeds required of Him. Jesus sacrificed his body for his believers (brothers and sisters). So we believers are to be found in Jesus protected by His righteous sacrificial body. **(Rom.12:5)**

ABRAHAM'S BIRTH DATE BC

We must use Abraham's birth date near the 2,000-year marks as they appear as the crossing points of AC and BC dating. Abraham was born in **1948 AC**[E] and **±2166 BC.** You will notice both lines on the chart below falls just to the left of the 2,000 AC/BC line. To average the difference between the two points, I take the difference from the 2,000 marks. The 1948 AC is 52 years short, and 2166 BC is166 years over the 2,000-year mark. So the difference between the two is 114 years. I divide by 2 to get an average of 57 years. So 1948 +57 = **1891 AC** and 2166 – 57 = **± 2109 BC** for a common point for Abraham's birth.

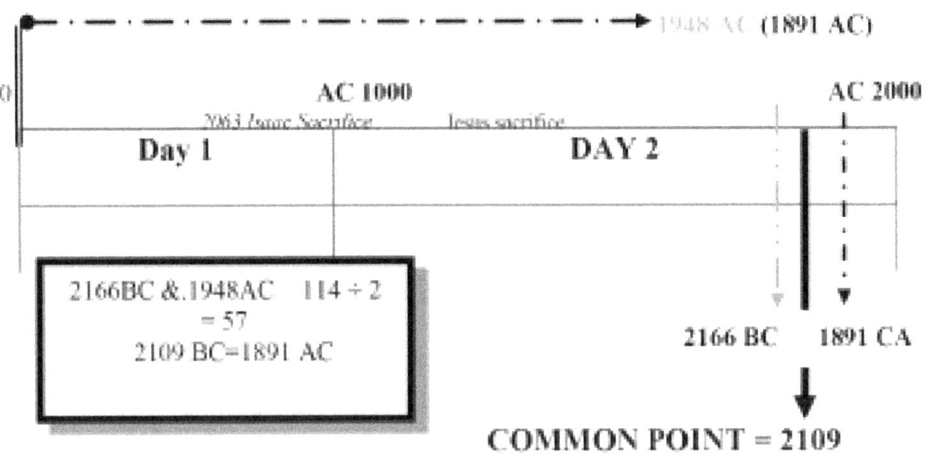

FAITH BEFORE LAW

Please note the location of Abraham's birth date as it falls in God's clock. It is near this transition point in creation (Day 3) where vegetation will be created (the Bloodless life day) but before the LAW (±1450 BC) was given to Moses. Abraham is known as *"The Father of Faith."* God placed Abraham before the LAW to tell us that FAITH has much more impact than the LAW. And this reveals the rescue of Jesus from the Law. Jesus also tell us that *not one jot or tillle will depart.will depart from the law* (**Mat.5:18**).

Therefore, we are saved by FAITH and not by the LAW. The High Priest, Levites Priests, and Rabbi's missed this foreshadowing of righteousness pointing to the Messiah's salvation. But initially, righteousness was imparted to the patriarchs of old because of God's Grace and their <u>deeds</u> to keep the Law. It is at this point that God establishes an exceptional focal point in his clock. The fact that Abraham and Isaac lives transition this 2,000 AC / BC line gives witness to the location of the initial sacrifice that was not sufficient. Near this point in time, God creates Bloodless life (LAW) and begins a system for atonement for sin. This system will transition time; until the sacrifice of the perfect sacrifice, the lamb (Jesus).

You can see that the 1,000-year per day is still holding reasonably true, as the difference ±2109 BC is relatively close to 2,000-years per day of creation in BC time.

But please remember, I am not trying to compute the exact day of Jesus' *2nd Return* (the Rapture). There is far too much information missing at this point. I am only trying to reveal how close his return appears, and we should be looking for his return. And that will require our learning from scriptures and our vigilance in looking for those *clues* for Jesus' *2nd Return*.

FULFILLMENT OF THE SACRIFICE

Abraham's sacrifice of his son Isaac was fulfilled some years later by God's sacrifice of his Son Jesus. *This event is the most critical point in God's clock! This point in God's plan is where God's grace provides a way for the forgiveness of all our sins, for all people, for all times. It is our faith in Jesus and Jesus' sacrifice that makes full payment for all our sins.* And the Blood of Jesus cleanses us in God's eyes. Therefore, we being without sin (in God's eyes) we are children of God and heirs to eternity in heaven. This is that point on God's clock (Day5) that *Blood Life* is created to replace the day of *Atonement Blood*.

It is the operation of the Holy Spirit, through the Blood Life of Jesus, that establishes the Church, and that operation will continue until the Church is complete at the end of Day 6. With such an important day, it would seem prudent to give the Church period some study as to its timing. Here the dates are more accurate for us but with still some inaccuracies.

One of the problems with dates is our use of BC (Before Christ) and AD (Anno Domini) "In the year of the Lord." AD was to begin at Jesus' birth. But there seems to be some error in man's calendar during BC's transition to AC, which is considered here. Also, the Bible speaks of Herod the Great in the passage of **Mat.2:1** with the Magi seeking baby Jesus, and we accurately know that Herod the Great, a non-Jew appointed Ruler of Israel by the Roman Senate, ruled from 37 BC to 4 BC. Therefore Jesus must have been born in 5 BC to 4 BC to be alive during Herod's reign. The 5—4 BC appears close, as Herod killed all the children who were two years old from the Star's date, which the Magi gave to Herod. Herod would bracket that date by a year ether side to assure that he covered any date error for Jesus' birth. However, many studies suggest 5 BC as the date of Jesus' birth, which could be reasonably accurate.

Also, we know that Jesus was 30 years old when he started his 3½ years ministry. That makes Jesus 33½ years old at his crucifixion. It is at this time that the sacrifice of Isaac reaches its fulfillment in the sacrifice of Jesus. Remember, Isaac's sacrificial blood sparing was the incomplete sacrifice pointing to the time of Jesus' sacrificial blood as the completed sacrifice.

Jesus' Resurrection that verifies, HE IS CHRIST, THE HEBREW MESSIAH, and SAVIOR OF THE WORLD.

This position on God's clock is at the beginning of Day 5, and his Blood will continue to clean for two millenniums until the 3rd Return of Jesus (end of Day 6) to this earth. And his 1,000- year Kingdom begins. The Rapture *(2nd Return)* will be at least seven years before Jesus' *3rd Return* and final return to claim the earth and punish the unrighteous.

Note

Please keep in mind that God's Creation Clock is different than the Creation Story. Creation Story events covered six days of 24 hours a day. These six days also reveal <u>the days of hidden clues</u>

to the life of God's creation, which appears to be 6,000 years; 7,000 years if Jesus' earthly kingdom of 1,000-years is counted. After which, a new Heaven and Earth will be created. **(Rev. 21)**

The 2,000 years after Jesus' Resurrection is an estimation of time-based on all the material as mentioned above. The 3rd Return of Jesus will occur after the 1st Harvest of Rev.14 (1st Resurrection) for the dead Tribulation Saints and Old Testament Saints. This period is also witnessed to in scripture by Hosea's prophecy.

WITNESS OF HOSEA (Most Revealing Witness)

Here I am revealing the most profound clue as to the correctness of 1,000 days equals 1,000 years. And we have history of Israel to help us understand this concept.

In Hosea **1,** we see the theme that God orders Hosea (analogous to Jesus) to marry (Gomer) an *adulterous woman* to be his wife; and each of their three children were given a symbolic name.

- 1st- Son "Jezreel" means *"God scatters."*
- 2nd- Daughter "Lo-Ruhamah" means *"Not having obtained mercy."*
- 3rd- Son "Loammi" means *"Not my people."*

God is revealing to Hosea that these names are pointing to Israel's future. They will be: 1.) *"scattered"* to all nations (70AD), 2.) God did not find Israel's death of Jesus worthy of his grace and *"mercies"* and 3.) God will separate himself from Israel temporarily, for Israel is *"not my people."*

In **Hosea 2,** God tells Hosea (Jesus) to rebuke her and put her whoredoms away from the children. This time occurred in 70 AD when Rome conquered Israel. In the future, God will be removing their blinders and bringing the truth to the

Hebrew people. The Hebrews will accept Jesus as their Lord Messiah, and all of Israel will be saved. We see this in **Hos. 1.**

> **Hosea 1:7** *"But I* (God) *will have mercy upon the house of Judah, and will save them by the LORD* (Jesus) *their God, and will not save them by bow, nor by sword, nor by battle, by horses, nor by horsemen."(KJV)*

This verse further identifies the 144,000 Jewish missionaries **(Rev.7)** as Jesus's emissaries to Israel, and Israel will not be converted by military might but by God's words. But, the Hebrew people will be scattered by the Romans in 70AD. However, in **Hosea 3,** we read of the Hebrew children returning to Israel and seeking Jesus. This event will occur *"in the latter days."* **(See Isaiah 2)**

God will punish Gomer (Israel), but it is for her repentance that God seeks **(Hos.2:23** and **3:3).** Hosea (Jesus) is ordered (by God) to continue to love Gomer (Israel) and take her back from her adultery. And the children (Israel) will have no king (No country). Hosea is to keep her in isolation for a period of time. This isolation is from 70 AD to 1948 AD when Israel won back her land and became a country again. However, this country, Israel, will end at the midpoint of the Great Tribulation to Jesus' final return to earth **(Dan. 9:23–27** and **Rev.12).** The Hebrews will be converted by the 144,000 Jewish missionaries and not by war or sword. This time is when Israel flees into the wilderness for 1,260 days **(Rev. 12:6).** This fleeing occurs after Israel's conversion to Jesus. **(Hos. 6)**

In **Hos. 6,** God tells Hosea to exhort Israel to repent (necessary for forgiveness) and reveals the timing set aside for Israel's return to God.

> **Hosea 6:1–2** *"(1) Come let us return unto the Lord: for he hath torn, and he shall heal us; he hath smitten, and he will bind us up. (2) After two days will he revive us: in the third day he will raise us up, and we shall live in his sight."(KJV)*

From Hosea's book, we see that Israel is to be punished for their whoredom, the worship of other gods, and the denial of Jesus's being the Messiah and Son of God. And Israel is to be put away for some time. That time set aside for Israel is two days (2,000 years), after which Israel will be revived. These two days are the same two days (2,000 years) for the Church period. Israel was scattered into all nations in 70 AD (after the beginning of the Church in 27AD) when Roman Legions destroyed the Temple and scattered the Hebrew people throughout the known world. During these 2,000 years and 70 AD to 1948 is 1848 years.

Christians have been trying to convert (revive) Israel to the saving grace of Jesus. After the Church's Rapture, the 144,000 Israelites **(Rev.7)** are sealed with the Holy Spirit and go to all nations to spread the Gospel of Jesus. This is Hosea's three days of total time, where Israel will be two days (2,000 years) for their revival and one day (1,000 years) to worship Jesus. It will also be that time after the Church Saints' Rapture, which will be an undeniable sign to Israel.

Many Jewish converts will be human sacrifices during the last 3½ years of the Great Tribulation. We find their souls under the Temple Alter in **Rev.7:14, Rev.6:9–11,** and **Rev.20:4.** But there will also be some pew-sitters, and gentile converts there too.

HOSEA'S PROPHECY (1 Day = 1,000 yr.)

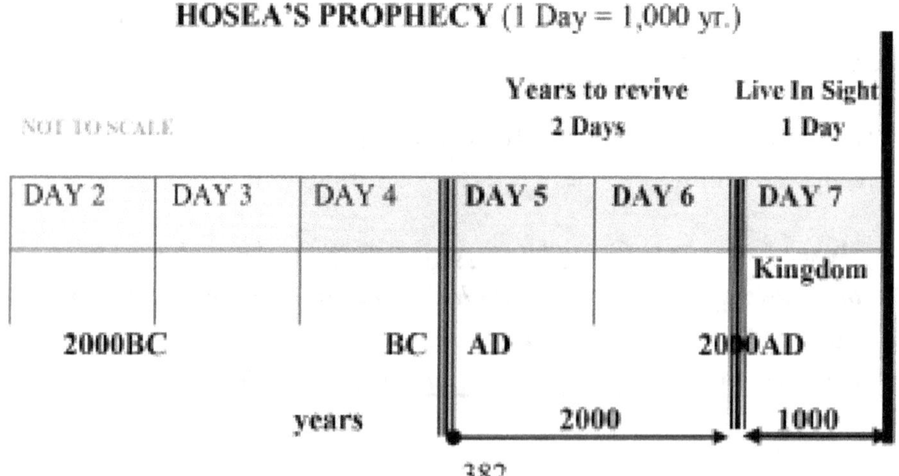

Please do not misunderstand!

> **I am not saying that Jesus' 3rd return is 2030 AD, or the Rapture will occur in 2023AD. I am only trying to reveal that the time is near for Jesus' return.**

This information presented is averaged and general in nature. There are too many historical dating errors and _unrevealed clues_ to accurately determine God's end plan's date. And this is in God's plan to hide the Rapture's exact date *(2nd Return)*. However, Jesus' *3rd Return* can be computed to the very day. [More on this later.] Next, God reveals an event that will occur between the Rapture and the *3rd Return* of Jesus.

In **Rev.7:9,** we read the results of the 144,000 Hebrew missionary's efforts. Then notice that in Hosea's third day (last 1,000 years), Israel will be revived (saved) and live in the sight of Jesus. **Rev.7** reveals these **144,000 will live in Jesus' sight** as they will serve Jesus day and night.

> **Revelation 7:14–17** *"(14) And I said unto him, Sir, thou knowest. And he said to me, These are they which <u>came out of great tribulation, and have washed their robes, and made them white in the blood of the Lamb.</u> (15) Therefore are they before the throne of God, and <u>serve him day and night in his temple:</u> and he that sitteth on the throne shall dwell among them. (16) They shall hunger no more, neither thirst any more; neither shall the sun light on them, nor any heat. (17) For the Lamb which is in the midst of the throne shall feed them, and shall lead them unto living fountains of waters: and God shall wipe away all tears from their eyes."(KJV)*

This event will occur near the end of Genesis Day 6 or just before the beginning of Jesus' Kingdom age *(3rd Return)*. During this coming 1,000-year Kingdom period, David will rule over the twelve tribes of Israel as was promised by God to his servant David **(2 Sam. 7:16).** This covenant with David further confirms that Israel will be revived and will live in God's sight. The statement that they will *"serve him "day and night"* is referring to the 1,000-year Kingdom period as there will be human survivors (Tribulations Saints) that will transition the Great Tribulation period and will still need the night for their rest and recuperation. Also, the children born to these survivors during the 1,000 years will require the Sun for health and night for rest. However, our home in Eternity will contain no night (darkness) as Jesus will be the constant light **(Rev. 21:22–23)**. Also, in **Zec. 8,**

Zec.8:1–3 reveals God's jealousy against Israel for worshipping other gods. Still, God will return to Zion (Jerusalem) as it mentions old-men and women present and appears to be speaking of this time of Jesus' Kingdom with boys and girls playing in the streets. Other verses appear to talk of survivors of the Great Tribulation. In **Zec.8,** it seems Jesus' headquarters will be in Jerusalem.

> **Zechariah 8:20–23 *"(20) Thus saith <u>the LORD of hosts</u>; It shall* yet *come to pass, that there shall come people, and the inhabitants of many cities: (21) And the inhabitants of one city shall go to another, saying, Let us go speedily to pray before the LORD, and <u>to seek the LORD</u> of hosts: I will go also. (22) Yea, many people and strong nations shall come to seek the <u>LORD of hosts in Jerusalem</u> and to pray before the LORD. (23) Thus saith the LORD of hosts; In those days* it shall come to *pass, <u>that ten men shall take hold out of all languages of the nations</u>, even shall take hold of the–skirt of him that is a Jew, saying, <u>We will go with you: for we have heard</u> that <u>God is with you.</u>" (KJV)***

This city is not the eternal New Jerusalem because all these individuals do not have the mind of Christ. They do not know all truths but need guidance from the LORD of *"Host."* Do you remember who these *Host* **(Gen. 2:1)** are? Therefore, this is after Armageddon. With all these people coming from all nations, God provides ten men with complete *knowledge of all languages of* *the Universe*. But, in the final Heaven, there will be one language again.-Also; **verses 16–17** point to those individuals as they still have the carnal mind. These individuals are living Tribulation Saints prodigy and survivors of the Great Tribulation transitioning into the 1,000-year Kingdom of Jesus. **Zec. 8** also speaks of the Kingdom.

> **Zechariah 8:16–17** *"(16) These are the things that ye shall do; Speak ye every man the truth to his neighbour; execute the judgment of truth and peace in your gates: (17) And let none of you imagine evil in your hearts against his neighbour; and love no false oath: for all these are things that I hate, saith the LORD." (KJV)*

In eternity truth will be a constant. Judgments will be unnecessary. Imagine evil in our hearts will be impossible. So this has to be speaking of some other period before eternity. Being this was written just before **Zec. 8:20–23,** it appears to be in the time of Jesus' 1,000-year Kingdom.

The New Jerusalem's population is after the *1st Harvest* **(Rev. 14:13–16 / 21:4)** and will be the incorruptible souls whose names are written in the Book of Life that survived the Beast (Satan). Those who blasphemed the Holy Spirit will be judged for every deed, and every word they have spoken at the Great White Throne Judgment after Jesus' 1,000-year Kingdom ends in War #2 and at the end of the *2nd Harvest*. It will be when all is revealed and laid bare. It will be God as judge, jury, and executioner. All lost souls will be cast into the *Lake of Fire* forever. How sad! They gained the world of sin but lost their souls. **(Mat.16)**

> **Matthew.16:26** *For what is a man profited, if he shall gain the whole world, and lose his own soul? or what shall a man give in exchange for his soul?*

For 70 to 80 years of sin, these individuals have lost their souls to Satan and will inherit with Satan the *Lake of Fire*. Those who have given their lives to

Jesus will inherit with Jesus: eternal life, Kingship, Lordship, and Priesthood. Jerusalem will be Jesus' headquarters and throne for 1,000 years. Humans from all over the world will come to worship Jesus for those 1,000 years. The incarcerated Satan will be paroled at the end of the 1,000 years. Then he will gather another army to fight Jesus. Satan's army will be instantly burned up by God **(Rev.20:7–15),** and all will be made new. **(Rev.21)**

The New Earth and New Heaven spoken of in **Rev.21** and **22** reveals all saved souls have the mind of Christ. No impurities will be permitted into eternity. Therefore **Zec.8** is speaking of that time of Jesus' 1,000 year Kingdom on earth. Here the Saints will rule with Jesus over the survivors of the Great Tribulation and their offspring's.

This book is to point out to you that most of the time necessary to complete God's plan for the Rapture is here; **NOW!** Also, don't be misled by the thought that God will not warn his children of the impending wrath coming onto this earth and our loved ones. ***Consider this a warning.*** How will you feel seeing that loved one sentenced to the eternal *Lake of Fire* because you failed to speak to them about Jesus and his or her need for salvation? Jesus said to the <u>children of the Kingdom</u> in **Mat. 8.**

> **Matthew 8:11–13 *"(12) And I say unto you, that many shall come from the east and west, and shall sit down with Abraham, and Isaac, and Jacob, in the kingdom of heaven. (13) <u>But the children of the kingdom</u> shall be cast into outer darkness: there shall be weeping and gnashing of teeth."(KJV)***

The ones that sit with Abraham, Isaac, Lazarus, and Jacob are saved by God's grace and not by Jesus' Blood. These are the Old Testament Saints that came from (Earth's Paradise) in the *1st Harvest*. Those that come to sit down with them are primarily the Jewish children of the tribulation survivors in Jesus' Kingdom. But the Tribulation Saints are saved by Jesus' Blood **(Rev.7:14)** and deeds. They will also be in the *1st Harvest* **(Rev. 14)** and attend God. **(Rev.7:14–17).**

The *"children of the kingdom"* reveal the children born during Jesus' earthly Kingdom of 1,000 years. They will still have the sinful nature given to them through Adam by their parent survivors. These children are the candidates for Satan's future army after his release from the Abyss **(Rev.20:7–10).** These unrighteous children are *"cast into outer darkness,"* and darkness is symbolic of unrighteous. The *"weeping and gnashing of teeth;"* is the trait of a sad and angry person who has not accepted Jesus. And they must remain outside the city of Jesus headquarters. Even this perfect kingdom of Jesus; will still have sin even though Satan is absent and incarcerated.

This earthly Kingdom will occur after the *1 Harvest* of **Rev.14:13–16**. The children spoken of here lived through the Great Tribulation or were born during Jesus' Kingdom, which will have the inherited sin. Many will eventually join with Satan in his final War #3 against Jesus at the end of the 1,000-year Kingdom. They (carnal) will be completely burned up, and their souls will meet God at his *Great White Throne judgment.* Their names will not be found in the *Book of Life,* and they will be *cast into the Lake of Fire to remain forever.*

Those **"cast into outer darkness"** will be those that reject Jesus after Armageddon and during Jesus' 1,000 year Kingdom. These are the children that are cast out of the kingdom into a miserable existence. They have rejected Jesus; and will only live to be 100 years old **(Isa.65:20).** They will be those humans that join Satan in his final war against Jesus. **(Rev.20:7–9**). This War #2 will occur at the end of the 1,000 Year Kingdom after Satan is released from the Abyss

> **Revelation 20:7–9"** *(7)And when the thousand years are expired, Satan shall be loosed out of his prison, (8) And shall go out to deceive the nations which are in the four quarters of the earth, Gog and Magog, to gather them together to battle: the number of whom is as the sand of the sea. (9) And they went up on the breadth of the earth, and compassed the camp of the*

saints about, and the beloved city: and fire came down from God out of heaven, and devoured them." (KJV)

In **Mat.24,** Jesus tells us about the evil servant's (present and future) destination. Who is the wicked servant but the person that denies Jesus as his Lord? They have allowed the world and its cares to control them. This evil nature was given to us by Adam's disobedience. And this disobedience will continue through time until God destroys Satan and his army **(Rev.20:7–9).** Then God creates a New Heaven and Earth after the final *Great White Throne Judgment* **(Rev.20:11–15).** But what will happen to the evil church servants?

Matthew 24:48–51 *"(48) But and if <u>that evil servant</u> shall say in his heart, <u>My lord delayeth his coming;</u> (49) And begin to smite his fellow servants, and to eat and drink with the drunken; (50) The lord of that servant shall come in <u>a day that he looketh not for him,</u> and in an hour that he is not aware of, (51) And shall cut him asunder, and appoint him his portion with the hypocrites: <u>there shall be weeping and gnashing of teeth.</u>"(KJV)*

There is a saying that captures these individuals, and it goes like this: *"They do not walk the talk."* In other words, they may appear to be Christians, but their actions are not according to God's word. They are the tree that produces bad fruit. These Scriptures diametrically oppose their actions, such as 1) actively practicing homosexual parishioners and pastors, 2) parishioners advocating abortions, 3) accepting unmarried couples living together, 4) and so many more actions against God's laws. Also, notice the *clue* "*he looketh not for him, and in an hour that he is not aware of,"* This reveals the Rapture. Also, they (evil servants) have the appearance of Godliness but deny its power. **(2Tim 3)**

2 Timothy 3:1–5 *"(1) This know also, that in the <u>last days</u> perilous times shall come. (2) For men shall be lovers of their own selves, covetous, boasters, proud, blasphemers, disobedient* *to parents, unthankful, unholy,(3) Without natural affection, trucebreakers, false accusers, incontinent, fierce, despisers of those that are good, (4) Traitors, heady, highminded, lovers of pleasures more than lovers of God;(5) Having a form of godliness, but denying the power thereof: from such turn away."* *(KJV)*

Notice that **verse 5** speaks to us of those individuals *"having a form of Godliness but denying his power."* These are Pastors, Teachers, Elders, Deacons, and ordinary people who appear to be righteous and belong to Jesus. But, they are unrighteous, self-serving, and not *"walking the talk."* There is also a scripture that transcends the Rapture and reveals the complete degradation of these people's unrighteousness before and during God's wrath on the earth.

This attitude will not occur instantly; it will overtake (if not already here) this world in a manner that appears normal or necessary. There will come a specific point in time that God will say, *"It is finished."* Then God will start his end plan of wrath for this earth and its people and specifically for Israel's conversion to Jesus. So by now, you may ask: *When will the Rapture occur?*

SOON BUT HOW SOON?

<u>CLUES</u>

In **Mat.25:14–30,** Jesus tells us a Parable of the Talents. Three servants were given talents from the master, and two servants put their talents to work, but one servant just buried his talent. When the master returned, the two profitable servants (sheep) were blessed, but the third unprofitable servant (goats) was cursed and cast into outer darkness where there shall be <u>weeping and gnashing of teeth</u>. This servant, too, will go through the Great Tribulation.

These verses of scriptures apply throughout time as evil souls will be present before, after, and during Jesus' Kingdom. But Satan will be cast into the Abyss. Humans will still have a sinful nature within them.

I have no knowledge of the exact time that Jesus will return to set up His Kingdom, but we have been given <u>many clues</u> as to the approaching Rapture. However, after the Rapture, the <u>*Tribulation Saints have been given the exact day of Jesus' 3rd Return.*</u> This specific day is anchored on one particular event. **(Dan. 12).**

Many scholars of end times agree that the Rapture will occur approximately seven (7) years before Jesus' final *3rd Return* to set up His earthly Kingdom. You do not want to miss the Rapture and live in the Great Tribulation during the end times!

Jesus will return to Rapture his Bride on God's timing, not mine, and I do not say that I have his timing down pat. So you ask, *"What is the purpose of this study"*? Fair question! **<u>Again,</u>** <u>*this plan of God that has been set in motion has an ending, and never before in human history have we been given so much information as to God's end time's schedule.*</u> Some of the Christians have fallen into Satan's deception spoken of in **2 Pet. 3**.

> **2 Peter 3:3–4 *"(3) Knowing this first, that there shall come in the last days scoffers, walking after their own lusts. (4) And saying, Where is the promise of his coming? For since the fathers fell asleep, all things continue as they were from the beginning of the creation."(KJV)***

But take courage and stand strong, my brothers; Jesus will keep his promises he gave us in **John 14.**

> **John 14:1–3 *"(1) Let not your heart be troubled: <u>ye believe in God, believe also in me.</u> (2) In my Father's house are many mansions: if it were* not **so,** *I would have told you. I go to***

prepare a place for you. (3) And if I go and prepare a place for you, I will come again, and <u>receive you unto myself</u>; that where I am, there *ye may be also." (KJV)*

Notice the underlined words refer mainly to the Jews, but it is also for the gentiles. Many gentiles believe there is a God but are not believers in Jesus. They claim to be Christians because they <u>believe</u> there is a God. But Satan <u>knows</u> there is a God!

SUMMERY

I hope all of the information above has revealed to you the **Clock of Creation,** which is measured in 1,000's of years or millenniums. It is not to be confused with each day of creation but as an overall look at the larger picture of God's time plan for the earth, 7,000 years. Day 7, if you remember, God rested from creating, and that day never ended (no evening and morning). So the 7th Day is representative of that future Day 7 when Jesus' Kingdom will be established on earth; and will last for 1,000 years (1 day).

After Day Seven's 1,000 years, Satan will be released from the Abyss to make another war (#2) with Jesus' Kingdom. How is this possible? This 1,000-year perfect Kingdom of Jesus has no external temptation from Satan. God is proving to us that <u>most of our temptations are internal.</u> This tempting is our Lust of the Flesh and Lust of the Eyes the Bible told us about 2,000 years ago. We have used Satan as our scapegoat, and I'm sure he enjoys that. Satan does not need to tempt us as we do an excellent job of that all by ourselves. But Satan is alive and well. If you are doing God's and Jesus' work, Satan or his Demons will attack you. But, if you are not involved in Jesus' work, why would Satan mess with you at all. You are doing exactly what Satan desires you to do, NOTHING! Do not deceive yourself by making decisions that benefit an unrighteous agenda **(1 Cor.3).**

1st Corinthians 3:18–19 *"(18) <u>Let no man deceive himself.</u> If any man among you seemeth to be wise in this world, let him* *become a fool, that he may be wise. (19) For the wisdom of this world is foolishness with God. For it is written, He taketh the wise in their own craftiness." (KJV)*

There are individuals in this world that will purposely use scripture *for their own agenda*. When looking for an answer but cannot figure out the solution, some will try to make scripture fit their own beliefs. This practice has occurred over the years since Jesus' resurrection. So many doctrines have been established to create the different religious groups of today. Some doctrines are from well-meaning people and some from Satan. The knowledge of righteous and unrighteous doctrines must come from God. Depend on God to show you the truth through earnest study of scriptures. Ask, and he will answer, seek, and you will find. Let the Holy Spirit give you peace and assurance in God's answer. If you are not at peace with your study results, continue studying for the proper peaceful solution.

Remember, no one knows *all the truths* in the Bible except the triune God. So test the spirit.

THE CLOCK OF EMPIRES *(Daniel)*

A little background history is necessary to fully begin to understand where and why Daniel was given this information to us from God. Nebuchadnezzar captured Daniel and his three friends (Hananiah, Mishael, and Azariah) in the third year of Jehoiakim (king of Judah) reign. You probably know Daniel friends by Shadrach, Meshach, and Abednego. Nebuchadnezzar took some young men of the Israelite Royalty and Nobility to serve in Nebuchadnezzar's Palace. These four young men's names were changed, and they were trained for three years and entered Nebuchadnezzar's service. After about two years, Nebuchadnezzar had a dream that the Wise Men were unable to tell the unknown dream, as Nebuchadnezzar would not tell them of his dream contents. Therefore, they could not interpret the dream. But Daniel, through God, could reveal and interpret the dream. Daniel was given this prophecy of five (5) empires to show to Nebuchadnezzar the future (4) empires that will arise. And we know three of them have existed through ancient documents from antiquity.

When you read this section, remember other empires surfaced in between these empires. But God chose to reveal these four empires for a reason. It appears their history and their empires' characteristics are the best help to explain the movement of earth time.

THE DREAM

Daniel 2:31–35 *"(31) Thou, O king, sawest, and behold a great image. This great image, whose brightness* was *excellent, stood before thee; and the form thereof* was *terrible. (32) This image's head* was *of fine gold, his breast and his arms of silver, his belly and his thighs of brass, (33) His legs of iron, his feet part of iron and part of clay. (34) Thou sawest till that a stone was cut out without hands, which smote the image upon his feet* that were *of iron and clay, and brake them to pieces. (35) Then was the iron,*

the clay, the brass, the silver, and the gold, broken to pieces together, and became like the chaff of the summer threshingfloor; and the wind carried them away, that no place was found for them: and the <u>stone that smote the image became a great mountain, and filled the whole earth</u>". (KJV)

THE INTERPRETATION

Daniel 2:36–45 *"(36) This is the dream; and we will tell the interpretation thereof before the king. (37) Thou, O king, art a king of kings: for the God of heaven hath given thee a kingdom, power, and strength, and glory. (38) And wheresoever the children of men dwell, the beasts of the field and the fowls of the heaven hath he given into thine hand, and hath made thee ruler over them all. <u>Thou art this head of gold.</u> (39) And after thee shall <u>arise another kingdom inferior to thee,</u> and <u>another third kingdom of brass,</u> which shall bear rule over all the earth. (40) And the <u>fourth kingdom shall be strong as iron:</u> forasmuch as iron breaketh in pieces and subdueth all things: and as iron that breaketh all these, shall it break in pieces and bruise. (41) And whereas thou sawest the <u>feet and toes, part of potters' clay, and part of iron,</u> the kingdom shall be divided; but there shall be in it of the strength of the iron, forasmuch as thou sawest the iron mixed with miry clay. (42) And as the toes of the feet were part of iron, and part of clay, so the kingdom shall be partly strong, and partly broken. (43) And whereas thou sawest iron mixed with miry clay, <u>they shall mingle themselves with the seed of men: but they shall not cleave one to another, even as iron is not mixed with clay.</u> (44) <u>And in the days of these kings shall the God of heaven set up a kingdom, which shall never be destroyed:</u> and the kingdom shall not be left to other people, but it shall break in pieces and consume all these kingdoms, and it shall stand for ever. (45) Forasmuch as thou sawest that the stone was cut out of the mountain without hands, and that it brake in pieces the iron, the brass, the clay, the silver, and the gold; the great*

God hath made known to the king what shall come to pass hereafter: and the dream is certain, and the interpretation thereof sure." (KJV)

THE STATUE EMPIRE

There is another of Daniel's prophetic visions of Beasts, which supports this vision, and it is found in **Dan. 7:1–14.** I have included the Beast's name under the empire title with the supporting scripture's location for that particular Beast. Both these visions and commentaries of Daniel reveal *"The Time of the Gentiles"* **(Luk.21:24)** as all of these empires are not Hebrew. This time is a duration that must be completed before Jesus' 2nd and 3rd Returns. But **Dan. 2:31–45** is the scriptures that reveal the time bases for this discourse. It establishes the base time of Millenniums.

These words found in **Dan. 7** are synonymous with the statue found in **Dan.2.** But the animals reveal the character of the statue's different empires.

One other item to keep in mind is that some of these metals used in these empire's weapons were unknown to Daniel or King Nebuchadnezzar in their lifetime. Especially iron, which was invented much later. There are other Empires, but God chose these as they were easily recognizable into the future by clear identification of their history and their characteristics.

You will notice these creatures mentioned come out of the sea. **(Dan.7:3)** Sea being water is referred to in the Bible: as nations, people, and tongues. Therefore, these animals represent the different Empires that will come up from the people on earth.

1st THE BABYLONIAN EMPIRE5

(605 BC to 539 BC)

<u>**THE LION**</u> **(Dan. 7:3–4)**

The **head of gold** is the representation of the then-present Babylonian Empire of Daniel's time. All other empires are future to Daniel.

Nebuchadnezzar was conquering Jerusalem when his father died, and he became king shortly after that. This was when Daniel and his three friends were captured to enter into training for the King's Court. All four proved themselves valuable to the King. But Daniel was exceptionable. In Daniel's interpretation of the King's dream, he first established that this interpretation comes from the God of Israel (JEHOVAH), and only Daniel's God could give him this interpretation. Also, this dream is to reveal the passage of time. And only the passage of time can fully reveal the intimate details of the dream.

Babylon is represented by the golden head due to the extensive use of gold in Babylon's shrines, buildings, and images. After Babylon's demise, a historian wrote that he was amazed at the amount of gold that was still there covering walls and buildings[5].

They had a god named Marduk, the god of gold. So it seems appropriate for God to use gold to represent this empire. For we know that this empire existed, and gold was their *god*.

Nebuchadnezzar was the King and was as vicious as the Lion. Also, Babylon's icon was a Lion with wings. But through Daniel's God's interpretation, Nebuchadnezzar received a man's heart to soften his character.

2nd THE MEDO—PERSIAN EMPIRE5

(539 BC to 331 BC)

THE BEAR (Dan.7: 5)

The **chest and arms of silver** are the representation of the Medo-Persian Empire of two peoples. The two arms combine the two King's power represented by Medes, and the other arm was the Persians. The Bear's body elevated on one arm, inferred the primary support and leader for this empire was Persia (Iran).

The three bones in the Bears jaws represent the three countries the Bear conquered: Lydia, Babylon, and Egypt.

The Medes and Persians came together as one but under their two Kings. At that time in history, silver was the standard of value for legal tender (money). And this Medo-Persian Empire worshiped silver or money and produced and collected it through an extensive taxation system.

This empire was inferior to Babylonian Empire because Medo-Persia was a partnership of two Kings, where one King controlled Babylon. But the Medo-Persia Empire was more superior in their military due to the size of their armies. This large army conquered Babylon.

3rd THE GREEK EMPIRE5

(336 BC to 323 BC)

Alexander the Great

THE LEOPARD (Dan.7:6)

The leopard is a fast and single hunter and can have different colored fur. Panther and Cheetah are included in this species. The Cheetah is one of the fastest animals on earth. Like Alexander, whose army was fast-moving. The wing also represents fast-moving but includes great reconnoiter ability of the battlefield. The four legs symbolize the ability to move quickly to change directions rapidly. These are the four generals under Alexander's leadership.

The statue's **Belly and thighs of brass** (some scripture use bronze) represent the Greek Empire under Alexander the Great. He unified that divided the Medo-Persian Empire (silver) into one powerful empire (brass). His military genius was as outstanding, as his tactics are still studied today by our military colleges.

Brass (or bronze) represents Greece because Greece developed this strongest metal at that time, and it was used extensively in military weaponry. Other military metals were inferior to bronze as it could render other military metal weapons useless very quickly.

Alexander was the first western empire to use elephants in his military. And his army is noted for the speed in which they could move. Alexander conquered the vast area of land, but he died at a young age. His empire was divided among his four Generals, represented by the four heads, four wings, and four legs of this Leopard. Generals Antipater and Cassander got Macedon and Greece. General Lysimachus got Trace and Asia Miner. General Seleucus got Syria. General Ptolemy got Palestine and Egypt[5]. This original empire was so great that the Bible says it covered the whole earth **(Dan.2:39).**

These are four divisional weaker empires that followed Alexander after his death. This is supported by the four heads, four wings, and four legs. The Greek Empire later fell to the Romans.

NOTE

There are different names for the metals used here. The King James Bible uses the word brass, but the NIV uses the word bronze. I am not sure why, as brass is copper and tin (weaker), and the bronze is copper and nickel (stronger). However, I believe I remember reading a commentary that said the word brass was commonly used for both metals in the past parchments.

4th THE ROMAN EMPIRE

(27 BC TO 395.AD)

FIERCE BEAST (Dan. 7:7–8)

This beast will have three empires in one: the Roman Empire, Antichrist #1 Empire, and last Antichristv#2 (Satan's) Empire. The legs of iron of this statue represent the 1st Roman Empire. And the feet of iron and clay represent the Antichrist #1 / #2 Revived Roman Empire. The ten horns (kings), with ten kingdoms, join the Antichrist Empire. These ten toes are the same kingdoms but will eventually become Satan's Empire. (feet!)

Iron is an excellent representation of Rome, as Rome was known for its extensive use of iron in its military implements. Iron was able to break and crush gold, silver, copper, and bronze because it is the strongest of medals at that time and for many years after. This material gave the Roman military its ability to crush and conquer much of the known world at that time.

Rome also introduced a form of democratic government with senates and assembles, but it was also divided politically between the Western Roman Empire and the Eastern Roman Empire. One division eventually became military motivated, and one could say the division was political and military. Therefore, the two legs reveal this division.

This empire was not conquered but died in 395 AD. The Western Part survived until 476 AD, and some of the Eastern survived until 1453 A.D. However, this statue's feet and toes (iron & clay) infer that it is not entirely dead because the iron mentioned mixed with clay is a future revived Roman Empire.

5th THE REVIVED ROMAN EMPIRE

OF THE ANTICHRIST #1

(RAPTURE to LAST 3½ YEARS OF GOD'S WRATH)

TEN HORNED BEAST (Dan. 7:7–8)

Here we read about the feet of a **mixture of iron and clay**. Iron is the identification of the old Roman Empire, but what does the clay represent? Clay (brittle), as you know, is an <u>element of earth</u>. In **Rev. 13,** we read of the <u>Beast from the earth</u>. This Beast of the Earth is the False Prophet representing the false religion to help conquer the planet. Remember, Jesus called Peter the Rock upon which the Church is founded. And we all know rocks come from the earth. We know from scripture that we humans were made from dust, and dust we will return. So it appears God is telling us that this fifth kingdom will be a mixture of **Roman Empire** (iron = military) and *a new earthly false (human made) religion (clay)*. This initial empire is the **Antichrist #1 Empire**. It will have great military and political power, as did Rome. But the clay (False Religion) will double his power to be expended on this planet.

However, clay is the weakest link in this empire as clay is a brittle material and easily broken. Therefore, being brittle, it will be destroyed **(Rev.18).** The Antichrist #1 Empire will be a ten nations (10 horns, 10 toes, 10 Kings) consortium as his political arm. This False Religion will increase his spiritual effectiveness of power over the world. But we read in **Rev.17:16** these 10 Kings hate the Whore (False Religion) and will in time destroy her just past midway (first 3½ years). But notice God will put into these 10 Kings hearts to support Satan later.

The two feet represent these two branches of the Roman government and religion. Antichrist #1 leadership will create this Beastly Empire with Satan's help, who will be covertly active during its creation. Satan's influence will continue for the first 3½ years of the seven years of tribulation to covertly assist Antichrist #1. The Antichrist #1 will be wounded with a deadly wound, but his empire (the Beast) will miraculously save him. However, this Antichrist #1's Empire *has an evil twist* to it! This Beast will become Satan's Empire halfway through the seven years of its existence. Satan places his spirit into Antichrist #1's body during the recovery from the deadly wound. This body invasion is as the demons have done in the past **(Mat.8:28–32).** People will see the same body, same face, but a greater evil will reside within. The government (Beast) will be the same, but a covert new leader. Satan will assume the Antichrist #1's role in world domination. It has been Satan's desire and plan ever since creation to become like God. And what is a better place for Satan to make his spiritual power known than in the rebuilt Temple for God? *This Satanic worship in the Temple is desolation at its greatest.*

6th *THE REVIVED ROMAN EMPIRE OF SATAN*

LAST 3½ YEARS OF GOD'S WRATH (Dan. 7: 8)

Dan.7:8 explains that a small horn comes up from within the ten horns and plucks up (destroys) three horns by that little horn. This small horn is the resuscitated Antichrist #1 arising. But this Beast, Antichrist's empire government, was already established **(Dan.7:7);** and this little horn has come up from within the Antichrist Empire. Remember the feet of iron mixed with clay? They represent the Revived Roman Empire that Antichrist #1 was the earthly principle creative architect. The people of the earth now: know, trust, and fear the Antichrist #2. But Satan will use the Antichrist's #1 familiar body to deceive the masses. This Satanic Empire will arise out of the Antichrist Revived Roman Empire when Satan (Small horn) takes possession of the wounded Antichrist's #1 body **(Rev.13:3–8).** This invasion is a similar technique used by Demons to possess a human's body mentioned in scriptures—**(Mat.4:24; 8:16,** to mention just a few).

This last 3½ years is the point in time where Satan will break the covenant with Israel, and Israel flees into the wilderness for 1260 days **(Rev. 12:6).** This point is also when Satan will set up his statue *(the abomination)* in the rebuilt Jewish Temple. He will require all nations to come and worship this satanic statue **(Rev.13:15–16).** And he will require all persons to wear the Mark of Satan on their hand or forehead.

If we go to **Rev.17,** we read the span of influence of one of the kings (Satan).

Revelation 17:8–11 *"(8) The beast that thou sawest <u>was, and is not;</u> and <u>shall ascend out of the bottomless pit,</u> and go into perdition: and they that dwell on the earth shall wonder, whose names were <u>not written in the book of life from the foundation of the world, when <u>they behold the beast that was, and is not, and yet is.</u> (9) And here is the mind which hath wisdom. The seven heads are seven mountains, on which the woman sitteth. (10) <u>And there are seven kings: five are fallen, and one is,</u> and <u>the other is not yet come; and when he cometh, he must continue a short space. (11) And the beast that was, and is not, even he is the eighth, and is of the seven, and goeth into perdition.</u>" (KJV)*

CLARIFICATION

I could not help but smile the first time I read this. As clear as mud; but, notice these words are hidden from none believers. But let us see if we cannot decipher these passages. First, I want you to realize that hidden here, you can read that Satan has covertly transitioned all these empires (except Jesus') to eventually establish his own empire from the Antichrist #1 Empire. But Satan's empire will last (*short space*) for the last: 3½ years, 43 months, or 1,290 days. And at the end, Satan will be incarcerated for 1,000 years in the Abyss. He also will be allowed (after those 1,000 years) to function for a short time after his release from incarceration from the Abyss. But he will shortly be destroyed by God and be cast into the Lake of Fire. These ten toes represent those 10 Kings of **Rev.13:12.**

The first sentence reveals the period these scriptures are speaking. The beast (was, is not, and yet ascends) is none other than Satan, who ascends at the end of Jesus' 1,000-year Kingdom. **(Rev.20:7–10)** And he will astound and deceive many people at his reappearing.

The seven mountains or heads on which the woman sits are the seven different types of governments (10 minus 3). Remember, heads are representative of the political intellect for a type of government. The woman is the false religion (whore) that has been present during the last two revived Roman Empires. But this woman can be traced back to the city of Babel, the beginning of pagan religions.

Notice that these lost souls shall be in wonderment as they have not the Biblical knowledge of this future occurrence. Now here comes another mystery in **Rev.17: 9–11.**

" Seven Kings five are fallen" These fallen are: (1) Babylon; *"fallen"*; (2) Medo—Persian, *"fallen"*; (3) Greek *"fallen"*; (4) Roman; *"fallen"*; **(5)** Revived Roman [Antichrist #1]*"fallen'*; (6) Satan "**one is** "*Satan Empire* last 3½ years *;* (7) Jesus future 1,000-year Kingdom; where Satan's **is not** and is incarcerated in the Abyss **(Rev.20:7–15).** But Adam's effect of sin will still affect human survivors during Jesus' Kingdom. Number 8 is when Satan is paroled from the Abyss after Jesus' 1,000-year Kingdom *and "is to come"* to war against Jesus. But Satan and his army are destroyed by God **(Rev.20:7–15).**

We appear to be located in time between the 4th and 5th Empires. The Rapture will occur before empire #5, but we have been given a *clue* by Jesus about what to look for just before the Rapture. And that *clue* is found in **2 Thes: 2.**

> **2 Thes.2:3** *"Let no man deceive you by any means: for that day shall not come, except there come a falling away first, and that man of sin be revealed, the son of perdition;' (KJV)*

Are we looking for these two clues? If not, why? As we have read previously, Jesus tells us to watch fervently so we will not be caught by a thief in the night. If we are caught, we will go into Empire #5 and #6. And there will be *"weeping and a mashing of teeth."* But what of Empire #8

This kingdom number 8 is also from the seven or the kingdoms or empires numbered 1, 2, 3, 4, 5, 6, and 7. This means that Satan has been the motivating factor behind sins in these six empires. Satan is imprisoned in the Abyss for the 1,000-years of Jesus' Kingdom (7) and cannot affect His kingdom's individuals. Satan's sin effect through Adam continues for human survivors during the 1,000-year Kingdom. These sinful, unrepentant individuals during Jesus' Kingdom will be coerced to join the paroled Satan, to fight Jesus in War #2. Being this released king is Satan; then he cannot come from Kingdom #7 as this is Jesus' Kingdom on earth. But Satan's sin effects will be present in Empire #7. Therefore, #7 will never be conquered or destroyed.

Satan's sin streams from Adam's day and will be present in the Great Tribulation survivors during Empire #7. Therefore, Satan's unrighteous stream effects will be from Adam to God's destruction of Satan in War #2. Roman Empire number 6 sure looks appropriate as a candidate, as it covers two empires in one. But it could be from any of the others. But let us not forget the ten toes.

These ten toes and ten horns represent the first 10 Kings of **Rev.13.**

> **Revelation 13:12-14** *"(12)And the ten horns which thou sawest are ten kings, which have received no kingdom as yet; but receive power as kings one hour with the beast. (13) These have one mind and shall give their power and strength unto the beast. (14) These shall make war with the Lamb, and the Lamb shall overcome them: for he is Lord of lords, and King of kings: and they that are with him are called, and chosen, and faithful." (KJV)*

These ten kings will join Antichrist #1 to develop the Beast (Antichrist Government). These kings' powers will be given to Antichrist #1 to magnify his Beast's army. This army will be powerful and will be considered unbeatable by the world at large. This army is a religious-backed (Islamic?) army, which doubles the Beast's power and creates much fear on the earth. But Jesus will conquer them. Notice Jesus is King of Kings, Lord of Lords of those called, chosen, and faithful. These are the entire saved individual from all the past: Old Testament Saints, Church Saints, Tribulation Saint, Converted Jews,

Converted Gentiles, Pew Sitters, and righteous Aliens (?). This is you and me; both the dead and alive brothers in Christ. Again, notice in **verse 14** all saved souls will come with Jesus. Here is the army of HOST that have been waiting for warfare **(Gen.2:1).**

We know that the Beast (government) spoken of in **Rev.17:8** speaks of Satan. *"Was"* is during the last half of the seven years of tribulation. *"Is not"* is during Jesus' reign of 1,000-years. The *"yet is"* is the last half, 43 months (1290 days) after the Antichrist #1 reign in the first 3½ years. This *"yet is"* should occur approximately halfway through the seven years of the Great Tribulation when Satan takes possession of the Antichrist #1 body (the wounded King **Rev.13:3– 9).** Satan will *War #1* with the Lamb (Jesus) and lose *War #1* of Armageddon to Jesus, and Satan will be incarcerated in the Abyss. *"**And is not**"* refers to that time for Jesus' 1,000-year Kingdom, as Satan is imprisoned in the Abyss. *"**And shall ascend**"*; is that time Satan is released to return to earth after his incarnation of a 1,000 years; to establish his *evil empire #8.*

Again an army to fight Jesus **(Rev.20:7–15).** You would think by now; Satan would have learned his lesson, but no. **Verse 14** clearly identifies *War #2 to End All Wars*. This time God himself will destroy his nemesis Satan and his revived army after Jesus' 1,000-year reign. Satan's destruction will be by fire from God, and God will judge all the lost souls from all the past to the present; at God's Great White Throne Judgment **(Rev.20:11–15).** The result of God's judgments is the casting of Hell (all lost souls) into the *Lake of Fire* forever. Remember, these individuals' eternal parts are their soul and spirit, plus *everything they have ever possessed.* Then God will create a New Heaven and Earth **(Rev.21:1).**

7th THE ROCK EMPIRE OF JESUS (Dan.2)

WAR of ARMAGEDDON to ALL of ETERNITY

Here we read that the 7th Kingdom will destroy the Antichrist's #2 Empire. This is referring to War #1 of Armageddon **(Rev.19).** There Jesus returns with

His Angels and Saints to take back his earth and establish Jesus' 1,000-year Kingdom. We read of this perpetual Kingdom in **Dan.2.**

> **Daniel 2:44–45** *"(44) And in the <u>days of these kings</u> shall the God of heaven set up a <u>kingdom, which shall never be destroyed:</u> and the kingdom shall not be left to other people, but it shall <u>break in pieces</u> and consume all these kingdoms, and <u>it shall stand for ever.</u> (45) Forasmuch as thou sawest that the <u>stone</u> was cut out of the mountain without hands, and <u>that it brake in pieces the iron, the brass, the clay, the silver, and the gold;</u> the great God hath made known to the king what shall come to pass hereafter: and the dream is certain, and the interpretation thereof sure." (KJV)*

To Christians, there is no doubt of what and who this rock is; it is Jesus! In **verse 44,** we read *"in the days of these kings,"* referring to all kingdoms before and after Jesus' Kingdom. This is Jesus' everlasting Kingdom #7, which God has set up. Paul tells us of this stone in **Rom.9.**

> **Romans 9:31–33** *"As it is written, Behold, I lay in Sion a stumblingstone and rock of offence: and whosoever believeth on him shall not be ashamed." (KJV).*

Here we read that Jesus Kingdom (#7) will *"break in pieces the iron, the brass, the clay, the silver, and the gold;"* in reverse order of their appearing. This prophecy was told to the prophet Daniel, then to King Nebuchadnezzar, thousands of years ago. And though the Bible we (who are alive today) have been told. And **Rev.19** also tells us and those before and after us of this destruction (Armageddon War #1) by Jesus. And **Rev.20:7–10** reveal the final and complete destruction, the *2nd War* to End All Wars.

8th SATAN'S PAROLED EMPIRE

Comes after the 1,000-year earthly Kingdom of Jesus.

This Satanic Empire is a little confusing, as it appears covertly with the Antichrist #1 Empire, which was at the beginning of the 1st half of the seven years of the Great Tribulation. After the first 3½ years, Satan will take over the Beast, the Antichrist #1's Government. This is Satan's last attempt to be God and will end by *War #2*, and the Final Judgment will shortly commence **(Rev.20:7–10).**

4 BEASTS

Dan.7:7--9

In **Daniel 7**, we read about his vision of 4 beasts.
>   1. Lion = Babylonian Empire ---------- history
>   2. Bear = Medo—Persian Empire ----- history
>   3. Leopard = Greek Empire ------------ history
>   4. Unnamed Beast = Revived Roman Empire [in the near future]

CLOCK of EMPIRE'S COUNT DOWN

Please consider this prophecy of Daniel as a window for you to look through at the passage of time for God's plan for man. Empires 1 through 4 have come and gone. Therefore, 6, 7and 8 are yet to come.

Never before in human history has humanity been so tormented as during these future seven (7) years, and especially during the 5th and 6th empires. If Jesus does not return, no life on earth will remain. Therefore, the 5th and 6th empires will exist, and Jesus will bring in the perfect 7th empire. Isn't it interesting that the number 6 is also the number of man? But also consider number 7 as the number for righteousness.

This information has been around for thousands of years, but how could scholars have missed it? This, in its self, should make us marvel at God's master plan for man created years ago. The fact that so much information is being revealed today should also convince us of Jesus' near return. And it would be prudent for ½ christians to be filling their lamps with oil (**Mat.25:9**) or buying Gold from God (**Rev.3:18**). Ancient history should teach us to be looking for Jesus' soon return.

We have looked at the **Clock of Creation** and now the **Clocks of Empires;** next, we will look at the final **Clock of Church History.** But first, let us look at some Hebrew lunar dating.

DATING

I have included Jewish lunar dating, hopefully for clarity.

1. One month = 30 days.
2. One standard year = 360 days, 12 Lunar months.
3. One Leap year = 390 days, 13 months.
4. Leap year added = every 2 to 3 years.
5. 3½ years = 1260 days (Compare **Rev.12:6** with **verse 14**).
6. Time, times, and half time = 1260 days, 42 months. or 1290 days, 43 months.
7. 3½ leap years = 1290 days, 43 months.
8. Start of Jesus Kingdom = 1335 days.

SEVEN-YEAR CHART

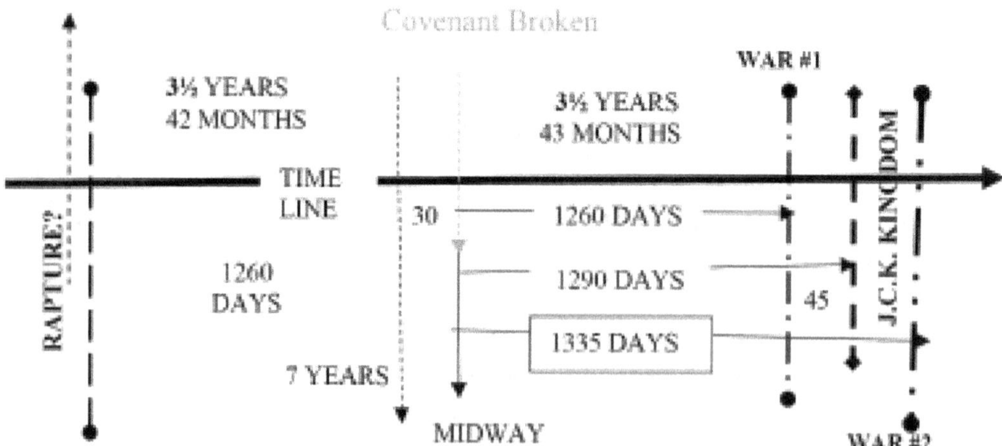

LEGEND

Time Line = starts with where you are presently located in God's timing.

Rapture = will occur before The Great Tribulation.

1260 days = that time in days from the start of the Great Tribulation to the midpoint in the **7 years of tribulation**.

  30 days = is the month added at lunar leap year.

1260 days = the normal 3½ year days.

1290 days = is that time from the midpoint; to the end of War #1; Jesus 3rd return. Proves Leap year (30 days) is added.

1335 days = is the time from midpoint to the completion of cleansing of the Temple; burial of the dead; removal of war implements; establish a human government.

45 days = is the time it will take to perform the previous actions. Except burial of the dead; that takes 7 months.

  J.C.K. = Jesus Christ's Kingdom and SIN WILL STILL BE PRESENT!

THE CLOCK of CHURCH HISTORY

I must first state that this is a very controversial concept for several scholars have some valuable opposing points to consider. But so is the complete book of the Bible and, in particular, the Book Revelations. In righteous scholars' efforts, they get information that is neither all correct nor all wrong. But it is in this process that they sift out the incorrect and slowly increase the accurate information. But with that being said, no earthling will ever have complete knowledge of God and his plan except when we receive the full mind of Christ.

MYSTERY CONTENTS

1. Pre Clock Information -- 411

2. Fruchenbaum's Chart --- 414

3. Ephesus -- 415

4. Smyrna --- 415

5. Pergamos --- 415

6. Thyatira -- 415

7. Sardis -- 415

8. Philadelphia --- 415

9. Laodiceans -- 416

10. Earth Best Clue --- 418

11. Daniel's Prophecy Unsealed -------------------------------------- 419

12. Falling Away -- 423

13. Salvation --- 426

It is significant why God chose these particular Churches. And it appears that consideration should be given to this selection; and its possible inferences. So here are some questions.

1. **Why these Churches?**
2. **Why in this order?**
3. **Are these Letters for this corporate Church or an individualized Church?**
4. **Are these conditions for the duration of the Church?**
5. **Can we get a general timing of the Church?**

<u>1. Why these Churches?</u>

The condition of these particular Church Letters represents some of the problems that could invade any Church in the future. And God wants us to know what to look for in our congregation. And how to correct it before it gets out of hand. And at the same time: comfort, evaluate correction needed, and rewards for that Church's efforts. So these letters are teaching tools for Church leaders, as measuring tools, to assess their congregation.

<u>**2. Why in this order?**</u>

This is an essential question because it lays out foundational movement, the Church's spiritual righteousness, external influences, Church's reactions, condition, and overall characteristics of that Church as it proceeds through its time into the future. And to compare these Churches as they adjust to conditions within and without the congregation. God has picked this order to reveal the passage of time.

<u>**3. Are these Letters for the corporate Church or individual Church?**</u>

These letters are both corporate and individualized. They are individualized by the statement, ***"He that hath an ear."*** If only one person believed in Jesus, that individual would be the Church, *The Bride of Christ.* Therefore, these letters allow you and me to evaluate our lives to see if we have these same problems or conditions within us.

They are also corporately because these letters pertain to a particular Church group's present condition. A Church assumes an attitude reflected by all the member's and its leadership's attitude. Like the military group, it is only as strong as its weakest member. The weakness I mention here is in righteous attitudes. Some individuals in a Church body are very influential, be it for righteousness or unrighteousness. Therefore, it behooves each member to know what constitutes righteousness. That can only be acquired by Bible study and the Holy Spirit's leading. Also, to be informed on how to exercise judgments for the health of the Church.

4. Are these conditions for the duration of the Church age?

Yes. Some of these earlier Churches no longer exist, but the information is still pertinent to all Churches overall times. They reveal the history of the Church in its growth and demise. Satan's attack on the Churches will remain the same over the years. God is telling us of these attacks, and we should not be surprised or confused. These attacks on the Church will be the same mentioned in these letters but will have a different face. Satan's final desired outcome remains the same: to confuse, challenge the intellect, separate, and prevent the growth of the Servants of Jesus.

5. Can we get a general timing of the Church age?

Why pick a progression of these Seven Churches? Could not God just combine all of these Church Letters into one discourse of information? Sure he could but would a single discourse provide the lessons God wants for us? Apparently not! Because if it did, God, the great economizer, would have most likely, done it that way. What is the purpose of inserting these Seven Churches in a particular order for a specific location in the Bible?

Interestingly, God placed this Church history in the Book of Revelation. The book of end times. God is revealing an order of historical movement! And the duration of these Seven Letters as tied to the Life of the complete Church age using individual Church history. And by an in-depth study of the: historical conditions facing the Church, the Church's reactions, and the results of the deeds of that Church, we can get the results for a given period of time.

A Messianic Jewish Bible scholar named Dr. Arnold Fruchenbaum did such a study[6]. But due to the complications of earthly history and Church history, some scholars disagree with his seven stages of Church history. Some of these disagreements appear to be looking at the grain of sand and not the beauty of the beach. But these letters have meaning and direction.

For example, why was the letter to the Church of Laodicea not presented first? It is because the First Church's characteristics were first of Love and excitement, and they knew they needed Jesus. In contrast, the Church of Laodicea was a church of apathy (no Love). They also have no need for Jesus or anything because they are rich. If they want it, they buy it. This contrast is so pronounced there must be a time where the Church grew and then regressed spiritually in their walk through this life.

This sounds much like our progression in our walk through our own lives. These letters reveal that we face these same problems, but they can strengthen us if we test and apply them in our own walk through this life. These letters give us corrections to apply in our life and reassurance of the outcome. And in **Rev. 3:14–22,** we can read the condition of The Church of Laodicea. Therefore, from Dr. Fruchenbaum's chart[6], we are taught the progression of the different Church periods.

However, even with these disagreements with this study, it is enlightening because *it is general in nature and not intended to claim extreme accuracy in its dates.* This list in an order appears to refer back to **Mat.24:32–34.** Also, these letters can reflect the changing of the fig tree leaves in its column. To Dr. Fruchenbaum's chart[6], I (with permission) replaced his far-right column with the **FIG TREE MINE[6].**

DR. FRUCHENBAUM'S SEVEN STAGES OF CHURCH HISTORY

CHURCH	CHURCH HISTORY	DATES	FIG TREE MINE
EPHESUS	THE APOSTOLIC CHURCH	A.D. 30 TO 100	*SEED IS SOWN*
SMYRNA	THE CHURCH OF THE ROMAN PERSECUTIONS	A.D.100 TO 313	*SEED'S EFFORTS TO GERMINATE*
PERGAMUM	THE CHURCH OF THE AGE OF CONSTANTINE	A.D.313 TO 600	*PLANT ACHIEVES FREEDOM*
THYATIRA	THE CHURCH OF THE DARK AGES	A.D.600 TO 1517	*PLANT GROWING & SURVIVING TESTING*
SARDIS	THE CHURCH OF THE REFORMATION	A.D.1517 TO 1648	*FORMATION OF THE LEAVES*
PHILADELPHIA	THE CHURCH OF THE GREAT MISSIONARY MOVEMENT	A.D.1648 TO 1960	*FIGS RIPEN*
LAODICEANS	THE CHURCH OF APOSTASY AND APATHY	A.D. 1960 TO PRESENT DAY	*PLANT WITHERS AWAITING REBIRTH*

LETTERS REPRESENTATIONS

<u>In the letter to Ephesus,</u> we see the apostles sowing the seed of the Gospel of Jesus Christ. Not one seed is sown, but several seeds are sown throughout Israel, and a small section of Asia Minor, namely Mysia, Lydia, and Caria

<u>In the letter to Smyrna,</u> we see the seeds sown are searching for water and nutrients to germinate and grow. They are struggling with the new Covenant from Jesus. It is so opposed to what the Priests have told them for decades. Traditions have invaded their minds and hearts. Change is difficult and dangerous. The beginning of the Church (Bride of Christ) is finding small footholds in society. Growth is beginning. Germination begins.

<u>In the letter to Pergamos,</u> we see the results of the seed's attempt to break free of the soil. The toil and efforts of the Apostil's teachings free the seeds to reach for the sun through faith. Once freedom is achieved, growth will speed **up, and** the Church will multiply. Freedom from persecution has finally come through Emperor Constantine's edict. Growth begins, the plant breaks free into the sunlight.

<u>In the letter to Thyatira,</u> we see the fast growth of the Church, bringing with **it** some confrontations from the religious community and governments. The weeds are trying to restrict the development of the seeds. Trials spring forth from all sides, and loyalty to Jesus and God is tested. The locusts have been eating at the leaves. But loyalty survives the trials of the *Dark Ages*. The fig roots, stalk, and leaves survive!

<u>In the letter to Sardis,</u> we see the beginning of enlightenment. The Catholic Church's false doctrines are challenged by several righteous men and priests that help change some of their doctrines. The protestant movement is started. New doctrine and information emerge that has been hidden by Satan for years. The fig leaves are forming; next comes the figs.

<u>In the letter to Philadelphia,</u> we see the seed of brotherly Love. And the desire to spread love to those individuals who have not the word of God. And great Missionary movements are started in this period. Both Catholic and Protestant missionaries start going to the lost world, spreading the seeds of

Jesus' Gospel. The Gospel of Jesus is spread throughout the world. This love is reflected in the fruit (figs) of the tree of life. It is the sweet taste of humanity's Love for humans that God wants us to share the Gospel and enjoy it with all souls. These are the partial results of Jesus' Great Commission. But more is needed.

In the letter to the Laodiceans, we see that this Church Letter is not to the city of Laodicea but the <u>Church of the Laodiceans</u>. This makes it appear this Church is not very committed to the people of Laodicea but for the people inside this Church and not for the city. This Church is singled out due to many years of neglect to care for the Gospel's seed. The weeds have taken hold **(Mat.13:24–30)**. In years past, God's people struggled with survival. It was in their need for God's intervention or help that motivate people to seek God. This final test of God has shown humanity that we will fall into a state of stupor without our attempt to follow Jesus' commands. **This church believes they have everything they need because they worked for it without God's help. If they need (more likely want) it, they go buy it.** *Vanity!*

At this time, God's demands are egregious to **man, and they make no sense! This period is very reminiscent of the '60s, unrestricted sex and drugs explosion on to our society. They needed Laodicea's healing salve for their eyes to see the truth. But they want to do whatever they want to do, so why have God's restrictions present in their lives. If they want to speed--- they speed, if they want to steal from God---they don't tithe, if they desire to speak in tongues without an interpreter--- they speak in tongues, if they do not want a child---they kill it, and if they desire homosexual relationship --- they perform homosexual acts. Society's efforts are expanded in removing God's Law and reverence from daily life, with little or no confrontation from the** Church. Today's society appears much like the warning in **Rom.1.**

> **Romans 1:29–32** "**(29)** *And even as they did <u>not like to retain God in</u> their <u>knowledge,</u> God gave them over to a reprobate mind, to do those things which are not convenient; (29) <u>Being filled with all unrighteousness, fornication, wickedness,</u>*

covetousness, maliciousness; full of envy, murder, debate, deceit, malignity; whisperers, (30) Backbiters, haters of God, despiteful, proud, boasters, inventors of evil things, disobedient to parents, (31) Without understanding, covenantbreakers, without natural affection, implacable, unmerciful: (32) Who knowing the judgment of God, that they which commit such things are worthy of death, not only do the same, but have pleasure in them that do them." (KJV)

If we cannot see these same conditions spoken of in these verses of scripture in our earth today, we are blind or have grown numb to God's Word. Open your eyes to the opposition to Jesus and God, the lack of human decencies, hatred, Church closings, entertainment growing more evil, and on and on. It is so obvious. God wants Laodicea's eye salve on our eyes so we can see clearly!

But, there is patience with God ----, but his patience will expire.

CLOCK SUMMERY

First, we have the **Clock of Creation** in Genesis, where God reveals the general overall life span of his time plan for humanity. Its foundation is in millenniums of 1,000 years. Starting at Creation and ending after Jesus' 1,000 year Kingdom (Seventh Day).

Second, we are given the **Clock of Empires** in Daniel, starting with Babylon and ending with the Revived Roman Empire. Its foundation is that of centuries of 100's years. This clock started with Babylon and moves to Satan's Empire. But Jesus' (Rock) Kingdom is the final empire that will last forever.

Third, we are given the **Clock of Churches** in Revelation, where this clock's foundation uses God's Church's evolution over the years. It started with the Church in Ephesus and ending in the Church of Laodicea.

With these three clocks, we should understand that this earth is about to run its course, and it is near midnight. And if we return to **Daniel 12,** we read when God will reveal his prophecy of the final days of this earth.

THE END OF EARTH'S BEST CLUES

These three clocks lead us to the time of the end of this earth and universe. But if we read the Book of Daniel, we will get a closer time pointing to this end. As you have read in Daniel, he was given information about the end of time. But the information has been hidden by God for many years. Notice in **Dan.12,** God commands Daniel to shut up God's words and lock them with a seal. Then God reveals when these words will find freedom for God's people. It will slowly occur over time.

> **Daniel 12:4** *"But thou, O Daniel, shut up the words, and seal the book,* even **to the time of the end: many shall run to and fro, and knowledge shall be increased." (KJV)**

God is giving his Bride (Church) and especially the Tribulation Saints the clearest *clues* to watch for as it will reveal the time for the Rapture. Notice this time is shown by an increase in *travel* and an increase in *knowledge*.

Also, you can compute the exact day of Jesus' *3rd Return* to this earth. And the exact day Jesus' Kingdom will begin. But first, let us look at the leading in of words to those *clues*.

Daniel was so confused by **Dan.11** and **12** prophecies God gave Daniel. **Daniel 11** reveals the movement of time and conditions of the empires we just looked into. Starting with Babylon, to Medo-Persia, to Greek, to the Roman Empire, and in **verse 40** says *"at the time of the end"* and moves to **Dan.12** where God makes a profound statement.

> **Daniel 12:1–3** *"And **at that time** shall Michael stand up, the great prince which standeth for the children of thy people: and there **shall be a time of trouble,** such as never was since there*

*was <u>a nation</u> even **to that same time: and <u>at that time thy people</u>** **<u>shall be delivered, every one that shall be found written in the</u>** **<u>book.</u> (2) And many of them that sleep in the dust of the earth** **shall awake, some to everlasting life, and some to** **shame** and **everlasting contempt. (3) <u>And they that be wise shall</u>** **<u>shine as the brightness of the firmament; and they that turn</u>** **<u>many to righteousness as the stars for ever and ever.</u>" (KJV)**

These verses speak of the *end time* spoken in **Dan.11:40.** But in **Dan.12:1,** we read Michael, the prince of angles will defend God's children. These words covered many years into the future. Then comes troubling times (the Great Tribulation) as never before in history. The following verses cover multi-events. The dead in Christ shall rise first, and those who are alive shall meet the Lord in the air (Rapture). Those spoken of, *to shame and everlasting contempt*, have rejected Jesus and whose names are not in the Book of Life. This statement covers both the *1st and 2nd Harvest* of **Rev.14**. But pay particular attention to **verse 3**. Who are the wise, if not the obedient, and who are those that turn to righteousness (obedience)? Christians?

We shall shine as the brightness of the stars. When we look at space, we see stars that are trillions of miles from earth. How bright does a star need to be to be visible at that distance? And those who help save individuals are also as the stars. How many stars do you think there are in the universe or space? And if we turn many to righteousness, then we too will additionally cause the growth of righteousness exponentially. This star is represented in our universe as our stars (saved) are uncountable. But God chooses to deny Daniel the meaning of these verses until the proper time.

PROPHECY UNSEALED

Here I will repeat some of the previous information as it will be vital to those who are looking for Jesus' returns. And for the Jews and Pew Sitters to look back and realize there were truths they missed. But take heart that if they

(Tribulation Saints) repent and get busy with deeds, they too will join with Jesus on his *3rd return* to earth.

> **Daniel 12:4** *"But thou, O Daniel, <u>shut up the words,</u> and seal the book,* even *to the <u>time of the end: many shall run to and fro, and knowledge shall be increased."</u> (KJV)*

Here we read this command by God to make <u>these verses of scriptures hidden and *non-interpretable until the end of time.*</u> God is opening these words to give us *<u>clues</u>* about the appropriate time for his children to understand.

1. **<u>Run to and fro</u>;** this *<u>clue</u>* is vast travel. And we have that today. We can fly anywhere and even travel to the Moon. Shortly to Mars! All one needs to do is go to any international airport to see the magnitude of today's travelers. Daniel time had nothing like this.

2. **<u>Knowledge increase</u>;** this *<u>clue</u>* is *the result of the computer different language software* that is overcoming God's curse at the Tower of Babel. Where the different languages confused the different tribes. Those who spoke the same language gathered together. Then they scatter throughout the known world.

God further gives Daniel (**Daniel 12**) the exact day of *Jesus' 3rd Return* to conquer the earth and set up his Kingdom

> **Daniel 12:11–12** *"(11) And from the <u>time</u> that <u>the daily sacrifice shall be taken away, and the abomination that maketh desolate set up,</u> there shall be* ***a <u>thousand two hundred and ninety days</u>. (12) Blessed is he that waiteth, and <u>cometh to the thousand three hundred and five and thirty days."</u> (KJV)***

The *"daily sacrifice"* is the Jewish reinstituted twice-daily sacrifice in the rebuilt Temple in Jerusalem. This rebuilding will be just before or just into the Great Tribulation period. This time is the seven-year covenant for Israel's protection from Islam, made between the Antichrist #1 and Israel. This rebuilding will infuriate Islam as the Dome of the Rock (3rd most important shrine to Islam) must come down. Because Islam's Dome of the Rock appears (at present) to be directly over the Holy of Holies geographic location inside the Jewish Temple.

The ***"abomination that makes desolate"*** is *Satan's statue set up for Satan worship (greatest abomination)* inside the rebuilt Jewish Temple of God. The Ten Commandments in **Exo 20** say:

> *Exodus 20: "(3) "Thou shalt have no other gods before me. (4) Thou shalt not make unto you any graven image* **and** *(5) Thou shalt not bow down thyself to them nor serve them." (KJV)*

This statue of Satan inside God's Temple is the greatest desolation and insult ever committed.

Satan has tried for ages to be the same as or greater than God. Satan is the force behind the killing of not only God's Son; but of God's children over thousands of years. And this point in time of this occurrence; is ***the anchor point to measure these next two sets of days!***

<u>1290 days</u> is the time duration measured from the setup of the desecration in the rebuilt Temple called the *"Abomination of Desolation."* And these days of 1290 point to the <u>*3rd Return of Jesus*</u> to take back his property, the earth, and destroy all evil individuals (Armageddon). 1260 days is 3½ years, but a lunar leap month must add 30 days, making 1260 days to 1290 days (43 months). This event will occur during the last half of the Great Tribulation.

<u>1335 days</u> is also the time duration measured from the temple desecration to the day the 1,000 years of Jesus' earthly Kingdom is started, And the *Rebuilt Temple is cleansed of Satan's statue of Abomination.*

These 45 days between 1290 and 1335 covers that period of time for War #1 of Armageddon. Then is when the rebuilt Temple cleansed, the establishing a human and spiritual universal worldwide government, beginning with the cleansing of the earth of the dead and all the needed infrastructure of the righteous human earthly government. Many Tribulation Saints will survive the Great Tribulation and enter the 1,000-year Kingdom of Jesus as mortal human beings. The last period is Jesus' earthly Kingdom of 1,000 years, after which God will destroy everything and recreate a New Heaven and New Earth.

These three clocks also have alarms about to chime and clearly point to the time for our awareness of the mysteries from God, Jesus, and the Holy Spirit (3 in one). The seven years will be revealed explicitly to the Tribulation Saints and those who study God's Word. It will be evident that the two witnesses will speak against antichrist #1 during the first 3½ years. And they will be killed but will return to life after three days and be taken up into Heaven. Now evil will rule on earth. The time of God's three clocks has all but expired.

These three clocks mentioned here are not intended to be very specific, except for the last half of the seven years of God's Tribulation. It will be part of the proof of Jesus' mission as Messiah, which the Jews have been looking for, for years. We of the Church Saints (The Bride of Christ) are to live by faith. But God gives us so much information in the Bible to prove not only his love but his plan for his children.

If we are God's children, how could we not be concerned for the lost souls and realize their time is growing short? ***Are we, too, apathetic to their peril like the Laodiceans?*** We Christians must attempt to bring this knowledge to man. It is our responsibility to bring the Gospel to the lost and not only the pastors. The Church is to teach us the knowledge to use in presenting the Gospel to lost souls and help us with our walk with Jesus. The time for creating Treasures is about to expire for the Church.   *Don't wait!*

And again, this is not an attempt to set a specific date for Jesus' *2nd Return* to Rapture us to Heaven, but to give some idea of how close his *2nd Return* can be. Remember **Amos 3's** words.

Amos 3:7 *"Surely the Lord GOD will do nothing, but he revealeth his secret unto his servants the prophets." (KJV)*

FALLING AWAY MYSTERY

This concept has been a very controversial subject for many years. Therefore, let's see if we can clarify this mystery in our minds. It stems from verses in the Bible that appear to contradict each other. Once saved, always saved is a statement we hear, but also we read of those who will fall away. So it appears we need to look first into information pertaining to salvation. So let's see if we can breakdown what salvation is and what it is not.

<u>*WHAT IS SALVATION?*</u>

Funk and Wagnall define **Salvation as**: "*1. <u>the process</u> or <u>state of being saved.</u>* 2 Theol. **Deliverance from sin and penalty, <u>realized in a future state,</u>** 3. Any means of deliverance from: danger, evil, or ruin[3]."

Notice the first explanation is a *"process or state of being saved," "And realized in a future state."* Then we must ask, saved from what? **The answer is not from Hell but the** *Lake of Fire* **(Rev.20:14).** But, this *Lake of Fire* is into the future for the unsaved **(Rev.21:8).** So it appears we need to look into the condition of where are those who have died before us. Those that have accepted Jesus by faith are in a state of rest in Paradise in Heaven with Jesus. But what of us who are still alive? Here is where it gets a little sticky. We read in **Rom. 8** about our hope to be saved.

Romans 8:24–25 *"(24) For we are <u>saved by hope: but hope that is seen is not hope:</u> for what a man seeth, why doth he yet hope for? (25) <u>But if we hope for that we see not,</u> then do we with patience wait for it." (KJV)*

Saved by hope! Hope in what? FAITH! It is our faith in God's covenants with Christians for our salvation. Think of it this way. If you hoped for a new home and God provided you a new home, then that hope would no longer be needed and would disappear. The same applies to our hope in salvation.

Salvation has two parts, one is the spiritual side, and one is the mortal side.

<u>The spiritual side</u> is the heartfelt disdain for all your previous sinful actions against God and man. This repentance is overpowering regret and a sincere desire to want to change to the righteousness of Jesus. And to feel the calmness, peace, love of forgiveness from friends, family, and especially God. Repentance is the most essential aspect of salvation. ***Without repentance, there is no salvation***.

> Repent = "1) To <u>feel remorse</u>, as for something one has done or failed to do; be contrite. 2. To <u>change one's mind</u> <u>concerning past action</u>: with of: He *repented* of his generosity. *–v.t.* 3. *To <u>feel remorse or regret</u> for (an action, sin, etc.)* 4. To <u>change one's mind</u> concerning (a past action). [< OF < L *re*-again + *poenitere* to cause to repent] -- re pent'er n^3."

<u>The mortal side</u> is your visual submission to God and Jesus and proof of your repentance. We call this visual event of Baptism (submersion). The repentant person is declaring visually to the world; they have repented and is declaring their own death and burial to this life. By their death (dying to this life) and burial (submersion) and rebirth (raised) out of their watery grave into their new life in Jesus. This physical act is the completion of the act for salvation. Without these two, there is no salvation given by God, and that person is still in sin. Don't wait! *But there can be a few exceptions to Baptism.*

Anyone who has genuinely repented and is not capable of receiving Baptism will find God's grace applied for their salvation. For example: if a person makes their declaration of faith (repentance) and is to be Baptized the following Sunday but is killed in a car wreck on their way home, they are saved. Also, some individuals will never reach the age of accountability. Therefore, *salvation is always by God's grace*.

Those of us, who are alive and have accepted Jesus as our Lord and savior, are in the state of GRACE of being saved; and when we die, we will meet Jesus at Jesus Judgment Seat. This event is the point that we hoped for, and we are, at this time, actually saved from the *Lake of Fire*. With that being said, let us look at our guarantor.

This is God, Jesus, and the Holy Ghost who has given us a guaranty (covenant) that if we are in Jesus, we can have assurance (the hope), we will be saved! What an outstanding guaranty we have from an absolutely trustworthy guarantor. But, what does it mean *"to be in Jesus."*

Think of *"to be in Jesus"* as sort of like being married; *you and your spouse are one.* You and your spouse are together almost every day and share good times and bad times together. You do deeds for her, and she does deeds for you. You share intimate times of pleasure and times of sadness. You two make covenants with each other and maintain that trust in keeping them. This is somewhat of a simplistic parallel to being in Jesus.

If this time is not spent together, then being in one starts becoming two. Same with Jesus; if you do not study God's Word and spend intimate time in prayer with Jesus, God, and the Holy Spirit, you will become separated to some degree. This separation is the perfect condition for sin to rear its evil head. Many people have given their life to Christ but have slipped into apathy. They come to Church on Easter, Christmas, Wednesday night meals, and a few times a year. Jesus speaks of these individuals in **Mat.25:14–46**. This individual who repented and accepted Jesus but did not perform any helps for the Church or lost souls; are saved (guaranty) but will not have or have very few treasures stored up in Heaven. *One treasure I see is the Rapture.* These pew-sitters will need to go through the Great Tribulation. It also appears that those who faked their repentance and Baptism are those in the Social Gospel group. In **Hebrew 6,** we see verses of warning for these individuals who fall away from Jesus.

Hebrews 6:4–6 *"(4) For it is impossible for those who were <u>once enlightened,</u> and have tasted of the <u>heavenly gift,</u> and were made <u>partakers of the Holy Ghost,</u> (5) And have <u>tasted the good word of God,</u> and the <u>powers of the world to come,</u> (6) If they shall fall away, to renew them again <u>unto repentance;</u> seeing they crucify to themselves the Son of God afresh, and put him to an open shame. (KJV)*

This receiving-only group will fall away from Jesus during the Great Tribulation to worship Satan and accept the Mark of the Beast. Many people believe if they have been Baptized (or sprinkled), they are going to Heaven. Nothing could be farther from the truth. **Baptism comes after** *a sincere desire to change one's spiritual and carnal life*. The realization of what Jesus has done for you, and you want Jesus to be the source of your changed life. Baptism is your outward visual declaration of your: inward spiritual change, dedication, and a fidelity covenant with Jesus.

To have God's guaranty of salvation, a person must:

1. Make a true repentance of the sins they have committed and the sincere regrets and desires to stop sinning.
2. A sincere want to alter their life's reactions to evil situations with good.
3. To commit their new life to Jesus and walk as Jesus did.
4. Study God's word regularly.
5. You must believe in your heart and mind: Jesus is the son of God, Jesus was a human man, Jesus died to pay for your sins, Jesus rose from the dead, and Jesus will come again for you to take you to Heaven.
6. Last and difficult for some people is DEEDS. If you are not motivated to work for Jesus, question yourself. Deeds have always been required.

<u>WHAT IS NOT SALVATION</u>

Without confessing the truth of these above items, your salvation is visual only, with no effect on your salvation (in most cases). Sprinkling is not Baptism. The word baptism is a Greek word that means submersion. In the 1600s (when scriptures were translated into English), King James was sprinkled instead of submerged. And the priest and scribes were afraid of the King's reaction to their ignorance of the Bible. So they included the Greek word instead of the proper English word. God's grace can still apply to those sprinkled. But, who can be baptized? Anyone; who is above the Age of Accountability when *they personally* understand *and accept* these above requirements. A baby needs not to be baptized as they are not accountable for their sins until they know right from wrong, Jesus died for them, and *they must repent of their own volition.* They must exercise their self-will for salvation. We see this in **Mat.19:13–14,** where Jesus acceptance of the children in heaven. Children are not accountable for their sin until they reach the Age of Accountability. God desires each individual he created to exercise their self-will for good or evil and are rewarded for their deeds, be they good or evil. We are all responsible for our own actions and not for others unless we are the instigator for their sin.

From these verses, we see the children (under the Age of Accountability) who have physically died are in Heaven with God and Jesus. But what of the *souls that have reached* the Age of Accountability? And have not exercised their self-will to sincerely ask Jesus into their lives and have not repented. They have deceived themselves, WOE! And what of the individuals that have accepted Jesus and baptized into Jesus but are not obedient in deeds. These are the pew-sitters (½ righteous) who will miss the Rapture (a Treasure) and will need to perform righteous deeds during the most grievous period, The Great Tribulation. Here is a verse of scripture that has caused some controversy in **Acts 2.**

> *Acts 2:38 "Then Peter said unto them, Repent, and be baptized every one of you in the name of Jesus Christ for the remission of sins, and ye shall receive the gift of the Holy Ghost." (KJV)*

Some individuals see *"be baptized"* as "for the remission of sins" and think that baptism removes sin. And in a sense, it is, as it is the final step in the salvation process, but not the most essential step. But they ignore the *"and"* in-between *"Repent and be baptized,"* which indicates these two steps are tied together. The first step is REPENT. Without this first step, the second step is null and void as it is the outward representation of the completion of the first step (repent). If this is the case of your first baptism, then I suggest you repent and be baptized again. Any time you see a baptized, it is referring to the completed process. See **Mark 16**.

> ***Mark 16:16 "He that believeth** and is **baptized** shall be saved; but he that **believeth not shall be damned.** (KJV)*

Here we see *"believeth and believeth not,"* which reveals those requirements, afore-mentioned in this book, for salvation. Think of Baptisms like high school or college graduation. The Graduation Ceremony (Baptism) is the visual statement of a successfully completed process.

The time of our hope in being saved will come to fruition can be found in **2nd Cor.5**.

> **2nd Corinthians 5:10** *"For we must all appear before the judgment seat of Christ; that __every one may receive the things__ done __in__ his __body,__ according to that he hath done, whether it be good or bad." (KJV)*.

But how can a truly saved person fall away? He or she cannot! But those individuals, who deceive themselves, can and will not be unable to resist Satan's threat of death for refusing the Mark of the Beast. We already see America's population in the late stages of falling away. The religion of Islam is presently recruiting non-religious individuals to the Islamic faith. Many of these converts are seeking vengeance, which radical Islam permits and supports vengeance. Just as Jesus said, *"you are for me or against me,"* so also the same is true for Islam. It is the non-radical Islamic population's responsibility to correct their own religion's failures and not other religions.

So if they are not making an effort to correct, then they are approving the radicals. But we see the same apathy happening in America. Local and national governments are removing our Judeo-Christian heritage symbols with minimal complaints from Churches or religious groups. Therefore, our ranks are dwindling away, and proof by rampant Church closings. What of the weak Christians in these Churches? Where do they go for strength and maturity in Jesus? They are very vulnerable to Satan's deceptions. And are targets for Satan to attack. Statistics prove we are losing the battle.

A South Carolina newspaper [The State] has acquired statistics showing this deterioration of Churches in their state. The Author Sarah Ellis article can be found in www.thestate.com/news/local/article215014375.thml. Statistics are from the S.C. Southern Baptist Convention. The United Methodist Church, from the years 2012 to 2016, lost 12,707 members and closed 30 churches in their state alone. In comparison, the Southern Baptist Church lost 130,000 members but held a constant 2100 churches. The Catholic Church appears to retain its own due to the influx of Hispanic newcomers, which offset the American departures. The S.C. Baptist Convention's leader stresses that there may be nothing left in 5 to 10 years if something isn't done soon. What of the other states?

The situation is becoming ripe **(Rom.1:16–32)** for the Antichrist (Beast from the sea) and the False Prophet (Beast from the earth **Rev.13)** to appear. To the weak, these two will solve both government and religious problems and make them seem desirable. This Beast will make war and defeat the righteous Tribulation Saints left behind **(Rev.13:4–8).** The weak will fall away from Jesus and God and accept the Mark of the Beast.   **SAD!**

FOR THERE WILL BE NO SALVATION POSSIBLE FOR THOSE WHO FALL AWAY AND TAKE THAT MARK.

TO THE ACTIVE BELIEVER

Be encouraged that your God loves you and is coming soon, and your rewards come with him. Be strong and finish the race strong. The race has been long and challenging at times, but the end is near. Then you will rest. You have treasures laid up in heaven for you that you cannot imagine their eternal value for your pleasure. Your loved ones await your entrance into Heaven. But the greatest Love of all is there as your advocate; Jesus is with God, speaking on your behalf. He is: leading you, encouraging you, protecting you, providing for you, and building you a mansion of unspeakable splendor **(Rev.21)**. And if Jesus prepares a place for you, *He will come* to take you home himself **(John 14)**.

> **John 14:1–3** *"(1) Let not your heart be troubled: ye believe in God, believe also in me. (2) In my Father's house are many mansions: if it were not so, I would have told you. I go to prepare a place for you. (3) And if I go and prepare a place for you, I will come again, and receive you unto myself; that where I am, there ye may be also."* *(KJV)*

> **Romans 8:18** *"For I reckon that the sufferings of this present time are not worthy to be compared with the glory which shall be revealed in us."* *(KJV)*

TO THE INACTIVE BELIEVER

There is still time for you to get busy with Jesus' work so he will not come and find you unprepared. Remember the parable in **Mat. 25** of the ten virgins, five were prepared, and five virgins were not prepared? The five *not prepared* were left behind, and even after they got their oil for their lamps (righteousness), they were not even permitted to the marriage feast. Those five virgins *prepared* to meet the Bridegroom; represent the faithful (Bride) in the worship of the one true God. If you are *not ready* for Jesus' return this very moment, then you must place yourself in the *company of the unprepared virgins*. You do not want to be left behind to face the Great Tribulation period coming onto the world. The Antichrist will make every effort to punish you or the ones you love with unspeakable torture and painful death. All Christians want you to go with us and, Passover, the wrath God is sending to the earth.

REMEMBER

<u>SALVATION</u> is by <u>FAITH,</u> but <u>TREASURES</u> are by <u>DEEDS.</u>

The Rapture is a Treasure.

Begin again your study of the Bible. *"Study to shew thyself approved unto God, a workman that needeth not to be ashamed, rightly dividing the word of truth."* Do not be slack in your responsibility to Jesus, as you will be caught in the Devil's snare.

> **Luke 21:34–36 *"(34) And take heed to yourselves, lest at any time your hearts be over charged with surfeiting*** (overindulging in food or drink)*, **and drunkenness, and <u>cares of this life, and so that day come upon you unawares. (35) For as a snare shall it come on all them that dwell on the face of the whole earth.</u> (36) Watch ye therefore, and pray always, that ye may be accounted worthy to escape*** (Rapture) ***all these things that shall come to pass, and <u>to stand before the Son of man.</u>"(KJV)***

In **verse 35,** notice, *"<u>For as a snare shall it come on all them that dwell on the face of the whole earth.</u>"* These are the individuals who are unaware of Jesus' soon *2nd Return*. These words are a warning, as <u>this speaks of the time before the Rapture.</u> Because it comes to active believers on the earth, but it is the practicing Christians that will be Raptured out of the world. This unawareness is the pew-sitters as they have not performed the required deeds. Therefore, watch for God's *clues* for Jesus' *2nd Return*. These *clues* are in the Bible.

Please do not be caught in the snare that thinks you can sit in the pew and do nothing for God's children. The complete book of **James** encourages you to work for God's Kingdom for a reason. Please be aware that deeds have always been required. God's creation required a deed (not to eat from the Tree of Knowledge of Good and Evil). The Law given to Moses reveals salvation

431

through deeds, which man could not keep. So God's grace was applied to those deserving souls who made an effort to keep all of God's Laws.

Notice the last statement, *"to stand before the Son of man."* This statement refers to Christians presents at the Judgment Seat of Christ and not at the Judgment Seat of God (The Great White Throne).

In the time before Noah, deeds were measured by God without his law. Except for *not to eat from the Tree of Knowledge of Good and Evil*. This broken command event gave man the knowledge of right and wrong. And God wanted them to do good! It was easier for them to be fruitful, multiply and replenish, subdue, and have dominion.

Pleasures (Lust of the eyes and flesh) take preference over doing good.

After the Flood, Moses received the Law of God, which revealed the deeds required for salvation and punishments for breaking those deeds. Then came Jesus with a new covenant for man's salvation. Faith only for salvation as he (Jesus) will pay (deeds) for repentant Sinners but, he still requires deeds. We read about deeds throughout the New Testament. One such admonition is the Sermon on the Mount **(Math. 5, 6,** and **7).** The most extraordinary deed required is the Great ~~Commission~~ Command of **Mat.28**.

> **Matthew 28:18–20 "(18***) And Jesus came and spake unto them, saying, <u>All power</u> is given unto me in heaven and in earth. (19) Go ye therefore, and <u>teach</u> all nations, <u>baptizing</u> them in the name of the Father, and of the Son, and of the Holy Ghost: (20) <u>Teaching them to observe all things whatsoever I have commanded you:</u> and, lo, I am with you alway,* **even** *unto the end of the world. Amen. " (KJV)*

Notice the words *"commanded you,"* this is not a *Commission* that you can accept or reject, but a command from Jesus. Next, you should test your salvation by whether are not you want to be active in doing the work God has for you. **1 John** is an excellent book of tests for your honest self-examination. If you do not want to be active, then do not be surprised when you are left behind at the Church's Rapture. *For then, the left behind will have to do the most difficult of deeds.* None of us Christians want you to be left behind, so we encourage you to get busy for Jesus. God's Army (Host) needs to be robust against this world's principalities and powers, while the Holy Spirit and angels wars against the spiritual world. We need to be vigilant, for the enemy is devious and cunning. The more soldiers Jesus has, the better. Come with us to stand before the Son of Man to hear *"well done good and faithful servant."* Jesus is coming soon!

> **Matthew 6:19--21** *"(19) Lay not up for yourselves treasures upon earth, where moth and rust doth corrupt, and where thieves break through and steal: (20) But lay up for yourselves treasures in heaven, where neither moth nor rust doth corrupt, and where thieves do not break through nor steal: (21) <u>For where your treasure is, there will your heart be also.</u>" (KJV)*

One of your Treasures is the **RAPTURE.** Some Saints will miss this Treasure by just sitting in the pews, and they will have to go through the Great Tribulation. And then, by their deeds, prove themselves worthy of Jesus' sacrifice. Please get busy with God's works; store up this Treasure for yourself. Remember, you are for Jesus, or against Jesus, period. You gather, or you scatter -- no gray areas here.

TO THE UNBELIEVER

Do you feel there is more to life than you are experiencing? Are you really happy with your life today? Do you feel you are going nowhere fast? Or do you want Jesus back into your life? Have you gotten yourself into a situation, which you see no way out? Do you feel worthless? Now is the hour to ask Jesus into your heart? The Holy Spirit is bring you to the Valley of Decision. Do not deceive yourself!

IT IS TIME TO CHANGE!

The time is coming when it will be very difficult to find anyone to talk with about Jesus. And for anyone to own a Bible, it will be a death sentence. This book is an attempt to prove to you that the time remaining is short. People will disappear from this earth (Rapture), but the government will be able to deceive most people about why they have disappeared. This same government will try to destroy all future Christians, and at the same time, the earth itself will be in great convulsions. The government will require you to wear a mark on your hand or forehead. Without this mark, you will not be able to buy or sell. **If you accept this Mark of the Beast, there will be no salvation possible for you!!!!! And you will have guaranteed your eternal place in The Lake of Fire.**

Without the mark, you will have identified your allegiance to Jesus Christ, and you will be hunted as a criminal to be destroyed. There is no gray, no gray area here at all. Either you will be for Jesus or the government, namely the Antichrist #1/#2 (Satan). There will also be a critical religious leader (False Prophet) that will also be in league with this Antichrist and will be very convincing of *government religious policies* to the people. These two will have such immense earthly power, and the spiritual leader will require all people to worship the Antichrist (Satan). God will also be causing great earthly convulsions, and over 1/3 of the earth's population (3.5 billion + as of 2019) will be destroyed. Horrible and unspeakable terror will be upon the world because of God's wrath. Jesus will return with Angels, Church Saints, Tribulation Saints, and Old Testament Saints; before man completely destroys the earth. Jesus will destroy all evil beings before establishing his earthly kingdom. There will not be any opportunity to accept Jesus at that time, so all evil persons will be mortally destroyed. Their spiritual soul eventually sent to Hell and later the Lake of Fire FOREVER.

Don't delay! Now is the time to establish your escape from the terrors that are coming upon the earth. But the most important is that you do not know what hour you will die, and to die without Jesus in your life, is a sentence to Lake of Fire forever and ever. The Lake of Fire is a place of unbelievable pain, loneliness, and tears.

Please keep in mind that these 70 to 80 years of life on this earth are not reality. Eternity is forever; **now that is reality**!

You are going to die, which is unavoidable but choose wisely where you want to spend eternity. **It is the most crucial decision of your life;** after death, that decision is unalterable. I plead with you to give this Jesus the same time and effort you would give to a major investment you are contemplating to purchase.

To be saved from the Lake of Fire, all you need do is: recognize you are a sinner, earnestly repent of your sins, ask Jesus to come into your heart and become your King. It is a gift that God gives to you because he loves you so much; that he sent his son Jesus to die and pay for your debt of sins. In **Romans 6,** we read.

> **Romans.6:23** *"For the wages of sin is death; but the gift of God is eternal life through Jesus Christ our Lord." (KJV)*

This free gift is here now; you can accept it or reject it. It is totally your choice. Please ask Jesus into your life. Study the Bible, let the Holy Spirit control your life with righteous deeds, and believe Jesus (the Son of God) paid for all your sins. There is no other name, in heaven or earth, which can save you but Jesus.

> **Acts 4:***12 "Neither is there salvation in any other: for there is none other name under heaven given among men, whereby we must be saved."(KJV)*

> **John 3:16** *"For God so loved the world, that he gave his only begotten Son, that whosoever believeth in him should not perish, <u>but have everlasting life.</u>" (KJV)*

NOW IT IS

HIGH TIME

TO AWAKE!

Roman 13:11

EPILOGUE

Never before in human history have so many prophecies been completed. And there are very few awaiting their completion. Most of these have to do with *"The Day of the Lord,"* the final days for earth's inhabitants. The world is becoming like the cold-blooded Frog. Satan has heated the water (the sinful world) with little notice to our society, and we have become so comfortable with the increasing heat that this evil world is about to be in really hot boiling water (God's wrath)

Jesus spoke many times to us about watching for his return to remove his Bride from the earth. But he also said that he would come; *"like a thief in the night."* This statement will be valid as no one (or very few) are watching for Jesus' *2nd Return*. These individuals left behind will experience the "Great Tribulation" of seven years. Hitler's antics will be as child's play compared to those last 3½ years of King Satan's rule.

God has given us the <u>clues to watch for,</u> and time is considered in this book. God has always revealed his intentions to his children. Time is an essential subject to God because he speaks of beginnings (Genesis) and endings (Revelation) and eternity.

I hope that this theory of The Three Clocks helps you realize just how close we are to the Rapture and then the Great Tribulation. I want all souls to be looking for and getting ready for the greatest and most wonderful trip we will ever experience.

<u>*REFERENCES*[X]</u>

1. All quoted scriptures are from the Holy Bible, King James Version Cambridge Addition: 1769; King James Bible Online www.kingjamesbibleonline.org.

2. "Strong's Exhaustive Concordance", Copyright 1890 by Mr. James Strong, Madison, N.J. Printed by Crusade Bible Publishers, INC. Box 90011, Nashville TN 37209

3. "Funk and Wagnall Standard Desk Dictionary", Funk and Wagnall Corporation, Harp & Row, Publishers Inc. All rights reserved except in case of Brief Quotations embodied in a critical articles and reviews.

4. "Wikipedia Foundation Inc." Public Domain, CCO, 149 New Montgomery Street, San Francisco, CA, 94105, <u>info@wikimedia.org</u>.

5. Commentary notes used are "from HOLY BIBLE, INTERNATIONAL VERSION Copyright 1973, 1978, 1984 International Bible Society, and Used by permission by Zondervan Bible Publishers".

6. The original chart may be found in Arnold G. Fruchenbaum, *The footsteps of the Messiah – A Study of the Sequence of Prophetic Events*) San Antonia TX: Ariel Ministries 2004), p.46.

Attachment -- A

THE 3RD HEAVEN OF
2 COR 12:2 - 4

3RD HEAVEN
GOD'S ABODE
SPIRITUAL REALM
(Can include all three)

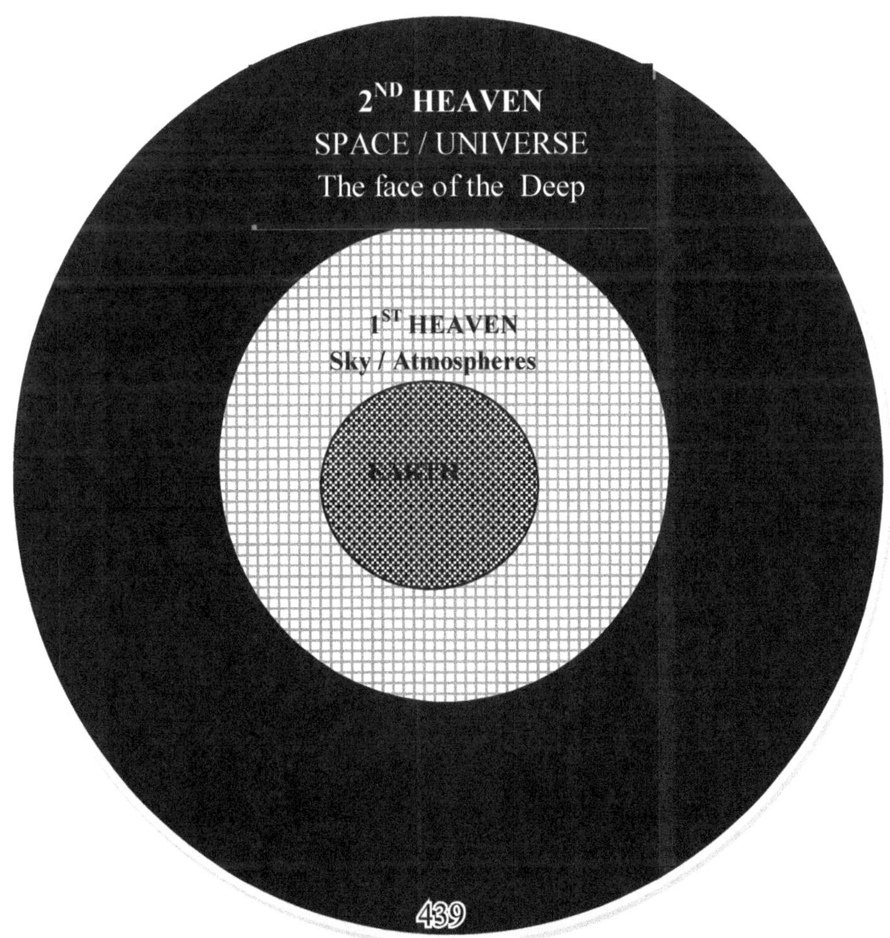

Attachment -- B

THE PLACES IN EARTH
PARADISE,
TORMENT AND ABYSS

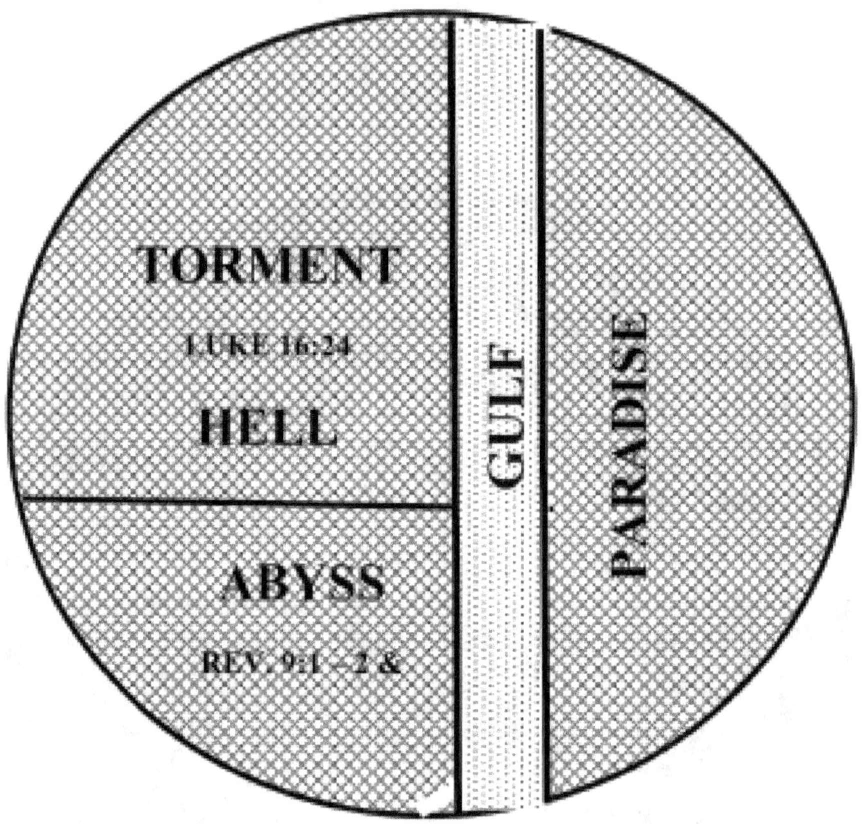

Matthew 25:33—"And he shall set the sheep on his right hand, but the goats on the left." *(KJV)*

Ecclesiastes 10:2—"*A wise man's heart is at his right hand; but a fool's heart at his left.*" *(KJV)*

COMPILATION CHART

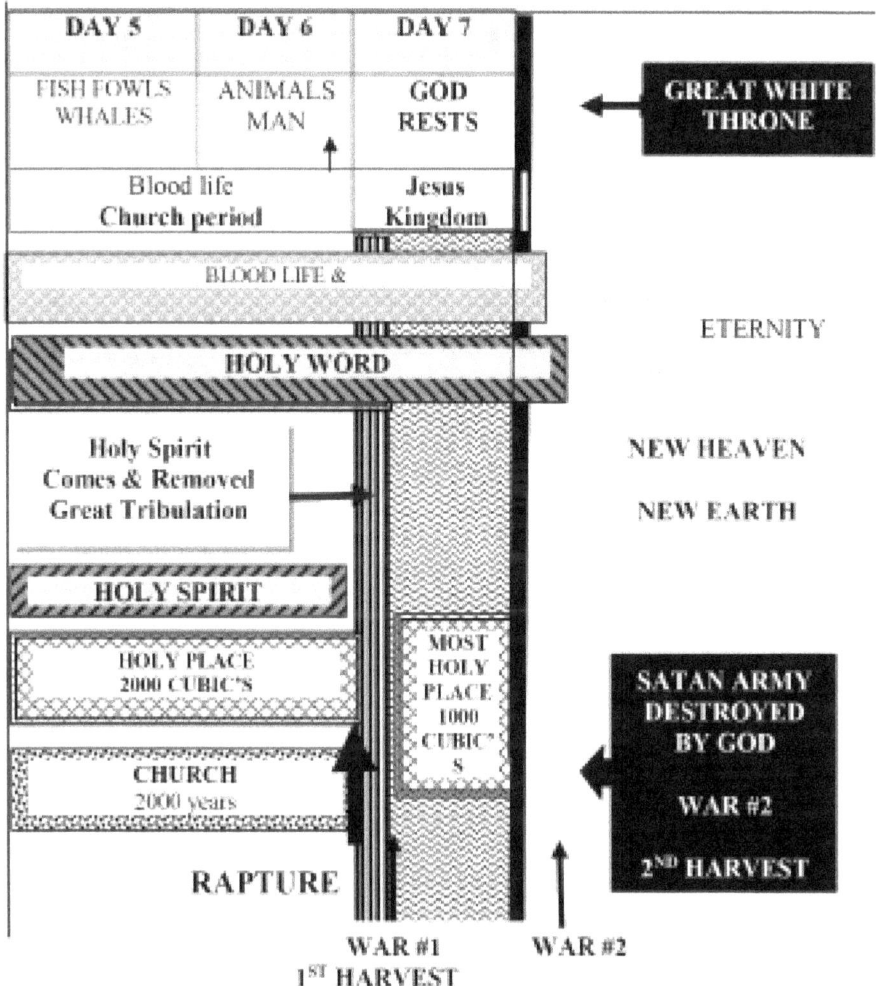

74 Bible Mysteries Solved

God's mysteries have been around since time began. They challenge us and, when solved, reveal in-depth knowledge to us. This knowledge is God's love message to you. Here is where you will see the intricacies which unlock God's plan for you. They also clarify erroneous traditions that fog up our understandings. One tradition is Faith and Deeds, which will reveal a condition for the Rapture left behind, that has been overlooked for many years.

DON'T DECEIVE YOURSELF AND BE LEFT BEHIND!

AUTHOR

Mr. Jones is a USAF retired aviator with 23 years of service, with 20 years as a USAF instructor and FAA Certified Flight Instructor since 1963. In his church, he has been an elder, Sunday teacher, and singer. The Book of Revelation is his specialty study for over 15 years. And has written "Fig Leaves are Forming Summer is near," and "Parables, Bible Building Blocks," both to be published soon, and "Formation Flying."